DISCARD

BAD MOON RISING

BAD MOON RISING

Tess Pendergrass

Five Star • Waterville, Maine

First Edition
First Printing: December 2004

Set in 11 pt. Plantin by Ramona Watson.

Printed in the United States on permanent paper.

Library of Congress Cataloging-in-Publication Data

Pendergrass, Tess.
    Bad moon rising / by Tess Pendergrass.—1st ed.
      p. cm.
    ISBN 1-59414-236-X (hc : alk. paper)
    1. Triangles (Interpersonal relations)—Fiction.
2. White supremacy movements—Fiction.   3. Missing persons—Fiction.   4. Psychics—Fiction.   5. Police—Fiction.   I. Title.
PS3566.E457B33 2004
813'.6—dc22   2004047165

Dedication

For my grandmother, Ann Longshore,
my most loyal fan and best publicist.

Acknowledgements

Once again I would like to thank Sergeant Ron Sligh for his generosity in answering questions about police work. Many heartfelt thanks to Michelle Dostal for sharing the details of her job as a hazardous materials technician, to Dr. John Longshore for ensuring Professor Nagle's geological accuracy, and to Dan Landando for car advice. And thank you to John Michael Farrington for his kind permission to use a line from his song "Shifting Gears."

Thanks also to Judy Longshore, Katy Longshore, and Barbara Kerley for their perceptive comments on the manuscript and for all their support.

And particular thanks to my editor, Russell Davis, for asking for Kermit and Serena's story—and for believing I could write it.

Chapter 1

"I need a cure for a low-down, lying, no-good, Pisces heart."

Serena Davis tried to slam the door to Callista's Herbal Haven for emphasis, but the automatic latch caught it, swinging it closed behind her with a gentle, holistic whisper.

"Have you tried arsenic?"

Callista perched herself on a three-legged stool behind the glass counter at the back of the small shop. The strands of silver in her wildly corkscrewing blond hair put her in her early forties, maybe ten years older than Serena, but granny glasses perched on the end of her nose as she glanced up from that morning's edition of the *Hope Point Register*.

Callista believed the glasses gave her a serious, knowing air. Serena didn't point out that the moon and stars bandanna holding back her unruly hair spoiled the intended impression. Serena's sister Destiny had achieved the same wild hair with a disastrous home perm, and Serena had learned the hard way not to point out hair faux pas.

Callista's enigmatic eyes, more gold than green, showed no surprise at Serena's dramatic entrance, but Callista never showed surprise. Serena supposed that was only prudent for a professional psychic.

"I was wondering why I hadn't heard from you since Destiny and Daniel's wedding last weekend," the psychic said. Despite Callista's imperturbable manner, she never pretended to know more than she did, which made her occasional flashes of second sight that much more convincing.

"I'm not talking about Daniel," Serena assured her hastily.

"No," Callista agreed. "If Daniel had hurt your baby sister, you'd be over at Hammer's Hunt and Feed buying a .45, not coming to me for advice. You've always been more protective of other people's hearts than your own."

Serena arched an eyebrow as she edged around a standalone bookshelf displaying a variety of tarot and other divination cards alongside books on astrology, therapeutic massage, and herbal menopause treatments. The gentle, woodsy fragrance of sandalwood incense mixed with the musty scent of drying mint and sage to fill her nostrils as she neared the counter. Quiet on a late Friday afternoon, the shop nevertheless never seemed quite peaceful, as if something mysterious and unexpected lurked around every corner.

"You think I should be taking care of Jesse with a Glock?" she asked. "Wouldn't that impact negatively on my karma?"

Peering over her glasses Callista gave a formidable stare. "It could hardly be worse than hooking up with him in the first place. I warned you. A Sagittarius falling for a slippery white-knight fish without a reality-check bone in his body is just asking for trouble."

Callista *had* warned her, when she'd first met Jesse Banos two years before, which was precisely why Serena hadn't called her friend in the five days since her sister's wedding.

"He found another damsel in distress," Callista guessed.

A jolt of fury stabbed through Serena, almost as much at Callista's casualness as at Jesse's stupidity. Her emotions must have flashed in her eyes, because Callista's eyes widened.

"He *did?* The bastard. And he told you at your sister's wedding?"

"He didn't show up at my sister's wedding."

The entire, surreal day replayed at high speed through her gut. Her annoyance at Jesse's being late, as he had been so often the past few months. Furtively scanning the little church from her position as matron of honor, hoping to see his thick, black hair above the crowd as he slipped in late. Annoyance turning to worry when he didn't appear at the reception at Daniel and Destiny's house. The growing, gut-wrenching certainty that the continuous busy signal on his cell phone meant another desperately important counseling session for his poor, pitiful high school sweetheart.

"She's rich, gorgeous and naturally blond. Just how much distress can she possibly be in?" Serena demanded. "She needs to be going to a marriage counselor with her husband, not calling up someone else's man to cry on his shoulder."

Callista shrugged, a motion made more graceful by the loose-fitting organic cotton dress draped over her generous curves. "I don't believe in interfering with free will, but if you've set your mind on preventing Jesse from wandering, I can put you in touch with some people who don't share my ethical principles. I'm sure we can dredge you up a love potion, though I don't have much faith in those things working for long."

She leaned forward, her pale eyes catching the reflected light from the glass countertop. "You know the girl is not the problem, Serena."

Serena wasn't going to give Callista the satisfaction of nodding, but her jaw tightened so hard it ached. She knew. She knew that even if she were rich and blond, with a supermodel's wistful pout instead of her own strong features, and had only a confirmation champion Lhasa Apso to feed instead of a teenage daughter, Jesse would still be pulling away from her, an elusive flash of a dream she couldn't hold onto.

Callista reached under the counter, pulling out the silk-lined box that held her favorite deck of tarot cards. She spread a square of black velvet on the counter and handed Serena the cards. "Shuffle."

"I don't need a tarot reading," Serena grumbled, though she ran the cards through her hands a couple of times before handing them back to Callista. "The last one you did said that I'd already found my soul mate."

"I didn't say it was Jesse."

Her friend's tart response brought Serena's first smile. Callista had given her unwavering support through some of the worst times of her life, including her painful divorce from her daughter's father. She'd seen Callista open her heart to anyone who came to her in need. But she'd never seen Callista admit she was wrong about a psychic reading.

"Who do you think it was, then?" Serena asked. "The single men I know at work are all at least sixty. Or they're eighteen-year-old students." She found her job as a hazardous materials technician at Pacific Coast Community College rewarding, but it didn't offer as many opportunities to meet eligible bachelors as some of her friends seemed to think.

Not that it mattered. She had been happy with Jesse, until he'd started pulling away. Until he'd started driving down to San Francisco to spend holidays with his parents without inviting her. Until he'd started missing meals she'd cooked and calling out of weekend plans at the last minute. Until he'd begun finding more things wrong with her than right. Criticizing her for being divorced, for not wanting to live in a big city, for not taking Sarah down to visit her father often enough, for her sister's ex-boyfriend getting himself murdered—as if that was somehow Destiny's fault!

The late-night emergency calls from Nadia that had turned into dinnertime emergency calls and then anytime emergency calls weren't the problem. They were only a symptom.

Serena shook herself. She'd cried her tears over the past week. Cried them over the past six months. She'd known in her heart the relationship was dead for some time. Known it was dying for longer. Maybe since that party at Roger Avalos's cabin on the Trinity River the fall before when Jesse had spent more time with his clinic partner, Lani Mitchell, and her sprained ankle than with Serena and her skimpy new bikini.

Tears weren't going to pay the mortgage or take care of Sarah. At least she didn't need Jesse for that.

"There are a couple of single guys who work in the acquisitions department at the Hope Point Library," she mused, forcing herself into a lighter tone. "They're always so attentive when Destiny takes me along to the library Christmas party. Of course, I'm not sure there's much of a chance for a long-term relationship there, since I think they're dating each other."

Callista snapped a card down on the black cloth. The queen of swords, a card that often came up for Serena, though Callista complained that Serena hadn't tapped into her inner wisdom deeply enough to appreciate it. The knight of swords came next. Callista pointed to it.

"How about a hunky cop?" she asked with curt sarcasm. "I'm sure your brother-in-law could introduce you."

"I thought I was already supposed to know him," Serena pointed out smugly. "But you could be right. One of the patrol officers, Garth Vance, was hitting on me pretty hard at the wedding reception. He said he wanted to marry me, but that might have been the beer talking. He couldn't walk straight, and he kept calling me Savannah. Kermit had to drive him home before they even cut the cake."

Callista's eyes flashed as she looked up from the pattern of cards she was laying. "Officer Kermit Riggs," she said, a dangerous smile curving her coral-frost lips. "I've seen him look at you. He's a steady, good-hearted young man."

Serena snorted. "*Young* being the operative word. He does *not* look at me. He's practically closer to Sarah's age than mine."

"Thirty-three and you're ready for the old folks' home," Callista said, not hiding her disgust. "You're not nearly as old as you think you are, Serena Davis. Not as mature as you think you are, either."

That finally made Serena laugh. "Look who's talking."

"And Kermit's not as young as he looks," Callista continued, refusing to be sidetracked. "You can see in his eyes that he has an old soul. But a young heart. A good combination." She smiled again, this one even more wicked. "And he'd be pretty hot, too, if he let his hair grow a little and wasn't always tangled up in his own feet."

"He's not nearly as clumsy as everyone seems to think he is," Serena objected, defending her brother-in-law's best friend and the man who had helped incarcerate the sociopath who'd nearly killed both Destiny and Daniel that past November. "You've never seen him cross-country ski. He's got a powerful grace for a tall man. He's only really clumsy when he's nervous. I haven't seen him trip over a doorway in months."

Except for at the wedding. But standing up as a best man would be enough to make anyone nervous. Of course, not just anyone would rip a hole in the pants pocket of his tuxedo trying to dig out the ring for the groom and then fall down the stairs off the chancel trying to dance the ring down the inside of his trousers.

"You're smiling," Callista noted, her voice like a portent of doom.

"True," Serena agreed, waving a stray wisp of incense smoke away from her nose. "Thank you. Smiling is something I haven't done much of this week."

"What do you want to do about Jesse?" Callista asked, turning another card.

"I've already done it," Serena said, her smile fading. The incense burned unpleasantly through her nasal passages, constricting her breathing. It wasn't tears. She wasn't going to cry anymore, not over Jesse. Not even over the dream of Jesse that she'd held onto for so long. "No need for love potions. Or arsenic, for that matter. I broke off the engagement."

Serena reached out to straighten the display of copper bracelets on the counter near the cash register. Her lips curled grimly. "I must say, he took it very well."

He's proud, Destiny had told her. *He's not going to let you know you broke his heart.*

He had pride, Serena thought. But that was all that she'd hurt. She could see it in his dark eyes, flattened of expression, hear it in the annoyance in his voice. They'd almost broken up before, just three months after they'd met. She'd been so wary of getting hurt again after her divorce from David, she'd panicked and picked a fight to drive him away. He'd come to her door later that evening with a picnic basket and a bottle of wine, driven her to the beach to watch the sunset. She'd seen the passion in his eyes that night, known how much he'd wanted her. She wondered

15

how she'd failed to notice when that passion had faded away.

Give him a chance to make it right, Destiny had insisted. *He's a little mixed up right now, but he'll come around.*

Daniel had turned Serena's sister into a hopeless romantic. Or maybe just brought out that natural tendency in her. But Serena didn't have only her own heart to think about. She had Sarah, and she wasn't going to let Jesse go on hurting Sarah, too.

Besides, she hadn't told Destiny everything that had happened over the past six months or so. She'd made excuses for Jesse's absences, for his distant behavior. She hadn't wanted to spoil her sister's happiness planning her wedding to Daniel. And her own pride had held her tongue, not wanting to admit to her baby sister that she didn't know what to do next.

"No, no. What's *that* doing there?"

Callista's muttering snapped Serena back to the herb shop. She'd been too deep in her own black thoughts to notice Callista's darkening frown at the cards.

"You could at least pretend to be sorry," Serena complained to the top of her friend's bent head. "Even if you weren't that fond of Jesse. It's only the second time I've been engaged, and the first one didn't work out too well, either, although at least I made it to the altar. I've decided to swear off men for good."

"You wouldn't need to be so drastic if you'd just open yourself to the patterns in your own life," Callista said, a familiar refrain.

Callista insisted Serena could learn to tap her own psychic powers, but Serena wasn't so sure. She couldn't even predict what breakfast cereal Sarah would be willing to eat from one week to the next.

"Don't do this to me," Callista said, and it took a second for Serena to realize her friend was speaking to the cards, not to her. Callista held an unturned card, talking to it more like a Vegas poker player than a mystic. "Bring me some good energy. Something positive. Clear this up."

"Talk like that is not going to instill confidence in your clients," Serena noted.

Callista's eyes flashed. "Shh! You're the one whose fate is in trouble. There's nothing I can do about it if I can't figure out what's brewing."

She flipped the card, the knight of cups reversed, and her indrawn breath hissed through her teeth. Serena saw nothing in the card to upset her. Callista had often described Jesse as the knight of cups—amiable and intelligent, but easily bored and led astray.

"What happened when you broke up with Jesse?" Callista demanded, not looking up. "Did he threaten you?"

"Threaten me?" Serena snorted. "He said I'd regret breaking up with him, but that was his ego talking."

"Did you threaten him? Strike him?"

"You're kidding, right?"

Callista's eyes snapped up to hers. "Did you kick his Honda? Did he flush the engagement ring down the toilet? Anything? Has anything happened this week that would account for the violence I'm seeing here?"

Serena glanced at the pattern of cards, but she hadn't been paying attention as Callista laid them down, and all she saw in them was a jumbled mess.

"No. I thought about killing him after the wedding, but Sarah would never let me live it down if I had to serve time. And, like I said, Jesse took it very well. I broke off the engagement Monday morning, and he didn't so much as leave me a telephone message until Wednesday. He wanted me to meet him at the Banana Slug Café this afternoon to talk things out, but he stood me up."

Her face burned at the memory. She should have known. He'd stood her up often enough that spring. On the positive side, it reduced her guilt at how relieved she'd felt since breaking up with him.

"This is not good," Callista muttered, picking one last card off the deck and holding it facedown over the others. "This is not good."

"What? That the cards got it wrong?" Serena shrugged. "I'm just as glad there wasn't any violence, thanks."

"If there hasn't been any violence this week, that doesn't mean the cards are wrong," Callista growled. "It only means it hasn't happened yet."

"Stop that," Serena ordered, resisting the sudden urge to glance behind her. "You were right about Jesse, all right? I give. You told me so. You don't have to try to spook me, too."

Callista's eyes narrowed. "I *never* play games with people's readings."

Guilt stabbed through Serena's irritation. "That wasn't fair. I'm sorry." She sighed. "As Sarah says, I've been a bit of a rhymes-with-witch since Sunday. It just really sucks to mess up another relationship."

She glanced at her watch. "Speaking of Sarah, I'd better get home and start that spinach pie I had planned for dinner tonight. Gemma's coming over after their Aikido class to spend the night."

"Serena." Callista's voice cut through her sudden distraction, her friend's tone tense with frustration and an undercurrent of strain that almost sounded like fear. "You're not listening to me. This isn't a game of poker. There is some kind of violence hovering over your life. Serious violence. And I don't see any clues as to what you can do to prevent it."

Serena glanced back down at the cards, gritting her teeth against the unwanted shiver that ran down her neck. Callista did prophetic with a particularly uncanny flair.

"You think it has something to do with Jesse?" she asked. "You think he's going to attack me in some way?"

Even with the chill from Callista's prediction taking up an annoying residence in her chest, she couldn't picture it. Jesse had a temper, no doubt about it. He'd once threatened to beat his brother senseless, but that had been when he'd found a stash of pot in Mark's glove compartment. Serena couldn't shake the feeling that Jesse just didn't care as much about what happened to her as he did about Mark.

Callista shook her head, her wild curls dancing behind the purple bandanna. "That's not exactly the feeling I'm getting. The violence I see is definitely connected to Jesse, but it doesn't seem to be coming from him. It might even be directed against him. Maybe Jesse is the one who is going to be the victim of this violence."

Serena snorted, trying for nonchalance as she searched her purse for her car keys. "Better him than me."

Callista's snort matched her own. "Unless you're the one who gets blamed for it. It definitely involves you, too. You and this unknown knight of swords. He might be a cop, or something else, something dangerous. You're not planning any sort of revenge, are you? If the police ask, I didn't ever hear you mention poison."

"My only plans involving Jesse Banos are to avoid him as much as possible." But the chill was back, running up and down Serena's spine. She wasn't trying to start any trouble; she certainly didn't want it to come looking for her. "What is going on? Is somebody going to slash his tires? Is one of

19

his counseling clients going to lose it and take him hostage with a letter opener? Just what kind of violence are we talking about?"

Callista tapped the unturned card in her hand against the velvet cloth on the counter, then flipped it over.

Serena's stomach dropped. She didn't need Callista to interpret the upturned card the psychic placed in the empty space next to Jesse's knight of cups. The stark figure of a black-clothed skeleton spoke for itself. *Death*.

Chapter 2

"This is so cool." Gemma Tasker's adolescent whisper squeaked with tension from the back seat of Serena's Subaru. "I've never broken into anyone's house before."

Serena eased the Outback to a stop against the curb between two generic fifties-era starter houses with identical salmon-pink trim. The driveway in front of her bumper, which consisted of two strips of concrete down a lane of shaggy grass, gave a clear view to Jesse's back fence and the street running up to his house.

"I'm not breaking in," Serena reminded Gemma sternly. She loved her daughter's best friend, but Gemma sometimes had difficulty grasping subtle distinctions. "I'm going to use a key."

"That you're going to steal from under Jesse's pelargonium planter," Sarah's voice pointed out, equally stern. "If that's not breaking in, then why do you need me and Gemma to be lookouts for you?"

Serena glanced in the rearview mirror at the two girls in the back seat. Her daughter's green eyes stared back at her accusingly from a serious, angular pre-teen face. Sarah's dark blond hair was pulled back in its typical ponytail, but Serena could still make out the uneven streaks of yellow from Gemma's late-night attempt at highlighting.

Gemma sat beside Sarah, her fiery red hair and sharp blue eyes belying an equable personality that tempered Sarah's fierceness, but did not preclude disastrous experi-

21

ments in makeup and hairdressing.

"You're here so I can keep you out of trouble," Serena told Sarah primly. "Gemma's grandmother would have killed you both if you'd managed to use that platinum dye on Gemma's hair."

Considering Pleasance Geary was nearly six feet tall and wielded a mean chainsaw, that wasn't as far-fetched as it sounded.

"On the box, it's the same color as Britney Spears's hair." Gemma sighed.

"Britney Spears would kill for your hair," Sarah told her friend, fiercely loyal. She glanced back at Serena. "If the cops arrest you for breaking and entering, I don't know you."

Serena gave her daughter a scornful glance. "I think Kermit might find that hard to believe, given that he watched me ground you for life in the police station after you cut school."

"Omigod," Gemma gasped breathlessly at Sarah. "What if Officer Riggs came and arrested your mother? Wouldn't you just die?"

"Yeah," Sarah agreed. "I'd die all right. Laughing. Where's your cell phone, Gemma?"

"Ha, ha. Just sit still and try to stay out of trouble for five minutes," Serena ordered, trying to keep an unexpected flush from filling her cheeks. She could just picture the look of reproach in Kermit's eyes as he put on the handcuffs.

The suppressed color surged up her face as the thought of being handcuffed by Kermit Riggs took on a wholly unexpected entendre.

He'd be pretty hot if he'd let his hair grow. She could see that sandy hair, tousled, about ear length. *Thank you, Callista. I didn't need that today.*

"I'll only be a minute," she said briskly, unhooking her seat belt. "If Jesse would answer his phone or return my calls, then I wouldn't have to do this, but it's my stuff and I have a right to go in and get it."

She ignored Sarah miming dialing 911 and got out of the car. Mid-morning sunlight dazzled her eyes, freshening the old paint on the houses, turning the damp grass a brighter green than emeralds, banishing the remains of early fog and the memory of the previous week of rain. But the price paid for a sunny morning in June on the northern California coast was a brisk breeze, and Serena tugged her black blazer closed against the wind as she hurried up the drive between the two houses in front of her and onto Jesse's empty driveway. She glanced around, trying not to look furtive, before sliding the bolt on his back gate and slipping into the yard.

She tried settling her mind into the responsive, quiet space Callista recommended for tapping into the wisdom of the universe. Sarah, ever the young scientist, insisted that any accurate psychic prediction that couldn't be explained by the supposed psychic's having a greater than average sensitivity to other people's facial expressions and personality traits was merely random luck.

At the moment, Serena hoped Sarah was right. She saw two images in her quiet psychic room. One involved interrupting Jesse and some new distressed damsel *in flagrante delicto*. The other was finding Jesse hacked to pieces in his bathtub.

She couldn't say which distressed her more.

Heart pounding, she crossed the overgrown lawn to the narrow back porch, her cheeks burning in anticipation of the horrified embarrassment she'd feel when Jesse opened up the back door and demanded to know what she was doing there.

23

Coming to get my cashmere sweater, as you'd know if you weren't playing games, refusing to answer my calls. That was the story she'd told Sarah and Gemma. And she did like that sweater—the deep burgundy brought out copper highlights in her dark chestnut hair.

But the truth was, she didn't like it well enough to have to face Jesse again to get it. But she hadn't been able to reach him to assure herself he hadn't succumbed to her friend's mysterious vision of possible violence. Even his cell phone, which he never turned off, shunted her immediately to voice mail without ringing.

Curse Callista for her irresponsible predictions of doom and herself for letting them bother her.

Serena forgot to feel guilty as she rocked back the heavy redwood planter on Jesse's porch and reached under it for the spare key. If the SOB couldn't dredge up enough common decency to return her calls, after all he'd put her through, he deserved to have his privacy invaded.

She stomped across the porch and turned the key with the savage wrench required to throw back the recalcitrant dead bolt. She pushed open the door and stepped decisively into Jesse's kitchen, but the sudden cool silence drained her courage.

The porch overhang left the small, cheerless room gloomy even on a bright summer morning. Jesse hadn't removed the daffodil-colored curtains she'd made, but nothing could brighten the institutional green vinyl or the battered faux-cherry cabinets. He'd laughed at her interest in Feng Shui, but anyone with any sensitivity would know this miserable little space would have a negative effect on one's psyche, regardless of which direction the oven faced.

Jesse had also left dirty dishes in the sink, something that had driven her crazy when they were together. Now, the cereal bowl and coffee mugs, soaking in cold, dingy water, only depressed her. He always seemed to expect someone to follow around after him, cleaning up. Maybe now he was free of her, he'd find someone who would.

She started forward, across the kitchen toward the doorway to the living room. Her boot toe knocked against an open cupboard door, clattering it closed. Her heart tripped with her feet, but she gulped down her panic.

It didn't take Callista's finely honed intuition to know the noise wouldn't bring anyone running. The silence, the cool air unmoved by so much as a cat's breathing—the very smell, slightly musty and stale—told her no one was home.

She stepped into the dim living room, and a sudden, cold chill raced up her spine. She froze, her breathing shallow, as she strained her senses to figure out why. *Disturbance* was the word that whispered in her brain. Nothing looked disturbed. That was to say that there was nothing strange about the half-empty bowl of stale pretzels decorating the long glass coffee table or the medical journals that had spilled off the antique end table beside the black leather recliner, and the cushions of the matching leather sofa looked reassuringly off-kilter, wrenched out of place by Jesse's latest search for the television remote.

Everything else looked much as it had the last time she'd been to Jesse's house, though the heavy green drapes made specific detail difficult to make out . . .

The drapes. That's what was wrong. She'd never seen the drapes pulled before. Even at night with all his lights blazing in defiance of her environmental and fiscal responsibility lectures, when the whole neighborhood could watch CNN with him from the sidewalk, he refused to cover the windows.

Serena breathed out. Convenient for her that he'd

chosen that morning to let the drapes air. The whole neighborhood would not be watching as she cased his house.

She crossed the room to Jesse's recliner. The black cordless telephone sat haphazardly off-center on the glowing teak end table. The steady red light showed the unit was plugged in. Nothing wrong with it. She knelt to check the switches on the side. The answering machine had been deliberately turned off.

So much for her vague nightmares of Jesse's having a heart attack and accidentally yanking the phone out of the wall while trying to dial 911. Trust Jesse to turn off his answering machine just to complicate her life.

With an exasperated sigh, Serena pushed herself back to her feet. Some previously undeveloped instinct for crime caused her to rub the end table with her sleeve, eliminating her fingerprints from the gleaming surface.

Again, that sudden chill down her back. She spun to stare at the coffee table, glinting dully in the faint light. The bowl of pretzels, the pile of opened mail, the scattered books, the abalone shell Jesse used as a catch-all for paper clips and rubber bands, all still looked undisturbed.

Serena bent forward and nudged the pretzel bowl aside with her elbow. It still looked undisturbed. There was no dust ring on the coffee table to show where the bowl had been. There was no dust on the coffee table. Or the end table.

Serena stood straight and looked around. No dust on the television cabinet. She edged toward the fireplace beside the entertainment center. A pale film coated the mantle and the candles she'd arranged above it. Just about as much as she would have expected since she'd dusted the room in disgust right before Easter. But there was none on the polished tile in front of the closed fireplace screen. She moved to the end of the couch. There was dust on the lamp and the top of that end table. But none on the pile of old journals on the shelf beneath the lamp.

All the newly dusted surfaces were things someone might touch or move if they were looking for something. Things they'd need to dust if they didn't want anyone to know they'd been moved.

Serena gritted her teeth. *Darn Callista.* If she'd wanted to pay Serena back for her skepticism, she'd certainly be enjoying Serena's overactive imagination. It was time for Serena to get her sweater and get out.

She stalked to the master bedroom. She ignored the trembling flutter in her heart as she pushed open the door. No tangled bodies going at it in the sheets.

She pushed open the door to the master bath with a bravado she almost felt. No bodies of any kind. Nothing wrong.

Even if the medicine cabinet was slightly ajar. Even if the waste basket had been freshly emptied. Even if the plastic pill dispenser she'd given Jesse to hold his herbal supplements still held all of Saturday morning's capsules.

A short, emphatic bleat sounded faintly through the bathroom door. A car horn.

Serena stepped back out into the bedroom. The horn sounded again. A quick succession of sick sheep noises in a familiar pattern. *Shave and a haircut?*

Sarah. A warning? Had Jesse driven up without her hearing the car? Had he seen the girls? If he was trying to frighten Sarah, he *would* be facing violence . . .

As Serena rushed out into the living room, another sound rattled into her consciousness, abruptly driving out thoughts of being arrested and of murder. Murder on her part. Murder in general suddenly seemed all too possible.

27

There was someone at Jesse's front door. More specifically, someone thumping against Jesse's front door.

It wasn't Jesse. He would be using a key. There *had* been an intruder. He hadn't found what he was looking for—money? credit cards? prescription drugs?—and he was back to try again.

Maybe the intruder hadn't killed Jesse and left his bleeding body to drain in the bathtub. But there was no telling what he might do if he found Serena there.

She might have time to escape out the back door. But if this intruder had done something to Jesse, this might the only chance to bring him to justice. How fast could the cops reach her if she ended up in serious trouble? Only one way to find out.

She was lunging for the phone on the end table when Jesse's mail shot through the slot in the door.

"If you two have any trouble, call us." Destiny Millbrook Parks had her purse wedged against Kermit's doorframe as a backboard and was writing her cell phone number on the back of an old receipt she'd dug from the depths of that same purse.

Officer Kermit Riggs glanced over at his soul mate, sprawled across the length of his faded black sofa. She grinned at him, seemingly unconcerned by the imminent departure of her family.

"We won't have any trouble," Kermit assured Destiny as she pressed her scribbled note in his hand. He didn't point out that he already had the Parks's Hawaiian hotel number stuck to his refrigerator door and written on a sticky pad by his phone, along with a dauntingly long list of emergency numbers, from poison control to Destiny's parents' house in Sacramento.

Destiny looked panicked and excited and volatile enough that he was surprised she even remembered her cell phone number. He didn't think she'd remembered to comb her hair that morning, though it was hard to tell with that wild perm.

"They'll be fine." Detective Daniel Parks squeezed an arm around his new wife's shoulders, though his own customary calm had a keen edge that morning. "Kermit's got everything under control."

"And I'd trust him with my life." Destiny's skeptical brown eyes tilted with mischief. "Not my grandmother's fine china, maybe, but my life."

"I think you're safe there. Fleur may be irreplaceable, but she's not exactly fragile," Daniel drawled.

At the mention of her name, Kermit's lanky houseguest raised her head and thumped her thick tail against the sofa.

"She's getting blond hair all over that black fabric," Destiny warned, shaking her head as she strode over for one last kiss on Fleur's forehead. The yellow Lab's tongue caught her nose, making Destiny snort.

"Our plane leaves in an hour, and we still have to take Edgar to Serena's," Daniel said.

"I could take Edgar, too," Kermit offered once more. "He's cool. For a cat."

Daniel's eyes narrowed as Destiny laughed.

"We don't want your new landlord to regret his pet policy," Destiny said, scratching Fleur's ears. "Fleur and Edgar together would destroy this place."

Kermit caught Daniel's incredulous look. Glancing around the tiny one-bedroom apartment with its remaindered carpeting and battered appliances, furnished in Spartan single cop, he thought Daniel probably had it right—Mr. Murray wasn't risking much by allowing Kermit to babysit Fleur for a couple of weeks. The mildew stains in the shower and the curling linoleum in the kitchen would have kept even Kermit from renting the little garage apartment behind the Murrays' hundred-year-old farmhouse, but their pet policy and the promised access to their fenced backyard had sucked him in.

He might not have found the perfect dog yet—well, Fleur was perfect, but she was taken—but he intended to be prepared when it happened.

Of course, his father had been all too happy to inform him that in renting a good home for a nonexistent dog, Kermit had found a dump designed to drive human companionship right out of his life.

But Kermit figured he was a lot farther from finding the perfect woman—one that wasn't just as taken as Fleur, anyway—than he was from finding the perfect dog. At least dogs weren't embarrassed by his clumsiness. Fleur wasn't even afraid to let him cook. She'd scored an entire uncooked hamburger patty off him at Daniel's last barbecue.

Destiny's voice brought his thoughts back from their downward spiral. "Thanks again for taking Fleur. I know she's in good hands."

"That's right," Daniel said, putting a hand on Destiny's shoulder to steer her toward the door. "No worries. Maddy's got your job, Kermit's got your dog—"

"Our dog," Destiny reminded him with a slanting grin.

"Now we've just got to take *our* cat to your sister's, before our plane leaves for Hawaii without us."

Destiny's eyes clouded as she blew out a worried breath. "Yeah, no worries except my sister. Who's got her?"

Daniel grimaced at his mistake. "Serena's a big girl. She'll be fine."

"Serena is not fine," Destiny said, her lips thinning.

"She puts up a good front, but this whole mess with Jesse has worked her over. I hate leaving her."

Kermit glanced over at Fleur, trying not to listen. Serena's broken engagement was none of his business. Daniel had mentioned it to him at the station, just to prevent Kermit from blundering into anything, since Serena was his backup babysitter for Fleur if he couldn't get away for a dinner break one night.

"I hope she's home by the time we get over there," Destiny continued. "I don't know where she's gone this morning."

"She's probably taking Gemma home," Daniel said. "We've got a key. Edgar will make himself at home."

"I can't just desert my sister in her hour of need without even saying good-bye!"

"Serena's got our hotel numbers on Hawaii and Maui. She can call you anytime." Daniel said it soothingly, but Kermit noticed the clenching of his teeth.

"My sister is not going to interrupt our honeymoon with her broken heart," Destiny insisted.

"That's like asking Fleur not to beg at the table."

"Daniel!"

Daniel dodged the punch she aimed at his shoulder. "I for one don't blame Jesse for missing the wedding. I'm not a big wedding fan myself. Though I am looking forward to the honeymoon . . ." He glanced at his watch.

Destiny shook her head in frustration. "Men."

Kermit held up a hand. "I didn't say anything."

"It wasn't just the wedding," Destiny told him. "She's not the kind of person to break off an engagement over a tiff."

"Of course not," Kermit agreed. "You don't have to explain."

He had seen Serena at the wedding reception the week before, seen her checking her watch. Seen her slip back into Daniel's house to borrow the phone. He hadn't realized she was worried about her fiancé. Jesse never seemed to be around anyway. But he could tell that whatever was bothering her went deeper than she wanted anyone to see.

"Maybe they'll work it out while we're gone," Daniel suggested. "Once things cool down."

Destiny shook her head. "I doubt it. She says they're through for good, and once she's made up her mind about something . . . I thought he was the one, though. He seemed good for her. There for her."

"He wasn't there at Christmas," Kermit said, the words out before he remembered it wasn't any of his business.

"He was down in San Francisco with his parents and Mark," Destiny reminded him.

"Thanksgiving, too," Kermit said. "And Sarah's birthday he was working late."

As Destiny and Daniel stared at him, he felt the same helpless vertigo as when he started down a flight of stairs or stepped over a curb and suddenly realized he wasn't going to reach his destination upright. He knew he ought to be able to stop himself, but he fell anyway.

"Destiny's the one who put up her new mailbox when that drunk kid ran down her old one. Daniel took Sarah to 'take your daughter to work' day. Sarah and I tightened her fan belt so her car wouldn't squeal anymore." Kermit was used to pretending his face wasn't turning red. "That's not how I'd show somebody I was there for them."

Destiny's wild curls and L.L.Bean attire bore no resemblance to Serena's smooth, dark hair and instinctive fashion sense, but their frowns, intense and thoughtful, matched them as sisters. "Kermit, would you do me a huge favor?"

"It can hardly be more huge than that one." Daniel pointed at Fleur, who took that as an invitation to heave herself off the couch and mosey over for him to scratch her ears.

"And keeping an eye on your house," Kermit reminded him.

"And keeping an eye on Lieutenant Marcy—"

"I never promised that!" Kermit objected. He did his best to stay out of the tension between his friend and his lieutenant. Kermit enjoyed working as Daniel's occasional partner on cases run out of Lieutenant Tiebold's Support Division, but Kermit's direct supervisor was Patrol Division's Lieutenant James Marcy, and he couldn't afford to antagonize the man if he wanted to make detective sergeant himself eventually.

Daniel shook his head. "Marcy looked much too pleased that I was going to be out of town for two weeks. Somebody's got to keep him under control while I'm gone."

"I thought we were going to be late to the airport," Destiny interrupted, tapping her watch.

Kermit laughed at her exasperation. "I'd be happy to do you a favor. Just ask."

In the brief moment between the end of his words and the flash of gratitude in Destiny's eyes, Kermit remembered childhood tales where heroes ignored warnings not to make rash promises and ended up losing limbs and firstborn children and other vital items that caused them to repent their hasty ways.

"It's nothing, really," Destiny said, with a relief that did nothing to ease Kermit's trepidation. "But if you could just keep an eye on Serena for me? Make sure she's okay whil we're gone?"

Kermit struggled not to look horrified. Based on Da iel's amused expression, he didn't succeed.

No. That was the only possible response. He had already promised Destiny anything she asked, but apparently his honor was not as sterling as those ancient story heroes, because he had to tell her no. He could not, under any circumstances, be left alone with Serena. He would find a way to make such a complete fool out of himself that she'd never be able to look at him without wanting to laugh again.

No. Serena had too warm a heart for that. She'd pity him, which would be infinitely worse.

Serena was easy to be around when Destiny and Daniel were there. With that sly sense of humor and her quiet enthusiasm for life, she lit up a room. He enjoyed the friendship the four of them and Sarah had together. Treasured it.

But if he didn't have the others as a buffer, he feared the warmth of her friendship might be too much for him. And he might not be able to hide the feelings he needed to hide. She was engaged to Jesse Banos, and . . .

Okay, she wasn't engaged to Jesse Banos anymore, which only made everything that much more complicated—

"I can't tell you how much I appreciate this." Destiny's voice jerked him back to his front door. She reached up to give him a firm hug. "She's not as tough as she looks, you know. David hurt her badly, and now Jesse . . . . I'll just feel a lot better knowing she's got a shoulder to cry on while I'm gone."

"Ah—" His voice stuck somewhere in the panicked constriction of his throat.

"I can't tell you how much I appreciate it, either," Daniel muttered, cuffing Kermit's shoulder as Destiny crouched to give Fleur a last kiss good-bye. "I love Serena. She does grow on you, after a while, sort of like Fleur. But this is our honeymoon."

"Be a good girl, Fleur," Destiny ordered as Daniel gently

tugged her out the door. After a final wave from Destiny, the door clicked shut, and they were gone.

Fleur stared at the door mournfully for a full five seconds before glancing up at Kermit with the gleeful expression of a teenager whose parents have left her the house to herself on a Friday night.

But Kermit didn't have the heart to worry about Fleur. The dog's wild party ideas held no terrors comparable to the thought of Destiny telling Serena to call him if she needed a shoulder to cry on.

A damp nose bumping his hand broke him free of his immobility. Fleur's tongue hung just beyond the tip of her muzzle and her forehead wrinkled in that immortal question: *Is it time for a walk yet?*

"Sure," Kermit agreed, his spirits lifting as Fleur's heavy tail went into overdrive. "Where's your leash?"

Fleur's simple joy in the moment shamed him out of his cowardice. After all, a classy, together woman like Serena was not going to call a clueless male cop for tea and sympathy. The only reason he could think of for her asking his help would be if she had car trouble, and, of course, he'd be more than happy to duck under the Subaru's hood for an afternoon. He'd even enjoy it.

As he clipped Fleur's bright new sunflower-patterned leash to her collar, he briefly succumbed to the pleasant fantasy of Serena's gratitude when he rescued her from a breakdown on Old Hope Point Road by nonchalantly re-attaching her loosened ignition coil.

Unfortunately for Kermit, the problem Serena needed help with at that moment had nothing to do with automobiles, or even sympathetic shoulders. Before the week was out, he would decide a cup of tea and some girl talk would have been getting off easy.

Chapter 3

In his dream, he was on a stakeout. The suspect burst out the front door of the house under surveillance. Even dreaming, Kermit was surprised to see the suspect was his straight-laced landlord. Seventy-five-year-old Cadwallader Murray ran across the expansive yard in front of his home with no trace of his chronic gout, firing rounds from an M-16.

"Let's go, let's go!" Kermit's partner, Graciela Martinez, shouted beside him. But when he glanced at her, she had long, chestnut hair rather than Grace's nearly black bob, and her eyes were Serena's catlike hazel rather than Grace's deep brown. "Step on it, Riggs!"

He threw the Crown Vic patrol car into gear and stomped on the gas, but the car just jerked and groaned.

"He's getting away!"

Mr. Murray had reached his forty-year-old Ford pickup, which started without a hitch.

"I thought you could fix cars," Serena-Grace accused, as Kermit desperately stomped on the gas, his tires spinning gravel behind them.

"Here, I'll do it." Serena pulled a 9mm Beretta from her belt and pointed it at the dashboard.

"No!" Kermit shouted, but he couldn't take his hands from the wheel.

Mr. Murray's truck spun in the driveway, and the M-16 poked out the Ford's window, firing toward the patrol car. But the rounds coming in didn't sound like automatic rifle fire. More

36

like incoming artillery. That long, shrill, descending note of im-pending doom. But not as loud as he expected. As if it came from a great distance. Round after round after . . .

A sudden, jangling explosion of noise jerked him awake, his eyelids flying open. Something black and yellow was poking toward his pupils. Kermit pulled back, struggling to focus. The sound of falling mortar shells came, very faintly, from the anxious dog nose prodding toward him over his pillow.

The telephone rang again, almost on cue, the explosion after the falling mortar round.

Kermit glanced at the alarm clock on his bedside table. The red display snarled a surly six-seventeen a.m. Kermit groaned and reached for the telephone receiver beside the clock. Not good. It had to be the police station. He'd been looking forward to this day off.

"Hello?" His dry throat choked the word, and he tried again. "Riggs here."

"Kermit! Thank God you're there. Are you busy? Do you have a minute?"

The feminine voice sounded familiar, but it wasn't Nancy Dennis, the department secretary.

"Busy?" Kermit squinted at the clock again. Maybe he'd missed something the first time. Nope. Six-eighteen. "I guess not. Just sleeping."

Fleur whined again, the soft, yet piercing noise raising the hair on the backs of Kermit's arms.

"Trying to sleep," he amended, swinging his bare legs out from under the covers. The shock of the cold floor-boards on his feet and Fleur's cold nose on his knee made him gasp.

"Sleeping?" the voice demanded. "Don't you have to be

at the station at seven? You're going to be late."

"It's my day off," Kermit explained, unable to keep the plaintive note from his voice as he struggled to pull his slippers on with one hand and push Fleur's tongue away from his face with his elbow.

"It's Monday." That sounded like Destiny, worried about his sanity. If it was six-eighteen in California, what time was it in Hawaii? Maybe that's why he hadn't recognized her voice.

"I'm off every other Monday. Is everything okay out there?" One slipper down, one to go.

"I woke you up. Damn. I'm so sorry. I was trying to catch you before you left for the station. I'm sorry. I was just so worried—"

Kermit sat up, barely missing cracking his skull on Fleur's jaw. "Are you calling about Fleur? We're fine. I'm just about to take her out."

At the word *out*, Fleur's ears pricked up, and she danced backward from Kermit's side, the whine coming again, with a little more lung behind it. Kermit ducked down to grab his second slipper, struggling past the telephone cord.

"Oh, right. I forgot about Fleur," the voice said. Definitely *not* Destiny. The apologetic note faded slightly. "I'm surprised she let you sleep this late. She came into my bedroom about five a.m. when I was watching her one time and stuck her cold nose into the back of my neck. I think the whole neighborhood heard me scream."

"Serena!" Kermit's head snapped up from his slippers, pulling him off balance just as Fleur head-butted his thigh. He grabbed for the bedside table, managing to knock the radio alarm clock to the floor and sending his departmental cell phone after it. The clock blared on with a local used car commercial as Fleur barked in consternation.

Kermit grabbed for the clock, but the telephone cord had somehow wrapped around his neck.

"Yes, it's me," Serena drawled. If she'd used that dangerous cat's purr of a voice earlier, he'd have had no trouble identifying her. "Who did you think it was?"

"Oh, I figured it was one of my legion of groupies," he said, trying desperately not to sound as though he were being attacked by electronic appliances. "They just won't let me be."

"Poor, poor, pitiful you," Serena agreed dryly.

The commercial break ended and country music blared from the radio. "I've got a wife," the baritone voice belted. "Her first name is Ex. And when we were married, we didn't get much—"

Kermit lunged for the switch, but the telephone cord wrestled him to the floor. Fleur took advantage of the situation to wash his face with dog drool. He sputtered as he tried to roll out of range of her attack.

"Are you all right?" Serena asked.

"Fine!" Stretching forward, Kermit managed to whack the clock's snooze button with his slipper. "Just fine. What can I do for you? Is everything all right over there?" Concern focused his struggle, and he managed to unwrap himself from the phone cord. "Is Sarah all right?"

"Sarah's fine. We're fine. Everything is fine. I just called because . . ."

As Serena's voice faded, music played again, this time something tinny with a rap beat. His partner had been playing with his cell phone settings again. *Very funny, Grace.*

"Hold on," Kermit said, using his slipper to drag the bugling cell phone toward him. "Hello. Riggs here."

"Riggs!" Officer Garth Vance's bullhorn of a voice

blared into his ear. "Get your lazy butt out of bed and get to work. Some of us have been at this all night, and we're ready to go home."

Kermit bit back a hasty reply. Ever since Garth's partner, Tom Yap, had been arrested for murder that past December, Garth had made an impressive effort to be more of a team player in the department. Kermit tried to reward that effort with patience, but although Garth might have been less of a loose cannon than he used to be, he was still loud.

"I'm off today, Vance," he said. "Every other Monday."

Garth's laugh boomed over the little phone. "I woke you up? Sorry, man, I'm not used to the new schedules yet. Hey, I just called to give you a heads-up before you came in. The lieutenant's gone on the warpath about our backlog of paperwork. Get this. He wants us to—"

"Garth!" Kermit interrupted him. "Go home and get some sleep. I don't have time to talk. I'm having a conversation."

Garth laughed again. "What a coincidence. Me, too."

"With *someone else*," Kermit growled. "Hold on." He shifted to the other receiver. "Sorry, Serena. It'll just take me a second to get off the other phone."

He moved back to the cell phone. "Look, Garth—"

"Just let me tell you what Marcy's planning. He thinks we can use our meal breaks to—"

"You can tell me later," Kermit said. "I need to get back to this conversation, so she can tell me—"

"A chick?" Garth asked. Kermit could practically see his ruddy face light up with glee. "Whoa. Sorry to interrupt there, buddy."

"Kermit?" Serena's faint voice jerked him back to the regular phone. "Kermit, never mind. Like I said, everything's fine, really. Or, at least, things probably are fine. I'll just—"

"No, hold on," Kermit told her, a sudden chill running down his spine at the anxiety in her voice. Cool, calm Serena never panicked.

He fumbled the cell phone, slammed it against his ear. "Garth, I'm hanging up on you now."

"Who is she, Riggs?" Garth boomed. "I can't believe you've got a hot chick in that ratty apartment with you."

"I don't!"

"You're at her place?" Garth asked, enjoying himself way too much. "Good for you!"

Kermit glanced toward the heavens for guidance, but all he saw was the peeling apartment ceiling. "No, I'm not at her place—"

"Hey, whatever, man. I can't believe you've got a hot chick anywhere."

Kermit moved to throw the phone across the room, remembered it was the department's property. He settled for knocking his forehead against the end table. "She's not a hot chick!"

"Who's not a hot chick?" Serena's voice pierced his frustration like an ice pick. He froze in horror. He'd moved the wrong phone receiver. "You have a hot chick on the other line? I'm so sorry. I'll just hang up now—"

"No! It's Garth Vance on the other line. I was just telling him you're not a hot chick."

"Gee, thanks, Kermit." At least sarcasm had driven the panic from her voice. "I needed a good dose of reality this morning."

He shut his eyes, but oblivion refused to swallow him. "That's not what I meant. Of course you're hot. I mean, in a totally objective way—"

"Why, Kermit," Garth's drawl was much more amused than Serena's. "I had no idea you felt that way."

"Good-bye, Vance," Kermit snarled. As he lowered the cell phone to punch the end button, he could hear Garth laughing.

"Serena." He paused for a deep breath. He could feel the heat filling his face. He'd done it. He'd made a complete fool of himself. Gotten it over with. Rather spectacularly. Good. Now he could move on. At least Fleur had quit whining. She had dropped to the floor with a sigh and was staring at him, her deep brown eyes warm with pity.

He figured he had two choices. He could go commit hara-kiri in the kitchen or he could pretend the last five minutes never happened. Considering his kitchen didn't hold a knife sharp enough to cut butter, he really had only one choice.

"Serena." His voice sounded admirably calm and professional. "What's wrong? What can I help you with? Are you okay?"

"I'm sorry to bother you," she repeated, amusement mixing with her earlier uneasiness to make her voice shake. She puffed out a hard breath. "Like I said, I'm fine. But things aren't fine. Or, they probably are fine, but they don't seem that way."

She paused. "No. They're not fine, and I know they're not fine, but you're going to think I'm overreacting. I know something terrible has happened, but no one will listen to me, and Destiny said something about giving you a call if I needed anything, and I hate bothering you, especially since it turns out it's your day off, but I didn't know who else to call—"

"Of course you can call me," Kermit said, his embarrassment fading as the uncharacteristic babble of words told him how upset Serena really was. "Is Sarah all right?"

"Yes. Yes, Sarah's fine." She paused again. "It's not Sarah. It's Jesse."

Isn't that what Destiny had said Serena needed help with? So there was no reason for the cold lump of disappointment that settled in his stomach. He'd promised Destiny to do anything he could to help. He could listen. He could do that for Destiny and for Serena.

Except, if Jesse had done one more thing to hurt Serena, Kermit was going to be hard pressed not to go right over to that clinic, drag the SOB out by his snobby silk tie and . . .

"I called the police station, but they said there was nothing they could do."

Kermit's jaw clenched in anger. Maybe there was nothing the police could do if Jesse had made no specific physical threat. But Kermit was off-duty.

"Tell me what he did," he said, not caring how dangerous his voice sounded.

"No, it's not like—"

"I'll make sure it doesn't happen again. Just tell me what happened."

"I'm trying to tell you," Serena said, exasperated with him. "I don't think Jesse's done anything. I think he's had something done to him."

She gave him a second to absorb that information. "I think Jesse's been kidnapped."

Serena watched Kermit's ancient tangerine-colored convertible pull up in front of her house. Fleur sat in the front passenger seat, her head stuck out the open window. Destiny never let her ride that way, for fear of wind damage to the dog's ears, but looking at the blissful expression on Fleur's face, Serena decided Destiny didn't need to know.

She pulled back from the living room window, taking deep yoga breaths to calm her nerves. The sergeant she'd spoken to at the police department had pretty much told her she was imagining things. She couldn't blame him. Couldn't blame her parents for telling her the same thing on the phone the night before.

But that made Kermit her last resort. If he refused to help her, she hadn't a clue what she was going to do next.

Then again, she felt that way about her entire life lately. Callista would tell her to trust the universe. Destiny would tell her to hold on to faith. Which was all well and good when you needed to decide what to do with your life when you grew up, but when your ex-fiancé was missing and possibly dead, and your psychic friend was warning you that you might get fingered for whatever happened to him, then you wanted something a little more concrete to hold on to.

So much for her spiritual growth.

She grabbed her fleece jacket from the coat rack as she reached the front door. Her hand paused on the knob. *I've seen him look at you.* She'd called a man before six-thirty in the morning, talked to him in his pajamas. If he wore pajamas.

She pushed that thought right out of her mind. It wasn't as though Kermit was liable to get the wrong idea. After all, she'd called him to help her with a kidnapping. Still, there was something about the earliness of the hour, the morning fog hugging dawn close to the earth, that felt . . . risky.

As she pulled open her front door, seventy-five pounds of ecstatic yellow Labrador burst into her house, nearly knocking her off her feet.

"Sorry!" Kermit tumbled through after the dog, trying to haul her back. "I thought I had a better grip on the leash."

Serena laughed, despite herself. So much for awkwardness. It was just Kermit, after all. Same painfully short crewcut blond hair, same tall, lanky frame, same sky-blue eyes that held a depth of humor at the dog's excitement and his own clumsiness.

"She's glad to see you," he said, as Serena bent to rub Fleur's ribs while the Lab's whole body wagged. "She got all excited when we turned onto your block."

"She was just hoping Destiny was here," Serena said, as Fleur left her to trot down the hall, searching for other inhabitants. "Sarah's left for school already, you fickle mutt!"

Kermit smiled. "You're right about Destiny, though. I know Fleur loves the rest of us, but she lights up when she sees her mom. One of these days I'll have a dog who feels that way about me."

"Fleur does light up when she sees you," Serena told him, touched by the wistfulness in his eyes. "You have that effect on people."

"What do you mean?"

Suddenly, she wasn't sure what she'd meant. Only that it had just struck her that Kermit was the sort of person whose presence warmed a room.

She shrugged, hiding her uncertainty as she zipped up her jacket. "Maybe it's your aura," she suggested. She turned to the hall. "Come on, Fleur! Let's go."

An unearthly yowling from deep inside the house told her Fleur had found Daniel's cat, Edgar, sleeping on Serena's bed. Heavy dog feet pounded down the hardwood hall, and Fleur skidded to a stop in front of Kermit, her eyes bright with glee.

"You're incorrigible," Serena informed her. Fleur's tail swept across the floor in happy agreement.

"My aura's irresistible, huh?" Kermit said, raising an

eyebrow as he grabbed Fleur's leash. "You never told me you saw auras."

"I don't, but Callista does. I'll get her to read yours one of these days. I bet it's white. Purity and protection."

"That's me," Kermit agreed, following her out the front door. "White knight. Have sports car, will travel. Dragons killed on request."

"Don't say that!" Serena spun around in protest, and Kermit and Fleur jumped awkwardly aside to avoid bowling her over.

Kermit raised warding hands. "It was just a figure of speech. I'd never harm a dragon. Promise."

Serena flushed as she locked the door behind them. "Sorry. I meant the white knight part. Jesse always said he was my knight in shining armor. I'm a little jaded about knights these days."

"Not a knight, then," Kermit agreed. "It's probably better that way. I'd be dangerous with a sword. To myself and others."

But the self-deprecating humor didn't hide the uneasy concern in his eyes. "You said you thought Jesse had been abducted . . ."

His tone gave her plenty of room to back out, to admit that no, she had simply overreacted.

"He's gone," she said, meeting his gaze directly. "He hasn't been home since at least Friday night."

"He's not answering his phone?"

"His car is gone. His answering machine is turned off. He's turned off his cell phone, too."

Kermit rested a hand on Fleur's head, maybe for moral support. "He went away for the weekend and wants to be out of touch."

"Out of touch from you, you poor, hysterical, scorned

46

woman," Serena finished for him.

Kermit shook his head. "I didn't say that."

Calm, cool, sympathetic. She bet he got to play good cop every time.

"Kermit Riggs, you can drop the attitude right now. Yes, I'm upset. I think a crime has been committed and a man's life could be in danger. I'm going to show you why, if you'll give me a chance. Not because I want attention from that self-righteous, unreliable, inconsiderate SOB and not because I'm hysterical."

Kermit's mouth twitched. "I didn't say you were hysterical. I didn't think you were hysterical. You're not the hysterical type."

Serena wasn't mollified. "The officer I spoke with when I went to the station yesterday afternoon thought I was. He was very kind to me as he ushered me out the door and told me to wait a few more days before I tried to have Jesse declared a missing person."

"With adults, it usually turns out that they've gone missing of their own volition. We'll start an investigation right away if there's evidence that they're in danger, but otherwise . . ."

"Let me show you the evidence, and you can decide." She strode across the lawn, shaggy from the recent rains, to her Subaru.

"I can drive," Kermit offered. "It's not every day you get a chance to ride in a vintage 'seventy-four Jensen Healey."

Serena eyed the treated rust spots marring the faded orange paint job. " 'Seventy-four, huh?"

She would have guessed the car was considerably more than thirty years old, but she could see the pride in Kermit's eyes. "Do you think the three of us will fit in your car?"

"Fleur can squeeze in the back." He glanced at Fleur, the big dog panting eagerly beside him, and glanced at his nonexistent back seat. "Okay. Maybe not."

"Next time," Serena assured him, unlocking the Subaru. Once Fleur and Kermit were situated, she headed for the Bottoms, across town from her neighborhood in the Cloverbrook area of Hope Point.

"I know what this looks like," she said, crossing Highway 101 where it bisected the town. "Trust me. It would be easier—" and maybe a little gratifying "—to believe that Jesse's so distraught over losing me that he ran off for a few days to clear his head, and that he'll be back in Hope Point any minute, making me look like a fool for worrying about him.

"But if he turned up dead—or never turned up at all—because I kept my mouth shut out of embarrassment, I'd never forgive myself."

Kermit nodded, blue eyes thoughtful. "Tell me why you're worried. Maybe we can figure out what's going on."

Serena turned onto Jesse's street. Wisps of fog still haunted the cow pastures beyond, but the sun had finally broken free of the hills to the east of town, spreading warm light across the neighborhood. "I told you that his cell phone is turned off. He never turns it off, even at the movies or church. He's always worried he might get an emergency call from the clinic."

"He wouldn't be able to respond to an emergency call if he went out of town."

"It wouldn't matter," Serena said. She wrapped her hands tight around the steering wheel as she pulled up in front of the house, but she turned to meet Kermit's gaze, prepared to stare down his pity. "He wouldn't risk missing a call from Nadia."

The expression that flashed briefly through his eyes looked nothing like pity, but all he said was, "Nadia?"

"His high school sweetheart," Serena explained, trying to ignore the fury searing through her heart. Sitting in front of Jesse's deserted house, trying to convince someone, anyone, that Jesse Banos needed their help, when she could happily strangle him herself, she suddenly wondered just how much more pain she was going to allow him to make her feel.

"Blonde, buxom, beautiful," she continued. "They broke up when he went off to college, but never lost touch. Nadia had a brief career as a fashion model before marrying some rich kid from down south. Sometime this year, she decided darling Biff was neglecting her, so she started calling Jesse for advice and consolation."

"Somebody actually named their kid Biff?" Kermit asked, surprised out of his professional detachment.

"No." Serena gave him a look. "It's Brock or Blake or Brandon or something. Jesse says that since it's his fault she married the guy—anybody would be a second choice after Jesse, right?—it's his duty to offer her moral support."

"And he thought you'd buy that?" Kermit asked.

The disgust in his voice nearly made her laugh, except that his assumption that she shouldn't have had to buy it struck too deep at the hurt she'd been keeping to herself for so long.

"She knew just where to get to him," Serena admitted. "He can't resist anyone who needs his expert help. I guess that's what drew him to counseling in the first place. I guess that's what drew him to me, too. We met not long after my divorce."

She tried a laugh, but it died in the silence of the car. "Karma."

"This isn't what goes around comes around." Kermit's voice sounded hard as stone. "When he met you, you weren't married, and he wasn't engaged. He should have told Nadia to buzz off."

Serena glanced at Jesse's little yellow house and shook her head. The signs were there. Jesse's perfect care when she was hurting or sick. The way he would fade from her life when she was healthy. She should have known, even without Callista's attempts at psychic training. She should have protected herself better.

"Anyway," she said, forcing the words through the constriction in her throat. "He wouldn't have turned off his phone. But that's not what worries me the most. I think someone broke into his house. Come on, I'll show you."

She climbed out of the car and headed up the walkway. There was no need to skulk around the back way. Jesse's car was still gone; she could feel in her bones he hadn't been back.

"*Somebody* broke into his house?" Kermit asked, his long strides bringing him to her side as she reached the front porch. "*You* haven't been doing any illegal breaking and entering, right Serena?"

Serena unlocked the front door and turned the knob. "It's not breaking and entering if you have a key," she said, flashing it at him. No need to tell him where it came from. As Destiny said, sometimes you had to protect a cop's legal sensibilities.

"Serena—"

She scooted into the house before he could object, and he followed behind her. The living room felt even colder and gloomier than it had on Saturday morning, dust motes dancing in the light from the open door.

"Hello?" Kermit called out, his low-pitched voice loud

in the emptiness. "Hello, Jesse? It's Kermit Riggs."

"He's not here," Serena said. She leaned into the kitchen. "The same breakfast dishes are in the sink as on Saturday morning. And look at this."

She took him on the same route she'd followed Saturday. Kermit followed her, reluctance in every step, as she pointed out the strange dust patterns, still visible, though less distinct after several days of dust fall. She showed him the empty trash basket in the bathroom, the closed drapes in the living room and bedroom.

But she could tell that what Kermit saw were the things she hadn't noticed until after she'd been interrupted by the mail delivery Saturday morning. The empty spaces in Jesse's chest of drawers. The empty hangers in his closet.

"There isn't a suitcase in here," Kermit pointed out, closing the closet door.

"He had a soft-sided bag," she said. "And, yes, it's gone. But that doesn't mean Jesse packed it. And it doesn't mean he didn't pack it against his will. I'm hoping it means that if he was kidnapped, whoever took him intends to keep him alive, at least for now."

"Serena—"

"And that's not all," she said, leading him back into the living room. Darn it, she couldn't blame him for the misgivings in his voice. Walking the house with another living person, it was hard to remember the subtle hints that had convinced her something bad had happened there.

"There was mail opened on the coffee table," Serena said, pointing to the pile. "But Jesse never returned opened mail to its envelope like that. It's too tidy. And then there's this mail."

She grabbed a handful of envelopes left on the seat of the recliner. "The mail carrier delivered these while I was here Saturday morning. They nearly scared me to death coming through the slot."

"Serena," Kermit repeated. "Tell me you did not interfere with Jesse's mail."

Serena stared at him. "It practically landed in my lap."

"Mail tampering is a federal offense."

She sighed and raised her right hand. "I didn't interfere with Jesse's mail. It just happened to be open when it came through the slot. Satisfied?"

He frowned at her. "You are not nearly as funny as you think you are."

"And I used to think Destiny was exaggerating when she said you were as anal-retentive as Daniel."

His eyes glittered. "Daniel would have arrested you by now."

She gave him her best smug smile. "You would have arrested me by now if we were driving your car."

He laughed. "I may yet. Just tell me what you found while you weren't tampering with Jesse's mail so we can get out of here before we *both* get arrested."

"I just looked at his phone bill," Serena said. That might not be virtuous, but the rules changed when someone's life might be in danger. "There were a bunch of calls to an Orange County area code. I'm assuming that's Nadia's number. But there were also several calls to Sacramento. I tried calling the number from home, just to see who it belonged to."

Kermit shook his head. "You know you sound like a stalker, don't you?"

That was precisely why she hadn't told quite everything to the police officer she'd spoken with the day before.

"Don't you want to know who it was?"

She could tell he wanted to say *no*. But his curiosity was as bad as hers.

"It doesn't matter if I do or not," he said instead. "You'll tell me, anyway."

"It was the FBI."

For the first time that morning, she saw his eyes narrow with interest. "The FBI?"

"The Sacramento main office." She let him think about that. "Officer Riley said all I had was a hunch, even when I told him Jesse had called the FBI. I don't think that's true, but I do have a bad feeling about all of this. Something strange is going on, and I think Jesse could be in real trouble."

"Or maybe Nadia is," Kermit said.

She could have hugged him for that tiny acknowledgment that she might not be delusional. Maybe she would have hugged him if he hadn't suddenly looked so much like a cop, a professional considering a case. She hadn't seen that steel in his eyes very often.

"I thought of Nadia, too," she said. "And when I checked the phone bill again, the three times he called the FBI were each just a few minutes after he'd finished a conversation with the Orange County number. Here, look at this."

She shuffled the mail from her left hand to her right. Then did it again. She turned back to the recliner, crouched down to feel behind its seat cushion. Her pulse quickened in her throat as she turned to look up at Kermit.

"The phone bill is gone." The words sounded strange. Surely that wasn't fear in her voice. "Someone's been in here and taken it."

Chapter 4

The Hope Point Life Integration Clinic was housed in a two-story slate blue Victorian house two blocks north of the town square. A marker stuck into the lawn named it the Broadside House, for the lumber baron who'd had it built in 1884.

Kermit climbed the concrete steps from the sidewalk to the lawn, terraced onto the steep H Street hill. The cement walkway led to another set of wooden stairs up to a front porch that creaked enough under his weight to be over a hundred years old. But geraniums spilled from window boxes in bright pinks and whites, and the doormat glowed with sunflowers, creating a welcoming ambiance.

Kermit guessed the clinic's clients could use it. The nameplates beside the door listed two general counselors, including Jesse Banos, who had an impressive list of letters ranged after his name, a social worker specializing in addiction, and one specializing in couples counseling.

The front door opened into a dark, narrow hall, but to the right a door stood open under a welcome sign. Kermit ducked under the low lintel and still managed to catch the top of his head on it. The plump young woman behind the long office desk glanced up.

"We have to get that fixed," she said. "It's just it's a weight-bearing structure, so it's going to be complicated. But I don't think it'd be a very good start to a session to have a client knock himself out trying to get through the door."

Bad Moon Rising

The waiting room looked like something out of one of those Jane Austen movies Destiny had rented after a barbecue one night: sweet rose wallpaper, lace curtains, high-backed chairs with brocade seats. Two of the chairs were currently occupied by a sullen youth with a nose ring and his long-suffering mother.

A photograph hanging on one wall showed four people in front of a rustic cabin. Kermit recognized Jesse, his perfect teeth showing in a broad smile as he stood with his arms around the other three figures, two men and a woman. Kermit guessed they were the clinic's other counselors.

"Do you have an appointment?" the redheaded receptionist asked, scanning down her book.

"No. I was just hoping I could speak with Mr. Banos for a minute. Is he in today?"

Bright brown eyes peered at him from under fiery, spiked bangs. "You're the second walk-in he's had today. Too bad, though, because he's not in. I can schedule an appointment for you for next week. Or maybe work you in with another of our counselors, if it's urgent. We're a little tight this week, with Mr. Avalos on that mission to Guatemala, but I'm sure we could squeeze you in with Ms. Mitchell or Mr. Crow."

Kermit shook his head, hoping he wasn't reddening at her kindhearted concern. He wouldn't feel awkward if this were a real case. But it wasn't, and he wasn't a licensed private investigator, and he felt like a fraud.

Yet every time he told himself he should back out and go home, he remembered Serena's fear when she hadn't been able to find Jesse's telephone bill. Probably she'd stuck it in her purse after reading it the other day and simply forgotten where she put it. But as little as he cared where Jesse Banos had run off to, he couldn't leave Serena to be afraid alone.

At least he'd convinced her to go to work and leave him to the footwork. Jesse's colleagues at the clinic might be more likely to share information with someone other than Jesse's recent ex. And if he did track Jesse down, he could feel free to let the man know just what he thought of him.

"No, I'm not one of his clients," Kermit said. And he wasn't going to use his job to pry information out of her, either. He gave her his best boy-next-door grin. "Jesse's a friend of a friend. Do you know where I can reach him?"

Her expression sharpened as she sized him up, but the grin brought out her own smile. "No, I'm sorry. But if you leave your number, I can have him call when he gets in."

"You expect him in today?" He couldn't keep the hope out of his voice.

She shook her head. "No, he's out for the rest of the—"

"Ouch! Damned door!"

Kermit turned at the thud and the exclamation that followed it. A tall, cadaverously thin man with unruly black hair entered from the hall, rubbing his forehead with one narrow hand, clasping a stack of files with the other. Kermit recognized him from the cabin photograph, the man on the other side of the attractive woman from Jesse.

"Mr. Crow," the receptionist said, gesturing at Kermit. "This gentlemen says he's a friend of Mr. Banos's. He's trying to get in touch with him."

"Kermit Riggs." Kermit offered his hand. Despite the other man's skeletal frame, he had a firm handshake. And he was just as tall as he looked. Kermit wasn't used to looking up to meet someone's gaze, even an inch or two.

"Nigel Crow," the man replied, setting the stack of files on the desk. The plaque outside the door identified Nigel Crow as the marriage counselor. So much for typecasting. Kermit would have pegged him for the addiction social worker, probably because he was thin and pale enough to look like a seventies rock star addict himself. "You're a friend of Jesse's?"

"An acquaintance," Kermit clarified, sticking to the strict truth. Serena could accuse him of anal-retentiveness all she wanted, but Jesse wasn't worth lying for. "I've been trying to get in touch with him, but he's not answering his home phone or his cell."

"You've got his home number?"

Counselor Crow probably asked questions like, "And you thought slashing your husband's tires with a chainsaw was a good idea?" in that same pleasant, neutral voice.

Kermit reached into his back pocket. Just because he didn't intend to lie didn't mean he had to let them think he was some kind of disgruntled ex-client come back to even the score on his therapist. He flipped open his wallet to his ID.

"This isn't an official investigation," he said, jumping in on the receptionist's gasp. "As I said, I'm just concerned because I haven't been able to reach Mr. Banos."

Nigel Crow's blade-like face sharpened further. "That's because Jesse's gone out of town, Officer Riggs."

Kermit declined to mention that he'd gathered that much himself.

"He left voluntarily?" He was embarrassed to ask the ridiculous question. It made the receptionist gasp again, covering her mouth with her hand, her bright red nails the same color as her hair.

"Sherry," Nigel warned, glancing at the sullen teenager and his mother staring at them from across the room. He looked back at Kermit. "Yes, he left voluntarily."

Kermit saw nothing antagonistic in the psychologist's intelligent dark eyes, but he knew stonewalling when he saw it.

"Did he tell you where he went?"

"No." The answer was not too quick, not too slow. In fact, Nigel looked much too pleased by the truth of the statement for it to be a lie. And yet, something about it bothered Kermit. Still, he didn't need to find Jesse. All he needed to do was determine that the man was alive and operating under his own power.

"I assume he told you when he would be returning?"

"He did." This time the man couldn't hide the tiny smile that twitched the corner of his mouth.

Kermit smiled back. It didn't bother him when suspects and witnesses underestimated him. He preferred it that way. "And can you tell me when that will be?"

The psychologist shrugged his narrow crane's shoulders, his oppositional stance easing slightly. "He should be in next Monday, if you care to try back then."

"I'll do that," Kermit said. "Your receptionist said I could leave a number with you?"

"Of course," Nigel agreed, relaxing further, his professionally supportive attitude finally emerging. "Just give it to Sherry, and we'll have Jesse ring you up when he returns."

Kermit smiled in gratitude, as if he weren't trying to search Nigel Crow's soul to find out why he'd been so recalcitrant to begin with. What was Jesse up to? Or did Nigel just have something against cops? Some people did, which could make it hard to tell when they were hiding something and when they were simply being obstructionist out of principle.

He took the sticky note Sherry handed him and wrote his name and number. She made a friendly show of sticking the note in a prominent place by the telephone.

Kermit gave her another grin. "If he happens to get in touch with you before next week, would it be possible to ask him to give me a call?"

"We'll give him the message," Nigel assured him, offering his hand once more.

"Thank you." Kermit turned toward the door, paused, turned back. "He really didn't tell you why he had to take this emergency leave?"

"No, he didn't," Nigel replied firmly, recognizing the trap too late. His thin face pinched, but he didn't rush in to compound the mistake by sputtering out a story about how it wasn't emergency leave at all, but a planned vacation.

Kermit admired the man's composure, though he would have preferred cooperation. He had to remind himself that this was not a police case. All he had to do was reassure Serena that Jesse was alive and well.

Still, the interview with Nigel Crow had aroused his curiosity. What had called Jesse away from home so suddenly, and why didn't his colleague want Kermit to know?

As he left the office deep in thought, the door lintel caught him smack in the middle of his forehead, a reminder of just how dangerous curiosity could be.

"No, Professor Nagle, it doesn't matter how careful you are about locking your door, it's not okay to keep containers of hydrofluoric acid sitting on your office desk." Serena put the steel of unbending certitude into her voice, despite the disappointment her pronouncement caused the anxious geology professor.

"But, Miss Davis—" He looked up at her with an ingratiating smile as he pushed his glasses into place with pudgy fingers. "—I need it for dissolving silicates. They're good, airtight plastic containers. Let me explain the safety precautions I intend—"

"No. I'm sorry, Professor. Not under any circumstances." She continued down the hall toward her office, checking her watch. One-fifteen. She still had time to finish writing up her inspection of the geology lab before she left to pick up Sarah from school. She'd volunteered Sarah for Fleur's afternoon walks, so Kermit wouldn't have to run home over his dinner break. It was the least she could do after waking him up on his day off for her wild kidnapping fantasy.

Today, Thursday, was Kermit's last twelve-hour shift for the week, so Serena wouldn't have to get to work early tomorrow and skip lunch in order to pick up Sarah and drive her to Kermit's. Sarah could take the bus home from school, though due to early dismissal for the last day of classes for the summer, that meant she'd be home by herself for almost four hours.

So far, Serena had resisted the impulse to ask her boss for another early day. Sarah had worked hard to re-earn the trust she had broken by skipping a week of school that past November. She deserved to enjoy her first afternoon of freedom without her mother hovering over her like a vulture.

Serena remembered that her own mother had developed a very good vulture impression when Serena hit junior high.

"Miss Davis?"

She whirled to find stout Professor Nagle scurrying to catch up with her. He had a personality like the badger he resembled. He never gave up.

"Miss Davis, I understand that your job is to protect the staff and students of the college from the dangers of hazardous materials, but I assure you that I—"

"My job is to help ensure compliance with state and federal regulations concerning the use and disposal of hazardous materials," Serena corrected him, gently but firmly. "I have no doubt you know what you're doing, Professor."

A white lie. Sometimes she wondered if any of the teaching staff at Pacific Coast Community College really knew what they were doing when it came to hazardous materials, whether it was wall paint or potentially explosive picric acid. She had grown fond of some of her repeat offenders over the past two years, like Professor Nagle, with his endless enthusiasm for his work. But she worried about them, too. It wouldn't surprise her a bit to learn they kept improperly labeled bottles of ammonia in their home refrigerators next to the salad dressing or experimented using small charges of TNT to get rid of their gophers, à la *Caddyshack*.

"Regulations, Professor," she reminded him, as she reached the door to the Environmental Health and Occupational Safety office. "Hydrofluoric acid must be stored properly in the storeroom at all times, except when it is under your direct control. Do you understand?"

The professor's round shoulders sagged, and he sighed, but she held his gaze sternly until he nodded. "I understand."

"I'll see you later, Professor."

She thought he murmured something about not if he saw her first, but he gave her a sad smile and headed back down the hall toward the geology department.

She sighed and entered the cramped warren of scarred wooden desks, overflowing filing cabinets, and tiny cubicles that formed the nerve center for protecting people like Professor Nagle from themselves.

"One of these days that man is going to burn a hole straight through his desk and down into the biology department downstairs," Serena announced in frustration to her boss, the only other current occupant of the warren.

With his long, knife-edge nose and small, even teeth,

Wyler Odom looked nothing like a rabbit, but his jerky, nervous movements as he shuffled through the papers strewn across the front desk made the rodent image appropriate.

"Oh? Serena." He didn't look up from the papers. "I don't suppose you know where I left that memo from Calvin about the oil leaking in the garage?" He ran both hands through his shaggy brown hair, making it stand up around his head. "I can't find a stapler, either, if you've got one in your desk. And some thumbtacks?"

He blinked at her hopefully before returning to the repetitive shuffling. "And I need you to run over to the chemistry department this afternoon and give that safety talk we had scheduled for next week. I guess Dr. Pooler called to change the time on Monday, but I lost the message until just now."

Serena sucked in her protest. It wouldn't do any good. Wyler wouldn't hear her, anyway. When he was in panic mode, he wouldn't hear the last trumpet sounding.

Instead, she opened the top desk drawer in front of him and pulled out a stapler and a box of tacks. "I think you stuck that memo from Calvin on the bulletin board."

He glanced over at the board beside the desk. "No, wrong one, there's a new one."

Serena struggled not to sigh. "What time is the presentation for the chem department?"

"One-thirty? Two?"

Serena glanced at the clock. She could try to pin Wyler down, or she could just decide it was at two. That would almost give her time to dig out her standard safety lecture, work up a few notes, and dash up the hill to the chemistry department. It would not give her time to bake the homemade cookies she sometimes used to bribe students and faculty to attend her safety talks, but if no one showed, she could come back and do her paperwork.

As she edged past the front desk toward her cubicle, Wyler glanced up again.

"Oh, there's somebody back there," he said. His pale brown eyes widened as they settled on hers for a second. "He's been waiting about fifteen minutes. He says he's with the FBI."

"With *who?*" Serena caught her foot on a table leg and stumbled forward to the entrance to her cubicle. The man sitting in her chair glanced up from where he was flipping through her appointment calendar.

He didn't look FBI. Oh, he had the obsessively short dark hair and the bland suit from a hundred B movies, but his Al Pacino nose, manicured nails, and shark-like smile reminded her more of the Mob.

"Dominick Johnson," he introduced himself, rising to offer his hand.

Serena didn't take it. "Don't you need a search warrant to do that?" she demanded, gesturing toward the appointment book.

He shrugged, lowering himself back into the only chair in the cubicle. "I got bored."

"And aren't you supposed to show me your badge?"

He reached inside his jacket, and Serena felt a split second of panic that he really was with the Mob, after all, and since she'd called him on it, he was going to have to shoot her. But all he pulled out was a flip-out wallet with a photo ID in it that identified him as FBI agent Dominick Johnson.

She was going to have to quit teasing Sarah about her overactive imagination. Then again, when your sister had been shot at by a sniper and your brother-in-law had been framed for murder, both in the same year, maybe you could be forgiven for occasional lapses in your faith in humanity.

"What can I do for you, Agent Johnson?" she asked. Not until the words left her mouth did the possibilities flash through her mind. What could an FBI agent want with her? "Oh, my God. Is my daughter all right? She hasn't been kidnapped from school?"

"No, no." His wide mouth turned down, more in irritation than compassion. "Your daughter is fine, as far as I know. I'm here to ask you a couple of questions about a man I believe is a friend of yours. Jesse Banos."

Serena sucked in a breath, let it out again. *Sarah is fine.* She had to repeat it to herself a couple of times before she could take in the rest of Agent Johnson's words.

"Jesse?" Ever since Kermit had called her Monday night to let her know that Jesse had left town of his own free will and had notified his coworkers of that fact, she hadn't thought twice about his disappearance—mostly because when she did think of it, she felt like a complete idiot. Kermit had kindly told her that he didn't mind in the least that she was a complete idiot, and the humor had helped. But not much.

She had called Callista and blamed the whole, embarrassing incident on her and the tarot cards. Callista had only intoned a sepulchral comment about how Serena should be extra cautious for the next week or so.

And Serena had promised she would be careful—you had to let a friend save face now and then. But perhaps she hadn't been careful enough. Had Jesse reported her for breaking into his house? Was her opening one piece of Jesse's mail really a federal offense?

She decided now was not the time to ask. "Is Jesse in some kind of trouble?"

"Do you have reason to think he is?"

She'd spent enough time dating a counselor to use the answering-a-question-with-a-question technique fairly well herself. "Is there something specific you want to know? I have a presentation to give across campus in fifteen minutes."

"How well do you know Jesse Banos?"

She'd wondered that herself over the past six months. "We were engaged."

"Were?"

"His interests turned elsewhere."

Agent Johnson's peaked eyebrows rose slightly. "He has a new girlfriend? Who is she?"

Serena stared back at him. "I don't know what he's doing or who he's doing it with, and I don't particularly care. What is this all about? Is Jesse all right?"

"You don't know where he is?"

"No. He doesn't feel the need to run his schedule past me." For some reason Agent Johnson's attitude brought out the worst in her. She tried again. "Really, we have no reason to stay in touch. He left town this past weekend without telling me where he was going. Do *you* know where he went?"

His grim expression told her he'd rather eat nails than admit he didn't. "Can you tell me who he left town with? You implied he had a new lady friend."

Serena shook her head. "Not in the area, that I know of. I assumed he went away by himself. Maybe he went to visit his folks in the Bay Area. Have you talked with them?"

"Did Jesse Banos ever hit you, Ms. Davis?"

"*Hit* me? Jesse?" If he'd asked her if she'd run Jesse over and left him lying in a ditch somewhere, it would have surprised her less. "No. Never."

"Did he ever threaten you with physical harm?"

65

"No." The only person she'd ever heard Jesse threaten to kill was his brother, Mark, and that was only after Mark had tried to buy black-market prescriptions less than a month after getting out of rehab.

"You don't need to fear telling the truth, Ms. Davis. We have the resources to protect you from retaliation."

And a cozy way of putting it, too, Serena thought, deeply grateful that she didn't need Agent Johnson's protection.

"I'm not afraid of Jesse Banos," she said firmly. "Unless you know something about him that I don't know?"

"I want to make sure you feel free to tell me what you know." Agent Johnson took a pen from the cup on her desk and wrote a number on one of her sticky pads. "I'll be staying at the Flyway Express Inn at the airport if you decide you need my help."

He pushed himself away from her desk and stood, the interview apparently at an end. Serena crossed her arms over her chest. He might have taken her chair, but that left her standing in the only exit to the cubicle.

"Just what is going on here?" she asked. "Jesse might be low on my list of favorite people at the moment, but he wouldn't hurt a fly. Where is he, and why are you asking me about it?"

"Ms. Davis, it's my experience that people's attitudes toward flies have very little to do with their willingness to harm their fellow humans. If Mr. Banos has gone away with a woman, she could be in grave danger. I don't know what he has or hasn't done to you, but I'm sure you wouldn't want another woman's death on your conscience, even if you see her as the 'other' woman."

Agent Johnson was scarcely an inch taller than Serena's five foot eight, but his dark eyes seemed to bore into her from a greater height. After a long moment, she stepped aside from the cubicle opening.

"I don't know anything that can help you," she said, trying not to look guilty. After all, she *didn't* know anything. She doubted Jesse had driven all the way down to Orange County to confront Nadia's philandering husband. Besides, she didn't know the woman's last name. And from what little Jesse had told her, she would be more concerned about Nadia's husband's temper than anything Jesse might do.

In fact, her overactive imagination might even point out that Agent Johnson's questioning seemed specifically designed to trick information out of a supposedly jilted lover rather than having any relation to reality.

"Call me if you change your mind," Agent Johnson said, brushing past her with a shiver of cold air that touched her like the wings of the angel of death.

Stop that, Serena! But as she watched Agent Johnson weave his way out of the Hazmat office, she wished Callista were there to read the man's aura. She would have liked to know how much of the man's sinister demeanor was a sulky attitude and how much was something darker.

All she got when she cleared her "inner mind" was a disembodied voice saying, "Leave the gun. Take the canolli."

Wyler, now digging through desk drawers like a terrier after a rat, shrank aside as the FBI agent passed, as if he could feel the menace, too. But then his darting glance fell on Serena. He blinked in surprise, though he must have been able to hear her conversation with Agent Johnson. "Aren't you supposed to be over in the chemistry building right now?"

Serena prevented her eyes from rolling by an act of will. "I'm on my way."

She ducked back into her cubicle and dug into her filing

cabinet—the one Wyler was not allowed to touch under pain of death. She grabbed the folder of standard safety information. She'd given this presentation often enough, she ought to be able to wing it.

She reached into the Cloverbrook Middle School mug on her desk, but after rattling it around twice, she couldn't find her red gel pen. The phone number on her sticky pad caught her eye. Red ink. Agent Johnson had pocketed her pen.

Her guilt at not mentioning Nadia to him evaporated. But as she scooted out through the office and started the long jog down the hall to the stairs, she could feel the return of the dark, niggling fear that had subsided with Kermit's investigation earlier in the week.

Once again, she could see the death card like a portent of doom on Callista's shop counter. Once again, she could feel the shiver of dread she'd felt when she'd realized someone else had been searching Jesse's house, the sickening drop in her stomach when she saw the phone bill was gone.

Maybe Jesse hadn't been kidnapped or murdered. Yet. But something strange was definitely going on. Destiny would tell her she had to let Jesse make his own mistakes. Her brother-in-law would tell her it was none of her business. Kermit would get that worried look in his eyes. But they hadn't been there when Callista had predicted trouble and said that she, Serena, would land right in the middle of it.

She burst out the hall door into a bright June afternoon freshened by a breeze straight up the Black Bear River delta from the sea. But the sunshine couldn't dispel the darkness in her heart.

What in heaven's name have you gotten yourself into, Jesse?

Chapter 5

"Do you really think this is a good idea?" Gemma asked for the thousandth time as Sarah reached up to pull the bell for the next bus stop.

"You don't have to come," Sarah responded, her patience run dry, as the short, orange Hope Point Municipal Bus swayed to a stop in front of Green River Hospital.

But Gemma hefted her backpack, crammed full as Sarah's of the year-long accumulation of junk from their lockers, and followed Sarah out onto the sidewalk in front of the hospital.

"Your mom's going to ground you for life," Gemma warned as they darted across the street toward the residential neighborhood stretching toward the cow pastures and the sea.

"She said we could take the bus downtown after school," Sarah reminded her best friend. She shifted her backpack from one shoulder to the other. They probably should have gone to her house first, to drop off their stuff, but she'd been too impatient to wait another hour for the next scheduled bus.

"This isn't downtown," Gemma said, struggling to keep up as Sarah set a ground-eating pace into the Bottoms.

"We did go downtown," Sarah said, trying not to sigh over her friend's literal-mindedness. "We transferred buses there, remember?"

"You know what I mean, Sarah Davis," Gemma

snapped, tossing her red curls with flair. "Your mom already looked through Jesse's place, anyway. And with Officer Riggs, too. I don't know what you expect to find."

"I don't, either," Sarah admitted, slowing her pace to let her friend catch up. "But he's got to have left some clue to where he went. And some clue to who that Nadia lady is that Mom was talking to Callista about on the phone last night."

"I still can't believe you were eavesdropping."

Sarah shrugged off her friend's approval. She didn't like to encourage Gemma's belief that junior high survival required ears like a rabbit's and a willingness to use them shamelessly. Her own strategy was to pretend that most of the rest of the seventh graders didn't exist and hope they'd do the same for her.

She especially ignored the whispers every time Brian Tilson stopped to talk with her in the hall or when she'd help him with his math homework at recess. She knew every time Brian smiled at her it meant another snide comment from Jennifer Bright—*What did you do to your hair this morning, Sarah, wash it in the toilet?* But as long as Brian smiled at her, who cared what jealous old Jennifer said?

She took the same route her mother had that previous Saturday, down the street behind Jesse's, so they could slip between his back neighbors' houses and into his yard, exposed only briefly to the side windows of his next-door neighbor's house.

"You're sure he's not here?" Gemma hissed as Sarah unlatched the gate.

"Do you see his car?" Sarah asked. The grass was tall with neglect and still wet from the morning's fog, despite the afternoon sunshine. Sarah's sneakers were soaked by the time they reached the back door.

As Sarah dug into her backpack for the key she'd pilfered from her mom's purse the night before, a sudden surge of nerves ran up the back of her legs. Gemma could have a point about this not being such a good idea. Except Gemma never thought anything bold was a good idea. If she backed out now, what kind of example would she be setting? A cowardly one, that's what.

She found the key and unlocked the door. After all, she was practically Jesse's stepdaughter. A stepdaughter had every right to enter her stepfather's house.

She stepped through the door into the kitchen before she could remind herself that Jesse and her mom weren't even engaged anymore, much less married, and that Jesse had never seemed that interested in being her stepfather, anyway. Detective Parks—it was still hard to remember to call him Uncle Daniel—had come to more of her school basketball and softball games that year than Jesse had. So had Kermit, for that matter.

Of course, that hadn't stopped Jesse from feeling free to lecture her every time he thought she messed up. Like forgetting to take out the garbage once was such a crime.

"If Jesse is such a jerk and you don't want to get him back together with your mom, why do you even care if he's shacking up with some chick named Nadia?" Gemma whispered, as they tiptoed through the kitchen. It smelled like stale dishwater.

"I *don't*," Sarah insisted, stepping into the dim living room. She doubted they'd find anything there that her mother and Kermit had missed. "What I care about is that he hurt my mom so bad. He kept making excuses all spring about why he couldn't spend any time with her, about all his clients needing help and about looking after Mark and going to visit his folks. Like he's some kind of saint. He

71

thinks he's such hot stuff he can get away with anything. Come on, his computer's down this way."

"You're not going to trash his files, right?" Gemma asked, following her into the bedroom. "I mean your mom's better off without him. Like my grandma says about my dad, he's not worth going to jail for."

"I'm not going to trash his files," Sarah promised, dropping her backpack next to the computer desk. "I'm just going to figure out where he is, so I can call up that FBI agent who talked to Mom yesterday and give him the information."

"That's a pretty good plan," Gemma admitted, settling onto her half of Jesse's desk chair as Sarah booted up the PC. "But I don't know how you're going to find him if the FBI can't. Do you think Jesse's in really big trouble? What do you think he did? You think your mom was in danger while they were going out?"

"Maybe," Sarah said. Then, remembering that Gemma's father had gone to jail for abuse, she answered more honestly, "Mom doesn't think so. She told Callista that Jesse might be a low-down, faithless dog, but he'd never hit a woman. She thinks the FBI agent was fishing for something, but she doesn't know what. She wants Jesse to come back and straighten things out so she doesn't have to field his crap anymore."

With a flick of the mouse, she started scrolling through the files on Jesse's hard drive. Most of the word processing and spreadsheet files had case numbers in the titles. Probably client files or research for the clinic. She didn't want to trespass on those.

"Look." Gemma pointed. "*Hazard Pilot*. He's got some cool games."

"Dig one of those CD-R's out of my backpack," Sarah

72

said, nudging it around the front of the chair toward Gemma. "Please."

"You're gonna pirate his games?"

"No." Sarah ignored Gemma's disappointment and popped the rewritable CD into Jesse's burner. "I'm going to copy his address book and stuff like that. Then we can go over it back home."

As the PC burned the files onto her CD, Sarah double-clicked on Jesse's mail program. *ShrinkRap@hplink.com.* Sarah rolled her eyes.

A password request popped up, and she typed in *freudianslip.* "Jesse was over at our house one night when he got a call on his cell phone and said he had to check his e-mail. He told me he was going to use my computer."

"And you scoped his password? Remind me never to let you stand behind me when I check my mail."

"I wouldn't have done it if he'd *asked* to use my computer," Sarah said primly. "Besides, you already told half the school your password's *ilovejustin,* so it wouldn't do you any good to hide it from me. Sheesh! Hasn't he ever heard of spamblockers?"

"He's got lots of offers to enhance body parts," Gemma commented as Sarah scrolled through a week's worth of junk mail. She snickered. "You think he needs help in that department?"

"He's got offers to enhance body parts he doesn't even *have,*" Sarah said, trying not to blush. "I don't see anything good in here. He hasn't even checked his mail since last Friday."

"It's almost three," Gemma said. "We've got to get back to the bus stop so we can get home before your mom does."

"Yeah, okay," Sarah said, her own nerves beginning to jitter. "Just let me finish looking through this list. I don't

73

want to miss it if he's gotten an e-mail from Nadia."

But she reached the screen of that morning's e-mails without seeing a single message she thought worth the risk to open.

As she moved the mouse up to quit the mail program, a window suddenly flashed open on the screen.

"Ohmigod," Gemma squeaked, ducking behind Sarah. "Ohmigod. We're caught! Somebody's instant messaging us."

So, you thought you could hide from me? The message read, in bright red ink. *You think you're so smart, but I knew you'd surface eventually. I have patience and resources you can't imagine. Are you scared, Banos?*

"Somebody's instant messaging Jesse," Sarah corrected, her adrenaline shifting from panicked terror to terrified excitement. "And look at the screen name."

"Shrinkwrecker," Gemma read, still pulled as far back on the chair as possible. "It's like Jesse's."

"It's like he picked it to threaten Jesse," Sarah said. She reached for the keyboard.

"Sarah! What are you doing?"

"Finding out what's going on." Her mother griped at her for hunting and pecking, but she could still type faster than anybody else in her class.

Who are you and what do you want?

The screen remained quiet for a long moment, and Sarah wondered if answering back had scared Shrinkwrecker off, but then another message scrolled under hers.

You know who I am. I'm your worst nightmare, and I'm coming after you.

Ooo. That's so original, Sarah typed.

"Sarah! He's going to kill us!"

"He doesn't even know who we are," Sarah said, though her own heart was pounding. She'd had friends—friends whose cool parents allowed them to IM, unlike her mother—who'd gotten weird messages before. She figured most of them were dumb pranks from other kids who didn't have anything better to do. But there was something about this Shrinkwrecker that felt serious. "If I get him mad, maybe he'll let something slip that will help us identify him."

It was a tactic she'd learned from watching *Law & Order*, but Kermit said it really did work sometimes. Most criminals weren't all that bright.

You want to be a wise ass? Good. I was going to make you an offer. Return what's mine, I won't kill you. But I don't think I want to make that offer. I don't even think I want to kill you. At least not until you beg me to. I'm sure you know by now that's not an idle threat. I'll be seeing you soon, Banos. I'm closing in.

In the cool, silent room, Sarah could hear Gemma's breathing, fast and shallow. Or maybe that was her breathing.

"Ohmigod," Gemma whimpered. "We've got to get out of here. Now. Come on, Sarah."

"It's just a dumb threat. If he knew where Jesse was, he wouldn't be hanging around waiting to instant message him." But her hand was shaking as she quit out of the mail program.

"Are you gonna tell your mom about this?" Gemma asked.

"She'd kill me." But for once, that was almost a comforting thought.

"So would Grandma." Gemma sat in thought while Sarah ejected her CD from the burner. "Maybe we don't have to tell them we broke into Jesse's house. You use the same mail program. You could tell your mom we logged on to Jesse's account from your house."

Sarah glanced at her friend with impressed admiration. "That would work. Then maybe we'd only get grounded, not killed."

She directed the computer to shut down and bent to heft her backpack from the floor. "Let's go home. Nobody will ever know we were here."

But a harsh male voice from directly behind her froze her in place. "Think again, kid. You're not going anywhere."

The smell of ink and incense and sweat struck Serena's nose as she pushed through the narrow Body Works Body Art front doorway into the tattoo parlor. The cramped space between the black-curtained windows and the counter usually held an assortment of pierced, dyed, and tattooed transients and college students, but today only a pair of shaggy, graying bikers in Harley jackets leaned against the counter chatting with the animated, open-faced man cleaning up the tattooing area in the back of the shop.

Serena's stomach twisted a little at the sight of the tattoo artist's high Greek cheekbones and thick dark hair. Mark Banos was smaller than Jesse, not any taller than Serena, and his features were softer, rounder. But when he flashed that welcoming grin the family resemblance was nearly painful—especially since any comparison between the two brothers had to take into account the muting of Jesse's sharp intelligence in Mark's wide eyes.

Mark had been clean and sober for over six months now, but Serena knew he'd never be the same quicksilver jester Jesse described him as being before drugs took over his life.

"Serena!" He set down the medieval-looking tools he was organizing and came to the counter to grab her hands in his. "Long time no see."

For a mortifying instant, Serena thought Jesse hadn't bothered to mention their breakup to his brother, but Mark's smile dimmed as he patted her ringless right hand.

"Sorry to hear about the dust-up, man. That's messed up. I told Jesse you were the best thing that ever happened to him. He said yeah, but some things just don't work out, you know? Guess it wasn't meant to be."

He turned to the bikers down the counter. "My brother let this lady get away," he announced, waving his free hand like a symphony conductor. "Can you believe it? What a flippin' idiot."

The two men turned to assess Serena through identical reflective silver sunglasses. They could have been twins in their black leather jackets, jeans, and ZZ Top beards, but the taller one wore a red bandanna tied around his scalp and the heavier one had a ragged scar puckering the left side of his mouth.

One lewd comment from the duo, and Serena swore to herself she'd disembowel Mark with his own tattoo needles.

But the two men just shook their heads, frowning in sympathy.

"That's rough," Bandanna Man said. "Classy lady like you, though, you won't have any trouble finding yourself another man."

"If you want one," Scarface added with a self-deprecating laugh. "We're all pretty much flippin' idiots, if you want to know the truth."

For once, words failed her. Serena managed a small smile before turning back to Mark. She'd had to gear herself up for the embarrassment of this visit all day, reminding herself of Agent Johnson's questioning the afternoon before and Callista's continuing premonitions of disaster. But somehow stepping into the twilight zone of Body Works Body Art turned it into just another absurd encounter with Mark Banos.

"It's Jesse I came here to see you about," she confessed. "I know he's gone out of town, but I need to talk to him. Do you know how to get in touch with him?"

Mark's guileless eyes widened even farther. "Whoa. I told him to beg you to come back, but he said you'd never go for it. He said he'd screwed up too big."

"He was right," Serena agreed hastily, even as her mind slowed over Mark's words. Had Jesse really wanted to work things out when he'd left her that message the Wednesday before he split? Had her lack of a quick response upset him so much he'd left town? Is that what Callista had picked up on? Could losing her have driven him to drastic measures?

Yeah, right. Snapping herself back to the present, she settled her rampaging imagination. That didn't jive with Jesse's sorrowful acceptance of her returning his ring the week before. And soothing to her ego as it might be to believe that Jesse regretted his reprehensible behavior and desperately wanted her back in his life, his returning to beg her forgiveness would mostly just be really, really annoying and inconvenient.

"He was right," she told Mark. "We were one of those things that aren't meant to be. No, this is about a financial investment we went into together. I got some paperwork in the mail that we need to send back soon. It's not a lot of money, but I need to find out what Jesse wants to do about it."

When high, Mark could lie with the innocence of an angel, but Serena knew he had no corresponding defenses against even her own pitiful attempts at deceit. Lying to him would probably damage her karma for years to come. But she hadn't been able to come up with any other way to convince him to give up Jesse's whereabouts.

She wasn't about to tell him the FBI was looking for his brother.

Mark raised his eyebrows. "That's a dilemma, man. I wish I could tell you where Jesse went, but, like, I don't know. He didn't even tell me he was leaving town."

Serena watched him shrug off his hurt at his brother's thoughtless slight, and reminded herself one more time that if she found Jesse alive and well, that didn't mean she got to kill him.

"He's not visiting your folks?"

Jesse wore his familial loyalty like a badge of honor, an implied criticism of her own failure to visit her parents for Thanksgiving, a criticism of Sarah's not getting to spend holidays with her father in Santa Rosa.

Aren't Sarah and I part of your family now? she'd asked at Christmastime. *Isn't that part of what getting married is all about?*

We're not married yet, he'd reminded her. *That's why I can't take you with me to stay with my folks. They wouldn't approve, especially with you being divorced.*

And she'd felt his own disapproval in the words, too. She'd shown a failure of judgment, getting pregnant and married too young, and a failure of character, getting divorced. He was willing to forgive her failures, but he would always be the one in the relationship with the moral high ground.

She felt her face flame at the memory. Had she really let him get away with that for a minute, much less two years?

"He didn't tell my folks where he was going, either,"

Mark was saying, his hands waving restlessly across his chest. "I called them after that other guy came in looking for him. Jesse told Mom and Pop he was going out of town, but not, like, where he went. I guess he told them he had something personal he had to take care of."

"Someone else was looking for Jesse?"

"Yeah." Mark's whole body shifted as he shook his head. "Kind of a scary dude, you know."

"About your height, short dark hair, nose like a knife?" She could just imagine Agent Dominick Johnson's blood pressure rising as he tried to get information out of Mark Banos. She almost wished she'd been there to see it.

Mark stilled, frowning, as he tried to peer back in time. "Like, there were a couple of guys with him, and one of them had black hair, I think. But this guy, he was pretty blond, you know? Like almost without eyebrows. And he had kind of weird eyes. He was taller than me, too, probably as tall as Jesse. He said if I was lying to him, he'd break my fingers, and he might've had the muscle to do it himself, even if he didn't have the goons for backup."

"He *threatened* you? Did you call the police?"

Mark stared at her. "What for?"

"He threatened you," Serena repeated.

Mark blinked. "No big deal, man. Guys come in here and sound off sometimes. Besides, Jimbo and Tank were in the back. I didn't have anything to worry about."

Down the counter, Bandanna Man and Scarface ducked their heads modestly and shrugged, their broad shoulders stretching their Harley jackets in a way Serena hadn't noticed before.

"Weren't you worried about Jesse?" she managed to ask.

"What for?" Mark asked again. "Like, they didn't know where he was, right? Besides, Jesse can take care of himself.

I used to think he didn't have a clue about the real world, you know? Like some of the dudes I've tangled with? But some of his clients at that clinic are kind of, like, whacked."

"This was one of his clients who was looking for him?"

Mark's hands started waving again. "Hey, I don't know, man. I don't think so. I mean, this dude talked like a lawyer. Like about me obstructing stuff and suing me for stuff and I better not mess with him, because he could get my business license yanked and my parole revoked and all this stuff."

"Was this before or after he threatened to break your fingers?" Serena asked. She glanced down the counter, but Jimbo and Tank didn't appear any more shocked by such goings on than Mark. She thought about Mark thinking Jesse didn't have a clue about the real world. She didn't believe her own world was any less real than the one Mark was describing, but there was no doubt it was different.

"He said he had business with Jesse," Mark continued. "I knew it wasn't anything illegal. I mean, Jesse's too straight-arrow for that. So I figured maybe Jesse was going to testify about something in this guy's court case or something? Like an expert witness?"

"You don't think this man was law enforcement himself?"

Mark frowned. "No, I mean, I know all the guys on the Hope Point Police force."

Serena clenched her fingers around the edge of the counter, but kept her voice calm. "But he didn't say he was FBI or anything?"

Mark shook his head. "Like I said, he talked about pulling my license and stuff, but he didn't have a badge or anything."

"He wasn't FBI," Scarface offered. His stocky physique

81

suggested he might rate the appellation Tank. "The Feds like to flash those badges. And he wasn't tight-assed enough, either. I didn't like his vibes. Not quite stable. Like a meth-head, without the meth."

Bandanna Man nodded thoughtfully. "I've seen a few guys like that before. Mostly they ended up in Pelican Bay for offing somebody."

Cold fingers crawled up Serena's spine like a premonition of death. She shook the fingers off. Her bad feeling had nothing to do with Callista's realm of psychic phenomena and everything to do with the physical world of creepy lowlifes and maximum-security prisons.

"We've got to find Jesse," she told Mark. "If he's in trouble, we have to find him before these other people do."

"Yeah?" It was more question than agreement. "How?"

Good question. Coming to Mark had been her one bright idea in that direction. "We need help from the police."

Mark's open face shuttered. "I don't know, man. I say let Jesse take care of it himself. Things just get worse when the police get involved. I mean, Daniel Parks is okay, for a cop, you know, but he's not even in town."

"What about Kermit Riggs?" Serena asked. "Would you at least tell him what you told me? He'd take it more seriously coming from you."

A depressing thought, but probably true after her crying wolf earlier in the week.

Mark sighed. "Hey, man, I guess. Like, for you. But don't let him come here in his uniform, okay? If this guy's keeping an eye on my shop, I don't want him thinking I'm talking to the cops, you know?"

"Thanks, Mark." Impulsively, she leaned over the counter to kiss his cheek.

"Yeah, yeah, whatever," he said, blushing, obviously relieved to be saved by the sudden ringing of the shop telephone. "Take care of yourself, you know?"

"You, too, Mark." She acknowledged the good-bye waves of Jimbo and Tank and turned for the door.

"Oh, hey, wait." Mark waved a cordless receiver at her across the counter. "It's, like, for you. It's Callista."

Serena took the phone, a funny chill once more running up her spine. "Don't do this to me, Callista. How did you know I was here?"

Her friend's voice held none of her usual mysterious smugness. "You told me you were planning to go see Mark after work when we talked last night, remember? Kermit said he'd already tried you at work and at home before he called me. It was the only other place I could think to call you."

"Kermit?" Could he have found out something about Jesse? She couldn't imagine why else he might send Callista looking for her. If he needed more help walking Fleur, he could have just left a message . . . "Oh, no. Tell me nothing's happened to Fleur."

"It's not Fleur," Callista said, her voice flat. "Serena, it's Sarah. Kermit said you need to get over to Jesse's house right away."

Chapter 6

Sarah's home with Gemma. They're giggling over their year-books and playing their music too loud to hear the phone. The thought repeated through Serena's mind like a mantra.

The squad car in front of Jesse's house, Kermit's tangerine jalopy a few yards beyond it, jolted her out of the fantasy. She accelerated the Subaru toward the house, jerking it hard into the driveway. The tires squealed protest, and she smelled hot rubber as she threw herself from the car.

Jesse's front door opened, and Kermit stepped onto the porch. She ran across the lawn, tripping as she reached the porch, and he grabbed her, his strong hands steadying her, holding her still.

"Sarah?" She pulled toward the door. "Where is my daughter?"

"Serena, wait." He held her back, his voice as steady and strong as his hands. "I told Callista to tell you she's all right. Sarah's all right."

Serena glanced up at him, into those clear blue eyes that had seen too much evil and suffering to be young anymore, and she knew he couldn't lie about that. Her heart still beat hard against her ribs. She tried to breathe deeply enough to quiet it.

"Callista told me." The words shook, and she realized dimly that her whole body seemed to be shaking. "She told me, but then I saw the patrol car here, and I didn't see

84

Sarah. Where is my daughter, Kermit?"

"She's inside with Garth Vance. He's the one who called me—"

"Mommy?" The thin voice belonged to a much younger, less self-assured Sarah than the one who had told her just that morning that *everyone else's mom* was going to let them hang out at the mall all weekend unsupervised, and Serena was the uncoolest mother who ever lived.

But the tall, gangly girl who flew out the door into her arms was that very same, whole, healthy girl, and Serena held her, crushing her tight, as if she could somehow hold her close enough that nothing bad could ever reach her.

"Mrs. Davis?" another small voice quavered.

Serena reached out her arms to pull Gemma into the circle, too, and she thought the sniffles she heard belonged to the redhead, though she could feel Sarah's tears against her neck. Kermit squeezed her shoulder, then stepped away, and she felt the loss of his steadiness.

"Are you all right?" she asked finally, time dragging them all reluctantly back to the front porch, the mildew stains on the yellow paint a shadow in the late afternoon sunlight. "Are you hurt?"

"No, ma'am," Gemma said, wiping her eyes with her sleeve.

"Sarah?"

Sarah pulled back, shaking her head. Moisture turned her green eyes dark, but she held her chin firm. "I'm sorry, Mom. It was all my idea. Gemma didn't want to come with me. Don't let Officer Vance arrest her."

Serena felt her blank, mother's shield face settle into place, coming to her rescue as so many times before. She glanced up. Officer Garth Vance stood in the doorway, his thick arms crossed over his broad chest, his uniform crisp and stern as his stance. He'd taken off his signature dark sunglasses, but his hazel eyes showed no more emotion than the reflective lenses would have. Without a twitch of the muscles around his grim mouth, he winked at her.

She shifted her gaze to Kermit, standing sentinel beside the door. He gave her a quick shake of his head. No arrests were imminent.

She didn't let her relief show in her face as she turned back to her daughter. Good Mom receded into the background.

"I'm going to let Officer Vance do whatever he needs to do with you two girls," she assured them. "But first, Sarah Constance Davis, you are going to tell me what in heaven's name is going on here, and it better be good, or you're going to be wishing Officer Vance already had you in a holding cell down at the station."

"Might as well bring 'em on inside," Garth Vance growled. He stepped slightly to one side, making the girls shrink aside nervously as Serena glared them into the house.

"Sit," Serena commanded, pointing to the sofa. The girls looked small and helpless huddled in the center of Jesse's overstuffed leather monstrosity. Serena stood in front of them while the two officers flanked her, providing backup.

"It was all my idea," Sarah spoke up again, but her eyes met Serena's with more appeal than defiance.

"*What* was your idea?" Serena demanded.

"Breaking into this house?" Garth Vance suggested.

"I didn't break in," Sarah said, shooting a look at Serena. "It's not breaking in if you have a key."

Serena gritted her teeth. The sins of the mothers. "You do not want to dig yourself any deeper," she warned. "You told me you and Gemma were going downtown after school to do some window shopping and get some ice cream. What the hell are you doing here?"

Sarah flinched. "I'm really sorry, Mom."

To Serena's surprise, she saw real contrition in her daughter's eyes.

"I wasn't planning to do anything bad. I just thought if I could get onto Jesse's computer, I could find out where he went."

"And why would you care about that?" Serena asked, surprised for a moment out of her anger. She'd always been grateful that Sarah and Jesse got along, but neither one had ever tried to bridge the distance between them. She'd asked Sarah about it when Jesse had asked her to marry him, if she thought they could all be a family. Sarah's reply, that she already had a dad and didn't need another one, had bothered Serena deeply.

Up until her engagement disintegrated. Then she had simply been glad that her latest example of poor judgment in picking men wasn't going to scar her daughter's psyche.

"I didn't know you missed him that much, sweetie," she admitted.

Sarah's appalled expression absolved her of that guilt. "I don't! Geez, Mom. I think he's a total jerk for the way he treated you. It's just that you've been worrying about him so much."

She glanced past Serena to Kermit. "It's not like Mom misses him, either," she assured him. "She just wants to get on with her life, and he's sort of like an albatross around her neck."

As Serena briefly closed her eyes against the looks the two police officers must be giving her, the familiarity of

Sarah's words penetrated her memory. Her eyes snapped back open.

"You were eavesdropping on my telephone conversation with Callista last night!"

Sarah's cheeks reddened. "I thought if I could find out where Jesse went, we could turn him over to the FBI, and you wouldn't have to worry about him anymore."

"The FBI?" Kermit asked.

Serena pinched her nose against the pain beginning between her eyes. "Later?"

He nodded, and she turned back to her daughter. "So, you broke your word, stole a key from my purse, and entered Jesse's house without permission. Does that about sum up the situation?"

Sarah leaned forward on the couch. "Yeah, but Mom—"

"But?" Serena cut in, the word an icy warning. She could hardly hold her daughter's gaze, caught between wanting to hug her again just to make sure she was really safe and wanting to beg Garth to lock her up and throw away the key until Sarah turned at least twenty-five.

"The neighbor saw them sneaking into the backyard," Garth said, flipping out a notebook and making a show of checking his notes. "She thought they might be looking for money to buy drugs or planning to vandalize the place. I found them in the bedroom, playing with the homeowner's computer."

"I thought we were dead," Gemma said, putting a hand on her heart in remembered terror.

"We were checking Jesse's e-mail," Sarah jumped in. "And while we were—"

"I recognized one of the perps as Sarah," Garth continued, his unforgiving stare quelling the girls. "She said she refused to say anything self-incriminating until she had a lawyer present." For an instant, his control slipped, and a smile twitched his lips. "I called Kermit instead. Figured he could track you down."

For the first time, it occurred to Serena that Kermit was supposed to be off-duty today and that he was out of uniform. Way out of uniform. The torn black t-shirt he wore must have been ten years old, from before he filled out his frame, because it stretched tight across his chest, showing off weight-room muscles Serena hadn't realized were there. His faded, mud-spattered blue jeans fit nearly as well.

"I'd just gotten back from the woods with Fleur," Kermit apologized, swiping at the dirt.

"Sure." Thank God he thought that was the reason she'd been staring at his pants.

Serena snapped her gaze and her wandering thoughts back to her daughter. "What would you like to do with these girls, gentlemen? I'd be happy to let you haul them off to jail and take them off my hands."

"I think we can release them into your custody, ma'am," Garth said, his eyes gleaming with humor, though his expression never relaxed. "Based on my own mother, I'd bet that's a scarier proposition for these two than coming with me."

"You're sure?" Serena asked, even as she took the strong hand Garth offered her. "Thank you, Officer Vance. I'm sorry these girls caused you any trouble. It won't happen again."

Garth shot Sarah and Gemma a look as he dug his sunglasses out of his pocket. "Somehow, I can't say I'm as sure of that as you are." He fitted the sunglasses in place. "Seems like I've told you this before, Miss Davis, but you've gotta leave the detective work to the police. You, too, Miss Tasker. Next time somebody might shoot first and ask questions later."

"Yes, sir," Gemma said. "There won't be a next time, sir. My grandmother is going to kill me, and there won't be enough left to bury."

"Sarah?" Serena prompted.

"I understand, sir."

Garth grinned and headed for the door, pausing to box Kermit on the shoulder. "You'd think you'd know better, Riggs, after what Detective Parks has gone through with that Millbrook woman of his. It's gotta be in their genes, man." His whisper could have been heard next door. "You just gotta resist how *good* they look in them jeans."

If looks could kill, Serena thought Kermit's would have dropped Garth in his tracks. But he only followed Garth to the door, bumping into the end table and nearly knocking the lamp to the floor.

"Mom," Sarah said, leaning forward again as soon as the door closed behind Garth Vance. "Listen, I've—"

"I don't feel like listening, right now," Serena told her daughter. "You and Gemma need to go get in the car and think about what your punishment is going to be, because I swear, if it gets left up to me, you're never going to leave your room again until there's gray in that ponytail."

"But this is important!"

She whirled back toward her daughter, but Sarah continued before she could speak.

"Mom, Jesse really *is* in danger. Somebody's planning to kill him."

Serena pushed closed the rear passenger door of the Subaru. Sunlight slanted off the window glass, fading Sarah and Gemma beneath a reflection of blue sky and house roofs. Serena subdued the sudden urge to yank the door back open just to make sure they were still solid, still real.

She knew they were safe, knew the sender of the instant messages they had received didn't even know who they were, but she wouldn't believe in their safety until they were back in her house, locked in Sarah's room. Preferably dragging balls and chains.

Kermit waited for her at the end of the driveway. The late afternoon light warmed his short, sandy hair and burnished the contours of his bare arms as he leaned against his beat-up muscle car. If it hadn't been Kermit, she would have said he looked like a classic bad boy, in that ripped shirt and molded jeans.

He definitely had a bad-boy body. How had she managed not to notice that before?

Of course, her first husband had cured her of her thing for bad boys. She reminded herself of that as she strode toward Kermit down the drive.

"I bet you're glad you're off-duty on this one," she said, giving him a half-smile. "That it's not your case, I mean."

"I would be," he agreed, pushing himself away from the car. "If there was a case. That way I wouldn't have to get involved." He half-smiled back. "Garth had a point about you Millbrook-Davis women."

"The part about us being irresistible?" she asked innocently, then froze. *Damn.* That almost sounded like she was flirting. She forced her eyes away from Kermit's bad-boy physique to his painfully cropped hair. No bad boy would be caught dead in that buzz cut. "Look, you don't have to get involved."

"I don't see anyone else volunteering. I'll see about getting authorization to check on Jesse's credit card use," he said, "but I can't promise that a seventh grader's claim that Jesse's been receiving instant message death threats is going to mean much to Lieutenant Marcy."

"Especially if the seventh grader is Detective Parks's niece?" Serena asked wryly. She knew something of the unspoken rivalry between the two men. "What about this guy who threatened Mark?"

"I'll have a talk with Mark tomorrow," Kermit promised.

Another day off spent solving her problems. She didn't know how to respond to that, so she only said, "Thank you."

"Serena, I have to ask this." His blue eyes caught hers briefly, wandered toward Jesse's house, then returned. "What does any of this have to do with you? Whatever is going on with Jesse, it's Jesse's problem. It isn't yours. Right?"

The slanting sunlight burned in her eyes as she turned toward him. "What do you mean?"

"I mean, I'm willing to look for Jesse Banos because it's important to you. That's what friends are for. But I don't want to walk into anything that's going to hurt you. There's something not-so-kosher going on here. If you have any knowledge about what it is, you need to tell me—"

"Kermit Riggs!" She glared at him. "If I had any clue what was going on, of course I'd tell you before I asked for your help."

Her outrage faded as her complete ignorance washed over her. "If I had any idea what was going on, I probably wouldn't need your help. I could tell all to Agent Johnson and wash my hands of the whole thing."

She'd described her meeting with Agent Johnson to Kermit after hearing Sarah's description of the instant message threats.

"You should wash your hands of it, anyway," Kermit said. "But since that would be completely out of character, I won't hold my breath. You've never suspected Jesse of being involved in any criminal activities?"

"You think it would be in character for me to be engaged to a criminal?"

"You're not engaged to him anymore," he responded, his mildness only feeding her indignation.

"I broke off the engagement because he was a jerk," she snapped. "And because he wasn't any good about hiding it. I don't think he would have had any more luck hiding criminal activities."

"No drugs? No financial improprieties?"

She snorted. "He's violently anti-drug, after what he went through with Mark. And he's barely organized enough to balance his own checkbook. He'd never make it as an embezzler."

"So he didn't get you involved with any suspicious investments. Didn't ask you to hold anything for him in a safety deposit box?"

"No." She couldn't blame him for asking, but it still hurt. "Damn it, Kermit, I can't imagine what this has to do with me. I can't imagine what Callista thinks it has to do with me. And I sure as hell don't intend to let it have anything to do with my daughter. But I can't sit around and let something terrible happen to Jesse."

"Why not?"

She paused at the harshness of his words, expecting him to explain them, but he merely waited. His eyes, sharp against the sinking sun, searched hers for something, but she didn't know what.

"Why not?" she repeated.

"Why not just let whatever happens to Jesse Banos happen?"

"What if that guy who threatened Mark finds him and breaks his fingers—or worse? What if the FBI arrests him on suspicion of some kind of domestic violence I know he couldn't have done?" It sounded weak, even to her.

"You think this might happen because Callista said he was in trouble? She saw it in some tarot cards?"

"I'm not saying a pack of cards can predict the future." Jesse had teased her about her flaky friends often enough that Kermit's skepticism shouldn't bother her. But she found herself trying to explain, anyway. "I do think Callista's got a sensitivity to things that might be difficult to explain scientifically. She could be wrong about Jesse. But I have a really bad feeling about the whole thing. I think Jesse could be hurt or about to be hurt."

She stopped, shaking her head. "Don't you care?"

"No," he answered flatly, glancing away from her to glare at the house. "After the way he's treated you? Not particularly."

Serena reached over to touch his shoulder, suddenly overwhelmed by the mess she'd made of her friendships and her life. "I'm sorry. I didn't want anyone to have to choose sides in this breakup. Just because Jesse gave up on having a relationship with me doesn't mean he's a terrible person. He's still a good counselor and a good brother and a good person to go to if you need a crusader. I don't want to interfere with my friends' friendships with him."

Kermit glanced down at her hand, then to her. She was close enough that she had to tilt her head back to see his eyes. They had turned nearly gray with some dark emotion she hadn't seen there before. Had she never quite noticed what a presence he had, when he chose to?

It struck her that Kermit Riggs could be a man to be reckoned with. But she didn't know what the reckoning would be.

"You have not interfered with my friendship with Jesse

Banos." He spoke each word carefully, as if concerned she might not understand. "That would be pretty well impossible, since I've barely ever had a real conversation with the guy, much less a friendship. If I'm doing anything to get him out of whatever trouble he's gotten himself into, it's not because he's a friend of mine."

He paused, as if considering his next statement. "It's because you are."

When Serena pulled her hand from his shoulder and glanced away, Kermit could have kicked himself—would have, if he hadn't been sure of falling on his butt and making an even bigger fool of himself than he already had.

He hadn't meant to say anything so personal. He just couldn't bear to see her apologizing for the creep who had broken her heart. He had only wanted her to see that her friendship was something of value to him, that her worth had nothing to do with Jesse Banos. Well, he had wanted that, and to brush the hair from her face and brush a kiss across her forehead.

At least he'd had enough self-preservation to stifle that impulse. *Idiot.*

The afternoon sunlight gleamed in the dark chestnut hair brushing her shoulders, and warmed her classic features with a hit of rose. He knew she inspected disastrously disorganized college labs, helped sort out stockrooms of dangerous solvents and corrosive chemicals, and supervised the clean-up of hazardous materials spills, but in her subtly sexy V-neck white blouse and camel-colored slacks, she looked like she could have just walked off a cover shoot for a J. Crew catalog.

Exactly the sorts of things he should not be noticing about a woman whose ex-fiancé was getting Internet death threats and who was preparing to remind him that her type ran to dark, handsome psychologists rather than clumsy beat cops with holes in their t-shirts from playing fetch with overeager Labs.

She crossed her arms over her chest, and when she glanced up at him, her eyes were damp and her smile slanted sideways. "We're friends, huh?"

Her smile tugged one from him, deflating his sudden, self-important panic. "Yeah. I didn't think that was going to be a life-changing revelation."

"Maybe it was just nice to hear." The sun flashed in her hazel eyes, and he thought for a second that he could see right through them into the gold of her heart.

"Hello?" A woman's voice broke the sudden silence, severing the connection. "You're Dr. Banos's fiancée, aren't you?"

Kermit turned with Serena to face the dark-rooted blonde approaching down the walk of the house next door. She moved forward in jerky steps, warily, and stopped several yards away, as if prepared to run back to the house in her faded fuzzy slippers if Kermit or Serena moved too quickly.

"Mrs. Jenkins, right?" Serena asked. "I'm Serena Davis."

The woman nodded, though her eyes still looked suspicious, deep set among her smoker's wrinkles. "I thought as how I recognized you. I saw the police car out here earlier. Did they catch those kids who broke into Dr. Banos's house?"

"Are you the one who called 911?" Serena asked. "I'm sorry about all that. It was my daughter and a friend. They weren't breaking in; they had a key."

Mrs. Jenkins peered up the driveway, where the two girls' silhouettes were visible in the back of the Subaru. "Is that right?"

Her eyes narrowed as she glanced back to Kermit. "I saw you there, too, with the policeman."

"Officer Kermit Riggs," Kermit said, managing not to drop his wallet as he pulled out his identification. "Officer Vance called me in when he arrived on the premises."

Mrs. Jenkins leaned forward to examine his ID, taking a careful look at his picture and comparing it to his face.

She glanced disapprovingly at his attire, but nodded, satisfied. "I'm sorry if I called you out for nothing," she said, without apparent remorse. "But I've been keeping an eye on Dr. Banos's house for him, picking up his paper and such, since he's been out of town."

"Did *Mr.* Banos happen to tell you where he could be reached?" Kermit asked, giving in to the temptation to lean on the title. It might be petty, but Jesse Banos wasn't a Ph.D., much less a medical doctor. "I would like to get in touch with him to ask him a couple of questions."

Mrs. Jenkins's lips pursed as she looked at Serena. "Don't you know where he is?"

"No." No explanation. A sigh of concern. The perfect combination to drive a busybody mad.

Kermit was impressed.

"It's important that we find him," Kermit said, using his best official-business voice. "Did he leave you a number where he can be reached?"

Mrs. Jenkins chewed her lip as she reluctantly shook her head. "He didn't say where he was going."

Kermit doubted he'd even told the woman that he was leaving town, but he wasn't going to make her admit it. He dug out one of his cards. "Thanks for your help, Mrs. Jenkins. If you do happen to see Mr. Banos, would you have him call me?"

She took the card, examining it as carefully as she had

his ID. "Is Dr. Banos in some kind of trouble?"

"Not that we know of, ma'am."

"I was just wondering, what with that IRS man looking for him and all."

"IRS man?" Serena asked.

Mrs. Jenkins shrugged. "He came by a couple of days ago. Said he was going to audit Dr. Banos, but couldn't get in touch with him."

Serena's eyes narrowed like a cat's preparing for a hunt. "He didn't happen to have short black hair and look a little like Michael Corleone, did he?"

"Like who?" Mrs. Jenkins asked, obviously not a *Godfather* fan. "No, this man was blond. A polite, well-spoken young man, carrying a briefcase. I did see a dark-haired man knocking on Dr. Banos's door yesterday, but I didn't open up when he came over to my house. I figured he was a Jehovah's Witness, but he looked like a gangster. I wouldn't send somebody who looked like a gangster out to spread the word of God, if I were them. Women who are home alone aren't going to open their doors to guys like that, you know what I mean."

"Did the IRS auditor show you some ID?" Kermit asked. Serena had said the man who had threatened Mark Banos down at the tattoo parlor was blond.

"He didn't have to," Mrs. Jenkins said, once more giving Kermit's attire a disdainful eye. "He was wearing one of them clip-on name tags."

"Do you remember his name?"

"A funny, foreign-sounding name. Othello Karenin."

"A blond Othello?"

Mrs. Jenkins ignored Serena's surprise. Apparently she wasn't a big Shakespeare fan, either. "I told him I couldn't believe Dr. Banos was evading his taxes. He's such a nice man. He's always been a good neighbor. You don't think he's gone off the deep end having a midlife crisis, do you?"

Since his father had been blaming a midlife crisis for his irresponsible behavior for the past twenty years, Kermit didn't have much patience with that excuse, but he merely asked, "Why do you ask, Mrs. Jenkins? Have you noticed anything different about Mr. Banos lately?"

"Well, just taking off like that," she said, shrugging a little too broadly. "It's not like him, is it?"

"It's all right, Mrs. Jenkins," Kermit said, playing into the sudden slyness in her manner. "We're not looking to get Mr. Banos in any trouble. We just need to find him. Anything you know could be helpful."

Mrs. Jenkins shrugged again, one side of her mouth hitching in a furtive smile as she glanced at Serena. "Well, it's probably nothing important. Probably just one of his clients or something."

"Somebody else came looking for Jesse?" Serena asked.

Mrs. Jenkins shook her head. "No, at least not this week. It was a week ago Thursday. Late in the evening, when I was sitting by my window, having a cup of coffee."

Spying on her neighbors. Kermit got the picture. "And?"

"Well," she glanced at Serena again. "A woman drove up in a fancy red convertible Beemer. Blond, leggy. A real beauty. Wearing one of those short skirts people do nowadays. She seemed really upset, which is why I watched to see where she went."

"She was visiting Mr. Banos," Kermit said. No wonder Mrs. Jenkins was enjoying her story so much, watching to see what Serena's reaction would be. "I'm sure you're right. It was probably just a client. Thank you again for your help, Mrs. Jenkins."

"Maybe she was just a client," Mrs. Jenkins said, her

voice rising to regain his attention as he crossed between her and Serena to walk Serena to her car. "She was only there for about half an hour."

"That's it, then," Kermit said, refusing to turn around. Serena's face was locked down. She didn't respond when he touched her arm as they reached the driveway.

"Except, when she drove away," Mrs. Jenkins called after them, "he went with her. He was carrying a big black bag with him. And he hasn't been back since."

Chapter 7

"Sit!" Serena ordered as Kermit collected a pile of dessert dishes off the table. Not that she didn't appreciate a guy who took the initiative, but . . . "Clearing the table is Sarah's job. I should have reminded her and Gemma to do it before letting Pleasance take them for the night."

"The girls played fetch with Fleur before dinner," Kermit said. A lazy tail thumped beneath the table, but Fleur didn't rise at the mention of her name. "They wore her out so well that she might even let me sleep in past five-thirty tomorrow morning. The least I can do is clear the table."

"But you're a guest. The least *I* can do after all your help today is to feed you without putting you to work."

She pushed back her chair, but Kermit cut around her on his way to the dishwasher.

"The truth is, you're just afraid to let me carry your plates over open tile."

She laughed. "You drop it, you clean it up, and the replacement money comes out of your allowance."

"Drill sergeant."

"I wish." Serena leaned back in her chair and rubbed her temples. "I'm so relieved Pleasance wanted to take Sarah along with Gemma tonight. I was trying to think up punishments all the way home, but I don't have a henhouse for them to clean. I'm sure Pleasance will keep them occupied with equally gross work all day tomorrow."

"I'd like to send a few of our habitual young offenders to Pleasance Geary's place for a week or two," Kermit said, returning to the table. "I'm sure she'd have a lower recidivism rate than Juvenile Hall."

Serena couldn't quite manage a smile. "Sarah's not even thirteen yet. I've got seven years of teenager to go. I'm not sure I'm going to make it."

He rested his elbows on the table, leaning over his tea mug. "She's a good kid. And smart. If she really does decide to go into forensic science in college, she'll be running the FBI eventually."

Serena grimaced. "It's her smarts I worry about. She cut class for an entire week last fall, and the only reason she got caught was because somebody broke into the house where she was hiding. And today—I wouldn't even have thought about checking Jesse's e-mail, much less known how to do it."

Frustration pushed her up from her chair, and she paced over to the sink to dump her tea, the scent of ginger wafting up from the drain. "I hate having to send her to David's every summer. I tell myself, I can do whatever I want while she's gone. It's like my parents have gone out of town for a weekend. I can stay out late, rent R-rated movies, mutter obscenities when I break a nail. There's nobody to worry about but me, nobody to nag about cleaning her room, nobody to tell me how gross soy milk is or how reading up on astrology is the sign of a weak, sloppy intellect."

She shrugged, turning back toward Kermit. "But I miss her. For that whole month, the house feels so empty. And even though I have friends and my sister to do things with . . ."

"It's lonely without her," Kermit supplied.

A picture flashed in her mind of Kermit watching the

late-night news in his mildew-ridden garage apartment behind the Murrays' farmhouse, and she guessed he understood about loneliness.

"It's lonely," she agreed. "But this year it's going to be a relief to pack her up and send her off to Santa Rosa. I'm only sorry it's still a whole week away. Let David play bad cop for a while. No offense."

He smiled, that smile that lit his blue eyes with mischief. "Hey, I get tired of playing a cop sometimes, myself. I understand why you're worried, but Sarah's not getting into drugs or trying to hack into the Pentagon's security system."

"Don't give her any ideas!"

"She showed poor judgment today, but she was only doing it because she thought she might be able to help you out."

Serena felt herself smile back. "I should be grateful she's using her powers for good instead of evil?"

"Exactly. At least she's not out chasing boys. They're the ones you've got to watch out for."

Serena arched a brow at him. "Personal experience?"

"Purely professional." He grinned. "Not for lack of trying. But it's a bit hard to be a teenage Lothario when you keep tripping over your feet every time a cheerleader looks at you."

He'd put on a long-sleeved denim shirt in deference to the coast's cool evenings, but she didn't have any trouble remembering what he looked like in the tight black t-shirt beneath it. Those high school cheerleaders must have had blinders on.

Serena moved to the refrigerator, welcoming the cool air washing over her embarrassingly warm cheeks. Apparently teenage hormones weren't the only ones she had to worry about. "Would you like something to drink? A beer?"

"You've got beer?"

"You don't have to sound so surprised." Though, as she dug back behind the fruit juice and kefir and organic two-percent milk, she couldn't say she blamed him. She paused as she hit the back of the fridge. "Okay, no, I don't have any beer. It was Jesse's. He must have taken it."

She closed the fridge. "At least I don't have to worry that Sarah drank it. She tried a sip of Daniel's at the Spicy Sicilian a couple of months ago and said it was the most disgusting stuff she'd ever put in her mouth."

She looked back at Kermit. He looked so comfortable there, sitting at her table, listening to her babble on about her daughter. Jesse'd never just listened like that. Whenever she'd bring up a worry about Sarah, Jesse would try to fix it. Tell her how to be a better mother, or, worse, how she'd failed Sarah as a mother already.

Whereas, if she told him something funny Sarah had done or how well she'd pitched at a softball game or about her good grades in school, he'd just nod and grunt and go back to his paper or watching the news. It felt good to have a friend sitting in her kitchen, letting her work through the fears the day had brought up for her, about her mothering skills, about Sarah's safety, about her daughter growing up and out of her control.

That was it. It was nice to have a friend to talk to. Like having her sister over for a chat. She tried to picture Destiny sitting in the chair Kermit currently occupied. But Kermit was too solid to budge.

She realized she still held the refrigerator door open, and closed it quickly. "I'm feeling more secure about the beer thing than the boy thing, actually. This kid in her class, Brian Tilson, has been calling Sarah every few nights so they can go over their pre-algebra homework together."

"Math, huh? I never thought of that one."

Serena leaned against the counter, clicking her fingernails on the reflective black surface. "I started dating David while helping him pass a calculus class at UC Davis. I intend to keep a close watch on this Tilson boy."

She closed her eyes against the sudden wave of weariness that swept over her. "I just hope Sarah got the good-man-picking gene my mother and sister got. It sure skipped me. First David and then Jesse."

Kermit's chair scraped back. "Destiny didn't get it right the first time. Look at Alain Caine."

Serena's eyes snapped open again to watch Kermit cross to the sink with his tea mug. "Alain was a pain in the behind. But at least he didn't leave a message asking Destiny to consider taking him back and then leave town with some married tart in a short skirt."

Kermit's mug clanked against the counter, but he managed to right it before it tumbled into the sink. "Jesse wanted to patch things up?" He glanced at her, just a flash of eyes she couldn't read. "What did you tell him?"

"Nothing." She bit down on her anger, but it didn't help. "He left me a message, then left town before I could respond."

Kermit's strong fingers played on the countertop a couple of feet from hers. He glanced from them to her. "Is that why you want to find him, Serena?"

"Why? Because I didn't get a chance to tell him hell would freeze over before I took him back?" Her anger flashed from the question to the subject. "Here I was, worrying myself sick that Jesse'd gotten himself into trouble with the law somehow or maybe one of his former clients had decided to make good on some kind of death threat."

She sagged against the counter, fighting back the week of fear and anger. "Even if Callista hadn't said his disappearance was somehow connected to me, I would have felt like I owed it to him to find out what was going on. And it turns out he's just run off with somebody else's wife."

Self-pity wrapped through the silence in the kitchen like a seven-headed hydra as Serena remembered the look on Mrs. Jenkins's face when she'd told them about the woman who'd driven off with Jesse. Blond, beautiful, rich. It had to be Nadia. Well, Nadia was welcome to him.

Better her than me. The truth of that thought burned through the hydra's heads.

"Better her than me," she repeated, surprising herself with a smile.

"Come on." Kermit's hand grabbed hers as he passed her, pulling her after him out of the kitchen. He grabbed her purse from the end of the counter and handed it off to her, glancing under the table. "You stay here, Fleur. Keep out the burglars."

The only response was a sleepy yawn. Burglars could have a field day while they were gone. *Gone?*

"Wait!" Serena caught the coat Kermit tossed to her from the coat rack by the front door. "What do you think you're doing?"

"I think I'm not the one who needs a beer," he said, pulling her out into the cool evening air. Twilight still lingered to the east, but stars hung like chips of diamonds across the redwood-furred shoulders of the hills to the west. "You've had a rotten week. It's Friday night."

They stumbled across the dark lawn toward his battered old—what had he called it? A Jensen Healey? She stifled a giggle. The ridiculous orange car made her feel like she was back in high school, sneaking out on a Friday night date when her parents thought she was doing homework in her room.

A *date? This is a very, very bad idea, Serena.* But Kermit's hand felt so warm wrapped around hers, warm against the cool night. Besides, this wasn't a date. And when the car door creaked as he opened it for her, and she glanced around guiltily for her mother, she couldn't stifle the giggles any longer.

"Don't laugh," Kermit said. "There aren't that many of these girls left. When I get her all fixed up, she's going to be a sight to see."

"It's not every day you get to ride in one," Serena murmured with a smile, as he closed her door and his long strides took him around the hood to his side of the car. As he folded himself into his seat, she realized the car wasn't as big as it looked. His shoulder was only inches from hers, and she could feel his body heat filling the space between them.

This is not a date, she reminded herself, but with slightly more panic than before. It was only a sweet attempt on Kermit's part to take her mind off her troubles. Better to stop it now, just to make sure he didn't get confused about its being any more.

Maybe to make sure she didn't get confused. Yet her protest didn't come out sounding as forceful as she meant it to.

"This might not be such a good idea, Riggs. Kidnapping is probably not a good career move for a police officer."

He grinned at her as he threw the car into reverse. "That's very true, Davis. But sometimes you've just got to live dangerously."

Music and the smell of hops spilled from the door of the Deepwater Brewery as Kermit held it open for Serena. Two guitarists, a drummer, and an electric bass player packed the tiny stage in the back of the bar's restaurant area. Several of the tables had been moved aside to form a small dance floor, though it was too early yet for anyone to have drunk enough courage to dance.

Kermit figured he'd be comatose before he'd drunk that much.

He steered Serena toward a small, empty table at the back of the bar. They'd be able to hear each other without shouting over the driving rhythm of the music—at the moment a rocking country blues song. The singer's baby had apparently left him, and his truck had died. He sounded most upset about the truck.

"What can I getcha?" their waitress demanded, dealing them coasters with practiced flicks of her long, red nails. She wore a skirt that barely covered her rear, but her Meg Ryan–haircut gave her a surprisingly innocent air.

"Deepwater Organic Wheat," Serena ordered without looking at the menu.

"Ginger ale," Kermit said. "I'm driving."

Serena's eyes slanted like a cat's. "I think your bodyweight can tolerate one beer without endangering your blood alcohol level. What happened to living dangerously?"

Looking into those teasing eyes, he thought he was living plenty dangerously already. What had he been thinking?

"Lost Coast Downtown Brown," he said.

The waitress patted his shoulder. "Don't worry, honey, I'll pace ya."

He watched her head for the bar, and when he turned back, Serena's eyes had narrowed even farther. "I bet you weren't wondering if her mother thinks she's old enough to wear an outfit like that."

He laughed. "No, I was actually wondering if she was

old enough to be serving alcoholic beverages. But Deep-water's out of my jurisdiction."

She shook her head, disgusted. "Cops."

"True." He shrugged. "The main reason I come all the way across the bay for a beer is that I don't usually have to worry about being served by someone I helped send to jail. The fact that I don't have to check IDs is just a bonus."

"At least she didn't card you."

He didn't think he was imagining the challenge in her eyes. He only grinned. "I had that happen once when I was out with Garth and Grace, and they've never let me live it down."

The waitress returned with their beers. Serena raised hers. "To locally brewed organic beer. Finally, something health-conscious that's still bad for you." She took a long drink from her mug and sighed. "You were right. I think I needed that."

Kermit smiled. "It's still a shock to see you drink beer. Destiny says you don't poison your system with alcohol. Just a little wine now and then for medicinal purposes."

"This *is* medicinal purposes," Serena assured him. Her smile turned down. "Destiny's never told you about my wicked past?"

He snorted into his ale. "I don't believe you had a wicked past."

"Because I'm a vegetarian?" She leaned back in her chair, still smiling that cat's smile, and shook her hair off her shoulders. "Destiny was like Sarah when we were growing up. Always getting good grades, mostly following the rules, making Mom and Dad proud. I was the one who did my homework in the five minutes before class started, tried smoking and drinking, and snuck out on the weekends with the bad boys."

She glanced at him. "Doesn't exactly fit in with my demure, health-nut, PTA image, does it?"

"I'd say it didn't fit in with your classy, professional, very together image," Kermit said. "Except I've seen that look in your eyes. Like now. It's time to watch out, because you're about to do something outrageous."

"No, I'm not." She sat back up, the tension returning to her shoulders as she wrapped her hands around her mug. "I've gotten myself into enough trouble over the years. Getting knocked up my second year of college. Marrying a man I barely knew because it was 'the right thing to do.' Falling into another poor relationship just because I thought I needed to be rescued."

"Aren't you tired of beating up on yourself? You graduated college, even with a baby to take care of. You supported yourself and Sarah after your divorce. You're good at your work. You're raising a terrific daughter." His eyes snapped down to his beer. He hadn't had more than a couple mouthfuls. But his mouth was running anyway. "You're creative, intelligent, organized—"

"Enough!" She raised a hand, laughing. "All right. I promise. No more feeling sorry for myself."

"No more bringing up Jesse?"

She shook her head, letting her hair fly across her face. "No more. He is now officially on his own." She paused with her mug at her lips. "Although Agent Johnson still bothers me. What do you bet he isn't really FBI at all, but a private detective hired by Nadia's husband?"

He watched her expression closely, but she only looked amused by the thought.

She met his gaze. "I don't miss him." She shook her head again, bemusedly this time. "I thought I would. I guess I think I should. We were together nearly two years.

110

But it's hard to keep loving someone who doesn't love you anymore, even if you're not willing to acknowledge that's what's happening."

Her gaze turned inward. "And I guess I like my life pretty well." Her smile was small, but strong. "I never needed Jesse for that. I love my family. I have good friends and a good job. I'm always learning new things. Not too bad for a middle-aged softball mom."

"You're only planning to live to fifty?" He loved it when he could make her eyes flash like that.

"My daughter's almost thirteen. I had a baby when I was young, not when I was adolescent." She waved a finger at him. "I'm not some sweet young thing, Kermit Riggs. I'm thirty-three years old."

"Ancient," he agreed solemnly.

She glared. "I don't expect a babe like you to understand. How old are you, anyway?"

The way she threw it out, a challenge, like her comment about his getting carded, he could tell it bothered her, that he was younger than she was. A lot. It didn't matter that it wasn't a large gap or that it would seem like even less in ten years. He could lie. He'd busted a guy down at the south end of Hope Point who had a real talent with fake IDs . . .

Then it struck him. It *bothered* her. It really bothered her that he was younger. It didn't bother Destiny that he was younger than she was. It didn't bother his partner, Grace.

Get a grip, Riggs, he commanded. But he had to struggle to hold down his grin. And he didn't say *almost twenty-eight.*

"I'm twenty-seven," he said, lifting his mug in a challenge of his own. "Afraid somebody here might think you're robbing the cradle?"

Her eyes flashed again, but her smile was pure Serena. "Forget that. I'm afraid I might get arrested for contributing to the delinquency of a minor."

Breathing beer and then laughing foam all down the front of one's shirt was a tried and true method for completely destroying a flirting atmosphere.

"I know some people in the DA's office," he said, swiping at his shirt with a tiny bar napkin. "I'll make sure you get off with community service."

She laughed, which was good enough to make up for his embarrassment. At least he hadn't dumped the whole mug in his lap. Or hers. There were some real advantages to sitting at a "just friends" distance apart.

"Come on." She stood and offered him her hand.

"What?" Not that he minded taking it. He glanced back at the table as she pulled him away from it. "You haven't finished your beer."

"I think I've had enough. I guess I'm feeling a little outrageous, after all. Know how to two-step?"

It was a little like that dream, where you step off a curb and it jerks you awake. But he was jerked awake to the realization that they were suddenly standing in the middle of the dance floor. Couples had drifted out onto it in the time he and Serena had been drinking their beers, but not enough to cover him if he tried to make a break for the door.

The band had swung into a rendition of that Alabama song about needing a fiddle to play in Texas. An interesting choice, considering they obviously didn't have a fiddle. Of course, they weren't in Texas, either.

"Kermit?" There was a dare in her eyes as she grabbed his other hand.

"You didn't have a wicked past," he informed her through gritted teeth as he tried to gauge when to start his feet so they wouldn't flatten hers. "There is nothing past about it."

Grace and Garth had spent most of an otherwise beautiful afternoon at a departmental picnic amusing themselves by teaching him how to dance. He'd never expected to be grateful to them for it.

"You're doing great," Serena said, managing to dodge a misstep and make it look graceful.

"It's all fun and games until somebody breaks a femur."

But it *was* fun. In a death-defying, no-guts-no-glory sort of way. Watching her laugh as they tripped around the dance floor. Literally. Holding her hands and feeling the music pulse through them both.

For a breathless moment, he even thought he had the hang of it, feeling the beat stomping out through his feet instead of counting it under his breath. But the band started wrapping up the song before he could try anything crazy, like the couple across the floor, where the man dipped his partner halfway to the floor as the music ended.

"Slow dance!" somebody shouted at the band, but even as Kermit felt the jolt of electricity that shot between his hands and Serena's, his eyes were still on the couple across the dance floor.

The woman had dipped, but the man hadn't quite caught her, after all. She seemed to slip in slow motion, but when her head hit the edge of the stage, time sped up again. She crumpled to the floor, pulling her partner hard to his knees beside her.

Even in the poor, orange lighting, Kermit could see red on the man's hands after he touched the woman's head.

Kermit turned to Serena, the music still echoing around them as the band slowly realized what had happened.

"Call the EMTs," he said, squeezing her hands to get her attention. "Possible concussion. If it's a scalp wound, she'll probably need stitches. Tell them I'll start first aid."

113

She nodded quickly, ready to help, her eyes full of concern for the injured woman. That didn't leave much room for relief that they'd been spared the awkwardness of whether or not to slow dance. Relief or regret.

He didn't know which he saw or which he hoped to see.

He tightened his hands on hers once more before turning to cross the dance floor.

The bartender was happy to let someone else make the call to 911. As she hung up the phone, Serena moved to the end of the bar to look around the divider into the restaurant area. The injured woman was conscious. She was sitting up, propped against her dancing partner, holding a handkerchief to her forehead.

Kermit crouched on her other side, holding her wrist, checking her pulse, and saying something that made her smile, despite a wince of pain. He'd already cleared the other Brewery patrons away from the area and sent the band to the bar for a break between sets.

"Your friend is a better medic than he is a dancer."

Serena turned to the man sitting on the stool at the end of the long, curved bar. His voice sounded friendly enough, but there was a curve to his smile that hinted at mockery. He was a rugged blond, and he lounged on the stool with an easy grace that showed off his muscular physique. He had a bold stare that suggested he found himself irresistible and expected everyone else to do the same.

"My friend has a number of talents," Serena said coolly. "I'm glad to have him around for any of them."

The man's pale green eyes widened as he raised his white-blond eyebrows. "I meant no offense. Please forgive me, Serena."

She stilled. "How do you know my name?"

He smiled, his teeth bright and even. "You would be surprised at how much I know about you. But forgive me, again, for failing to introduce myself. Othello Karenin."

She didn't take the hand he offered. "The IRS auditor?"

His smile deepened. "I see you've been paying attention. Then you must know already what information I'd like you to share with me."

He was still friendly, still lounging on his stool, but his stare disconcerted her enough to cause her to step back. He didn't seem to blink.

"You're the one who threatened Mark Banos," she said, remembering Mark's comment about the man's strange eyes.

He clucked disapprovingly, finally rolling his eyes away from her. "*Threatening* makes it sound so ugly. I merely wanted to convince him that it would be better if he told me what he knew. I'm sure I could have found a violation or two of code in his shop that could have resulted in a revocation of his license. But I believed his story, and . . ."

He raised his hands, gesturing away his benevolent generosity.

"You told him you'd break his fingers." Even as the words left her mouth, Serena remembered what Jimbo—or was it Tank?—had said about the man who threatened Mark reminding him of acquaintances in Pelican Bay. She was standing in the middle of a crowded bar, with Kermit just yards away, yet the thought of making this man angry sent a chill down her spine.

But he only smiled again, with evident amusement. "His fingers? Our Mr. Banos has been watching too many gangster movies. I like to hope I could come up with something more creative than that if I felt the need to hurt someone."

The beer in her stomach turned cold. She couldn't

115

imagine Jesse trying to cheat on his taxes. But if he'd made an error on his returns, he could be in real trouble with this man.

But it was not her business to rescue Jesse. She'd already gotten herself and Sarah in enough trouble worrying over him. Besides, she'd promised Kermit. And she had the advantage of being able to tell the truth.

"I don't know where Jesse is."

Othello Karenin sighed. "But you two are . . . involved. Surely you have some ideas?"

"Jesse Banos and I are no longer together," she said, her voice cold and hard. "I haven't seen him in over a week."

"A whole week?" Othello's good humor slid over into thinly veiled scorn. "Thank heavens you found a youthful balm for your aching . . . heart . . . before you wasted completely way."

Serena decided she preferred Agent Johnson's open hostility to this man's slimy insinuations. "No part of my life is any part of your business, Mr. Karenin."

"Jesse Banos is *all* my business at the moment. I have no tolerance for his brand of moral corruption, and I intend to make him pay for his misdeeds."

Serena stepped back. "Jesse may be your business, but he is no longer mine. And I have no idea where he is."

"For your sake, I do hope you're telling the truth." The low-pitched intensity of his voice held her against her will. "I hope so, for your sake and for your friend's sake over there and for the sake of your sister and her new husband. I'm not the sort of person you want to be lying to, Serena."

She managed to suppress the flash of temper that wanted to tell him off. She didn't doubt he was the sort of man who would audit everyone she knew just to prove his point.

Calling him a pathetic, ego-maniacal bureaucrat would probably not help matters.

"Fortunately, I'm not lying. I don't know anything more than Mark does."

Karenin shrugged. "I'm not certain Mark Banos could come up with a consistent lie to save his own life, much less his brother's. But I get the feeling you're a bit more cunning than Mr. Banos. You're a beautiful woman, Serena." His pale eyes blinked, slowly, as he smiled once more. "I've learned the hard way never to trust a beautiful woman."

Serena's good intentions slipped right through her self-control. "Mr. Karenin, you're wasting my time as well as your own. Excuse me."

"Yes." He sat straighter on the stool. "Please return to your dancing. Just remember that I will have an eye on you. And on your friend there, just in case. I notice he matches the description of the man one of my associates saw with you at Jesse Banos's house earlier today."

His eyes brightened at her surprise. "Of course, we're keeping an eye on our man's house. I assume one of those two lovely girls was your daughter? But the man . . . who is he? Possibly a physical therapist, with his knowledge of first aid and that athletic physique. But the haircut suggests a more military option." He grinned. "I see that touched a nerve! Sheriff's deputy perhaps?"

Serena scowled at him, but held her tongue. She feared anything she said would give away more than she wanted him to know. He already knew more than she wanted him to know.

He laughed. "I'll have his identity by tomorrow, have no fear. Enjoy your evening, Serena. Here comes your law enforcement stud now."

She turned to see Kermit crossing the restaurant floor

toward the bar. Two EMTs had arrived and were conferring with the injured woman and her partner at a table in a corner. The band had returned to the stage and was preparing to start their next set.

"She's going to be fine," Kermit said as Serena hurried forward to meet him. "Just a few stitches. Fortunately, she's actually got insurance, so the EMTs can give her a ride to the hospital. She was the designated driver tonight, and her husband probably shouldn't be behind a wheel for an hour or two."

His grin faded as she reached him. "What's wrong? Serena, are you all right?"

She shook her head, surprised to find her throat too tight to speak. He touched her shoulder to steady her, and she managed a calming breath.

"The IRS auditor who was looking for Jesse," she told him. "He's over there at the bar. He's the one who threatened Mark, and he was trying to pull the same number on me."

His hand stiffened on her shoulder and his blue eyes cooled. "He harassed you? Which one is he?"

Having a police officer for a friend occasionally came in handy. "The pale blond. The guy who thinks he looks like Brad Pitt."

Kermit's brows pulled together. "The one with the cowboy hat?"

"No. At the end of the bar." She hadn't wanted to give Othello Karenin the satisfaction of looking back at him, but at Kermit's puzzled expression she had to turn. Karenin's barstool was empty. "He's gone."

She glanced around the brewery. She didn't see him, but she could still feel his unblinking gaze roving over her. She shuddered.

"What did he say to you?" Kermit scanned the building himself with a practiced eye, though the anger in his voice belied his professional calm. "If he made inappropriate remarks, I'm sure his superiors will be interested to hear it. And if he said anything about your fingers, I will personally ensure that—"

"He's a slimewad," Serena said, Sarah's favorite pejorative helping to restore her equilibrium. Still, the man's comments about stalking Kermit slithered in her memory. Surely he had better things to do, but if Kermit confronted him, Othello Karenin would do his best to make trouble. She'd already caused Kermit enough grief for one week. "Can we just forget about him? I think I'm ready to go home."

"Sure. Of course. I'll get your jacket."

As Kermit made his way back to their table, the band started up again. A slow, easy beat. Serena remembered Kermit's hands on hers, the music pulsing in her blood, pausing in that instant before stepping closer for a slow dance.

Othello Karenin's snide comments came back to her. She'd broken off a wedding engagement not quite two weeks before, and here she was out dancing with another man. A younger man. Not that she cared what it looked like to an IRS auditor.

But she cared what it looked like to Kermit. Did he think she'd wanted to move closer? To slow dance? To feel his breath against her hair, his strong hands on her waist?

She felt her face heat at the thought. Had they even flirted, a little, earlier? She wasn't looking for love. Had no intentions of looking for love again. And she sure wasn't looking for anything less. Especially not with Kermit. She valued his friendship too much for that.

She would have to be more careful, make it clear that all she wanted was friendship. Make sure he didn't get the wrong impression.

But as she watched him walk back to her from the bar, concern for her in his steady, clear eyes, she had to squash the tiny voice in her heart asking her what the wrong impression was.

"You sure you're okay?" Kermit asked, holding her jacket for her.

"Fine." She managed a grateful smile. "This was just what I needed. Except for the IRS. And I'm not going to think about that petty little tyrant."

But even as she said it, she felt the menace of those unblinking eyes following her out the door.

Chapter 8

"You went out dancing? With *Kermit?*"

In counterpoint to her sister's disbelief, Serena heard her brother-in-law's voice echoing from somewhere deep in their Hawaiian hotel room, "She did *what?*"

Serena stretched the phone cord so she could drop into a chair at her kitchen table. She'd refused to buy a cordless, in hopes of limiting Sarah's phone time, but sometimes she was tempted to give in for the ease of her own conversations.

Not now. At the moment, she wished Destiny hadn't decided to interrupt her honeymoon by calling to check up on her sister on a Sunday afternoon. It was a sweet thought, and Serena would have appreciated it if she hadn't had anything to hide from her sister. She'd done a pretty good job of not mentioning finding an FBI agent in her office or Sarah's nearly getting arrested. Unfortunately, that hadn't left her much to talk about when Destiny asked what she'd been doing with herself, and she'd made the mistake of mentioning going to the brewery Friday night.

"Neither of you ended up in the hospital?" Destiny asked, though Serena couldn't quite tell if she was serious or trying to be funny.

"He's not a bad dancer," Serena insisted. "He just needs more practice. I guess Grace and Garth gave him a crash course at some department barbecue."

"I was there," Destiny said. "I nearly broke my collar-

121

bone, and I wasn't even the one dancing with him."

But Serena could tell her sister's heart wasn't in the teasing. Silence hummed across the line for a moment.

"Serena, I know it must have hurt that Jesse left town with another woman only a few days after you broke off the engagement."

Serena snapped up straight in her chair. "Who told you that?" *Dumb question.* "You called Mom before you called me. I told her not to bother you with that on your honeymoon."

"She and Dad are worried about you."

"So everybody else has to be worried, too?" Serena blew out a frustrated breath. "I wasn't too thrilled when I found out about Jesse running off with another woman," she admitted. "Especially if it really is this Nadia person. She's married. I'm sure her husband feels a lot worse than I do. I'm just lucky to be out of the whole situation."

"So going out with Kermit wasn't a subconscious attempt to make Jesse jealous?"

Glaring at the telephone wasn't terribly satisfying. "What kind of person do you think I am, Desty?"

"I think you're a wonderful person, Reenie. Not that I wouldn't care about you, anyway. You *are* my sister, but—"

"Honestly!" The words came in short bursts around the lump of emotion in her throat. "How could you think I'd use Kermit's friendship like that? And for Jesse! A man who apparently doesn't even understand what friendship is."

"Reenie, you can yell at me all you want. But I remember how devastated you were after your divorce from David. Jesse came along and rescued you, and—"

"And I let him do it," Serena said. "I wanted a white knight, and Jesse fit the job description."

She sighed. There was no point in being angry with Destiny. This was payback for all the good relationship advice she'd given Destiny when Destiny hadn't realized she'd needed advice. The difference was, Serena really *didn't* need the advice.

"I don't need anyone to rescue me from this disaster with Jesse," she said. "I got myself into it, but I also got myself out. Maybe I don't know how to make a relationship work, but I'm pretty good at taking care of myself and my daughter. I'm even pretty good at enjoying my life. I don't need Jesse back in it. I don't *want* Jesse back in it."

"Mom said you've spent the past week trying to find him."

"I thought he'd been kidnapped!" Okay, she could understand if that sounded a little crazy from her sister's perspective, but it happened to be the truth. "Callista said he was in trouble and that I was involved—and don't you dare say a word." She waited, but Destiny obeyed. "I was trying to find him so I could absolve myself of responsibility for him once and for all."

"Great. Good. I'm glad to hear it."

Serena narrowed her eyes. She could hear the unspoken *but*. "You think I'm in denial?"

"No. I knew you were certain of your decision when you first told me about breaking the engagement, and it doesn't sound like you've been having second thoughts." Her sister paused. "I'm sorry, Reenie. I didn't realize how Jesse's behavior had changed lately. I guess I wasn't paying attention to all the times he wasn't there for you. When Kermit started pointing them out before we left on our trip . . . I'm just sorry, that's all. I should have been there to give you support."

Kermit pointed them out? *Great.*

"Desty, you had enough to worry about, what with

Alain's death and Tom Yap's arrest and then planning your wedding." Serena closed her eyes against the truth that rose in her heart, but she spoke it, anyway. "And I didn't want your support. I didn't want to admit that I couldn't fix yet another broken relationship."

"Oh, right. Two strikes and you're out." Her sister's sarcasm helped. "Look at me and Alain."

"That's only one."

"Yeah, but at least no one you know has been accused of murdering one of your exes."

"Yet." Serena was getting very tired of that little shiver of worry. She did *not* have premonitions. Except this premonition wasn't hers; it was Callista's. And psychic or not, Callista's premonitions made her nervous.

"Forget Jesse," Destiny said. "I'm not worried about him. Just you. And that's the only reason I'm—"

"Interfering?"

"—asking. Why exactly did you take Kermit out dancing?"

"Kermit suggested it!" Serena protested. "To get my mind off things. And it did. We had a good time."

Even as the words left her mouth, she could picture her sister's expression. She dropped her forehead onto the heel of her free hand.

"How good, Reenie?"

Her head popped back up. "Damn it, Desty! Kermit's a friend. He's been a good friend to all of us. He's a good man. He's not some one-night stand. He deserves better than that. And so do I. I'm not a one-night stand kind of girl."

"I know," Destiny agreed mildly. "I never meant to imply you were."

"Then just what *were* you implying?"

124

Her sister didn't answer immediately. Never a good sign. Serena wondered if she should pretend to lose the phone connection and hang up. But that had never worked when Destiny tried it on her.

"I don't know if I should even say anything," Destiny said, finally. "But you must have noticed that Kermit's kind of sweet on you?"

"Kermit?" Shock jolted through her. Or maybe not shock, maybe some other shocking feeling. "I'm too old for him! God, Desty, I found three gray hairs this morning. I'm the mother of an almost-teenaged daughter, for heaven's sake. I have a failed marriage and a failed engagement to my credit. He only invited me out to the brewery to cheer me up. He probably thinks of me as an aunt or something." She paused. "A cool aunt."

"Give me a break. Kermit's mother might have died young, but she'd be nearly fifty by now."

"Okay, a cool older sister."

"Trust me, Reenie, Kermit Riggs does not think of you as a sister."

"Does, too." Although she remembered the flash in his eyes at the thought of slow-dancing.

"Does not."

"Does, too." Remembered her own response to his touch.

"Not."

"Too." Remembered the unreadable expression on his face when he dropped her off at her house and she'd told him she didn't need him to walk her to the door. "Too. Too. Too. Give it up, Destiny. You know I always win."

"Fine," her sister agreed, although the smug tone in her voice didn't admit defeat. "You think Kermit thinks you're too old. But what I don't hear you saying is that you think

125

Kermit is too young. I don't hear you saying that he's never been married and doesn't understand how hard it is. That he lives in a bachelor apartment with paint peeling off the roof."

"And he listens to country music. I don't have to say it! You know all that."

"Uh-huh." The smugness disappeared from Destiny's voice. "I don't pretend to be a relationship guru like my dear, busybody sister. But I can tell when I've hit a nerve. You don't have to tell me everything, but remember to be honest with yourself. You've been hurt. And I know you don't want to hurt Kermit, either. Just be careful. I wish I was there for you now."

"To take care of me?" Serena had to smile. "No you don't. I don't need any more white knights, remember? Not even my own sister. And you're having too much fun with your own knight in shining armor. Just go back to your honeymoon. This phone call must be costing you big bucks."

"Ouch. Probably," Destiny admitted. "Okay, I'll try not to worry." She laughed. "At least I'm not worrying about you and Jesse anymore."

Serena shook her head. "I haven't even thought about Jesse since Friday night. One of Jesse's partners at the clinic told Kermit that Jesse was supposed to be back to work to-morrow. I wonder if he's home yet. I bet Othello Karenin was waiting for him on his doorstep."

"Othello Karenin?" Destiny asked. "Come on."

"He's an IRS auditor," Serena said, reliving the feeling of his gaze boring into her back. "A very creepy man. He's out to get Jesse for something."

She shivered. "I told Kermit he was a petty tyrant, but I don't think 'petty' is the right word. There was something wrong with the man, Desty. I think he'd enjoy hurting people. I'd almost feel bad for Jesse, if this guy hadn't threatened to audit me and everyone I knew just because I couldn't tell him where Jesse was."

"He threatened you?" Destiny voice was sharp. "That's not very professional."

"Mark said he threatened to break his fingers," Serena told her.

"What?"

Karenin had claimed Mark was exaggerating, but recalling the auditor's manner, she didn't doubt he was capable of threats. And capable of carrying them out. "Mark can blow things out of proportion, but he had two friends out of sight in the back when this guy came by. They agreed that Mark had been physically threatened."

"That's a little odd for an IRS auditor."

"Othello Karenin is more than a little odd," Serena agreed. "He's jock good-looking and thinks he's God's gift to the world, but he also enjoys needling people. And he approaches his job like he's the angel of judgment. He called Jesse morally corrupt and said he'd pay for his 'misdeeds.' "

She shrugged her shoulders, trying to shake off the shadow of menace the man's memory threw. "Maybe I need an aura cleansing or something, to get rid of this paranoia. If someone had asked me what the guy's profession was, I'd never have guessed IRS auditor. I would have said vampire."

The attempt at humor only deepened the shadows. She glanced behind her involuntarily. "What if he's not an IRS agent? Jesse's neighbor said he was, but I never saw any ID. And he's never said what he was looking for Jesse for. I mean, don't they usually inform you in advance that they're going to do an audit?"

She tried to chuckle. "Okay, go ahead. Tell me I really am paranoid."

"I wish I thought you were." Destiny didn't laugh. "Reenie, didn't you notice anything odd about his name?"

Serena snorted. "You mean besides the fact that he's neither a Moor nor a Russian?"

"I mean, isn't it a little strange that he's got those two names?"

"What do you mean?" Serena asked.

"Othello, the tragic Venetian general who killed his wife because he thought she was cheating on him. And Karenin, the husband of possibly the most famous adulteress in literature, Tolstoy's Anna Karenina. That didn't strike you as strange?"

"Oh, lord." Serena's stomach dropped heavily. "You were the literature major, Desty. We didn't study a whole lot of Tolstoy in chemistry."

"As Daniel likes to say, I believe in coincidence, but . . ."

But. Jesse disappears with a married woman. A man shows up looking for Jesse bearing the names of a jealous murderer and a stoic cuckold. IRS agent?

Serena might not have studied much Russian literature, but she'd always done well in math. A scorned husband with incipient sociopathic personality traits was looking for Jesse and Nadia. What were the chances all he wanted to do to them was perform an audit?

The high-pitched whine of incoming mortar shells penetrated Kermit's restless dreams, but he was getting better at ignoring it.

"Go back to sleep," he muttered, and rolled away from Fleur's questing nose. He felt groggy, as if he hadn't slept at all, though dreams had chased him through the night. He could remember only the feeling of dread that had pervaded them, dread and loss and flashes of hot desire, dancing with a beautiful, chestnut-haired woman in his arms.

No, he did remember *that* dream. Serena had entered them both in a ballroom dance contest, and he'd been so clumsy that the judges had shot him in the knees so he couldn't come back to try again. He'd tried to explain it wasn't fair to ask him to tango to Tim McGraw, but they hadn't listened.

The abrupt blare of his radio alarm nearly drowned out the ringing of the telephone.

He rolled back over. Even Fleur's ears, raised in eager anticipation of going out, couldn't block the red numbers glowing on the clock's face. Maybe that Tim McGraw song hadn't been a dream, after all. Apparently he'd already punched the snooze button. More than once.

"Riggs," he answered the phone, slapping at the alarm. The department would have called the cell phone. If Serena was calling at this hour, it could only mean trouble. "What's wrong?"

"Kermit? Please tell me I didn't wake you up."

"Destiny?" He sat up, running a hand through his hair. Only a week since Serena had called him last Monday, and he knew he would never mistake her voice again. After what? A few days spent trying to chase down her runaway ex-fiancé and one lousy dance? Well, lousy on his part. *Idiot.* "No, I'm just getting ready for work. Is everything okay? What time is it there?"

"Early. Late. We haven't gone to bed yet."

Kermit glanced over at Fleur. "Your mom is a party animal."

"How's my baby?"

"She's good," Kermit said. Neither the phone nor the

radio had tried to ambush him so far, so he risked reaching for his slippers. "She's ready for her morning walk. She misses you, but she's been great. Except for that dead salamander yesterday."

"She didn't roll in it."

"She did."

Fleur's tail waved merrily at the memory.

Kermit reached over to scratch beneath her ears. She leaned her head into his hand, brown eyes glowing warmly. "You don't need to worry about us. We'll be fine for another week. Now go to bed or you'll be too tired to lie on the beach this afternoon."

"Not a chance." Destiny paused. "Kerry, I'm not calling about Fleur. Did Serena talk to you last night?"

"No." After their Friday evening at the brewery, Serena had made it clear enough that she was happy to go home. Alone. And though he'd picked up Sarah the afternoon before for a walk with Fleur—and a run-in with a decomposing salamander, he hadn't seen Serena. Sarah had told him her mother was out running errands. Maybe it was paranoia on his part, but it felt like she was avoiding him.

Destiny sighed. "She said she didn't want to get you involved, that she's put you out enough already. But even if she won't admit it, she needs help. And I can't be there."

"It's Jesse again."

"Yes."

Of course it was.

The steps up to the Hope Point Life Integration Clinic didn't challenge Kermit's calves quite so much as they had the week before. Working out at the gym was one thing, but walking a high-energy dog up and down the hills in the community forest had definite cardio-vascular advantages.

He paused on the sunflower doormat outside the front door, settling into a working frame of mind. Lieutenant Marcy had predictably ruled that the vague possibility of a jealous husband impersonating an IRS agent was not high on the department's priority list of crimes to solve. However, he had given Kermit permission to look into the problem on his lunch hour.

Rather, he hadn't forbidden it, which was better than Daniel's pessimistic predictions on the phone earlier that morning.

Kermit rolled his shoulders back to loosen the tension there. At the moment, he might not care whether Othello Karenin, or whatever his name was, sent Jesse to jail for tax evasion or simply broke his kneecaps. But he wasn't doing this for Jesse.

Serena had convinced him Friday night that she really was over the jerk, but that didn't mean Jesse's problems were no longer hers.

If Jesse's married girlfriend's unstable husband had been unhinged by her desertion, there was no telling whom he might take his revenge on if he couldn't find Jesse. He'd already threatened Mark Banos with physical harm and made veiled threats to Serena.

Whether Serena wanted his help or not, Kermit had no intention of letting some lowlife creep assuage his vulnerable masculinity by frightening her.

So much for professional detachment. Kermit gave up and entered the clinic. He remembered to duck his head moving from the hall into the waiting area, which was empty of clients for the moment.

Sherry, the plump, fiery-haired receptionist, looked up from the desk. Her eyes widened at the sight of his uniform, before she recognized his face.

"Oh!" she said, her expression losing its nervousness. "You told me you were a police officer, didn't you? Officer—" She looked down at the desk, brushing papers off of her desk calendar. "Officer Riggs. You were looking for Mr. Banos."

"That's right. Is he in today?"

He'd already determined that Jesse's answering machine and cell phone were still turned off, and Jesse's car hadn't been in his driveway when Kermit had driven by to check before heading to work that morning. So he was disappointed, but not surprised, when Sherry shook her head, her spiky bangs dancing.

"I'm sorry," she said. "He's still out of town."

"Do you know when he'll be back?"

"No." She gestured at the appointment book beside her computer. "I've been busy all morning rescheduling his appointments for this week. He might not be available until next Monday."

"He didn't let you know that until this morning?" Was Jesse having too good of a time with Nadia to be bothered to return to work? Despite his antipathy for the man, it didn't sound like the dedicated therapist he'd thought Jesse to be.

Sherry shook her head again, worry clouding her face. "I don't know. This morning's just the first I heard about it. It's going to be a crazy week, with Mr. Avalos still in Guatemala and all."

"You didn't speak with Jesse yourself?"

"No. Mr. Crow told me Mr. Banos wouldn't be in and to change his appointments. I thought for sure he'd be in today. I told everyone who was looking for him he would be." She grimaced. "They're not going to be happy."

"Other people are looking for him?" Kermit asked, too quickly.

Sherry's face closed up. "I think you'd better talk with Mr. Crow about that."

Kermit thought so, too, but he would have liked to have more ammunition for the encounter. "Are any of the other counselors available?"

"Like I said, Mr. Avalos is still on that mission with his church group. He's had it scheduled for forever." Unlike Jesse's unplanned absence, though, the receptionist's manner was careful not to imply criticism of one of her bosses. "And Ms. Mitchell is with a client. Mr. Crow's on his lunch hour."

She punched an extension number into the office phone.

Kermit doubted Nigel Crow was eager to see him, but he was apparently less eager to leave him alone with Sherry. Moments after Sherry said he'd be right down, Kermit heard the marriage therapist's long strides in the hall and a thud at the door.

"Ouch! Blast it!" Nigel's narrow face contorted in a grimace as he advanced on Kermit, one hand outstretched for a handshake, one gingerly probing his hairline. "Somebody's going to sue us if we don't get that fixed. And it's probably going to be me. What can I do for you, Officer Riggs?"

"You can tell me where Jesse Banos is," Kermit said. Nothing like the direct approach.

Nigel's grimace settled into an apologetic frown. "Sorry. I'm afraid you'll have to wait until he returns, like everyone else."

"Like the IRS and the FBI?"

The man's self-assured expression flickered with uneasiness. Kermit suspected he had been prepared for cat and mouse games, not direct questions.

"I don't think it's my place to discuss Jesse's affairs."

"If it were only Jesse's affairs, I wouldn't be bothering you," Kermit said bluntly. "But I think Jesse is in trouble, and it's spreading. At least one of the men looking for him may be an imposter and may be dangerous. I think Jesse's in more trouble than he realized, and that's why he's not back at work this morning like he planned."

Nigel Crow's face settled into a still mask, his dark eyes glittering deep in their sockets. "You have the right to think what you choose, Officer. However, I don't see how I can help you."

Kermit pulled a card from his wallet and held it out. "You can tell Jesse Banos that Kermit Riggs wants to speak with him. My cell phone number is on that card. He can reach me any time, day or night."

Nigel waved the card back. "I don't know how to get in touch with—"

"You can tell him," Kermit continued over his objection, "that his trouble has spilled over onto people I care about. He can either call and tell me what is going on and request my help, or I will find him on my own, regardless of who else I lead to him. What I'm not going to do is sit around while other people get hurt because Jesse can't face up to his own mistakes."

If Nigel Crow had considered Kermit a pushover rookie cop on their first encounter, the consternation in the man's eyes suggested he was reevaluating that opinion.

"If you don't know how to get in touch with him, that's unfortunate for Jesse." Kermit thrust his card out once more, and Nigel's long fingers reluctantly closed on it.

"I don't know what this is all about," Nigel insisted, his frustration convincing. "But I do know that a couple of the men who have come in here looking for Jesse are not pleasant people."

"You can tell Jesse that I can arrange for a certain amount of protection," Kermit said. Unofficial protection, perhaps. But between his friends and Mark Banos's, they could come up with a few scary types to keep the hounds at bay.

"I can't tell him that," Nigel corrected. "Not unless he contacts me first."

He sighed, his belligerence sagging. "Officer Riggs, I may not know what is going on, but I do know Jesse hasn't done anything illegal. He's trying to help out a friend in trouble. That's just the sort of person he is."

"I understand," Kermit said, his jaw tight. "He's the sort of man who feels compelled by duty and honor to help his friends, especially the sexy, blond, married ones."

Nigel's pale skin flushed as Sherry's eyes widened, but his words became only more urgent. "I'm a counselor, Officer Riggs, not a mind reader. I try not to judge my clients—or anyone else—by first impressions. But I must also be willing to make judgments about an individual's frame of mind, whether a given person might be suicidal or even potentially homicidal."

"Killing Jesse Banos might be tempting," Kermit admitted dryly. "But I'm not a fan of violence as a way of solving problems."

Nigel grimaced. "This isn't a joke, Officer. I believe you don't mean to do Jesse any harm. What I am trying to tell you is that I believe some of the others who are looking for him may. I don't suppose I will change your determination to find him, but I would ask that you not doing anything to help them. As I said, they are not pleasant individuals."

Before Kermit could respond, a smooth voice with a dark edge interrupted them.

"Tsk, tsk, Mr. Crow, I do hope you're not talking about me?"

The man in the doorway wore a dark, tailored suit and a smile that would alarm a shark. He stepped through into the reception area, his trim, black hair not quite brushing the low lintel.

"And you are?" Kermit demanded.

"Out of your league, Officer Barney." The man pulled out his ID as his dark eyes flicked dismissively over Kermit's uniform. "Agent Dominick Johnson, FBI. Jesse Banos is my investigation. Why don't you run along back to your donut shop?"

Chapter 9

A twenty-minute drive from Pacific Coast Community College north to Hope Point. A twenty-minute drive back. Serena figured that left her a good twenty minutes of her lunch hour to get some answers about Jesse's activities.

Unfortunately, she'd already wasted ten of those minutes on Mark.

"Like, I wish he *would* call me," Mark was repeating, a little too vehemently. He didn't glance up from the eerily lifelike snake's head he was scoring into the upper arm of the squirming college student seated behind his counter.

The boy's forehead dripped with sweat under matted blond dreadlocks, and his stoic scowl looked more like a quivering grimace of pain, convincing Serena that her decision to put off that dragonfly tattoo she'd been considering ever since high school should be extended another couple of decades.

"Don't forget to breathe," Mark ordered, causing the kid to gulp for air. Mark's eyes shifted briefly to Serena, waiting for the young man to stop twitching. "If Jesse's really in that much trouble, he could use my help. I mean, I know I'm not exactly a scary dude—" The kid he was tattooing rolled white-rimmed eyes in disagreement. "—but I've got some bad-ass friends."

The tall, bandanna-bedecked biker—Jimbo?—wasn't in the shop that afternoon, but the shorter one with the scar, Tank, sat in the free chair behind the counter. He gave Serena a bashful grin.

"If you do hear from Jesse, tell him he needs to call me," Serena said. Mark's evasive manner, such a change from the week before, suggested he had heard something from Jesse. And the way Mark talked about helping him . . . *What kind of help would Jesse want from Mark?* She couldn't ask Mark to betray his brother, but he might be willing to relay a message. "He's dragged me into his mess, and I want out."

"I hear that," Mark assured her, wrinkling his nose in guilty distress. "If this Othello dude bothers you again, you can call me. I mean, Jesse's my brother, so it's like, my duty to watch his girl's back when he's gone."

"I'm not his girl," Serena reminded him.

"Ex-girl," Mark corrected, turning back to the college kid's arm. "Like, you're still cool in my book, right?"

"You, too," Serena agreed, more touched than she would have expected, despite her realistic sense of Mark's reliability. With Destiny and Daniel in Hawaii for another week, the thought of Othello Karenin loose in Hope Point had her feeling disturbingly alone. The night before, Destiny had practically ordered her to call Kermit.

But she couldn't forget Karenin's veiled threats against anyone he thought she was close to. Against Kermit, in particular. She had no intention of exposing Kermit to that.

She would feel better, too, if Sarah were already with her father in Santa Rosa. Still, Sarah should be safe working as a junior counselor at the Hope Point Community T-ball camp all week, and Gemma's grandmother, Pleasance Geary, would be keeping both girls under close surveillance from the time camp ended until Serena picked Sarah up after work. Serena figured Pleasance was at least as dangerous as Tank when riled.

"I'll call if I need you," Serena promised, even as she

hoped she'd never be in enough trouble to need to rely on Mark Banos for help. "You be careful, too."

"I won't offer to shake the dude's hand, that's for sure," Mark said, grinning as he wiggled his free fingers at her.

"I don't think this man would stop at fingers if he got angry," Serena warned.

What had he told her at the Deepwater Brewery? He'd hoped he could find something more creative to do if he needed to hurt someone.

She shuddered. If *she* could tell Mark had something to hide, Karenin would be all over him. "Just keep your eyes open, Mark."

Tank straightened in his seat. "Don't you worry, ma'am. I spent eight years in the Rangers, but Jimbo learned how to fight on the streets. We won't let anything happen to our friend here." He winked at Mark. "At least not until he's finished detailing our bikes like he promised."

"I feel better already," Serena said, nodding her gratitude to Tank.

"Don't be a stranger," Mark said, once more turning his full attention to his young client's arm.

"How long is this tattoo going to take, man?" the kid demanded, finishing on a plaintive gasp as the tattoo gun connected with his skin.

"Not nearly as long as it took you to get those dreads, dude," Mark assured him with the detachment of a professional.

"They're not even my dreads!" Serena heard the kid wail as she left the shop. "I bought them, man. They're weaves!"

The determined sea breeze blasting along Tenth Street raised goosebumps on Serena's bare arms as she glanced at her watch. Just enough time to hike the two blocks to the

Life Integration Clinic, find out they had no intention of telling her where Jesse might be, and make it back to her car to head back to work.

Rounding the corner of Twelfth Street, she registered the patrol car parked across from the clinic. Her eyes narrowed as her gaze flicked to the number on it. Three-three-four. Kermit's car.

"Destiny Millbrook Parks, you interfering, meddlesome busybody. With relatives like these . . ."

Her boot heels clacked with satisfying force as she stomped up the steps to the slate blue Victorian house. Movement on the roof of the porch overhang halted her advance momentarily. Her first thought was that a desperate client was trying to escape from a bad counseling session, but then she saw that the man on the roof wore coveralls and a hard hat and carried a white bucket. He was only replacing missing shingles.

Serena shook her head. That overactive imagination again. Maybe Othello Karenin's malevolence was all in her head, too. Maybe he only wanted to audit Jesse's taxes. Maybe Jesse had merely run off to Cancun for a midlife crisis vacation with a supermodel. Maybe Agent Johnson's visit had been a bad dream brought on by too many tarot readings. Maybe that patrol car out front was mere coincidence, and she wasn't going to find Kermit Riggs talking to Sherry in the front office.

As she pushed through the front door and turned into the waiting area, ducking her head just enough to avoid the lintel, she grimaced in disappointment. No such luck.

"Miss Davis," Agent Johnson said, with sarcasm sharp enough to draw blood. "How delightful to see you again."

"What are you doing here?" Serena demanded, careful to include Kermit, who wasn't looking nearly as guilty as she felt he should, going behind her back at the prodding of her sister. In fact, he looked almost as grim as Agent Johnson.

She wondered what she had interrupted. Sherry, the receptionist, looked ready to hide beneath her desk. And Nigel Crow's face had paled to an even more sickly color than usual.

Besides Mark, she would have guessed Nigel would be most upset by the possibility of Jesse's being in trouble. Jesse had helped Nigel get his life together after the collapse of his marriage and a suicide attempt. *Another of Jesse's rescue projects.* Though at least Jesse hadn't dumped Nigel as a friend when Nigel no longer needed his help.

"I don't suppose you have any new information you'd like to share about Jesse Banos?" Agent Johnson asked, redirecting her focus.

"I don't suppose you're about to tell me why you're investigating him?" Serena replied, matching his acerbic intonation.

"It's none of your concern."

"It is *my* concern, though," Kermit said. He stepped into the space between Serena and the FBI agent, adeptly controlling the lines of tension in the room. "You're conducting an investigation in my jurisdiction. Any illegal activities in Hope Point are my concern."

Johnson's narrow, dark eyebrows rose. "You're right, of course. I assure you that if I discover Mr. Banos has a stack of unpaid parking tickets or has forgotten to clean up after his dog on a city street, I will notify you immediately. Now, why don't you tell me what you've discovered, if anything, and quit wasting my time."

The ironic twist to Kermit's mouth appeared to Serena to be equally dangerous as Johnson's sarcasm. "I assure you

141

that if I discover Mr. Banos has tampered with U.S. mail or removed the tag from his mattress, I will notify you immediately."

"Aren't you all supposed to be working together?" Sherry asked, her face turning nearly as red as her hair at her own temerity. "I mean, in the face of international terrorism and all?"

"The FBI takes all reports of terrorist activities very seriously," Agent Johnson said. "And when hell freezes over and the local police force has significant information to report on such activities, you can be assured we will treat it with all the seriousness it deserves."

"We're all inspired with confidence by the great strides both the FBI and the local police force have made in locating Jesse," Serena put in.

"The local police force isn't *trying* to locate Jesse Banos," Kermit said, stepping more firmly between her and Johnson. "And you shouldn't be, either. Leave it to the FBI."

Not bad advice, overall, but that didn't improve her reaction to being told what to do.

"If you're not here on an official investigation, I don't think you're in any position to be giving me orders," she said. Her voice was tight with control, but she could still hear the heat in it.

Kermit didn't flinch. "This is private property. I have the authority to remove trespassers."

She stared at him, unable to believe he'd use such a dirty trick. "I'm not trespassing. I have Nigel's permission to be here."

They both glanced at Nigel, whose dark eyes began to gleam. "I'm sorry Serena. We have a clinic to run. All this conflict isn't good for our clients."

"Nigel!" Of all Jesse's colleagues, Nigel was her favorite. He didn't have Roger Avalos's gregarious charm or Lani Mitchell's sparkling intellect, but his dry wit and open heart—his obvious, unrequited crush on Lani was enough to break Serena's heart—drew her to him. She'd thought the feeling was mutual.

He only smiled at her furious glare.

"I don't believe Agent Johnson's shown me a search warrant or anything else requiring me to allow him on the premises, either," Nigel continued, enthusiastically expanding on Kermit's theme. "Although I hope he will leave of his own accord without Officer Riggs being forced to remove him."

Johnson's white, even teeth looked ready for blood. "No, there's no need for that."

Serena eyed Kermit, considering civil disobedience. He wouldn't actually heft her off the floor and drag her outside.

He raised an eyebrow at her, gesturing to the door.

Okay, maybe he would. *Whatever happened to Good Cop?* She shot Nigel a last glance, to let him know she wasn't through with him, then swept back through the door. Silence followed her for a moment, then she felt a storm cloud of irritation flow out into the hall ahead of Agent Johnson. She heard Kermit's forehead hit the lintel, and she shot him a grim smile as she led the way out the front door.

"That was amusing." Agent Johnson adjusted his dark suit with sharp jerks on the jacket. "I hope you both are enjoying the experience. I assure you, I won't forget it."

"Any time you want to cooperate with the local authorities, I'm on your team," Kermit said, his hard expression only slightly marred by the fingers he had pressed into the knot forming on his forehead.

Johnson's lips thinned to a tight line. "You two have no

idea what you're involved in. I recommend that you stay out of my way and stay away from Jesse Banos. It's not that I'd mind dragging your mutilated bodies out of a drainage ditch, but I hate the idea of doing all that paperwork."

He stalked down the stairs, his shiny black shoes ticking smartly on the wood.

Serena turned on Kermit. "Do you really think it was a good idea to antagonize an FBI agent?"

"Me?" He stared at her. "I was trying to get things under control before you got arrested for assaulting a fed."

"Oh?" She glared right back. "So you embarrassed me in front of Agent Johnson and Nigel and Sherry for my own protection."

"That's right."

She gave him a smile as shark-like as Johnson's. "Thank you. Thank you for coming to my rescue, Sir Kermit. But I think I can take it from here. You can go now."

His blue eyes narrowed. "If you go back into that clinic, I will arrest you for trespassing."

"Why would I go back?" Serena snapped. "You and Agent Johnson obviously got all the information we could ever need from Nigel and Sherry. What the hell were you doing here, anyway? There's no criminal case for you to investigate."

"Tell me about it!" Kermit's voice rose to match hers. He gripped the post supporting the porch overhang. "There's no case. No crime, unless Agent Johnson decides to share whatever he's got with us. No reason for me even to care about where Jesse Banos has gotten himself to. Except that he seems to have put some psychopathic jilted husband on your trail."

He paused, his voice grinding downward. "Why do you think I'm here? I'm afraid you could get hurt. I'm trying to help."

"I didn't ask for your help!" The intensity of her response shocked her as much as it did Kermit. "I don't want it, and I don't need it. And I didn't ask for it!"

"I'm sorry." He dropped his hold on the porch support, his face hardening, even as the ice in his eyes cracked. "I thought you had. I thought you called me at oh-dark-thirty last Monday morning worried about Jesse Banos being kidnapped."

"Last week!" She was nearly shouting from exasperation. "But he wasn't kidnapped, was he? We already decided that. Who called you this morning about Othello Karenin? Me? No, my interfering sister. If I needed your help, I would have called you myself."

"I'm sorry," he repeated, stepping back toward the stairs. "I guess I was under the mistaken impression that we were friends and that friends help each other out when they're in trouble. I thought we were kind of in this thing together after last week. I guess that's what Destiny and Daniel thought when they called this morning. I guess we were all wrong. I should have known that, when you didn't call me yourself."

"Damn it, Kermit! That's not what I meant." She slammed the heel of her hand down on the porch railing. A splinter from beneath the weathered paint dug into her palm. She shook her hand against the sudden pain. "It's not that I don't want your friendship or appreciate all your help."

She glanced down at her hand and wished she hadn't. It looked like she might have dug an entire two-by-four into her palm. "I didn't call you about Karenin because I'm sick and tired of interrupting your life for Jesse Banos. You've got better things to do."

She grabbed the splinter between lacquer-strengthened

nails and tugged. And cursed. "Look, I asked for your help when I thought I needed it, but I don't need any more white knights. I don't need anyone to rescue me."

"Are you sure about that?" Humor eased the strain in his voice as he pointed at her hand.

"Yes!" She tugged again. Tears sprang into her eyes, though whether from the pain or from emotion, she didn't know.

"All right." He shrugged and stepped back. "I'll just get back to work then. Criminals to catch, scofflaws to ticket."

She glanced at him, a smile tugging around the lump in her throat and the sting in her palm. "You'd just leave me here with a tree stuck in my hand?"

He raised his hands. "If that's what you want me to do."

She eyed him skeptically. "What about Jesse?"

"You don't need rescuing." A smile tugged at his mouth. "But I'm going to send Fleur home with Sarah after their walk this afternoon. Just in case *Sarah* needs a little extra protection from our literary psychopath."

"You fiend," Serena said, forgetting the splinter for an instant. "You just want Fleur to wake *me* up at five in the morning instead of you."

"See?" Kermit raised his hands in a shrug. "You don't have to worry about me playing white knight. I'm not really helping you at all."

"Good," Serena snapped, jutting out her hand. "Then you can take out this blasted splinter."

He grinned as he grasped her wrist, turning her hand. His fingers, blunt and strong, moved with surprising dexterity. A sharp sting, and the splinter was gone.

"There you go," he said, but his palm still cradled her hand. He glanced at her, blue eyes dark under his pale lashes. "I wasn't trying to interfere. I was trying to help."

She nodded, wishing she still had the splinter to explain her damp eyes. "I'm sorry. I might be a little sensitive about that."

"Not much. I really didn't notice."

She tried to glare at him again, but couldn't manage a good burning stare when his eyes glinted with humor like that.

Yet she needed that glare. If she couldn't distance him with a frown, she'd notice that the humor in his eyes was muted by the memory of their argument, by whatever feelings had sparked off that ridiculous clash between them. She'd notice how his hand felt strong and steady against hers. She'd notice the pattern of darker flecks in his eyes, the faint dusting of freckles across his nose. And she'd wonder if she leaned close, if his freckled skin would smell like summer.

Her gaze drifted down to his lips. She bit hers to bring her wandering thoughts back, but it didn't seem to help. Kermit's hand felt suddenly very warm against hers. She wondered what he would do if she *did* lean in close.

She jerked her hand away.

He stumbled back a step. "I'd better get back to work."

"Right. You'd better," she agreed. Her arms moved with a jerky energy of their own as she waved at his patrol car across the street. "Does Lieutenant Marcy know you're asking questions for Daniel Parks's sister-in-law?"

Kermit's nonchalant shrug nearly unbalanced him, and his smile looked as awkward as hers felt. "I mentioned your name. If he didn't connect Serena Davis to Destiny Millbrook, that's all right with me."

She squelched the sudden urge to reach out and take his hand again. "I'll let Sarah know about borrowing Fleur."

"Sure." He ducked back, out from under the porch overhang, but the grace that had carried him through the confrontation with Agent Johnson appeared to have deserted him.

Serena saw his foot slip off the second step, and she lunged forward to grab for his arm, but his momentum tugged him out of her reach. She cried out as he spun, windmilling toward the cement walkway across the lawn, but her voice was drowned out by a rumble from the roof over her head.

She jerked back instinctively, and a white plastic bucket plummeted past her, smashing into the porch steps with a noise that made her ears ring. Roof shingles and nails exploded from the bucket like shrapnel, spraying across the steps and shredding half a dozen pansies in a planter beside the bottom of the steps.

For a moment she stood frozen, watching dust float over the cracked step where Kermit had stood just seconds before. Then she grabbed the handrail beside the steps and jumped the damaged stairs. She barely noticed the jolt the landing gave her ankles as she ran across the walkway to where Kermit lay sprawled on the lawn.

"Are you all right?" She dropped beside him, ready to shout for help, but he was already pushing himself up to a sitting position.

"That," he said, blinking as he took in the mess on the stairs, "was a little close."

Serena choked out a laugh, though her breathing refused to return to normal. "You think? Did you get hit by anything? Did you hurt anything when you fell?"

He shook his head, though he let her check the back of his skull and he wiggled his fingers and feet for her. "I'm pretty good at falling. I've had some practice." He managed a grin. "First time being clumsy ever saved my skull."

"Officer Riggs?"

Nigel and Sherry had run out onto the front porch and now stood at the top of the steps, eyes wide as they surveyed the damage.

"Officer Riggs? Serena? Are you all right?" Nigel's long legs vaulted the stairs with more ease than Serena had done, and he hurried over to them. "Should I have Sherry call for medical help?"

"I'm fine," Kermit said. He glanced at Serena. "None of that debris hit you? Are you sure?"

Serena glanced down at her slacks, half expecting to see them studded with nails, but other than her ankles protesting her doing hurdles in high-heeled boots, everything seemed to be in good shape.

"I'll get something to rope off the stairs," Sherry called, obviously glad not to have to leap off of them herself. "Before someone gets hurt."

"You're sure you're both all right?" Nigel repeated, hovering over them like an anxious stork. "What happened?"

"The roofing guy's bucket fell onto the stairs," Serena said. She glanced up at the steeply pitched roof over the porch, where she had seen the man before, but he was gone. "He must have left it sitting up there when he went on break, and it slipped."

"Roofing guy?" Nigel asked.

"The one fixing those holes in the shingling?" Serena suggested, pointing.

Nigel sighed. "Roger. He does this all the time. Schedules repairs without telling anyone. He had a painter over to do the front door a couple of months ago. The rest of us ended up with white palms."

He bent down to offer Kermit a hand. Serena took Kermit's other arm, and together they helped him to his feet.

"I'll have to talk with the contractor about safety," Nigel said. "Thank God no one was hurt. I'm terribly sorry."

"No harm done," Kermit assured him. "At least not to us. Your stairs are going to need some work."

Nigel nodded, his expression somewhere between misery and helpless amusement at the mess. "Everything happens at once. Just what we need with Roger and Jesse out of town."

"Jesse's little drama sure left you shorthanded." Serena had strong feelings against hitting someone when they were down, but Nigel *had* threatened to have her arrested for trespassing. "And he left me receiving threats from a man who might be an unbalanced, jealous husband. Don't you think it's time someone contacted Jesse and suggested he get his butt back here to clean up the mess he's made?"

Nigel's pale face flushed a light rose. "I can't help you with that, Serena. I already told Officer Riggs that I don't know where Jesse is."

"But he's been in touch with you," Serena said. She didn't bother to make it a question.

"I thought he was going to get in touch with you," Nigel countered. "He said he wanted to see you, try to talk things out."

"He stood me up." Serena was pleased to note the words no longer made her blush. "Without bothering to mention he was leaving town. You're the only one he's deigned to contact since."

At least, the only one who would admit to it. The more she thought about it, the more certain she was that Mark had heard something since the first time they had talked.

"You're worse than a pit bull." Nigel's expression softened in a wan smile. "I remember the first time Jesse introduced me to you, at one of Roger's summer parties at his cabin on the Trinity a couple of years ago. I thought you were one of his typical fragile beauties. Another damsel in distress."

"How long did that last?" Kermit asked.

Nigel shrugged. "Until I tried inner-tubing down the rapids just upriver of Roger's property."

"He was too tall for the tube. He looked ridiculous, jackknifed into that thing," Serena said, giving back as good as she knew she was going to get. "He should have known better."

"It wasn't the inner-tube," Nigel objected. "It was the river."

"It was late August," Serena told Kermit, "and the river wasn't really deep enough for tubing."

"My esteemed colleagues were ready to call in the Air National Guard or something to airlift me to a hospital," Nigel said, his face turning rosy again, though his smile was purely wicked. "But our delicate, sophisticated Serena commandeered a pen knife and a tube of antiseptic and proceeded to dig the gravel out of my behind, one pebble at a time."

"I still have nightmares," Serena growled.

"I still have scars," Nigel countered. His smile faded. "I'm worried about Jesse, but I'm also worried about his clients and the clinic. If he contacts me, you can be sure I'll try to convince him to come home. And I'll ask him to call you both, for what it's worth."

"Both of us?" Kermit asked, raising an eyebrow at Serena.

She thought she'd resisted those blue eyes and the freckles on his nose with admirable restraint. She'd made it clear she didn't need a white knight. But glancing at the nails and shingles spread across the cracked stairs in front of the clinic, a rush of shaky adrenaline coursed through her once more, and she could admit she needed a friend. Needed Kermit's friendship.

"Ask Jesse to call either one of us," Serena told Nigel. "Day or night." She smiled at Kermit. "And if it's really late at night, Officer Riggs is the one with the cell phone."

Chapter 10

Serena was twisted like a pretzel when the telephone rang that evening. She considered letting the machine pick up, then realized it could be Jesse responding to Nigel's request that he call her.

"I can get it, Mom."

She heard Sarah's feet hit the floor out of a headstand, as Serena was unwinding out of her half-bound lotus pose.

"Let me," she said, then regretted it as her knees protested when she jumped to her feet. Fleur leaped up on her other side, ready for whatever adventure might have interrupted the yoga session. Serena rested a grateful hand on the dog's head as she shook out her legs.

Sarah had already reached the kitchen and was grabbing for the receiver. Kermit might argue that thirty-three wasn't middle-aged, but it wasn't thirteen, either.

"It's for you," Sarah said, holding out the phone as Serena hobbled over.

"I thought the point of yoga was to keep you limber," Serena complained, reaching for the receiver. "Not cripple you."

"How many people your age can even do a pose like that?" Sarah asked, with a warming pride. "You're scientific proof it works. That's why I do it."

"Maybe it will keep you from having to use a walker when you reach my advanced years," Serena retorted, pulling her daughter's ponytail before lifting the phone to her ear.

"Hello?"

"Hello, Serena."

It wasn't Jesse. She'd only heard that eerie, mocking voice once before, but there was no mistaking it. It might be time to consider de-listing her phone number.

"Mr. Karenin?"

"I suppose that little fiction will do as well as any," the voice responded, amused. "You're actually the first person to see through it. Not very many literate minds here in Podunkville. I knew you were smarter than average when we met. It's one of the things I like about you."

She suppressed her first reaction, which was to give in to a case of the creeps. Instead, she opted for sass. "What makes you think I did see through it?" she asked. "Maybe you just now told me what I needed to know."

He clicked his tongue with exaggerated regret. "Only moments ago I said you were smart. Didn't you hear me when I told you I'd be watching you?"

The flare of alarm must have shown in her eyes, because both Sarah and Fleur were staring at her in concern from the living room. Suddenly, Karenin's scare tactics seemed more worthy of her anger than her fear.

"Look, I don't know who you are, Mr. Karenin, and I don't really care. I don't care whether or not you find Jesse. But I do care when you invade my privacy. I'm only going to tell you this once. Leave me the hell alone."

Sarah's eyes widened at her language, but she gave Serena the thumbs-up sign.

"My, my. That sounded like a threat." Karenin's amusement turned sharp in her ear. "Leave you alone, or what? You'll sick your lovelorn puppy of a police officer on me?

154

Kermit Riggs. Definitely a name better suited to frogs than to humans."

She knew she was supposed to be surprised that he'd discovered Kermit's name. She had no intention of giving him that satisfaction.

"I'm not making threats," she said, her teeth gritted against her anger. "And I'm not counting on anyone else to fulfill them for me. I'm simply telling you. Leave me alone."

"That is indeed a relief." Laughter rippled under his words. "I'd hate to think of you putting your faith in poor, ungainly Officer Riggs, as well-intentioned as I'm sure he is. But that's beside the point. You don't need any protection from me. I only want your help."

"I'm not that interested in what you want," Serena said, even as she wished she had her sister's knack for diplomacy. Destiny had faced two dangerous psychopaths in the past twelve months, and Serena was fairly certain she hadn't goaded either one of them.

"But we want the same thing, Serena. Your peace of mind. Just help me to find Jesse Banos, and I will be content to leave you alone as you request."

"If I knew where Jesse was, I'd have dragged him back home by his hair by now," Serena snapped back. "I can't help you."

"I think you can."

"You can think whatever you want. That doesn't make it true."

"I'm afraid it does." Karenin's voice had lost its undercurrent of amusement. "If I think you can help me, it doesn't matter whether *you* think you can or not. What matters is that if you don't help me, the consequences will be unpleasant."

"You *are* threatening me."

"Of course not. Serena, Serena," he singsonged mournfully. "It's not a threat, because even if you really don't have any information for me tonight—which I don't believe, but I will allow as your own little power play fiction—you will soon find out something which you can share with me."

The mocking tone returned. "You are resourceful and persistent. You have access to Jesse's friends, colleagues, and family, which I do not have. When I call you back in a couple of days, you will be able to tell me what I need to know."

"I'm sorry, but I don't think so."

"I'm not a patient man, Serena." Karenin's voice hardened. "I am a man of action. If I can't act to find Jesse myself, I will act to encourage those who can. I don't think you want me to have to encourage you any more forcefully than I already have."

"I have nothing more to say to you, Mr. Karenin," Serena said. "I'm tired of your vague threats. You were actually more frightening as an IRS agent."

He had a hearty laugh that was only a little too practiced to be charming.

"I *do* like you, Serena," he said as his laughter faded. "But I can't allow you to think you don't need to fear me. I tried to take the serendipitous opportunity to give you a demonstration of my methods earlier today, but fate stepped in at the last moment."

The ice sliding into his voice sent an unwelcome chill through Serena's blood.

"What are you talking about?" she asked, the question dragged from her against her will.

"Your Officer Riggs is a very clumsy man," he said, without a trace of humor now. "And a very lucky one. I don't know if those shingles would have cracked his head the way they did those stairs, but if you don't want to find out, I suggest you discover for me what I want to know.

"Good-night, Serena. Sleep tight. I'll be in touch."

The Hope Point Square on a summer evening. *Not exactly Palm Springs,* Kermit thought, swinging his arms against the chill. The morning fog had decided to hang around all day, and though sunset wasn't officially scheduled for another couple of hours, the heavy gray blanket sagged like twilight above the town, sucking color from the Victorian storefronts and warmth from poor cops assigned to foot duty on a slow Tuesday afternoon.

Lieutenant Marcy had decided on a proactive response to the problem of escalating encounters in the downtown area over the past few days. Local teenagers, already bored with vacation, had been provoking verbal altercations with the yearly influx of transients who spent the summer panhandling and hanging out on the Square.

Kermit had to agree with the lieutenant that the presence of uniformed police officers patrolling downtown discouraged trouble. But once the trouble had been discouraged, the patrolling quickly descended into boredom. Ticketing leash law violators, citing sneering Southern California teenagers for aggressive panhandling, and discouraging inebriated college students from dressing the incongruous statue of President Garfield in the center of the Square in drag wasn't the crime prevention he'd joined the force to perform.

Standing in the cold on a nearly deserted patch of lawn, with most of the foot traffic driven to more protected environs by the damp and gloom, all he could think about was Othello Karenin's threatening call to Serena the night before. The more he thought about it, the more he chafed under his forced inaction on the Square.

He knew the only reason Serena had even told him about the call was because of Karenin's intimation that he'd been the one trying to bean Kermit with the bucket of roofing shingles the day before.

The threat against himself didn't bother him. Nigel Crow hadn't yet been able to determine if his colleague Roger Avalos had arranged to have the roof fixed or not, but even if the falling bucket had been a purposeful attempt at injuring him, it could only have been a chance attempt, a seizing of an opportunity by Karenin—or an accomplice— already in position to spy on the clinic.

Kermit figured he was in at least that much danger every day from disgruntled former arrestees. He was used to keeping his eyes open.

What he *wasn't* used to was the simmering fury in his gut whenever he thought of Karenin, that . . . *slimewad* . . . invading Serena's home with his threats and intimidation.

Kermit had learned to divorce his emotions from his work. The things people did to each other often made him angry. Sad. Discouraged. But he didn't allow that to affect the way he did his job. He didn't allow it to become personal.

This problem of Serena's felt all too personal.

"Hey! Riggs!"

He turned, startled, to see Garth Vance approaching him across the Square, two steaming Styrofoam cups in his hand. So much for keeping his eyes open. He hadn't even noticed Garth's patrol car parking in front of the coffee shop up the street.

Garth extended one of the Styrofoam cups to him. "You might need this more than I thought. I saw you standing here like old Garfield up there, and I was afraid you'd died of boredom and just forgot to fall over."

As the smell of hot coffee worked into his brain, Kermit forgot the acerbic response he meant to make. "Thanks."

"Yeah, well, I hope somebody does the same for me when I'm getting ready to go off shift. Anything exciting happen this afternoon?"

Kermit grunted. "Does it look like anything exciting happened?"

Garth grinned with all the humor of a pit bull. "Have you noticed that ever since we got Detective Parks cleared of murder, Lieutenant Marcy gives us all the really great patrols?"

"He'll get over it."

"Easy for you to say. Odds at the station are that you'll make sergeant next year." Garth chugged the last of his coffee, burning away the injustice of it all. "You can head on back to the station if you want. You only got about half an hour left."

"I'll walk one more pass around the Square," Kermit offered, to make up for his earlier inattention.

"Suit yourself," Garth said, settling in to a surveillance of the Square. "But you might want to see what that lady's been waving to you about first."

"What lady?" Kermit turned the direction Garth had indicated with his cup. The woman standing on the sidewalk across G Street had her wild blond curls trapped in a twist behind her head, and her granny glasses, reflecting the faint afternoon light, hid her gold-green eyes, but even in Hope Point, one of the last hippie bastions in America, her fiery orange and pink muumuu caught the eye. Having got Kermit's attention, the woman gestured impatiently for him to cross over to her.

"I thought she just wanted a cop, but she waved me off. She wants you," Garth said. "I guess I'm not her type. She's got two good legs. Don't know why she can't cross the street."

Kermit took a quick sip of coffee to fortify himself for the coming encounter. "She doesn't want to leave her shop unattended."

Garth glanced at the row of businesses behind her. "Which shop? She's not the woman that runs the lingerie place."

"You would know that."

"Hey, I had to arrest a weirdo in there once. I check in from time to time, make sure she hasn't had any more trouble."

"I guess herb stores don't attract too many flashers," Kermit said wryly.

"Who said anything about flashing?" Garth asked. "Guy was trying to shoplift a black lace teddy and garters. Had 'em on under his business suit." He nodded across the street. "So she's the lady that runs Callista's Herbal Haven? Grace Martinez says she's psychic."

"That's Callista," Kermit agreed. "And she claims she's psychic, anyway."

"Martinez says she has a friend who went in there when her ex was threatening to kill her. That Callista woman gave her some kind of protection charm. The ex showed up at the friend's house that night with a knife. He trips over the neighbor's cat and stabs himself through the upper arm. Never bothered her again."

Kermit wasn't about to get in the middle of the exaggerated tales Grace and Garth told each other. He lifted his coffee cup in a last salute to Garth and headed across G Street.

"Come on inside," Callista commanded, glancing around the square in irritated scrutiny before ducking into her doorway. "I thought maybe I could get your attention without the entire world knowing about it, but I guess not."

Kermit followed her into the shop. Scents assaulted him, from the sage hanging over the front door to the cinnamon candles burning on the register counter in the back.

He'd been in Callista's shop a couple of times before to buy the ginger pills and vitamin supplements Serena had suggested when he'd hurt his shoulder a few months back throwing tennis balls for Fleur. He supposed the shop was a welcoming place, with its warm lighting and free samples of herbal tea by the door, but he still felt out of place. The remedies for female hormonal imbalances discreetly placed on the shelves to his left, the books on feminine spiritual power on the shelves to his right, the prints of ancient fertility figurines and moon cycles in a bin by the door, all suggested a sphere in which he had no competence whatsoever.

And, psychic or not, he always got the feeling that Callista enjoyed his discomfort much more than was strictly necessary.

"What can I do for you, Callista?" he asked, setting his coffee cup on the counter. There were way too many lacy scarves and things to spill it on.

"Do you have any leads on this nut who's stalking Serena?" she asked, sweeping around the counter to take her place on the stool behind it.

"No." Sometimes monosyllabic answers defused argumentative people.

"Why not?" Sometimes they didn't. "You do realize that she's in danger, don't you? I mean, it's not that New Agey, touchy-feely, unscientific fluff you can ignore anymore, right? Physical threats are supposed to be the sorts of things you're allowed to investigate, aren't they?"

"The police department has nothing to investigate," Kermit said, keeping his voice level. "We don't have the resources to investigate every strange telephone call people receive."

Callista's eyes blazed as she glared at him over the tops of her glasses. "How can you say that? This is Serena! And this isn't just some prank call. Anyone who's spent any time around criminals ought to be able to tell this man is dangerous. Are you waiting for her dead body before you do any—"

"I said the police department has nothing to investigate," Kermit cut her off. It occurred to him that he could have pretended not to see Callista and simply returned to the station. Why did he never think of things like that until it was too late? "I didn't say I didn't think it was serious or that I wasn't going to do anything about it."

Callista relaxed slightly as she began the process of closing down her cash register. "Then you're going over to Serena's tonight?"

Kermit gave her his best blank stare. "Serena has made it clear she doesn't want me trying to force protection on her."

Callista waved her hand in a dismissive gesture. "I'm sure she did. But she's inviting you over for dinner. I think you should accept."

His sense of the ridiculous began to dispel Kermit's discomfort in his surroundings. "You've had a psychic vision of Serena inviting me to dinner?"

Callista's smile wasn't friendly. "I just spoke with her on the telephone. I mentioned that I could see you out on the Square, freezing your rear end off defending law and order, and she said I should invite you over to dinner at her place.

I got the impression she thought she'd hurt your feelings and you wouldn't come."

If Callista wanted to know his feelings, she'd *better* be psychic, because he wasn't about to share them with her.

"I never turn down a home-cooked meal," he said.

Callista nodded. "Based on the astrology reading I did for Serena today, I think it's a good idea that you be there."

Kermit said nothing, but apparently his reaction didn't need to be spoken.

Callista's sharp eyes narrowed. "You're not one of those people who believe anyone who reads tarot cards or believes in astrology is a Satan-worshiping occultist, are you?"

"No."

"Because I find astrology is a useful way to help people to see the patterns in their lives. It helps me to focus my own ability to see those patterns."

Gold fire sparked in her eyes. "You know the three wise men were astrologers, right? I've seen things other people don't see all my life, and I don't think that makes me evil. I believe there is evil in the world. I choose to serve light."

"So do I," Kermit said mildly. "I don't believe you're a Satanist." He'd actually met a pair of Satanists once. He had no trouble telling the difference. "But that doesn't mean I believe you can predict what is going to happen to Serena or to anyone by looking at the stars. I don't believe our fates are written in stone."

"Of course not," Callista retorted, snapping shut her cash drawer. "If they were, then I could tell you exactly what was threatening Serena, and there would be nothing you would be able to do about it. As it is, all I can tell you is that danger appears to be hovering around her and that she may need your help if it decides to strike."

She rose from her stool, giving him a sly smile. "And

since you're the one with the badge, the gun, and the muscles, you don't even have to believe I'm psychic to know that I'm right."

Kermit almost smiled back. "I believe we both want what's best for Serena."

She shook her head with a sigh. "You may not be able to feel the connections linking you to the great tapestry of life, Kermit, but that doesn't mean they're not there. And your connections to those you care about are strong."

She paused, assessing him as she pulled a hand-woven shawl from a hook on the wall behind her. "Your fate may not be written in stone, but it's written in your heart. That's not a bad thing."

She pulled a book bag with a sequined yin-yang symbol on it out from under the counter and blew out the cinnamon candles.

"Are you joining us for dinner?" Kermit asked, squelching a sudden surge of disappointment. He should be grateful. Callista would be on his side when it came to suggesting safety measures Serena should take until Jesse returned or Karenin left town.

And Callista's presence would effectively solve the problem of how he was going to act normally around Serena when he kept thinking about how warm her hazel eyes had looked the day before when he'd almost gotten flattened by that bucket . . .

"No, Serena invited me, but I had to decline." Callista came out from behind the counter. "She's cooking vegetarian chili. My digestive system isn't up to the challenge. Consider yourself warned; it will take the roof of your mouth off."

She dug a large ring of keys from her bag. "I could use a big cop with a big gun to walk me to the night deposit at the bank, though."

Kermit lifted his coffee cup from the counter and followed her toward the front door. "I'm your man."

She glanced up at him out of the corner of her eye as she pulled the door closed behind them and inserted the key. "I don't think so. I think Serena has you all wrapped up."

He snorted in surprise, then took a swig of coffee, using the cup to hide the sudden heat in his face. The cold sludge only jolted the surge of alarm in his gut. What had he allowed to show in his face? He almost wished he believed in Callista's psychic abilities—at least he wouldn't have to worry that anyone else had noticed his inconvenient feelings.

"Serena's a good friend," he managed, choking a little on the coffee.

"Of course she is," Callista said, amused. "You're not interested in anything more? Do you think she's too old for you?"

"No, of course not!" Kermit snapped, then had to keep himself from striking his forehead. *Cool and detached, that's you, Kermit, my boy.*

"Good. I don't think so, either," Callista agreed, dropping her keys in her bag and starting up the block toward the bank. "I think you're good for her. You know the last time Jesse dragged her out dancing? Never."

Serena had told Callista about going to the Brewery? Because she'd had a good time? Or a bad one? Kermit opened his mouth to ask, stopped himself just in time with another sip of coffee.

"Serena broke up with Jesse barely more than two weeks ago," he said, instead. "She's not looking for another relationship. And she doesn't need anyone pushing her to find one."

"I'm not pushing," Callista insisted, waving her free

hand airily. "What's meant to be, will be."

"I told you I don't believe our fate is written in the stars," Kermit said. He gestured his coffee cup up toward the fog-blank sky. "Even if you could see them to read it."

Callista shot him a look that might have been sharp enough to pierce the shroud across the sky. "Be careful what you say about the stars," she said, with more humor than warning. "It's only three days until the full moon."

"You're a werewolf, as well as a psychic?"

She laughed, and he liked the honesty of it, despite himself. "Just watch your heart, if it's so necessary for you to protect it. June's moon is the lover's moon. And Serena—"

"Serena needs time to get over Jesse."

"I wouldn't worry about that," Callista said, her tone acerbic. "The two of them would have been terrible for each other, though she would have loved him to the end if he'd only loved her, too."

Kermit nodded, justified, though the thought stabbed at his heart.

"But I don't think Jesse is capable of that kind of lasting love," Callista continued. "I don't mean he's a sociopath. But he needs someone to take care of. Someone he can control with his love. Serena thought that's what she needed when she met him, but she's basically too strong a person to satisfy the ego of a man like Jesse Banos for long."

"I can't imagine anyone controlling Serena," Kermit agreed.

Callista glanced at him, the humor still glinting in her eyes, despite the gravity of her tone. "Maybe that's what she saw in you in the first place."

Kermit shook his head. He didn't want to talk about this with Callista. Didn't want to bring any of it out into the open, where he couldn't pretend it wasn't there. But he surely didn't want Callista saying something to Serena to ruin the friendship he'd built with her.

"Serena sees me as a friend," he said. He met Callista's gaze with all the honesty he could muster. "That's all. And that's good enough for me."

Callista tossed her head, loose curls flying from her careful twist. With her dark shawl and gold eyes, she looked like a gypsy fortuneteller. "I said that if Jesse had loved Serena for herself rather than as a project, she would not have stopped loving him. But he didn't. And she did. And she's known that in her heart for a lot longer than two weeks."

She sighed as they waited on the corner for a car to pass, the amusement gone. "If I weren't so worried about her, I wouldn't tell any of this to you, you know. I don't like to interfere."

Kermit laughed, despite himself.

She glared at him, though a smile tugged at her lips. "I think she would have broken off the engagement months ago, except her relationship with Jesse protected her from something much more dangerous."

Kermit stopped dead in the crosswalk. "What danger?" he demanded. "From who? She didn't say anything to me."

"Of course not." Callista grabbed his arm to tug him across the street. "Of course she didn't say anything to you. *You* were the danger."

"Me?" Kermit was too annoyed by her joking to laugh.

"You," Callista said. But there was no teasing in her eyes. "I doubt she was conscious of it. But her heart knew. If she broke up with Jesse, she wouldn't have anything to protect her from you."

"Serena is not afraid of me," Kermit said, suddenly feeling very dangerous indeed. "I've never given any woman any reason to be afraid of me."

He raised his coffee cup, glad to see that it wasn't shaking with his anger.

"I'm not afraid of you," Callista said blandly. "Even as much as I've provoked you. But then, I'm in no danger of falling madly in love with you. And I'm afraid Serena has."

The coffee cup dropped from Kermit's hand as he choked in disbelief, splashing coffee all over Callista, effectively wiping the smug smile from her lips.

Chapter 11

"I think it's time we take Othello Karenin on at his own game."

Serena glanced up from the crockpot she was scrubbing to where Kermit and Sarah were loading the dishwasher. China clattered as Kermit closed the dishwasher door. She'd thought he'd seemed restless all through dinner, and she guessed so had she.

The tension had nearly choked her, even the searing chili unable to burn through it. Tension from the uncertainty of what had happened to Jesse, of wondering what Karenin might be up to, of what Agent Johnson might be discovering.

That was more than enough to account for the ache in her shoulders and the knot in her stomach. Forget the tension from wondering what Kermit thought of the dinner invitation, from hoping he hadn't gotten the wrong idea. Of course, she couldn't come right out and tell him Callista had extended it without her permission.

Forget the flash of . . . something . . . that had burned through her when she had opened the front door to him and the fact that his cheeks had gone red and he'd dropped to his knees to hug Fleur in order to hide his eyes from her.

She took a deep breath and reminded herself that she was too old for teenager-style crushes and too young for a stress-induced stroke.

"We don't have to sit around waiting for Karenin to

make the next move," Kermit continued. "We need to uncover his real identity and let him know we know who he is."

Serena glanced at Sarah, seeing an echo of Kermit's determination flash in her daughter's eyes. She would rather not have involved Sarah in any of this. Sarah had been through too much already. Specifically, that mess at Thanksgiving, when she'd nearly been abducted. Serena could happily throttle Othello Karenin for frightening her again.

"Can you imagine, him calling up, acting all cool, and you calling him by name?" Sarah asked, with a steely grin.

Of course, Serena had to admit that so far anger had by far outweighed her daughter's fear. But Sarah's gutsiness wasn't the point. Karenin's smug malice was.

"Anonymous threats are a coward's ploy," Kermit said.

"Knowing the police had his name and address might back him off," Serena agreed. "But I don't know how we're going to figure out his real identity. Even if we assume that Jesse left town with Nadia and that Karenin is Nadia's husband—both pretty big assumptions—I don't even know Nadia's last name, much less her husband's name."

"Biff?" Kermit suggested. "Didn't you say something about Biff?"

Serena grimaced. "Maybe I should have paid more attention when Jesse mentioned him, but I didn't want to know that much about Nadia's problems. It wasn't Biff, but it was something like that. Started with a B, anyway. I think."

"Mark might know," Kermit said, then reconsidered. "Okay, maybe we can't count on Mark's memory. Jesse's parents would know."

"Her maiden name," Serena said, doubtfully, rinsing out

the crockpot. "I suppose we could try to track her that way, if they're willing even to talk to me."

And she supposed she'd have to try, though she really didn't want to call Jesse's parents to ask about one of his old girlfriends.

"I know how we can find her name," Sarah said. Her confidence wavered under Serena's questioning gaze, and she twisted the toe of one foot into the kitchen tile. "You remember when Gemma and I were over at Jesse's house?"

"Gee, no, I'd forgotten that," Serena said darkly.

Sarah made a face. So much for parental intimidation. "When I was on his computer, I kind of copied some stuff onto a CD."

Serena's calming count reached all the way to three before she spoke. "I don't remember you mentioning computer piracy to Officer Vance when you were confessing your crimes."

"He scared us so bad, I forgot all about it until I found it in my backpack the next day," Sarah said, with enough self-righteousness that she was probably telling the truth.

Serena glanced at Kermit, whose carefully neutral expression was somewhat spoiled by the amusement in his eyes. "Officer Riggs, if you took her down to the station and booked her, how long could I leave her there before I had to come pick her up?"

"I didn't steal any of his software or anything." Sarah planted her hands on her hips. "I wasn't there playing video games, you know."

"I can only detain her for a 'reasonable' amount of time without formally charging her," Kermit said. "Of course, once the reasonable amount of time was up, I might just forget she was in there. I could probably forget her for days."

Sarah rolled her eyes. "I copied Jesse's address book. Do you guys want to take it into evidence or do you want to come see if Nadia's name and address are in it?"

"Nadia Alexander."

Kermit thought Sarah sounded a little smug, but then a kid had to enjoy the times she proved she was smarter than the grown-ups. He leaned over Sarah's left shoulder, Serena on Sarah's right, as they all peered at the screen of Sarah's laptop.

"Laguna Beach," Sarah continued. "Nice."

"I guess she's not after Jesse for his money," Serena muttered.

"Her husband's name isn't in Jesse's address book?" Kermit asked. Not too surprising. Kermit doubted Jesse sent the couple a Christmas card.

"No problem," Sarah said. "We'll just check the Web." She clicked the icon to connect to the Internet. "Of course, this would be a lot faster if we had a DSL line."

"You spend too much time on the Internet already," Serena told her. "And not enough time cleaning your room."

"I wouldn't need to spend so much time on the Internet if our connection was faster," Sarah said. "And I like my room this way."

Kermit took a surreptitious survey of the dirty clothes Sarah had kicked under the bed when they walked in, the dresser strewn with scientific debris—he recognized the fingerprint kit he'd given her for Christmas, and the piles of books and school papers covering the only free chair and every inch of Sarah's desk. Fleur had taken up residence on Sarah's bed while they fussed over the computer, and Kermit knew from personal experience the surprising amount of shedding such a seemingly short-haired dog could do.

He would have expected someone with Sarah's scientific bent to be a little more organized in her personal space. He had to smile at her wall décor, though. A photograph of the Milky Way, a periodic table of the elements, a map of the world, and two huge posters of Orlando Bloom.

"I'm going into a reverse telephone directory," Sarah said, pointing at the screen. "We already have Nadia's name and number, but I'm guessing that her home telephone number is going to be in both her and her husband's name." She glanced up at her mom and then Kermit. "See, with a reverse directory, you can type in a telephone number and get the person's name and address."

Kermit nodded, struggling to hide his smile. "The police department does use the Internet occasionally."

Sarah looked skeptical. "Okay. So, let's see what we get." She shook her head as the screen changed. "No information. See that notice? They tell you it's a real number, but if there's no name or anything, you know it's probably unlisted. You can get a name from an unlisted number, but you have to pay, and it takes a few days."

"How do you know all this stuff?" Serena asked, looking equal parts suspicious and impressed.

Sarah shrugged, her studied nonchalance not hiding her pleasure at surprising her mother. "It's not like it's secret information or anything. You can find all kinds of stuff like that in books on being a private detective and finding missing persons and stuff."

Kermit didn't have any trouble reading Serena's expression: *How many twelve-year-old girls read books on stuff like that?*

Serena pulled her daughter's ponytail and kissed the top

of her head. "Okay, Miss Marple. What do we do next?"

"Miss Marple?" Sarah grimaced in mortification before getting back to work on the keyboard. "Next we can check to see if Nadia Alexander's name comes up on a Google search."

"You think it will?" Serena asked.

"Yours does," Sarah informed her mother. "Your office at Pacific Coast Community College."

Serena nodded. "Sure. The Environmental Health and Occupational Safety Department has a website."

"Maybe Nadia's in an organization that has a website," Sarah said.

"Try searching the news section," Kermit suggested. "If the Alexanders really are wealthy, chances are they've had their names in a society page somewhere."

Sarah made the shift, and after a pause the results began to scroll down the screen.

" 'Former fashion model,' " Serena read, pointing to the blurb under the second heading. "That's her."

"The *Coast Gazette*," Sarah said, noting the paper the article appeared in. "And it's dated just a month ago."

" 'Hatchet Buried at Charity Event,' " Serena read.

Given their current circumstances, Kermit hoped the headline wasn't meant literally.

"Bart!" Sarah exclaimed, bouncing in her chair. "Listen. 'Multi-millionaire landowner, Hugh Alexander, his son Bart, and daughter-in-law, Nadia, the former fashion model, hosted this star-studded charity ball in honor of slain union organizer, Eddie Johnson.' "

Sarah looked up. "Bart Alexander. We've got him."

"Bart," Serena agreed. "I knew it started with a B. Bart, Biff, whatever."

Kermit frowned at the screen. "Our 'Othello Karenin' is

174

Hugh Alexander's son? That seems kind of far-fetched."

"You've heard of him?" Serena asked.

"Grace Martinez has family down in Southern California, and she's talked about some of the labor disputes with Alexander's farming conglomerate. One of her cousins was working for Eddie Johnson before he got killed."

"He was the union guy who was murdered last winter?" Serena asked.

Kermit nodded. Grace had come to work in tears that morning. "A drug gang working out of one of the migrant camps he was trying to improve objected to his interference. They murdered him and left him in a ditch for some children to find. I'm surprised to hear Hugh Alexander would throw a charity event for him. Union organization of his workers could cost Alexander big bucks."

" 'Asked why he would make such a gesture for a man he'd once described as "the Jimmy Hoffa of agriculture," Mr. Alexander made this statement,' " Sarah read. " 'Eddie and I may have had opposing political philosophies, but we both wanted the same thing, to better conditions for immigrant workers in California. You may not know that Eddie's deep commitment to this cause came from the fact that three of his grandparents immigrated to this country from Italy before the war. My own great-grandparents were immigrants, as well.

" 'I may not have liked Eddie's methods, but I appreciated his goals. His death at the hands of a vicious gang should not stop his good works. Every penny raised here tonight will go to fund the series of medical clinics Eddie and I began for migrant workers. They will bear his name.' "

"I don't suppose there's a picture of Bart?" Serena asked.

"Just Hugh Alexander and Eddie Johnson," Sarah said, clicking the photo to enlarge it.

The grainy newsprint photo showed two men shaking hands at the opening of a small medical clinic. Neither looked happy about the photo op. Eddie Johnson was the shorter, slender man on the right—Kermit had seen photos of him after the murder, so he looked familiar. The man on the left was taller, with a trim mustache and an old-fashioned hat, like a thirties movie star.

Kermit looked at Serena. She shrugged.

"He could be our Othello Karenin's father," she said. "He's tall and maybe blond. But based on that, he could just as well be your father."

"My father would be wearing a Hawaiian shirt, have a drink in his hand, and it wouldn't be his son who had the fashion model on his arm," Kermit corrected.

He pushed himself away from the desk. "Good work, Sarah. At least we know Nadia's name and who her husband is, whether or not he's our obnoxious Mr. Karenin. On the off-chance he is, we have a big lever to make him leave your mom alone. I'm sure Hugh Alexander would not want any negative publicity from his son going around threatening people."

"I can keep looking on the Net for a photo of Bart Alexander," Sarah suggested. "I bet there are lots of Nadia as a model, and he might be in some."

Serena glanced at her watch. "Sorry, Squirt. It's bedtime."

Sarah stared at her. "Mom! Hello? This is important."

Serena stared back, basilisk calm. "So is bedtime. I can do some Web searches myself tomorrow, on my lunch break."

Sarah sucked in an outraged breath, then let it out again.

"Mom, please. I just want to help."

Serena's face softened as she bent down to give her daughter a hug. "I know, sweetie. You've been a huge help already tonight. I just don't want anybody losing sleep over this slimewad." She made a face. "Fifteen more minutes. Then it's lights out."

"Okay," Sarah agreed, turning back to her computer. "But I'd get a lot more done in fifteen minutes if we had a DSL line."

Kermit moved to where Fleur lay on the bed. Her tail thumped Sarah's pillow as he scratched her ears.

"You okay staying here again tonight?" he asked.

Fleur glanced from him to Sarah and back, her forehead wrinkling as she tried to tell him something with her warm brown eyes.

"That's right, keep an eye on Sarah and Serena," he said. She licked his wrist. He patted her head one more time.

"Fleur doesn't need to watch out for me," Serena said, as Kermit reluctantly left the dog and followed Serena back down the hall toward the living room. "Edgar's taken up residence on my pillow. Any bad guy who tries to move that cat to get to me is going to find himself with a severed artery."

She gestured toward the kitchen. "Would you like a cup of tea for the road?"

Kermit shook his head. "Working a twelve-hour shift seems like a great idea on my days off, but it doesn't leave much time for anything but eating and sleeping when I'm working. If I sat down on your couch, I'm not sure I'd be able to drag myself up out of it again."

He paused, trying to sound off-hand. "Of course, if you don't mind the neighbors talking, I'd be happy to crash on your couch for the night. I may not have as loud a bark as Fleur, but I think I could discourage potential intruders just as well."

"That's all right," she said, turning into the kitchen so he couldn't see her face. "We'll be fine. I'll just fix you up a container of chili for your lunch tomorrow and send you on your way. You need your rest."

Fat chance of that. Just the thought of sleeping on Serena's couch had burned away his weariness. Or maybe that was the chili. Maybe he could trade lunches with Grace tomorrow.

"I'm sure your couch isn't any less comfortable than my lumpy mattress," Kermit said, leaning against the kitchen doorway. "I'd sleep better if I knew for certain you and Sarah were safe."

Maybe not better, knowing Serena was right down the hall. But not any worse than he had the night before, worrying about her. Worrying about his feelings for her.

She turned from the refrigerator, a plastic container of chili in her hands.

"I don't need a white knight, remember?" she said. But what he noticed were her cheeks. Definitely pink.

"How about a black knight?" he suggested, suddenly feeling a little wicked. "No dragon-slaying, just lots of ale-guzzling and peasant-oppressing."

She rolled her eyes, and the brittle tension he'd felt stretching between them all evening eased. "I don't require knights of any color, thank you. And I don't think anyone's going to have to be oppressing Othello Karenin, now that we know he's Bart Alexander."

"*If* he's Bart Alexander." Daniel had taught him to look for patterns of evidence in complicated cases, and somehow the pieces of this pattern didn't quite fit together.

Serena looked up from scooping the chili into a smaller microwave container. "Karenin has to be Nadia's husband. The pseudonym, the fact that he's so angry at Jesse. It's the only thing that makes sense."

Kermit had to agree that even sociopaths usually had a reason for their actions, twisted as those reasons might be. But they didn't always make sense. "There's too much we don't know about what's going on. We've been assuming that the woman Mrs. Jenkins saw Jesse with was his friend Nadia. But we can't be sure. Maybe it was a client."

"Or a different old girlfriend with a sob story," Serena said, acerbic, but acknowledging his point. "The description Mrs. Jenkins gave fit. I've seen Jesse's pictures of Nadia, and she *is* blond and leggy. But that's not exactly a rare breed, even up here in Jasper County."

She ran a hand through her hair, the chestnut length falling softly back to her shoulders. "But Othello Karenin has to be her husband. Why else would he be looking for Jesse?"

Kermit pulled his thoughts back from Serena's hair. "I don't know," he admitted. "But he seems awfully determined to get you involved."

Serena snapped the chili lid closed and leaned against the counter, uneasiness settling into her face. "Before this whole thing started, Callista said something about me possibly getting blamed for whatever happened to Jesse. That's one of the reasons I was so worried that he'd been kidnapped or might show up dead. Like Alain."

Kermit could understand her fear. Destiny's old flame had proved it was possible for an ex-boyfriend to be more trouble dead than alive.

"If he did show up murdered," Serena continued, "his running off with an old girlfriend might make the authorities take a closer look at me, mightn't it?"

"They always look at the deceased's closest family and friends first," Kermit agreed. *Very comforting, Kerry. Very comforting. Maybe next time you could think before running your big mouth?* "But what little evidence we have suggests that Bart or Othello—or whatever his name is—is looking for his wife. There's no reason to think he's trying to set you up for murder."

Serena threw up her hands. "Hey, maybe he's doing both at the same time. Why not? I'd be a perfect fall guy. Everybody in town knows I'm looking for Jesse now."

Kermit moved forward to put a hand on her shoulder. "Look, it was a stupid thing for me to say. I'm just as clumsy with my mouth as I am with my feet."

"True." She tried to smile at him. "But I'll still feel better when Jesse turns up alive. Then *I* can kill him."

"Even if Sarah can't dig up a photograph of Bart Alexander, there ought to be a few of Nadia out on the Internet somewhere," Kermit said. "We'll take one over to Mrs. Jenkins, see if she recognizes her. Then we can plan our next step."

Serena's smile deepened. "We? How diplomatic. I see Good Cop is back and Lancelot is in remission."

"I'm a fast learner."

"Maybe your mouth isn't as clumsy as you let on."

He knew what she meant, but suddenly he was very conscious of her looking at his mouth. And he was looking at hers. Without lipstick, her lips were the soft plum color of clouds at sunset. *Very* soft.

And very close. Had he leaned forward or had she? Callista couldn't have been right about what she'd said. He'd be an idiot to believe Serena felt anything for him. An idiot to think about finding out.

He felt a flicker of electricity under his hand as he dropped it from her shoulder and stepped away.

"Your chili." Her hands fumbled on the counter, and she was the one who sent the container spinning toward the floor. He was the one who caught it.

"I'll see about finding a picture of Nadia," she said, scooting around him out of the kitchen toward the front door.

"Good idea," he agreed, surprised to hear himself sound so normal. Surprised he could breathe. But it seemed to be someone else moving his limbs, walking him to the door. "I can just see trying to explain surfing the Net for fashion models to Lieutenant Marcy. 'It's work, sir, I swear.' "

Serena's laugh sounded distracted, but she managed to play along. " 'Sure, Riggs. That's what you said the last time. Now quit ogling and get to work.' "

"You're uncanny," Kermit said, shuddering dramatically at her imitation of the lieutenant's sharp, seagull bark. "I'll stick to less hazardous searches. I can find out if Nadia Alexander has a red BMW registered in her name."

"Maybe you can put out an APB." Serena reached for his coat on the rack by the door. He thought she wouldn't meet his gaze as she handed it to him, but her eyes suddenly flashed to his, all her awkwardness vanished in a blaze of energy.

She thrust his coat into his chest, holding it there against him as he clutched it by reflex. For a second he had the crazy thought she was going to kiss him. Or maybe push him out the door.

But she was shaking her head, her intense gaze moving inward. "Nadia—or whoever it was—drove up in a fancy red convertible Beemer."

"That's what Mrs. Jenkins said," Kermit agreed, though

the weight of her fists leaning into his chest was making thinking problematic.

"And Jesse came out with a bag and got into her car, and they drove away together?"

. "And Mrs. Jenkins hasn't seen him since," Kermit said. "And nobody else has, either, as far as we know."

Serena's gaze sharpened, knifing into his. "So, what happened to *Jesse's* car?"

Chapter 12

At seven-thirty on a clear June evening, the soft blue of the sky spread overhead like a sheer silk tent. A cool breeze raised the hairs on Serena's arms, but it merely prickled the restless energy heating her skin.

The thrill of the hunt, she told herself, matching Kermit's long strides as they followed the walk up to Mrs. Jenkins's house. And she could pretend that accounted for the electricity snapping between her and Kermit, as well.

She could feel Kermit's irritation, despite his carefully cool exterior. He'd wanted to interview Mrs. Jenkins alone, but she hadn't been home on his lunch hour, and Serena had insisted that since she'd been the one to figure out they had a missing car to deal with, she should go with him when he tried again this evening.

Of course, maybe his annoyance wasn't solely at Serena's presence. She glanced back at the girl and the dog watching impatiently from the back seat of the Subaru. Bart Alexander—or whoever Othello Karenin might be—hadn't called her back since his threatening phone call two evenings earlier, but she couldn't leave Sarah and Fleur alone at home.

Lights shone through the living room curtains of Mrs. Jenkins's tidy little house, and Serena heard the sound of television voices as Kermit rapped sharply on the door.

Serena caught a flicker of movement at one of the curtains. Mrs. Jenkins apparently decided they might be worth a good story, for after a moment she opened the front door. She didn't remove the chain, however, and her face looked thinner than Serena remembered, with the frizz of her peroxided hair hidden by the narrow opening of the door.

"It's you two," she said, sizing them up. "Have you found Dr. Banos?"

"No, ma'am," Kermit said, detached and polite. "I was hoping you'd be willing to answer a couple more questions."

"I told you all I know, Officer," Mrs. Jenkins answered, with a hint of regret.

"I wondered if you'd look at this picture for me," Kermit said, holding out a photo Sarah had printed of a woman modeling red lace underwear.

Sarah hadn't found a picture of Bart Alexander, but there had been several of Nadia on various websites, apparently wearing just enough to slip through the parental filters on the Internet service provider they used. Serena would have preferred a photo of Nadia fully clad—in a bulky sweatshirt and baggy jeans—but that hadn't been one of their options.

"Could you tell me if this is the woman you saw Jesse Banos leave with two weeks ago?" Kermit asked.

Mrs. Jenkins pulled the printout through the crack in the door and backed up to hold it in the light. Her eyebrows rose. "Yeah. That's her, all right."

With more wrinkles and saggier thighs, Serena thought at her, but her psychic powers of persuasion were wasted on Mrs. Jenkins. Still, the news sent a shiver of relief through Serena's stomach. They were on the right track.

"You're sure?" Kermit asked.

"She was wearing a little more," the woman said, passing the printout back through the door. "But not much. It's her."

"And you said she and Jesse left together in her car?" Serena put in.

Mrs. Jenkins and Kermit both frowned at her interruption of the flow of questioning.

"That's right," Mrs. Jenkins said, less enthusiastically. "Drove off together in that shiny new Beemer of hers." Her eyes flickered with a hint of malice. "I guess it wasn't just a working weekend, if they're not back by now."

"Mr. Banos still hasn't returned?" Kermit asked, signaling Serena to stay quiet.

Mrs. Jenkins shook her head, with a little smirk. "Nope. Haven't even seen anybody break into his house lately, either."

"Then where is his car?" Kermit asked, with an innocent puzzlement Serena could never have pulled off. It occurred to her Kermit was good at his job.

"His car?" Mrs. Jenkins's eyes gleamed, and she straightened as she realized she did have information they wanted to know. "A friend of his came to get it the next morning."

She paused, making Kermit ask the question to draw her out.

"A friend? You recognized him?"

She nodded. "He's been over to visit Dr. Banos quite a few times. A tall man with mangy black hair. He looks like a daddy longlegs."

Serena turned to catch Kermit's stare. *Nigel Crow.*

Perhaps if Nigel had practiced Mrs. Jenkins's caution, he would have checked through his living room curtains before answering his doorbell and might have decided to pretend not to be home. As it was, his eyes widened in satisfying shock when he opened his door to find Serena and Kermit on his front step.

Serena gave him her best displeased-mother smile. "Nigel. Can we come in?"

"You've had news from Jesse?" he stammered, stepping aside as Serena pushed forward, Kermit close behind. Serena moved to the center of Nigel's living room.

She'd been there several times with Jesse and had always been impressed at a bachelor whose house actually felt like a home, with the brick fireplace the centerpiece of the room rather than the small television. Twining ivy poured out of its pot down a narrow bookcase, and an asparagus fern provided healthy energy from a brass perch by the window. An amateurish hand with a luminous touch had painted the scene of an English cottage that hung on one wall, and a framed photograph of the four partners in the Hope Point Life Integration Clinic graced the mantelpiece.

Serena's gaze lingered on the photograph for a moment, the alter-ego of the more posed picture that hung in the reception room at the clinic. She had been the one to snap both, after an afternoon of fishing up at Roger Avalos's cabin on the Trinity. Roger held the huge steelhead he had caught, giving the camera a muscle-bound body-builder's pose while his colleagues clowned around him, Nigel making bunny fingers over Roger's head, Jesse lifting Lani Mitchell up in his arms to show off the makeshift splint on her sprained right ankle.

Jesse playing white knight again, she thought with a twinge of irritation, but she had to admit it looked good on him, his tan arms looking nearly as buff as Roger's, his teeth even and bright as he grinned at the camera. Looking at that grin, she could remember how his solicitous chivalry had once made her weak at the knees, but the thought now brought only a melancholy regret.

Lani didn't seem to be minding it, though. Her narrow,

usually serious face glowed with laughter, and her blue eyes had a twinkling fire that turned her beautiful.

"I really can't tell you anything more than I already have," Nigel was saying, his hands moving anxiously as he tried to find a place to settle them. "Jesse didn't tell me where he was, and I haven't heard from him since Monday morning."

"I was hoping you would have some news by now," Kermit said, shaking his head with concern. "Did he say anything about when he might call you again?"

"No," Nigel said, relaxing a little at the predictable question. "He said he didn't know when he'd have the chance."

"Do you expect him back Monday?"

"I certainly hope so." Nigel sighed and leaned against the fireplace. "We really need him at the clinic."

Serena kept still, not wanting to interrupt Kermit's technique. Patience, stealth, and an innocent face—a potent combination. She was glad she wasn't the one trying to hide something from him.

A flash of guilty warmth heated her face. She *didn't* have anything to hide from him. As long as she didn't think about how close she'd come to maybe . . . well . . . kissing him the night before.

She focused on Nigel's unsuspecting face.

"It's been a long week," he was saying. "Lani and I have barely had a moment to breathe. We've been talking about chaining Jesse and Roger in their offices when they get back and escaping to Cancun."

Was that a hint of color in Nigel's pale face? Serena wondered if he hoped it wasn't just talk on Lani's part. She wondered if Lani knew about Nigel's crush. If the woman was stringing him along . . . Serena shook herself. She couldn't afford sympathizing with Nigel. It was time for Kermit to go in for the kill.

"Did he ask for any other help?" Kermit asked. "Besides covering for him at the clinic?"

Nigel turned his palms up, deliberately nonchalant. "I offered to help if he was in any trouble. He said he could handle the situation himself."

Kermit nodded, as if accepting the non-answer. "I guess that's that, then. We figured if he'd contacted anyone, it would be you."

He took a step toward the door, then turned to fix a hard blue gaze on Nigel. "Especially since you're the one who went by his house and took his car."

Serena saw Nigel's throat constrict, but other than freezing to a preternatural stillness, he showed no other sign of panic.

"Jesse's car?" he asked finally.

"One of his neighbors saw you take it the morning after Jesse disappeared," Kermit pressed. "Would you like to explain why you did that, if Jesse didn't ask you to?"

"I didn't . . . I don't have Jesse's car." Nigel glanced at Serena, as if for help, but she steeled her gaze to be as stern as Kermit's. Nigel twitched briefly, like a cornered rabbit.

It wasn't until she saw the subtle shift in his weight that Serena remembered how violently a rabbit could react to being cornered.

"Kermit, watch out!" she warned, as Nigel pushed past him and broke for the kitchen.

Kermit grabbed the man's arm. Serena stifled a scream as Nigel whirled, but rather than fight to pull away, he only glanced down at Kermit's hand in surprise.

"This isn't a police investigation," Kermit said, his voice low and steady despite the shot of adrenaline Serena knew they'd both received. "Yet. If you can help us answer a few questions, there won't be any need to involve anyone else."

Nigel blinked. "I told you I didn't have Jesse's car. I just wanted to show you." He pointed to the kitchen door. "Through there, in my garage."

Kermit released his grip on Nigel's arm as Serena surreptitiously scanned Nigel's kitchen counters for overly handy carving knives. But Nigel only shrugged his shirtsleeve back into place.

"All right," Kermit agreed. "Show us."

If, in fact, Nigel hadn't simply met Jesse somewhere to give him his car, Serena could think of any number of places where he might have hidden the little silver Honda besides his garage, but she guessed Kermit was only giving the man enough rope to completely entangle himself.

Nigel sidestepped across the small kitchen, half-turned to keep a wary eye on Kermit and Serena as they followed.

"Jesse and I are both tall and dark-haired," he said, slipping aside the bolt on the kitchen door. "We've had new clients mistake us for each other before."

Blind clients, maybe, Serena thought. Although, glancing at Nigel from the back . . . And Mrs. Jenkins had a way of peering at the world that suggested near-sightedness as much as nosiness. But Mrs. Jenkins would have expected Jesse to be taking his own car. Why would she imagine it was Nigel?

Serena wrinkled her nose. Because it made a better story. But that didn't change her instinct that Nigel was trying to throw them off the right track. If they only knew what the right track was . . .

Nigel opened the side door into a dark, cool space that burst into fluorescent brightness as he flicked a switch beside the refrigerator.

"You see?" Nigel waved triumphantly at the two vehicles parked in his garage. "You know Jesse's car, Serena. I don't have it."

Serena had to admit that Jesse's Civic was not hidden in Nigel's garage. But that wasn't what struck her voiceless as she stared into the cramped space. A jumble of cardboard boxes and lawn tools crowded a narrow strip at the back of the garage, barely leaving enough room for the two cars Nigel did have.

She recognized the green Jeep Nigel had driven for the two years she'd known him. And she was afraid she recognized the other car, too, even though she'd never seen it before.

Sitting in Nigel's garage was a hot red BMW convertible.

Chapter 13

Once, early in his career, Kermit had opened a suspect's car trunk expecting to find a stash of marijuana, an expectation based on the joint which the suspect had tried to hide from Kermit and Grace by dropping it down the front of his shirt. While Grace had treated the man for second-degree burns, Kermit had claimed probable cause and the man's car keys and opened the trunk.

The variety of road kill in various states of decomposition which the man had been collecting for his freezer had come as a bit of a surprise. But it had been the sudden hissing of a possum that had been merely stunned when acquired rather than actually dead that had made him yelp and jump back, falling flailing into a ditch.

Grace's hysterical laughter had cured him of showing surprise in many more serious situations since. Yet, facing Nadia Alexander's convertible in Nigel Crow's garage, he could only freeze, hoping his face didn't betray his shock.

"Wow. Hot car," Serena said, giving him a nudge with her elbow as she passed him into the garage. "I didn't know you'd gotten a BMW."

"Oh, that." Nigel's eyes blinked nervously as he followed Serena toward the convertible. "Got it used. Pretty recently. Good deal. I couldn't pass it up."

Kermit shook himself free of his paralysis and hurried after the two of them, mentally begging Serena not to tip off Nigel that they knew where the Beemer came from.

"It's too cute," she was saying, running a hand along the car's leather seats. "I bet it drives like a dream."

"Uh, yeah." Nigel followed her, his hands working nervously once more.

"You'll have to give me a ride sometime."

"Oh. Sure. Sometime. Too cool outside to go topless tonight. Er, I mean top down." Nigel waved toward the kitchen. "It's a bit cool out here, in fact. Shouldn't we go back inside?"

Kermit might have laughed at the man's discomfiture, except he was too busy taking stock of the hoes and shovels and hammers and various other dangerous implements hanging along the garage walls. He had his Beretta in his ankle holster, but it would take him a few precious seconds to reach it in an emergency.

"It looks like you've been driving it off-road," Serena said, gesturing to the mud splattered on the bumpers and caked along the undercarriage. "I thought that's what the Jeep was for."

Nigel's forced chuckle sounded high and tight. "Forgot I wasn't in the Jeep, you know. I'm so used to driving it."

Serena was toying with Nigel like a cat with a mouse. She obviously hadn't realized that this particular mouse was half a foot taller than she was and outweighed her by fifty pounds.

Kermit eyed Nigel's lanky frame. Okay, maybe thirty pounds. But in close quarters, he'd overpower Serena without much trouble, and she didn't seem to have a clue of the danger.

They'd been assuming that Nigel had absconded with Jesse's car at Jesse's request, either taking it to him at a prearranged meeting place or hiding it for him in order to throw searchers off the track.

But why would Nigel have Nadia Alexander's convertible? If it *was* Nadia's.

Nigel was hovering over Serena while she checked out the stereo system. Kermit stepped back and risked a quick glance at the license tag. He could check the plate with the DMV, but Nigel didn't seem the type to sport a vanity plate reading "BMSHLL."

"I would *kill* for a convertible," Serena was saying as she struck a suitably bombshell pose on the hood. "What do you think, Kermit, am I a BMW kind of woman?"

More like a problem kind of woman. Watching her dark hair spilling across the bright red paint, a seductive smile on her face, he could imagine just what trouble she'd put her parents through in high school. What was she doing?

"I think maybe more a Subaru kind of woman," Kermit said.

Serena pouted at him. "You really know how to charm a girl. Make her feel old and matronly. Here." She pushed herself up off the hood and beckoned him closer. "Take a look at the engine and tell me what you think."

Low blow. How was he supposed to resist that?

Nigel dutifully popped the hood, looking like a condemned prisoner resigned to helping the executioner sharpen his blade.

Kermit whistled. "Six cylinders."

"Three hundred thirty-three horsepower," Nigel pointed out glumly.

"Nice. That cylinder block—"

"It's cast iron. None of BMW's other six cylinders have that cast-iron cylinder block."

"Is that right?"

"And the gear box—"

"This is my fault, isn't it?" Serena leaned in between

them, casting a doubtful eye over the engine. "I should know better. Is there any chance I can drag you two away from the awesome majesty of this oily mess before my sister's dog eats my car's upholstery and my daughter decides to hack into the Pentagon through the cigarette lighter?"

Kermit glanced at Nigel, and for a second they were just two car guys shaking their heads over the blasphemy of a nonbeliever.

Then Nigel came to himself and dropped the hood down, barely missing Kermit's fingers.

"You have to go already?" he asked, his dry sense of humor reasserting itself as he ushered them back toward the kitchen. "Too bad. We'll have to do this again. Maybe I'll steal Roger's Explorer next, and we can make it a weekly date."

"Sorry about disturbing you," Kermit said, jumping in before Serena could return to grilling Nigel about Jesse's car. But she was already through the kitchen and heading for the front door. "We're just following up any lead we have at this point."

"Of course, I understand," Nigel said, relief making him magnanimous. "And I do promise to pass your messages along to Jesse if he contacts me. I'm surprised he hasn't called you on his own, Serena, or come to see you. I know he meant to before he left."

"You know, you don't have to apologize for him anymore," Serena said, pulling open the door before Nigel could do it for her. "I don't even want an apology from Jesse. All I want from him is to get his trouble off my back."

"I understand," Nigel said again, and, looking at the circles under the man's dark eyes, Kermit thought he probably did. "I wish I could be more help."

"I do, too," Kermit said, unable to muster any sympathy. He followed Serena down the walk and folded himself into the front seat of the Subaru.

"Did he have Jesse's car?" Sarah demanded from the back. She and Fleur both scooted up so their heads poked between the front bucket seats. "You were in there so long, I thought maybe he killed you and stashed you in Jesse's trunk. I would have called the police, but I don't have a cell phone."

"And that's a good argument for not getting you one," Serena said, calmly starting the car. "He didn't have Jesse's car. Sit back and put on your seatbelt."

"But you did find out something," Sarah said, her voice muffled for a minute as she fought Fleur off long enough to secure her belt. "I can tell. You look way too pleased with yourself."

"We don't really know what we found," Kermit said, but Serena wasn't having any of it.

"He didn't have Jesse's car," she said, heading the Subaru back toward Cloverbrook. "But he did have Nadia's BMW."

"*Nadia's* car?" Sarah leaned forward again, jerked short by her shoulder strap. "Why would he have Nadia's car? Mom, watch the road."

Kermit swallowed his own warning as Serena swerved to avoid an oncoming Beetle.

"Jesse must have traded cars with him," Serena said, the self-satisfied curl at the corner of her mouth not a bit disturbed by the near collision. "That convertible is too flashy for a pair of fugitives. Jesse must have decided to come back for the Honda, so they wouldn't stand out so much."

Kermit liked that theory. He liked it a lot. It sounded plausible. Much more plausible than the wild scenario that seeing the BMW had immediately conjured up in his mind.

It seemed to satisfy Sarah. She demanded they tell her exactly what had happened during their visit with Nigel, and Serena made her laugh, describing Kermit getting all worked up over the car engine.

"Cool car," Sarah sighed, glancing around the Subaru.

"Very cool," Serena agreed. She glanced at Kermit from the corner of her eye. "Not as cool as a Jensen Healey, of course. But no rust, either."

"Kermit's car is cooler than any fancy new Beemer," Sarah insisted loyally.

"It's a classic," Kermit said, mustering enough composure to play along.

"It's practically an antique," Serena agreed.

"It's almost as old as you are, Mom," Sarah jibed, which pretty much set the tone for the rest of the conversation until they reached Serena and Sarah's house, where Kermit's classic heap sat waiting for him out front.

"If I can get my walker moving fast enough to catch you, you're going to be sorry!" Serena called after Sarah as her daughter ran laughing up the walk, Fleur bounding happily after her.

Kermit smiled, too, but only until Sarah disappeared into the house with the dog.

"Looks like I'm leaving Fleur with you another night," he said.

"If it will make you feel better." Serena heaved a dramatic sigh. "At this rate, I won't need to set my alarm clock until Destiny and Daniel get home Sunday."

He'd feel better sleeping on her couch, but Fleur had proven to be tougher than she looked when it came to facing down bad guys in the past.

"Just be careful. Bart Alexander is still out there some-

196

where. If anyone surprising shows up on your doorstep, don't let them in."

"Anyone surprising?"

During the car ride, he'd tried to find a diplomatic way to put what he wanted to say next. He hadn't found one. "If Nigel Crow comes by or wants to meet you for any reason, stay in your house and call me."

"Nigel?" She stared at him like he'd lost his mind. Maybe he had. Or maybe it had merely been the photograph on Nigel's mantel, sending his mind down twisted paths. He didn't want to frighten her unnecessarily, but better that than risking her stepping unknowingly into danger.

"I know Nigel wants to protect Jesse," Serena said. "But he wouldn't hurt me to do it."

"I'm sure he wouldn't," Kermit agreed. "But if all he's doing is protecting Jesse, then he won't need to meet with you."

Her eyes narrowed. "What are you getting at?"

"I'm not sure." He didn't know if he could find the words to explain. "You know that photograph Nigel has on his mantel?"

"Of the four counselors? Sure, I took it."

He brought the image back into his mind's eye, Nigel hunching in back in order to fit in the picture, Jesse dominating the frame, despite Roger's pose with his fish. Seeing that vivacious smile on Lani Mitchell's face, he could well understand Serena's claim that Nigel had a crush on her. Probably the other two men did, too, to some degree, and half her clientele.

"You said Nigel has a crush on Lani Mitchell. What do you think must go through his mind every time he looks at that photograph and sees her laughing in his best friend's arms?"

Serena frowned at him, her eyes suddenly sharp. "There was nothing going on between Jesse and Lani. He just couldn't resist taking care of her after she twisted her ankle climbing the path up from the river." Her mouth twisted wryly. "Lani is too smart to fall for that. I'm sure Nigel has that photo up because it's such a good picture of Lani."

Kermit was sure of that, too. He himself had a photograph Destiny had taken of him, Serena, Daniel, Sarah, and Fleur during a walk on the beach one afternoon. Kermit had been trying to turn Fleur's nose toward the camera and away from the dog cookies in his windbreaker pocket. The Lab's tongue was hanging out and her eyes were rolling back toward him, and it looked like he was strangling her. But Serena was laughing at them both, beautiful and happy, and so he kept the snapshot in a little frame on his dresser at home—where no one would ever see it.

But Jesse hadn't come to the beach with them that afternoon. He was supposed to have come, Kermit remembered. But he'd called at the last minute to say he couldn't make it. Typical.

"It was just the camaraderie making Lani laugh," Serena insisted. "Nigel knew that."

"You're probably right." But Kermit knew he would not have that beach photo on his dresser if Jesse were in it.

Nigel's photo had twisted at his heart, reminding him of the occasions he'd had to spend time with Serena and Jesse together. Handsome, successful, un-clumsy Jesse. Fighting down outrage at the cavalier way Jesse sometimes treated Serena. Unable to say anything, dreading appearing jealous. Which he had assured himself he was not.

Maybe Nigel told himself the same thing. Or maybe homely, ungainly Nigel Crow had finally tired of playing second fiddle to Jesse Banos.

Serena had been the one to point out only the evening before that she would be the perfect fall guy if Jesse turned up dead. And it was Nigel who kept insisting that Jesse had meant to see Serena before he disappeared. As if to plant the seed that she might have been the last person to see Jesse alive . . .

"It's just a feeling," Kermit said, frustrated at allowing his own irrelevant emotions to color his perceptions of a case.

"A feeling?" Serena prodded.

"Just a feeling. Maybe Nadia Alexander's husband isn't the only one with a reason to want Jesse out of the picture." Literally, as well as figuratively.

"I'm going to have to warn Callista that she's got some competition," Serena teased, her eyes laughing like a cat's.

"All right. I'll be careful. Even around Nigel. At least until we figure out where Jesse's holed up. At least now we've got a clue."

The Cheshire Cat's smile couldn't have been more self-satisfied.

"You mean the car?" Kermit asked.

"Nadia's car."

"Maybe." Though even Kermit wasn't going to suggest coincidence. "I'll check with the DMV to make sure."

"It's Nadia's car," Serena said. "The same car that Mrs. Jenkins called a 'shiny new Beemer.' "

"Actually, it's last year's model."

Serena gave him a look. "Whatever. Did you also notice that it's not so shiny anymore? Wherever it's been between the time Mrs. Jenkins saw it and the time Nigel traded cars with Jesse, that's probably where we'll find Jesse and Nadia."

She looked so pleased with her deduction that Kermit

didn't have the heart to list all the flaws in it. All he said was, "So we just need to look for a patch of mud with matching tire tracks in it, and we'll have them."

Instead of punching him, Serena reached into her purse and pulled out a tissue. She unfolded it to reveal a sizable sample of pale, sandy mud. "Why do you think I wanted you to distract Nigel with the engine? It gave me a chance to collect this. Now all we need to do is get it analyzed and find out where it came from."

Kermit pinched his nose. "Serena, the chances of that mud coming from anywhere that could lead us to Jesse . . ."

"You don't have to say it. But I have a feeling, too." She folded the tissue carefully.

Kermit shook his head. "Lieutenant Marcy is never going to authorize spending taxpayer money to send that sample off—"

"He doesn't have to." She tucked the tissue back into her purse, giving him another satisfied smile. "I'll take care of it. Don't you worry about a thing."

He couldn't suppress a choked laugh. *Gee. Why on earth would he worry?*

"Unless there's something highly unusual in this sample, I'm not going to be able to give you a precise place of origin," Professor Nagle warned as his pudgy fingers slid the thin section slide into place under the petrographic microscope. "We can hardly hope for that."

"It would just be helpful to know if it came from around here at all," Serena assured him.

Her "feeling" of the night before had deserted her by the cold light of a foggy northcoast morning and left her feeling merely foolish for wasting Professor Nagle's time, though he had assured her that with the slow summer schedule, she wasn't taking him away from his preparation for classes.

"I really appreciate your help," she repeated for the fifth or sixth time.

"I love a good puzzle," he assured her as he adjusted the microscope. "Especially if it involves geology. People are always coming in wanting to know the composition of the fascinating rock they collected over their summer vacation in Utah or over spring break in Death Valley."

He glanced up at her. "I've had a few people sure they've found gold. Even had one fellow who wouldn't believe me when I told him it was just pyrite, fool's gold. He was sure I wanted to jump his claim."

"You do have a piratical air about you," Serena told him.

He grinned, running a hand over his balding head. "It's the dashing resemblance to Yul Brynner, isn't it?"

He set his glasses aside and peered into the microscope, adjusting the focus. "There is often some trace gold in the river sands around here. That's not what you're looking for, is it?"

"No."

"Good. Because you're not likely to find enough to cover the cost of extracting it. We do see lots of good agate around here, of course, including some beautiful moonstones. And local jade. You've seen our specimens, haven't you, on your inspections?"

Serena glanced around the lab as he fiddled with the microscope some more. Glass-fronted cabinets showed off some of the geology department's rock and mineral samples, including some dazzling geodes and some fine quartz and amethyst crystals, along with the less flashy chunks of local greywacke and deep green serpentine, the state rock.

The rest of the room was gray and drab, from the

scratched and battered lab tables to the scuffed industrial tile, and it smelled of rocks and dust and chemicals. Maybe the Feng Shui balance was a little off, but it still felt reassuringly solid and familiar, unlike some of the other areas of her life lately.

What had Kermit been thinking, to suggest Nigel Crow might be dangerous? And why was she looking forward so eagerly to seeing Kermit this evening to discuss the day's findings, when she was beginning to think he could be more dangerous to her peace of mind than Nigel, Bart Alexander, and Jesse put together?

"Look at you, you little devils," Professor Nagle muttered, pulling her attention back to him. "Very interesting. Here, come and take a look at this."

Serena took his spot at the microscope, adjusting his myopic focus to her own. A dazzle of crystals suddenly burst into clarity beneath her eye.

"Plagioclase and quartz," Professor Nagle said. "Those gray crystals. About what you might expect to see. It helps that your sample has so much sand in it. We can actually see what we're looking at here."

"What we expect?" Serena asked, her flagging hopes fading even farther. "You mean if it came from around here? Or from anywhere?"

"From anywhere in a couple hundred mile radius," Professor Nagle said cheerfully. His smile faded as she saw her expression. "No, no. Look again. This is good."

She peered back at the tiny sand grains. Anywhere between Portland and San Francisco, pretty much. *Terrific.*

"Plagioclase and quartz, as I said. But do you see those clear gray crystals with the single cleavages?"

Serena looked more carefully. "Yes. I see them." Sharper than the others, as if less weathered.

"That's potassium feldspar!"

Serena glanced up at the professor's beaming face. "That's interesting?"

He reddened slightly. "Well, I'm always glad to see some real rocks. Don't tell the sandstone lovers I said that. But interesting for you, too, I think. You said you thought this mud probably came from somewhere near Hope Point, but you're not going to find a concentration of potassium feldspar like this along the coast."

"What are you saying?" Serena straightened, nearly knocking the professor backwards. Her shivery, anticipatory feeling returned, with a vengeance. *Look out, Callista, you've got competition.* "Are you saying you can tell me where this stuff came from?"

Kermit hunched over the telephone at his desk, already regretting dialing the number on the crumpled sticky note in front of him. Dominick Johnson wasn't going to give him the time of day, and the FBI agent would undoubtedly do everything in his power to make Kermit feel like a dumb hick while he was at it. Serena hadn't been too thrilled the night before when he'd told her his intention of calling the man, either. Still, Kermit figured protecting Serena from harm was worth a few blows to his ego.

"Red ink?" Grace's voice asked, reading the note over his shoulder. "You know you're not allowed to call nine hundred numbers from the station."

Kermit glanced up to glare her off, but she'd already settled a hip against his desk. She grinned down at him, an unusual perspective, since he normally towered a full head over her.

"If you're having that much trouble finding a date, I hear Garth's got a cousin looking for a man. She's got a mustache, but she's got all her teeth."

"The way I heard it, Riggs was dating your mother, Martinez, but he couldn't keep up with her." Garth strode up beside Grace, his jeans and t-shirt as neatly ironed as Grace's uniform.

Kermit closed his eyes. Why worry about Johnson bruising his ego, when he had friends like these?

Grace picked the sticky note off his desk planner. "The Flyaway Express Inn? Vance, Kermit's been holding out on us. He does have a hot date."

Kermit snatched at the note, but at that moment the maudlin Cat Stevens song on the phone gave way to a human voice.

"Officer Kermit Riggs," he identified himself. "I was trying to call room two-fifteen, but there's still no answer. Can I leave another message for Dominick Johnson? Just ask him to call Officer Riggs. I left my cell phone number earlier."

"Whoa! Kinky date," Garth said.

"He's an FBI agent," Kermit growled, dropping the receiver.

"*Very* kinky." Garth grinned, taking a seat at his own desk right across from Kermit.

"Is this related to that problem you've been looking into for Serena Davis?" Grace asked.

"Serena Davis. Now, there's one hot mama," Garth said appreciatively. "If you're gonna be making hotel reservations for anybody, it oughtta be her. She's been single for what, a whole couple of weeks already. Why the hell haven't you asked her out yet?"

"You're not even supposed to be at work today," Kermit accused.

"Hey, I just happened to be in town and thought I'd

drag my buds Kerry and Gracie out for a bite to eat, but I see you're way too busy for food."

"If Lieutenant Marcy would let him start a case file on this thing, he wouldn't have to work through lunch," Grace said. Kermit appreciated her loyalty, though he couldn't really blame the lieutenant.

"You're trying to get in touch with that FBI agent who's looking for Serena's ex?" Grace continued.

There was no use trying to hide anything in a police station, especially when you didn't have a private office. "He's ignoring my messages. Either that or somebody finally got tired of his attitude and dumped his body off Cypress Head."

"He doesn't have a cell phone?" Garth asked.

Kermit gestured at the sticky note. "That's all he gave Serena."

"What do you want him for, anyway?" Garth asked. "If he had anything on Jesse Banos, he could have said so. He's just blowing smoke up your ass, if you ask me."

Kermit leaned back in his chair, refraining from reminding Garth that he *hadn't* asked. "My thoughts exactly. But at least he's got some kind of approval for his investigation. I could ask him about this guy who's been bothering Serena, find out if Johnson knows who he is."

And maybe find out if Johnson was investigating anyone else. Like Nigel Crow.

Garth shook his head. "I'm telling you, if it was me, I wouldn't be so hot to solve this thing. I'd be over at her house, day and night, offering my professional protection and a very broad shoulder to cry on."

"He's already doing that," Grace said, with a sly wink.

"Hey! Way to go, Macho Man."

"I'm just trying to help out a friend," Kermit snapped.

"A true friend offers physical comfort when necessary," Garth said.

"Stop it," Grace said. "You're making him blush."

Kermit knew from experience that the earth wasn't going to swallow him up and that no amount of glaring would reduce either officer to a pile of ash. That didn't stop him from trying. "Don't you two have anything better to do? Serena could be in serious danger."

Grace pulled a hurt, innocent face. "We're just here to help, right, Garth? Look, if this FBI prick is blowing you off, why don't you just call his supervisor? Pull his chain for not cooperating with local law enforcement, blah, blah, blah."

Garth grinned. "I like the way you think, Martinez."

Kermit was already reaching for his phone. He did, too.

"I can't give you an exact location for this sample, just as I feared," Professor Nagle said, forestalling Serena's excitement. "But I *can* say with a high probability that this mud came from east of the Coast Range. You're not going to find potassium feldspar until you get farther inland to the Klamath Range."

"Like the Trinity Alps?" Serena asked.

"Like the Trinity Alps. Possibly even from the Ironside Mountain batholith. Could this car you got the sample from have been over near Willow Creek any time in the past week or two?"

Serena's breathing caught in her chest. *No. Impossible.* "You mean this mud came from the Trinity River watershed?"

Professor Nagle raised his hands in caution. "Maybe. Perhaps. Not necessarily."

No, not necessarily, Serena thought. *Almost certainly.* The more she ran the impossible through her mind, the more possible it seemed. Willow Creek was only a little more than an hour from Hope Point, yet that was far enough to make the chances of Bart Alexander or Agent Johnson looking for Jesse there almost nonexistent. An easy enough distance to keep tabs on what was happening in Hope Point and to arrange a car swap with Nigel.

And if Jesse was willing to destroy an engagement and inconvenience his clients for a damsel in distress, why should he stop at taking advantage of a friend?

"Thank you," she said, restraining herself from embarrassing Professor Nagle with a hug. "Thank you. This was exactly the help I needed."

"Miss Davis—"

"I know." She acknowledged his unspoken warning. "But even if it doesn't help me find what I want to know, I still appreciate your help. More than you can know."

Professor Nagle replaced his glasses, not quite hiding his pleased smile. "I'm glad to help." He glanced up at her. "It's the least I can do after your work to keep us absent-minded scientists safe."

Serena studied his face to see if he were teasing her, but his eyes were serious.

"I know I don't always make your job easier," he said.

It was her turn to feel her cheeks redden. "I like my job, and I like the people I work with," she said, truthfully.

"I'm glad to hear it."

"And if there's anything I can do for you . . ."

He glanced at her as he removed the slide from the microscope. "Well, there is one thing. Just . . . don't look in the department refrigerator on your way back to your office."

Through the open lab door, she could see across the hall to the Geology Department office. She glanced from the office door back to Professor Nagle, frowning.

He gave her a sheepish grin. "I'll have it all taken care of by this afternoon. Scout's honor."

"I'll have to come by and check on that."

"Of course."

Shaking her head, she shared his smile and left the lab. She forced herself to pass the Geology Department office without so much as a glance. She owed Professor Nagle a couple of hours. She owed him big time.

He'd told her right where Jesse was.

Maybe she should have thought of it herself, but she knew she wouldn't have done so without the prodding of that mud. Maybe it was a long shot. She reminded herself that so far her attempts at psychic prediction had fallen far short of even the pure chance of fifty percent accuracy.

But this wasn't a psychic prediction. This was a deduction based on solid scientific evidence. More or less.

And it was also based on her knowledge of Jesse. Jesse, whose agenda was always more important than anyone else's. Jesse the white knight, who wouldn't think twice about protecting his damsel in distress by endangering his friends. Or by breaking and entering.

Chapter 14

"I know where Jesse is."

Serena's pronouncement sent Kermit stumbling over her threshold. He grabbed for the wall to steady himself and caught the coat rack instead, which might have been enough to keep him upright if not for Fleur bodyslamming into his knees at the same moment. He somehow managed not to crush the dog on impact, and the coat rack missed impaling him by a good two inches. However, it pinned him well enough to give Fleur excellent access to his face.

"Fleur! Off! Bad dog!"

He could hear Serena's voice quite clearly, but Fleur's selective deafness apparently muted the commands. He twisted his face out of the way of her eager tongue, ordering her to sit, but it was almost impossible to breathe and shout and stave off drowning in dog saliva all at the same time.

Just as he thought these might be his last moments on earth, Fleur's tongue swipe missed his nose by a whole inch, and he heard the scrabbling of dog claws on the hardwood floor as Serena dragged her off.

"I've got her for the moment," Serena gasped, though it sounded more a result of laughter than physical effort. "But you'd better get up fast."

Kermit managed to roll out from under the coat rack and get it straightened before turning back and opening his arms to the dog. Fleur lunged forward out of Serena's hold, nearly knocking him flat again as she pressed up against his legs for a thorough head and back rub.

"That animal is a menace," Serena said, mostly fondly, brushing yellow hair off her dark slacks.

"She's just reintegrating her pack," Kermit said, scratching Fleur's chin.

"She was just softening up the wounded member of the herd for the kill," Serena corrected, reaching down to tug one of the Lab's ears. "Isn't that right, Cujo?"

Fleur grinned at her happily.

Serena's gaze paused on Kermit's face. "And it was a close call for the clumsy caribou."

She caught the end of her sleeve in her hand, raising it to wipe the damp spot next to his ear. It brought her close enough for him to smell the herbal shampoo she used in her hair and the hint of fresh basil from whatever she was cooking for dinner. The comfortable intimacy of the gesture nearly took his breath away. If he lifted a hand, he could rest it on her waist, feel the warmth of her skin through the closely fitting knit of her dark green shirt.

Fortunately, a cold dog nose found his hand, pulling him back to reality as Serena stepped back and gestured him forward to the kitchen.

Of course she's comfortable wiping Fleur slobber off your face, you idiot. She'd do the same for any six-foot-two kid who got knocked over by her sister's dog.

"You said on the phone that you had news," Serena said, crossing to the stove to check a simmering pot of something that smelled temptingly like marinara sauce. Not that Kermit wasn't grateful for any home-cooked meal Serena chose to make, but Tuesday's chili and yesterday's Thai curry made a nice, mild spaghetti sauce sound heavenly.

"You obviously have news, too," Kermit said, remembering her announcement at the door. He crossed his arms over his chest as he leaned against the counter, pressing back the surge of mixed relief and embarrassing regret. "You've heard from Jesse?"

She paused her stirring to give him an impish smile. "I didn't need to. I figured out where he's hiding."

"You didn't go looking for him without me!" The words burst out before he thought how she would react.

"No, I didn't. You want to know why not?" She slammed the lid back on the sauce pot. "I had to pick up Sarah from Pleasance Geary's on my way home from work. She's apparently gotten lost on the information super-highway somewhere and forgotten to set the table, but I did get her home. Do you think I'm going to drag my daughter along to confront an ex-boyfriend? That's about as likely as me dragging along a cop."

"You *are* going to drag me along, Serena. This situation is too dangerous for you to face alone. You have to promise me not to do anything foolish, or—" Or what? Her eyes flashed the same challenge. The more he pushed her, the more outrageous her defiance would be.

He sucked in his fear for her and risked a little shrug. "I thought we were in this together. It wouldn't be fair for you to play white knight if I don't get to."

Her mouth twitched. "Nice save, Riggs."

"I thought so." He could tell she wasn't completely mollified, but then, neither was he. He forced himself to relax against the counter. "All right. Where do you think Jesse is?"

She hesitated. He knew she wanted to make him suffer for spoiling her story. But she was obviously too pleased with herself to be able to hold out long. So he couldn't help smiling.

"Darn you, Riggs." She tossed a potholder at him,

catching him squarely in the chest. "Okay. You remember that mud I scraped off Nadia's car?"

"Sure." That and the heart attack she'd nearly given him, pulling Nigel's chain.

"Professor Nagle analyzed it for me. It's got some grains of potassium feldspar in it that he thinks must have come from the Klamath Range."

She paused, waiting for something.

"Like the Klamath Mountains?" he tried. "Or the Trinity Alps?"

She nodded.

He nodded. "Sure. That narrows it down." To a couple hundred square miles or more.

"It didn't have to tell me exactly where he was," Serena said, unfazed by his lukewarm response. "All I needed was the general area, and I had him."

An image of dousing crystals and topographic maps popped into Kermit's head. "Does this knowledge have anything to do with Callista Hawthorn?"

She propped her hands on her hips. "I came up with this one all on my own. No thanks to psychics or police officers. Do you want to hear it or not?"

"Yes."

"Jesse's got Nadia holed up at Roger Avalos's summer cabin on the Trinity River."

Kermit's memory flashed to the photographs of the four Hope Point Life Integration counselors at Roger's cabin. Peaceful. Out of the way. Not a bad thought. But . . .

"Isn't Roger Avalos on some kind of humanitarian trip out of the country somewhere? How would Jesse get in touch with him?"

Serena smiled. "He wouldn't need to. We all know where the front door key is hidden. And with Roger out of the country, there's no chance of him making a surprise trip out to his cabin. It's perfect."

"Jesse could just as easily be renting a cabin anywhere within twenty miles of there. Somewhere he wouldn't be trespassing." But even as he said it, the logical conclusion followed. "Except this way he wouldn't need to use a credit card to secure his reservation."

"Which would be prudent if he knew the FBI might be looking for him," Serena said. "And Roger keeps the place well stocked with staples in the summertime. It has to be Roger's cabin."

"It *could* be Roger's cabin."

"It's worth taking a drive over to Trinity County on Saturday to find out." She raised one perfectly curved eyebrow. "I may not be psychic, but even your buddy Daniel believes in working hunches."

"It's a decent hunch," Kermit agreed, sorting through the possibilities in his head. "And there's no reason to wait until Saturday. I'm off tomorrow. I can go in the morning."

"Well, I've got to work Fridays, so that's no good—" Then she caught on. "Oh, no. I did not tell you where Jesse was so you could sneak up there without me, Kermit Riggs, you low-down—"

"Serena." He held up his hands, warding off her outrage and any more potholders she might have up her sleeve. "I just want to get this sorted out as soon as possible. To keep you safe."

She crossed her arms over her chest. "Bart Alexander, or whoever he is, hasn't contacted me since Monday night. He's probably gotten bored and gone home."

"Maybe," Kermit said, though he could tell she didn't believe it any more than he did. "But he's not the only one I'm concerned about. I told you I had news. I said I was going to try to get in touch with FBI Agent Johnson today. That didn't work out. He didn't respond to any of the messages I left at his hotel."

Serena shrugged, checking her sauce again before flicking on the burner under the pot of spaghetti water at the back of the stove. "Helpful as ever, I see."

"So I called one of the FBI agents I know over at the field office in Deepwater and asked if he could track Johnson down for me."

His tone alerted her, and she turned to him from the stove. "What? What did he say? Has something happened to Agent Johnson?"

"I don't know." A fresh shadow of apprehension darkened the evening as he recalled the conversation. "Bill asked around for me, then called back to let me know he couldn't help me reach Agent Dominick Johnson, because Agent Johnson is on vacation."

"Vacation?" She frowned. "Could that mean he's on some kind of secret operation or sting or something?"

"I wondered that, too," Kermit said. "Bill assured me that in this case vacation just meant vacation. Or, more likely, administrative leave. He didn't come right out and say so, but he gave me the distinct impression that Agent Johnson's current vacation isn't entirely voluntary."

"Administrative leave? Then what's he doing here investigating . . ." Serena's voice faltered. "Pretending to investigate. Pretending to investigate Jesse?"

"I don't know. But I don't like it."

"If the guy we've met even *is* the real Agent Johnson . . ."

He'd been hoping she wouldn't think of that possibility. He reached out to wrap his fingers around her right hand as she hugged herself against the sudden chill. She squeezed his fingers tightly.

"Serena, if there's a chance that Jesse's up at Roger Avalos's cabin, I don't think we should wait until Saturday to find out. The sooner we clear this up, the better."

Rebellion warred with the trepidation in her gold-flecked eyes. He suspected he knew which would win, but he never got the chance to find out.

"Mom? Kermit?" Sarah's shout broke the tense silence. Even from down the hall, the fear rang through. "Come here!"

Kermit and Serena broke for the kitchen entryway at the same time, but Fleur beat them to it, charging past them toward Sarah's bedroom.

"Mom!"

The door stopped Fleur, and Kermit would have paused to bend down for his gun, but he missed Serena as she flew by, so all he could do was follow as she flung the door open and burst into Sarah's room.

It's not fair, Sarah typed, jabbing the keys with satisfying force. *Mom's in trouble and all she wants to do is get rid of me. I even e-mailed my dad and asked if I could come down a week later and he said it was okay and she said no way.*

She glanced down at the Agatha Christie mystery she had propped against the desk while she waited for Gemma's instant message reply. Gemma's grandmother had restricted her phone time for forgetting to feed the chickens, but hadn't thought to restrict her computer use. Still, IMs were too slow for decent conversation.

She's just trying to protect you.

Sarah said that a lot to Gemma about her grandmother, but that was totally different. Gemma's father was a wacko.

SHE'S the one in danger, Sarah typed back. *And she thinks she can take care of herself. Please. I bet the only reason that guy hasn't called her back is because Fleur and I are here. What's going to happen when I leave on Saturday? Who's going to protect her until Aunt Destiny and Uncle Daniel get back?*

They get back Sunday, Gemma's message reminded her, which wasn't the point. A lot could happen in twenty-four hours. *And Kermit will be there.*

Which might have made her feel better if her mom would ever let him stick around, but she practically chased him away every night, even though Kermit seemed perfectly happy to hang out. He liked to play games, even if it was just three-handed Hearts, which didn't work as well as four. And he and Sarah were trying to teach Fleur to play dead when you pointed a finger at her and said, "Bang," before Aunt Destiny got home. But so far Fleur's only response was to check and see if your finger was a dog cookie in disguise.

You know Mom won't let him stay overnight or anything, Sarah wrote. *So she'll be here all alone. It's like she's worried about propriety or something. It's not like I don't know she had Jesse over sometimes when I wasn't here. And Kermit would be a gentleman.*

Kermit's way cooler than Jesse.

Way cooler, Sarah agreed. He would never run off with somebody else's wife.

He's got a huge crush on your mom.

Sarah could almost hear the defiance in Gemma's typed words. She couldn't really blame her. The first time Gemma had said Kermit liked her mom that way, Sarah had told her she was gross and stupid. But that was when her mom was still engaged to Jesse, and Sarah didn't want Kermit to feel like a loser because it was never going to work out.

Besides, she knew from the divorce that it didn't matter

who she'd like better as part of their family. If Jesse made her mom happy, that was cool. Except it seemed for a long time like maybe he hadn't cared if he made her happy or not.

Kermit would be so much better for her than Jesse, Sarah typed, thinking of all the times Kermit had come over with Auntie Dess and Uncle Daniel and just seemed to belong instead of always having to be smarter and cooler and more important than everybody else. *He makes her laugh. It's like she's not trying so hard to be perfect all the time.*

She should go out with him.

Like that was going to happen. Her mom was so set on this being-fine-by-herself kick since she broke up with Jesse. *Dream on.*

Why not? He's sexy.

KERMIT??? Sarah felt her ears burn, and was glad Gemma couldn't see her.

For an older woman like your mom's age, I mean, Gemma wrote back. *Didn't you see her checking him out in that muscle shirt when we got caught at Jesse's house?*

No. She'd been too worried about getting grounded for the rest of her life. But Gemma seemed to have a sixth sense about stuff like that, so it was probably true.

Did you hear from Brian tonight? Gemma's message interrupted thoughts of her mother's love life with the potential for her own. *I know he wants to know—Oops. Grandma's calling about chores. I gotta run. See ya tomorrow. Bye!*

Bye.

Sarah punched send, but Gemma had already signed off. Sarah glanced at the clock in the upper corner of her screen. Her heart jumped. Talking about chores, Kermit was supposed to get to their house fifteen minutes ago, and she hadn't set the table.

But Gemma's message reminded her that she hadn't checked her e-mail yet, either. The longer it took her to get out to the kitchen, the more ticked her mom was going to be about the table. But even if she got out there that second, her mom was going to ground her from the computer for the rest of the night.

She clicked her e-mail program open and hit retrieve mail. She'd just check real quick for a message from Brian and then—

The first message to scroll onto her screen was titled, "Hello, Sarah," but it was the address that caused her to suck in her breath in surprise. *ShrinkRap@hplink.com.* Jesse? Why would he be sending her an e-mail?

She clicked on the message and it popped onto her screen.

Hello, Sarah. It hasn't been easy getting in contact with you. Your mother would be glad to know how well your service provider screens your e-mail. Fortunately, I finally realized I knew an e-mail address your program would accept.

Sarah frowned. Of course her program accepted Jesse's e-mail. Back when he was bothering to try to be all stepfathery, he'd started passing along Internet jokes to her. Most of them were pretty lame, with a punch line about Freud or something.

I saw you coaching at T-ball camp today, you and your little red-haired friend.

Jesse was there? At the rec center? Sarah glanced around behind her. Yeah. Like he was going to be hiding in her closet. She should have been paying more attention that morning. If she'd seen him today, she could have saved her mom a lot of trouble.

Who was the old Amazon who picked you both up? It doesn't matter. I have her license plate number. I can find her when I need to.

A chill ran up Sarah's bare arms. Jesse knew Gemma's grandma, Pleasance Geary.

I hope you check your e-mail regularly, Sarah-Lee, because I have a message I need you to deliver to your mother tonight. I'm terribly disappointed that she hasn't found Jesse Banos for me, yet. And when I'm disappointed, I sometimes make hasty, rash decisions that I regret later. And I would hate so much to regret doing something rash and hasty to you and little Red.

Sarah sucked in a deep breath, but it still took several tries before she could get sound to come from her throat. "Mom! Kermit! Come here!"

She wasn't Jesse's biggest fan, but she knew he wasn't sick enough to play games like this. Bart Alexander had gotten Jesse's e-mail address—of course he had; it was probably on Nadia's computer. He'd wormed his way into her computer. He'd been watching her at T-ball camp that morning. He could be watching her right that minute through the crack in her window curtains . . .

"Mom!"

She turned as her bedroom door slammed open and her mom and Kermit tumbled into her room. Fleur yelped, her toes caught under someone's shoe, but she still reached Sarah first, the fur on her withers ruffled with alarm as she checked Sarah for hurt and then checked around her desk for intruders.

"What's wrong? Are you all right?" her mother asked, her eyes blazing, as ready to attack prowlers as Fleur.

"My e-mail." Sarah pointed to her screen, her panic ebbing with the arrival of the two adults and Fleur's solid presence. "It's from Bart Alexander. He sent me an e-mail using Jesse's address."

Her mother and Kermit crowded in on either side of her.

"He instant messaged you?" Kermit asked. "Like that time in Jesse's house?"

"No!" Sarah's hand beat his to the mouse as she realized the end of her conversation with Gemma was still partially visible behind her e-mail screen.

She should go out with him.

Dream on.

Why not? He's sexy.

The text disappeared as she clicked on the instant messenger's close screen button. She sent a quick prayer that neither her mother nor Kermit had seen any more, and pointed directly at the e-mail in the center of her screen.

"There. He says he wants me to give you a message, Mom."

As the two adults read through the message, she finished the final paragraph.

Tell your mother she has one more day to bring me Jesse Banos's head on a platter—metaphorically speaking, of course. If she can't tell me what I need to know by the time I call her tomorrow night . . . Well, I don't make threats. I just give examples. You can tell her you will be the example.

Sweet dreams, Sweetheart.

Shrinkwrecker.

"That's the name the instant messenger used to threaten Jesse. When he thought I was Jesse, I mean," Sarah said. "What a slimewad."

"The little bastard." Her mother's profanity startled her. "How dare he threaten my child. If he comes anywhere near her, I'm going to kill him."

"You'll have to get in line." Kermit's voice sounded equally grim.

Sarah could hear the apprehension underlying the fierceness in their voices, but her own fear was fading. If Bart Alexander thought he was going to get to her through her mom and Kermit, well, Kermit had a gun and Bart had never seen her mom mad.

She glanced up at the two adults flanking her. "What are we going to do?"

"Fleur's going to sleep in here with you tonight," Kermit said, moving over to the windows to pull the curtains tightly shut. "And I'm going to sleep on the couch."

Sarah expected an explosion, but for once her mom only nodded.

"And I don't think we're going to wait until Saturday to check out Roger Avalos's cabin," Kermit added.

Her mom shook her head, meeting his gaze straight on. "I'm calling Wyler and taking tomorrow off."

Chapter 15

Serena dropped her cup of tea, splashing it across the table when she heard Kermit pull up out front—there was no mistaking his car; he must have trouble finding mufflers for a vehicle that old. She grabbed her denim jacket off the coat rack. She wouldn't need it once they crossed the Coast Range, but the morning fog was cool.

Despite her best intentions, her eye caught her reflection in the hall mirror. With her hair thrown up in a hurried ponytail, she could see the resemblance to her daughter, her long face and prominent cheekbones, but she thought she looked more like Sarah's grandmother that morning, with the dark circles under her eyes and the lines etched more deeply around her mouth than they had been a couple of weeks ago.

Bitter pride helped push her out the door. She wasn't out to impress Jesse, if they found him. And it was better that Kermit see her this way.

The words on Sarah's instant messaging screen blazed neon in her memory. *He's got a huge crush on your mom.* Best she cured him of that now. Before some sweet young thing came along and showed him what he was missing.

She could still see him as he'd looked that morning, asleep on her couch, one of his long legs stretched over the overstuffed armrest. She'd offered him the guest bedroom, but he'd wanted to be where he could see the front door. Fleur had escaped Sarah's room sometime during the night to lie on the floor beside him, and he'd rested a hand on her side, his arm rising and falling in time with her breathing.

He had looked so innocent and at peace.

He must have felt her gaze, though, because his eyes had opened before she could glance away. And the ancient emotion that had momentarily blazed in them had nearly dragged her to his side.

The man now leaning against his battered Jensen Healey, however, looked almost as old and grim as she felt. He acknowledged her with a quick nod and held the passenger door for her before climbing into the driver's seat.

"You got Sarah to Hideaway Hill all right?" she asked, wrestling the stiff seatbelt into place as he pulled away from the curb. He'd insisted on driving Sarah and Fleur over to Pleasance Geary's farm that morning, the dog crushed into the front foot well, so he could look over the security measures Pleasance had in place.

Serena had ensured he had to return to retrieve her before going after Jesse by refusing to give him directions to Roger Avalos's cabin.

"Pleasance says she won't let Sarah and Gemma out of her sight until we get back this afternoon," Kermit said. His car might have been old, but it hugged the on-ramp securely as he accelerated onto the freeway. "She's got good locks on the doors and latches on the first-story windows. And she assures me she knows how to use that shotgun she's got."

"She does."

Maternal instinct wanted Sarah right beside her where Serena could assure herself that her daughter was safe every second, but taking Sarah out to a remote cabin where a hunted man might be hiding was not the wisest plan. And no matter how dangerous Bart Alexander might be, she'd bet on Gemma's grandmother every time.

But if anything happened to Sarah . . .

"You remembered to ask Garth to go out and check on them?" she asked.

"And I programmed his cell phone number into Gemma's cell phone," Kermit assured her, his blue eyes dark with understanding as he glanced at her. "She'll be safer with Pleasance than she would be with us."

Serena nodded, then leaned her forehead against the cool side window, watching the mist-filled cow pastures flow by as they turned away from the ocean, toward the mountains.

"Besides," Kermit said, pressing the accelerator to hit the first slow rise at a good-deal-faster-than-strictly-legal clip, "Alexander gave you until tonight. We'll be home long before then."

The doorbell of the old farmhouse rattled like a train's wheels on the track. Sarah jumped, nearly dropping the Ball jar she was washing into Mrs. Geary's huge porcelain sink. Beside her, Gemma squeaked and jingled the canning lids, making Sarah feel a little less self-conscious about her nerves.

Pleasance Geary pushed herself back from the kitchen table where she was preparing the plums for the preserves she planned to cook that day.

"Before nine on a Saturday morning," Mrs. Geary growled, stretching herself to her near six-foot height, particularly imposing in her bright aqua polyester pantsuit. The steel gray in her eyes matched her iron-colored hair. "Probably those overeager teenagers with their magazine sales. They never take a bit of notice of that 'No Soliciting' sign by the door. You girls keep at those dishes while I chase them away."

Sarah shared a glance with Gemma. Despite Mrs. Geary's unworried calm, she was keeping them out of sight. Mrs. Geary had plenty of practice at this sort of thing. She had been keeping her eye out for trouble since she'd gained custody of Gemma from Gemma's father.

Sarah touched her belt loop to make sure the small canister of pepper spray was still there. Auntie Dess had bought it for walking Fleur, in case another dog attacked the gentle Lab. Kermit had loaned it to Sarah that morning.

"Sarah!" Mrs. Geary's gravelly voice rang down the hall and echoed into the huge kitchen. "Come here a minute."

Sarah glanced at Gemma, who shrugged. They set down the canning materials and headed down the short, straight hall to the front door. Fleur heaved herself up from the kitchen floor to follow them.

Mrs. Geary stood in the doorframe, blocking most of their view of the foggy morning, the heavy gray sky sinking down to the bright green pastures out front. She edged aside as Sarah came up to the door, but didn't back away to allow the man on the front porch to enter.

The stranger wore a black hat, a fedora, Sarah thought, like something Humphrey Bogart would wear, over unkempt black hair. He matched Mrs. Geary for height and wore a dark suit that even Sarah could tell must have been tailored to fit him so well.

His sharp gaze fixed on hers. "Miss Davis?"

Sarah's stomach dropped. *Mom.* Something had happened to her mother, and the police department had sent this man to tell her. It couldn't have happened so fast. Kermit had only dropped her off at Mrs. Geary's half an hour ago. He and her mom would barely have had time to get on the road.

Fleur's nose pushed against her hand, and Sarah dug her

fingers into the hair on the dog's neck and hung on.

"Sarah?" Mrs. Geary's unruffled voice brought her back from the edge of panic. "This is Agent Dominick Johnson, with the FBI. He says he needs to find your mother."

She's okay. Sarah sucked in a quick, steadying breath. So, this was Agent Johnson. Her mother had said he reminded her of the junior Godfather. Sarah couldn't see much of Al Pacino in his football hero looks, but there was definitely something chilling in his stare.

"Can I see your badge?" she asked.

The agent glanced at Mrs. Geary, as if expecting her to tell Sarah to behave, but Mrs. Geary just raised an eyebrow and nodded at his jacket. He offered a sharp smile and pulled a leather ID holder from his pocket. Sarah could tell he was annoyed as he snapped it open, but there was real amusement in his eyes.

"Satisfied?"

She took a careful look at his ID. The photo matched, and she recognized the FBI symbol, but she'd never seen an FBI identification before to compare it to. She wanted to phone in his badge number, but you could only push grown-ups so far.

"Are you planning to go into law enforcement some day, Miss Davis?" Agent Johnson teased, slipping the ID back into his pocket.

"Yes."

His smile widened. "Don't forget the Bureau. We can always use bright new talent."

But he didn't mean it. He wasn't even trying that hard to charm her. He was in a hurry. "Miss Davis, I need to find your mother as soon as possible. I need your help."

"Why?"

His grin stuck in place. "FBI business."

"She'll be back tonight. If you give me your card, I can tell her to call you."

The grin disappeared. He hunkered down a little, as if she were a toddler needing reassurance, though she'd been one of the taller girls in her seventh-grade class last year.

"I think your mother may be in danger, Miss Davis. I can't say more than that, as it relates to an ongoing FBI investigation. But I can assure you that I don't play games. This is serious."

She knew her mother hadn't liked Agent Johnson much when she'd met him, but having an extra law enforcement officer backing up her and Kermit if things didn't go well with Jesse didn't sound like such a bad idea.

"Sarah." Mrs. Geary rested a strong hand on her shoulder. "It's the FBI, child. I told him your mom's going over the hill to a friend's cabin, but I thought you might be able to tell him where it is better than me."

"You said the owner of the property is one of Jesse Banos's partners?" Agent Johnson asked.

Mrs. Geary nodded. "But I don't have an address for it."

Agent Johnson turned back to Sarah. "This is important, Miss Davis. I'm sure you know your mom's looking for Jesse Banos. Maybe you know that a man named Bart Alexander is looking for him, too. I've been on Alexander's trail a long time. He's a much more dangerous man than your mother realizes. And I have reason to believe he's following your mom right now. I need to find her first."

A chill ran down Sarah's spine as she remembered the e-mail she'd received from Bart Alexander the night before. She had no doubt he was as dangerous as Agent Johnson said. Kermit had said to keep their destination a secret, but Kermit had told Mrs. Geary. And Mrs. Geary had already told Agent Johnson.

"Do you know the name of the man who owns the cabin?" Agent Johnson asked.

"Roger Avalos," Sarah told him.

"The one who's off in Guatemala on the guilt-relief mission," Agent Johnson mused, scorn mixing with satisfaction. "So that's how Jesse disappeared off the face of the earth. Smarter bastard than I thought."

Sarah began to understand why her mom didn't like him.

He pulled a notepad and pen out of his jacket pocket. The pen was a fancy ballpoint with what looked like a diamond chip on the clip. But the notepad read Cypress Head Lodge, obviously picked up from his hotel room.

"All right, sweetheart. Now I just need you to give me directions to this cabin."

Cypress Head Lodge. That was a bed and breakfast inn up in Shell Creek, near Uncle Daniel and Aunt Destiny's house. A little fancier than most Jasper County destinations.

"Past Willow Creek, Mrs. Geary said," Agent Johnson prompted.

"I don't know," Sarah said, trying to give herself a minute to think.

When they'd filmed that B-horror movie about the zombies up in the redwoods of Herbert Jasper State Park, the stars had stayed at the Cypress Head Lodge. Why was she thinking about that?

"Sure you know. Just concentrate," Agent Johnson said, impatient now. "Is the turn-off before or after Willow Creek?"

Uncle Daniel always said he believed in hunches. For a long time that had sounded too much like Callista's talk about psychic powers to Sarah. She'd finally figured out that Daniel's hunches were really just deductions based on all the detective work he'd done in his career. His subconscious was noticing stuff that he didn't even realize consciously.

But she didn't have any detective experience. Why was she suddenly so sure she didn't want to tell Agent Johnson how to find her mom?

"I don't know where the cabin is," Sarah said.

His irritated gaze suddenly snapped into focus, as if he could bore into her head. "A cabin on the river? The perfect place for summer fun? And you can't remember how to get there?"

A yellow sticky note. Written in red pen.

"I've never been there." The lie might have come from someone else, the words were so certain and calm. Not like her pounding heart at all. "None of the counselors at the clinic have kids. Well, Mr. Avalos does, but they're all grown up. They don't want kids hanging out with them while they party. I never got invited."

His face went blank for a moment, and Sarah couldn't tell whether he believed her or he wanted to shoot her. Maybe both. She couldn't see past the flat plane of his eyes.

Then he shrugged, and all the tension seemed to flow out of his body. He even grinned at her. "I can't say I blame him. Kids are a pain in the ass."

He tucked away his notebook and pen and touched the brim of his hat to Mrs. Geary. "Thank you for all your help, ma'am." He nodded to Sarah. "And for yours, sweetheart. Thank God for Internet property listings and GPS."

He shot her a wink and strode down the porch stairs toward the black Mercedes sedan waiting at the edge of the gravel driveway. The car windows were tinted, so Sarah couldn't make out the driver, but Agent Johnson got into the passenger seat, and the car rolled away.

Mrs. Geary blew out a worried breath as she pushed the front door closed and locked it. "I wish he'd told us what he knew. Serena should know how dangerous this Alexander fellow might be. I figured you knew how to get to that cabin, Sarah. I wonder why Serena didn't think of that and leave directions."

"I don't think she thought they were going to be gone long enough to worry about it," Sarah said, scooting down the hall toward the kitchen to avoid Mrs. Geary's gaze.

"I suppose."

Sarah risked a glance back at her friend's usually unflappable grandmother. "Do you think she and Kermit could be in some kind of danger Agent Johnson didn't tell us about?"

Had she made the wrong decision not to give him directions to the cabin? The lie had slipped out, almost without her thinking about it. She knew her mom would want to confront Jesse without interference. But what if she and Kermit were walking into danger?

"Now don't get all worked up." Mrs. Geary gave her a steadying nod. "Your mom will be careful, and Kermit will take good care of her. Don't you worry. They'll be fine. I was just saying I hope that FBI agent catches up with them."

"Uh-huh," Sarah agreed, though she honestly didn't know whether she meant it or not. She didn't like Agent Johnson, but that wasn't what had stopped her from giving him directions. It had been the memory of that yellow sticky pad with the red ink, the one Agent Johnson had given her mother with the phone number at his hotel.

He'd been staying at the Flyaway Express Inn. The cheap chain hotel at the airport. So why was he carrying a notepad from the Cypress Head Inn? And riding in a Mercedes?

That's what her hunch had been trying to tell her. But did it mean anything or not?

"May I borrow your phone?" Sarah asked, suddenly realizing she could get a second opinion. "I can call Kermit's cell phone and tell him and Mom what Agent Johnson said."

"Young brains." Mrs. Geary shook her head. "My doctor says I don't have any signs of Alzheimer's, but he's nearly as old as I am. What does he know? Go ahead, hon. Give 'em a call."

But Kermit's phone sent her directly to voice mail. No signal. Which only meant that Kermit and her mom had hit one of those pockets of dead air deep in the mountains somewhere. She might be able to catch them when they drove up over the next pass. She *had* to catch them.

Regardless of whether or not she'd made the right decision about lying to Agent Johnson, she had to let them know that he was on his way. Because he'd been right about what he'd said when he left. He'd almost certainly be able to find the address for Mr. Avalos's cabin on the Internet.

Of course, finding the actual cabin down those unmarked dirt roads might be a little more complicated . . .

Chapter 16

"Are you sure this is the right way?" Kermit asked as the low-slung Jensen Healey jolted along the deeply rutted drive. The dusty leaves of a red-branched madrone brushed across the windshield and knocked the side mirror askew. "Are you sure this is even a road?"

He was glad of the smile that pulled at Serena's mouth, despite the rising tension he knew they both felt.

"I suggested bringing the Subaru," she reminded him.

"You didn't say it was because we were going to need four-wheel drive. It's a good thing we stopped to buy those sodas in Willow Creek. They could save our lives until the search team finds us."

The road turned abruptly down a steep drop through a tangle of oaks and pine before leveling onto a flat terrace. Kermit could smell the river, though he estimated they were still a hundred yards from the cliff edge and at least fifty feet above the valley bottom. The heavy, deep scent of the water ran like a bass counterpoint through the high, dry violin smells of the oaks and the smooth melody of the pines.

He thought he could hear the river, too, or rather almost feel it, the low rumble drowned out by the car's engine.

The dirt road crashed through a snarl of blackberry bushes, then suddenly split around a high-fenced field crossed by lines of short green corn and rangy green beans, mounds of squash, and rows of sharp-smelling tomato plants too small yet to need their mesh supports.

"That's the neighbor's garden," Serena said. "He brings over fresh-picked corn for Roger's barbecues. All you have to do is dip it in the hot water and eat it."

For a second he could imagine owning a place like that. A little garden. Hard work on a weekend morning with a rototiller, an afternoon in a hammock under the trees. Picking home-grown organic vegetables for Serena's wild vegetarian dishes.

Of course, at the moment this idyllic setting was serving as Jesse Banos's love nest. Or possibly a death trap. *Get a grip, Riggs.* "Which way?"

"Roger's cabin is to the left. It's another couple hundred yards along, but there's a place you can pull off the road and park just ahead."

Kermit nodded agreement. They didn't want to warn Jesse of their approach. He wrestled the car off the drive and onto a smoother space cleared of underbrush beneath a stand of old pear trees.

A sense of peace struck Kermit as an almost physical force as he climbed out of the car. The constant, muted roar of the river drowned all distant sound, including the highway on the other side of the valley, making the rustle of a breeze in the trees, the call of a bird, the ticking of the car engine, all stand out sharp and clear.

He took a deep breath of the fresh air, already warming in the morning sun, and felt the stress of the past twenty-four hours breaking up inside his lungs. Too soon. They hadn't found Jesse yet. Sarah was still in danger.

"I can see how Nadia's convertible got all mucked up," Kermit said, taking a futile swipe at his bumper. Two weeks without rain had dried the mud in the road ruts, but dust and grit still sprayed the car's undercarriage.

"I told you this was the place," Serena said. In the bright sunlight, her eyes flashed with a glint of predatory gold, the look of a hunting cat scenting her quarry.

Not at all the appearance of a woman about to confront a straying man she still loved, Kermit was relieved to note. But he grabbed her arm before she could stalk down the road and gestured toward where he could see a cabin roof through the trees the drive wound through. "That's it?"

"That's it."

"Can I approach it from behind without being seen?"

One of Serena's perfectly curved eyebrows rose. "*I* can. I'll yell if I need you." The distress darkening her eyes belied her tough attitude. "Please. Wait here."

"You know I can't do that."

Even if he could be sure Jesse and Nadia were all they would face at Roger's cabin, even if he didn't still have nagging questions about Nigel Crow's role in this situation, about the possibility that someone was setting Serena up for a fall if Jesse's disappearance turned out to be of a permanent nature, he couldn't have let her face the situation alone.

"I told you, I don't need a white knight." She waved toward the hidden cabin. "I've had enough trouble with the one over there."

"I'm a police officer," he reminded her. "Nobody goes into a dangerous situation without backup."

He reached for her hand, and she met it with hers, small compared to his, but not delicate. The hint of a smile touched her lips.

"I see Good Cop is back." Then she made a face. "Kermit, the man I planned to marry is holed up over there with a rich fashion model. I really don't want anyone to see this."

"Jesse's the one who's acted shamefully." The force in his voice brought her gaze to his. "Don't you forget that."

She tilted a half-smile at him. "Walk in there with my head held high?"

"Metaphorically speaking." He dropped her hand to motion toward the trees. "After I scan the area for shallow graves and booby traps."

A laugh snorted from her as she followed him off the road. "Remind me again why finding Jesse in a shallow grave would be a bad thing?"

But she moved as carefully as he through the trees. Earlier in the spring someone had mowed swaths through the blackberry vines and other underbrush, opening paths to once-cultivated walnut and apple trees, but there was still plenty of cover to mask their approach to the cabin.

Serena touched his arm and pointed to a tangle of alder saplings. He nodded, dropping down to crawl forward under their shelter. Blackberry vine suckers snagged at his clothes, and he was glad he hadn't discarded his denim jacket in response to the warm inland climate.

Through the screen of trees and brush, he got his first clear view of Roger Avalos's cabin. A small, single-story building, the cabin sported a steeply pitched roof and high windows that probably went most of the way around. Kermit couldn't tell for sure, because the windows facing their hiding place were currently covered by roll-up blinds. There was a narrow walkway to a door in the wall he faced, but he guessed the main cabin entrance was on the other side of the building, facing the river gorge.

The dirt drive they had left emptied into a grassy clearing on the right of the cabin. As Serena crept up beside him, he pointed across the clearing to where a Honda coupe parked off to one side, its silver paint chameleon-like against white and gray tree trunks.

Serena nodded. "That's Jesse's car," she whispered. "He's here. I told you Nigel traded cars with him. Nigel couldn't have brought both cars up here and left one."

"Not without help."

"Help? From who?"

He glanced at her. "Bart Alexander? Vacationing FBI Agent Dominick Johnson? Some other jilted husband Jesse's managed to tick off—"

"Oh, for heaven's sake." Her whisper hissed with exasperation. She shook her head, squirming back the way she had come. "He's here. I can feel it. Alive and well."

"That's one possibility." But he wasn't going to let her wiggling rear end distract him from the others. "Or maybe he's dead and locked in his Honda's trunk. Or dumped in the river with rocks in his pockets. Or—"

She wrinkled her nose at him. "And I thought Sarah had an overactive imagination."

But he'd made her nervous enough that she waited for him to pull his gun from the shoulder holster under his jacket and check it before joining him in a quiet sprint to the back of the cabin. The blinds prevented them from seeing the cabin's interior, but also shielded them from view from anyone inside.

Kermit gestured Serena to keep her head down as they turned the corner around the left side of the building, opposite the drive where the Honda was parked.

As they moved toward the front of the cabin, the ground sloped down toward the cliff edge. By the time they reached the front deck, the cabin floor was even with Kermit's chest. A concrete block holding one of the deck posts gave him a hard surface to boost himself from. He heaved himself up onto the deck, rolling low to the front windows.

These were cracked open against the coming afternoon heat, and the blinds had not been pulled. With a quick, quieting breath, Kermit lifted his head up for a rapid survey of the cabin's dim interior. Seeing no one, he paused for a more leisurely view.

The cabin appeared to consist of one large main room, with a wood stove for heat, a foldout sofa for sleeping, a long, picnic-style table, and a small kitchen area. A black carryall bag and two pieces of cherry red luggage had been pushed against the far wall. A laundry line was strung across a pair of the bare rafters below the roof, decorated with a selection of lacy panties in a variety of colors, a yellow string bikini, and a pair of men's Speedo briefs.

"I told you they were alive," Serena muttered as she crawled up beside him. She sounded almost disappointed.

"In the other room?" Kermit asked, nodding toward the small section of the cabin cut off from the main room by a bare wooden wall.

"Bathroom," Serena told him. "Could be."

"Wait here." Kermit raised himself to a crouch and paused. *Fat chance.* "Warn me if you see them coming."

She nodded, her eyes dark and serious as she stared into the darkened cabin. Kermit squelched a grin. That ought to keep her out of the way.

He tucked his gun into his jacket pocket. He didn't expect to need it. Generally couples sequestered in a bathroom together weren't carrying a lot of firepower. But he wasn't going to let it too far out of his reach, either.

He tried the door. Unlocked. Jesse and Nadia had been staying in this remote, hard-to-find location undisturbed for two weeks. It would be easy to get complacent.

And if Nigel Crow had told the truth about not hearing from Jesse for a week, they might not fully realize the trouble they had caused back in Hope Point. Maybe Nadia figured her husband would have given up the chase by now. They might be completely unprepared for anyone to be breaking into their little love nest.

In fact, Kermit thought, ducking under a black lace thong hanging from the laundry line, if it weren't for Bart Alexander's threat against Sarah, he'd be feeling pretty silly about this whole business right about now.

But the thought of that malicious, arrogant e-mail kept him focused and cool as he slipped around the sofa, toward the edge of the bathroom wall. If the cost of protecting Sarah was embarrassing the hell out of himself, well, it wouldn't be the first time he'd caught a couple *in flagrante delicto*. Though that had previously involved investigating illegally parked cars, not trespassing on private property. Of course, Jesse and Nadia were trespassing, too.

Kermit paused at the end of the wall. He heard no movement, no water running. Despite his caution, they might have heard him enter, be waiting for him to show himself. He waited another minute. Nothing.

In one smooth motion, he turned the corner, ducking low. The back door was to his right, a closet door to his left. The bathroom lay directly in front of him, door wide open, obviously empty.

Clenching his teeth against the burst of adrenaline that had carried him that far, Kermit checked the closet. A few towels, a beach ball, a vacuum cleaner. And the shower stall in the bathroom. Floral shampoo and body wash.

A sound behind him spun him on his heels, but it was only Serena, skidding around the end of the wall.

"I found them!" Intensity burned in her harsh whisper. So much for her waiting on the porch for him.

"Where?"

"Down on the beach. I thought I heard voices, so I sneaked a look through the trees."

Kermit glanced at the swimsuits on the laundry line as he joined her by the sofa. "Are you sure it's them?"

"Oh, I'm sure." She strode purposefully toward the front door. "I couldn't get a clear shot—er, view—through the trees, but they were stretched out on beach towels. I could see enough to make an identification."

"Sunbathing? They must have brought extra suits."

Serena snorted. "Not exactly."

Kermit's foot caught on the end of the sofa, tripping him forward. Black lace fluttered in front of his face, snagging his nose. He brushed at it as he stumbled, ripping it off the laundry line. The thong snapped like a rubber band, zinging forward to strike Serena in the side of the head.

She caught it before it fell, holding it gingerly between two French-manicured nails.

Laughter choked from her like a suppressed cough. She met his eyes. "This is awful."

He nodded, compassion for her warring with his own embarrassment and laughter.

"One thing's for sure," she said, setting the panties on the kitchen table. "They're going to be surprised to see us."

Kermit followed her to the door, the heat in his face subsiding as he once more checked the gun in his pocket. He hoped so. It would be nice for once in this whole mess to be the one doing the surprising.

The path down the cliff to the riverside dropped in a series of steep switchbacks through the trees before emptying out onto a landscape of large, pale boulders deposited during floods of years past.

At the base of the river gorge, between the cliff they'd

climbed down and the even higher, steeper cliff across from them, the roar of the water coursing by effectively drowned all noise of their approach. Through a thicket of small willows, Serena could see the deep green water as it headed for the rapids at the river bend to their right, but the narrow strip of sand where Jesse and Nadia were sunbathing was hidden by the boulders.

"Wish I'd brought *my* swimsuit," Kermit muttered beside her as the sun pounded down on their heads and reflected back at them from the light-colored rocks.

"And a lunch," Serena agreed. If she concentrated on what a great day this would be for a picnic by the river, instead of on Jesse and Nadia, she might be able to get through this.

"Sunday," Kermit said, starting gingerly into the boulder field. "We'll come up to the river for fun. We'll bring Fleur and Sarah and some inner-tubes."

A funny ripple ran down Serena's arms at the picture that conjured in her mind. The four of them hanging out on the beach down near Willow Creek. Fleur swimming strong as an otter as Kermit threw sticks for her in the swift-moving water. Sarah insisting she wasn't too cold to keep swimming, even as her lips turned blue. Eating organic corn chips and Fig Newtons as the sun baked them warm again.

They looked almost like a . . .

Serena shook her head, trying to shatter the image. "Sarah's dad is picking her up tomorrow afternoon to take her down to Santa Rosa. And Destiny and Daniel will be back Sunday morning to pick up Fleur."

Kermit glanced back at her. "Just you and me, then."

The emotions stirred by the thought of Kermit in swim trunks, the muscles she'd glimpsed beneath his tight t-shirt the other day bared for all to see, turned out to be no more disturbing than picturing him as part of a family outing.

It was the dare that gleamed in his eyes, and the flash of something behind his smile, something deeper—and hotter—that caused her sheer, sudden panic. She opened her mouth to turn him down, but her powder-pink sneakers betrayed her, slipping her foot off the top of the boulder she was stepping toward.

As she pitched forward, Kermit's hand grabbed her elbow, pulling her into him, preventing her headlong fall into the rocks. Serena took a few quick breaths, letting him hold her steady, her shoulder against his chest.

It felt good to be supported that way. It felt good to imagine wrapping her arms around his chest and leaning in for a hug. Good to imagine coming to the river for a lazy afternoon of sunbathing and swimming with a man.

With Kermit. A man who would go on an outing if he promised to go. Who would love to spend the afternoon with her daughter and a dog.

Unlike the man a dozen yards ahead across the rocks.

She pulled away from Kermit's arms, forcing herself back into balance. This was no time for fantasy. "Let's get this over with."

He nodded, the challenge still bright in his eyes. "Right. Sunday will be our reward."

He headed off across the rocks, striding from boulder to boulder, and it occurred to her that Kermit wasn't having any trouble keeping his feet.

She almost tripped again at the disconcerting heat that coiled through her. He was serious. She wasn't ready. For what? To tell him she was too old for him? That he needed to find some hot chick his own age who didn't have a teen-aged child and a mortgage? To make it clear she wasn't going to risk getting hurt again?

Not that he meant the Sunday outing as a date. Right. He didn't. But if it turned out that he did, if he put his arms around her, hell, if he just looked at her . . . would she even be able to tell him any of those things?

She shook her head and followed him across the rocks. *Let's get this over with.* She might not be ready to deal with her feelings for Kermit Riggs, but she was more than ready to deal with Jesse Banos.

She could tell when Kermit saw Jesse and Nadia. His pace faltered for an instant, and his ears reddened. But he only glanced back to make sure she wanted to continue. She nodded, and they dropped down to the sand as the boulders became more widely spaced near the narrow beach.

The couple lay on their stomachs side by side on Roger's tropical print beach towels. Barely five feet from their toes, shallow water lapped against the sand, and an inflatable two-person kayak rested half on the beach, half in the water a few yards away.

The scene had all the trappings of an *Outdoor Magazine*–style romantic interlude, except that Jesse's concentration was buried in a medical journal and Nadia had turned her face away from him in what looked like a pout, though that might have simply been the result of collagen implants.

In person, Nadia was every bit as beautiful as in her photographs. Her tanning-salon-toned skin showed off her perfectly enhanced figure and her glowing blond hair.

So much for it's all being airbrushing.

Beside her, Jesse had the long, lean figure and black curls of a Greek god. He had tanned a deep bronze over the past couple of weeks, though Serena noted some peeling on his rear end from a healing sunburn.

Her smile was purely involuntary. "Ouch. That must have hurt."

242

The two sunbathers exploded up as if she'd thrown a hand grenade in their faces. The raw panic in their expressions was almost worth the embarrassment of the flash of nudity.

Nadia's scream echoed off the cliffs as she struggled to her feet, pulling her towel up to cover herself. Jesse lunged sideways, scrambling for the pile of clothes and shoes they'd left in the shade of a scraggly bush.

"Stay away from me!" Nadia shrieked, backing away from them, her face twisted by fear. "Don't touch me!"

"It's all right, ma'am," Kermit assured her, his voice calmly professional, despite the redness of his ears. "We're not going to hurt you."

But the woman only screamed louder. "Stay back! Jesse! Don't let them hurt me!"

"Oh, for heaven's sake," Serena snapped, turning to where Jesse was scrambling through the pile of clothes. "Jesse, would you please tell her to calm down. I didn't come out here to kill you both in a fit of jealousy. I might be disgusted, but not jealous."

But when Jesse looked up from his search through the clothes, he didn't turn toward Nadia. He was looking directly at Serena.

Down the barrel of a very large handgun.

Chapter 17

"Don't move." Jesse's order rang thinly across the sand. "Damn it, Serena, who else did you bring up here with you? Just tell me what I need to know. I don't want to shoot you."

"That's good to hear, Jesse." To his own ears, Kermit's voice sounded as though it belonged to someone else, someone cool and in control. His arms were steady, too, as he held his Glock trained on Jesse's heart. "That's good to hear, because I'm pretty sure I'm a much better shot than you are."

Jesse glanced at him, his eyes widening at the sight of Kermit's firearm. The Ruger he held shifted slightly with the turning of his head.

Kermit gritted his teeth, praying he wouldn't regret not taking the opportunity for a shot. He'd never had to shoot a man before, and he didn't want to start with Jesse Banos.

"Kermit Riggs?" Jesse blinked in recognition.

"You know these people?" Nadia demanded, edging up behind Jesse.

Jesse nodded. "This man is with the police." He glanced between Kermit and Serena. "Did you come alone? If you promise not to come any closer, I'll lower my weapon."

"No!" Nadia crouched down beside him, jostling his shoulder and giving Kermit another tempting shot. "Jesse, no. You can't trust anyone. He can buy the police. Don't let him take me away!"

"I didn't come here planning to take anyone anywhere, ma'am," Kermit said, mild and calm, though his aim never wavered from Jesse's chest. As long as he couldn't see Serena's fear, he could do this without murder. "We just want to have a little chat with Jesse here."

Jesse's hand wavered as he lowered the .45, carefully setting it down on the windbreaker from which he'd pulled it.

"Slide it away from you."

Jesse did as he was told, pushing it a yard away, before leaning back on his heels.

Kermit was pleased to note his own hand remained steady as he lowered his gun.

"Are you all right?" he asked, keeping his attention focused on Jesse.

"No, I'm not all right!" Nadia sobbed, wrapping her arms around Jesse's neck as she glared at Kermit. "Attacked by thugs with guns!"

"I wasn't talking to you," Kermit said. He risked a glance at Serena. The sight of her standing at the edge of the beach, whole and unhurt, sent a jolt of relief through him that nearly knocked him to his knees. "Serena?"

She nodded firmly, though her face looked pale as she crossed her arms over her chest, glaring down at Jesse. "What the hell was that all about?"

"I didn't know who you'd brought with you," he said, disengaging Nadia's arm from around his windpipe. "We have the right to defend ourselves." He glanced at Kermit. "We'd like to get dressed."

"Please," Kermit agreed. He slipped his gun back into his jacket pocket and moved to stand closer to Serena. With her eyes flashing like an avenging angel's, she didn't look like someone who needed protection, but he was sure glad he'd come along for backup.

"What are you doing here?" Jesse demanded, zipping up his denim shorts. "Did Nigel guess we were here?"

Kermit bet himself ten bucks the guy was too vain to throw a shirt over his deeply tanned chest. He won.

"I don't think Nigel knows you well enough to believe you'd break into a friend's private cabin and make yourself at home," Serena said.

"You have no business being here, Serena," Jesse said. "And no right to judge my actions. I can see why you'd be jealous, but we broke it off, remember?"

Kermit's fists clenched involuntarily. *Once an arrogant slimewad . . .*

"No, *us* breaking it off is not exactly how I remember it," Serena said, with chilling restraint. "The way I remember it, I dumped you."

It took Jesse only a second to recover from that. "So, that's why you came running after me, dragging Barney here along with you?" He cocked a patronizing eyebrow. "Really, Serena, I'm sorry I upset you, but I expected you to have a little more self-respect than this."

Kermit was glad Serena didn't have a gun. He was already regretting not shooting Jesse when he'd had the chance.

"You don't have any idea what your little display of misplaced possessiveness could cost," Jesse continued, working his feet into a pair of worn Birkenstocks. "You've just put Nadia in a great deal of danger. Didn't realize that, did you? You have no idea who could be following you."

"How about Nadia's psychopathic husband, for one?" Serena suggested, her expression cold as a stalking cat's.

"Bart?" Nadia gasped, jerking down the hem of her short, body-hugging, knit sundress. "Oh, my God. Does he know where we are?"

"Then there's the FBI," Serena continued, ignoring her. "I'm pretty certain the IRS was just a ruse, but I'm sure your counseling partners would give a good deal to know where you ran off to when you left them in the lurch. And then there's your family—"

"I didn't leave anyone in the lurch!" Jesse objected, finally struck where it hurt.

"They've seen Bart." Nadia jerked on his arm. "Jesse, he's here. He could find us any minute."

Serena shrugged. "Your clients might disagree. Did you give a thought to them when you ran off with your distressed damsel here?"

"Oh, that's rich," Jesse spat back. "Coming from a woman who divorced her first husband and then couldn't even stay engaged the second time. Who hangs out with psychic charlatans. Who lets her daughter run around with white trash teenie boppers. Who—"

"Gemma Tasker is not white trash!"

"Her mother's a drug addict and her father's in jail!"

Kermit might have been tempted to aim a swing at Jesse's nose for his comments about both Serena and Gemma, but he was too busy assimilating the exchange between Jesse and Serena. He'd believed her when she'd told him that she no longer loved Jesse. At least, he'd believed she was getting over loving him. That hadn't kept a whole host of unacknowledged fears from building up in his heart in anticipation of this encounter today.

But watching her body language and Jesse's, all those fears washed away. Serena wasn't the one wallowing in resentment and a bruised ego. She wasn't the one who'd been nursing a hope of reconciliation.

Kermit kept his sudden desire to grin carefully off his face. *Poor bastard.*

"Bart's coming!" Nadia yelled, trying to get anyone's attention. "We have to get out of here! He'll kill us all!"

Maybe Jesse was just comparing what he'd lost to what he now had. Nadia's histrionics were wearing Kermit's patience thin, and he'd only spent five minutes in the woman's company. Jesse'd had two weeks of it.

"Your husband doesn't know we're here," Serena said. "But you can't hide in your little love nest here forever. You're going to have to face him."

"This isn't a love nest," Jesse objected, his nostrils flaring. "I'm protecting Nadia's life!"

"You don't know what you're saying," Nadia told Serena. "I can't face Bart. He's crazy. He'll kill me."

"Maybe you should have thought about that before you cheated on him," Serena said, though Kermit could see her protective barrier of anger cracking at the woman's distress.

"I had to run away from him. I didn't have any choice." Nadia's chest heaved with suppressed sobs. "He would have killed me eventually."

"Did he hurt you?" Serena asked. "There are shelters that help abuse victims."

"Do you think any shelter could really hide me from the son of one of the richest men in California?" Nadia demanded.

"Probably better than Jesse could," Serena retorted. "Have you spoken with a lawyer about filing for divorce? Maybe there's a way to convince Bart—or his father—that letting you go would be better than the negative publicity if anything bad were to happen to you."

Kermit almost snorted. And *she* accused *him* of trying to play white knight.

"He's not going to let me go." Nadia shuddered, and Kermit remembered the hint of fear that had haunted

Serena when she described the man who called himself
Othello Karenin.

His annoyance with Nadia faded. He guessed she knew
what she was talking about.

"He's not going to let me go," she repeated. "I know too
much. He was already worrying about that, even before he
found my cell phone bill and found out I'd been talking
with Jesse."

"Knew too much about what?" Kermit asked.

"His father's business practices," Nadia said, the words
brittle and bitter. "And what Bart was willing to do to—"

"That's enough," Jesse interrupted, putting a protective
arm around her shoulders. "We don't have to talk to them.
There's no police case here, *Officer* Riggs. This is none of
your business."

He wants to be the only one who can help her. The insight
flashed in Kermit's brain. *He wants to play the hero.* No
wonder Serena was wary of being overprotected.

Nadia hadn't learned that lesson yet, however. She
closed her mouth, though fear still spoke from her smoky
gray eyes.

"Unfortunately," Serena said. "It is *my* business, Jesse.
You've landed everyone who knows you in the middle of
your mess, and I've come to let you know it's time for you
to clean it up."

"Forget the dramatics," Jesse said, his voice gentling.
"It's not going to do you any good. I know Nigel and Lani
can survive without me at the clinic for a while. Mark's a
big boy. He's been clean and sober for over six months.
He'll be all right. And so will you, Serena. I like to think
that over the past couple of years I've helped you learn how
to stand on your own two fee—"

"Screw you."

Kermit could tell those weren't the exact words she wanted to use, but she repeated them.

"Screw you, Jesse Banos. You think I'm being dramatic? Fine." She stepped toward him. Her own two feet might stand her only as high as Jesse's nose, but he was the one who took a startled step back, nearly tripping over Nadia.

She cocked her head at him. "You haven't seen dramatic yet. Dramatic will be when I promise to break every bone in your body unless you agree to come back to Hope Point immediately and help me convince Bart Alexander to quit threatening my daughter."

Jesse frowned. "He's got no reason to bother Sarah."

"Threaten," Serena corrected. "He threatened her. Kermit could have been killed by one of his little games last week, and he promised me more of the same and then told Sarah she would be next."

Jesse shook his head. "Why?"

Serena shrugged. "Because he thought I could tell him where you were."

"And you did." Nadia's voice shook, a thin, high whisper against the river breezes. "You told him."

"No," Serena said. "Not yet."

"And we don't have to," Kermit stepped in. Good cop to the rescue. "If you have a criminal abuse complaint against your husband, Mrs. Alexander, we can arrest him. The police can arrange for your safety."

"You *told* him." Her voice quavered louder, and she trembled despite the sun's heat.

Kermit kept his voice calm against her rising hysteria. "No, ma'am. As I said, if you're willing to help us in this investigation—" Okay, maybe there wasn't an official investigation at the moment, but if Bart Alexander had beaten his wife, there would be. "—then we can provide protection—"

"You *told him!*"

Kermit glanced at Jesse in exasperation. "Would you please tell her that we didn't tell her husband anything?"

Her gaze fixed and distant, Nadia lifted her hand and pointed a perfectly sculpted orange nail back across the boulder field. "Then who are those two men with the guns?"

Serena heard the first bullet sing past, heard the explosion of its report, heard the echo crash back from the opposite side of the river, heard another echo—or maybe another shot—

And then something hard and solid struck her in the shoulder, knocking her to the sand. Holding her there.

"Stay down!" Kermit's voice came from right beside her ear, but the deafening gunshots muted it. "Are you hit?"

"No." At least, she didn't think so. With all the noise it was hard to tell.

Kermit's weight shifted off her back. Turning her head, she saw him pulling his pistol. Chips flew off a rock inches from his shoulder.

Another gunshot blast nearly knocked her sideways. She whirled, pure adrenaline whipping her spine like a snake. The shooters were right on top of her . . .

No. It was Jesse. He'd retrieved his gun from his windbreaker and crouched behind a boulder beside her, firing wildly back at the men at the base of the trail down from Roger's cabin. Nadia huddled behind him.

Serena turned back to Kermit, who had sent off another shot, but had stopped firing. "Who are they?"

"I didn't recognize them." He glanced past her toward Jesse. "Hold your fire."

The gunshots stopped, ringing silence drifting down in their wake, but Serena heard the click of Jesse's trigger, and knew it wasn't Kermit's order that had stopped his gun.

"Who are they?" Serena asked again. She'd always heard that time slowed in times of physical danger, but the only thing moving unusually slowly seemed to be her brain.

"They're Bart's men," Nadia said, her voice cold with what Serena feared might be shock. "I recognized the hulking one. Bart uses him to intimidate people."

"Well, if they're trying to intimidate me, they're succeeding," Serena said.

"Those weren't warning shots," Kermit said, his profile set in grim lines as he scanned the boulder field before them. "They were firing like they meant to kill somebody."

"They'll kill all of us," Nadia promised. "Bart can't let me live."

"Why not?" Serena demanded, her annoyance at Nadia and Bart and Jesse and the whole stupid situation snapping through her fear. "I know he's got an ego problem, but can't he get a grip? A cheating wife isn't worth a lifetime in jail."

"It's a lifetime in jail he's trying to avoid," Jesse said. "That's why he wants Nadia dead, and that's what I've been trying to protect her from."

Even considering that he'd managed to endanger all their lives, even though they were pinned down by killers on a narrow beach, even though he'd emptied his gun and they had no escape route, he still managed to imbue his words with the haughty superiority of the moral high ground.

But Serena's anger was directed fully at herself. How on earth could she have put up with such a self-satisfied egomaniac for so long? If only she'd broken off the engagement six months ago, when she first started realizing things were going downhill, she and Kermit would be safely out of this mess.

Her heart stalled in her chest. *Kermit.* If anything happened to him because of her poor judgment in men . . .

"Nadia is a witness to a murder conspiracy," Jesse said.

"You saw Bart kill somebody?" Serena asked. No wonder the woman was shaking with fear. Nadia might be a beautiful Barbie doll with all the depth of cotton candy, but Serena had looked into Bart Alexander's eyes. She could sympathize with Nadia's terror.

"She didn't witness the murder," Jesse corrected. "She witnessed the conspiracy."

"Bart planned it from our hotel room in Vail." Resentment edged the sniffles in Nadia's voice. "We were supposed to be on our second honeymoon, and all he did was work the whole time. I told him I didn't see why that agitator threatening to sue Daddy Alexander over that union-busting stuff meant we couldn't have a romantic weekend together, but Daddy always came first for Bart. Always."

"Agitator?" An image of a grainy photograph flickered in Serena's mind, two men grudgingly participating together in the opening of a medical clinic. "Bart arranged to have that labor organizer killed? What was his name?"

"Eddie Johnson," Kermit said. "But he was murdered by a drug gang."

"Bart did a good job," Nadia said. "He thought of everything. Daddy Alexander wanted the body disposed of where it would never be found, but Bart said that would just make the authorities suspicious. So he had the body dumped in a ditch and made it look like the local gangs had done it."

"You can prove this?" Kermit asked. His sudden turn shifted his body position, and a bullet whizzed past his head.

Serena choked on a scream, but Kermit sent a single

shot toward the trees, then turned back toward Nadia. "You have proof?"

"She recorded it," Jesse said, with smug pride.

"Probably couldn't get that admitted into court," Kermit said.

"She recorded names and dates and bank account numbers," Jesse countered. "Enough to build a case."

Serena would have thrown her hands in the air, if she wasn't worried one of them might get shot off. She looked over at Nadia. "So, why didn't you go to the police?"

"Bart would have killed me!"

"Unlike what he's trying to do right now?"

"Serena," Jesse snapped. "Stop being so judgmental. The poor thing was terrified."

"The poor *thing?*" Serena sucked in a breath and held back the rest of her tirade. Jesse's patronizing attitude really wasn't the biggest issue on her plate at the moment. "Can we hold them off, Kermit?"

Kermit's expression told her all she needed to know. He pulled his cell phone from the holder on his belt, shook his head. "No signal."

He replaced the phone. "I've got seven bullets left in my clip, but those men are not going to cross that open area of boulders so I can shoot them. My guess is, they're searching for a spot somewhere along the cliff that will give them a clear line of sight down onto the beach."

Tilting her head up, Serena could make out the trees along the cliff top that hid Roger's cabin from view. That meant the trees had a clear view of all of them, stretched like drying salmon on the beach. *Not good.*

"Their aim at that range won't be so hot," Kermit said. "But, then again, it won't have to be. We need to get off this beach."

"Who are you? MacGyver?" Jesse spat out. "Are you going to dig us a tunnel? Or maybe you've got a rope and grappling hook in your jacket pocket, so we can swim across the river and climb the cliff up to the highway?"

Kermit turned his back to his protective boulder to survey the river behind them.

Serena rolled her head to follow his gaze. River. That was pretty much it. Perhaps twenty-five feet across at this point, and still running fast and high from the late spring rains, the Trinity hugged the opposite cliff, curving sharply around their beach.

Just east of Roger's cabin, the river poured down steep rapids that were a favorite with summer inner-tubers. When the water dropped in late summer, it was possible to work one's way up the river along the bank and take the rapids again, but Serena knew that wouldn't be the case so early in the season. Downriver, to the west, the river ran into another, even narrower passage of white water. The only way off their dead end of boulder-strewn land without getting wet was back up the path to Roger's cabin.

And as for crossing the river . . . Even if they could swim all the way across before the swift-running current slammed them into the rapids downstream, there was no way they could climb the sheer, hundred-foot cliff looming above. Even a professional climber would think twice about taking on that unstable amalgam of rock.

As if to underscore her thought, a small shower of rocks and dirt slid free from the cliff face, bouncing down to the river and disappearing with a faint splash.

"Can't walk, can't swim," Kermit summed up. "Time to ride."

Serena followed his gaze to the inflatable kayak resting quietly beside a stand of scraggly willows on the beach a few yards downriver. "Oh, no."

"If we can get around the river bend, we should be able to find a place where we can climb up to the highway and flag down help," Kermit said.

"No," Serena repeated. The river's roar suddenly swelled in her head, bringing up years of news reports of drowned tourists and vanished tubers. "We'll never make it down those rapids. The river is a killer this high."

"At least the river isn't armed with semiautomatic pistols." Kermit's gaze met and held hers, his eyes steady with a fierce determination. "These rapids aren't that bad. We can do it."

He'd grown up in Jasper County. He'd probably tubed these waters as a kid. Maybe he had more river kayaking experience than she did. That wouldn't be hard, since her experience was zero. She wasn't going to ask. "It's our only choice?"

"Pretty much." The flash of keenness in his eyes was more reassuring than his words. He trained for life and death situations. If he was up for it, she had to give him the respect of trusting him.

"I'll get you through those rapids," he promised.

"Then let's do it."

"We're going to be exposed when we cross to the kayak," he warned. "Stay low, and move fast. Those little willows won't stop bullets, but I'm hoping they'll at least shield us from view while we push off into the river. Then everybody needs to stay down until we hit fast water and round the bend, out of sight."

"Great plan." Jesse's lip curled with scorn as he gestured toward the narrow craft. "I don't know if you've noticed, but that's a two-man kayak. It's barely big enough for Nadia to sunbathe in."

"You're welcome to volunteer to stay behind," Kermit offered. "You ready, Serena?"

No! She glanced at the stretch of sand that separated them from the kayak. It suddenly looked as long as a football field. No, she wasn't ready. She wanted to lie right where she was behind her nice, solid boulder, until some better plan suggested itself.

"Ready," she said. "Nadia?"

"This is suicide!" Jesse objected.

"So is staying where we are," Nadia pointed out, her trembling chin steadying at the prospect of action.

"Right," Kermit agreed. "You three are going to have to get the kayak off the beach and into the water. I'll cover you."

"No way," Jesse objected. "Why should we go out there to get shot at while you stay safely here behind your rock?"

Serena didn't know if Jesse was aware enough to be scared or if he just didn't like the fact that someone else was daring to take control of the situation. Either way, he was getting on her nerves.

"With Kermit covering us, there's less chance of us getting shot," she said. "Unless *he* decides to shoot you, which I would personally consider justifiable homicide."

"He's got the longest, youngest legs," Jesse said, his tone scolding her for not seeing the obvious. "He's best suited to getting the kayak. Why should he get to stay back covering us?"

"Because I'm the one with the loaded gun," Kermit pointed out calmly. "And I'm not about to give it to you. On three. One—"

A puff of sand erupted by Serena's knee, the following report cutting off Jesse's next objection. Sound cracked around them. The gunmen had found their vantage point.

"Three!" Kermit roared, lunging to his feet to fire back.

Precious seconds sped by as Serena scrambled up and whirled to throw herself down the beach toward the kayak. Pain stung her temple, though she thought a rock chip had struck her, rather than a bullet.

Her breath sobbed from her with adrenaline and fear as she reached the inflatable boat. She grabbed the bow and hauled at it, stumbling backward toward the river.

Jesse had followed, after all, and grabbed the other end of the craft, shoving her along as she splashed into the frigid water. The shallows near the shore stretched only a few feet before plunging her waist-deep into a dark green pool.

"Hurry up!" Jesse was shouting at Nadia. She'd had the presence of mind to grab the craft's paddles off the beach, and she tossed them into the kayak before trying to climb in.

Serena struggled to hold the narrow craft steady as Jesse helped Nadia into the middle of the kayak. He still stood in the shallows, so he had an easier time climbing into the back.

"Get in! Come on, Serena!" Kermit had splashed into the water, too, though he still faced the cliff across the boulder field with his gun.

Serena knew his aim had to be even worse than their attackers', since he was firing uphill into tree cover, but maybe the gunmen hadn't figured that out, yet, because their shots continued to hit wide of their targets.

"You're holding us up!" Jesse shouted. He'd grabbed a paddle out of the boat, and dipped it over the side as if to shove off, but Kermit grabbed the kayak and swung it toward the beach, pulling Serena back into shallow water.

She heaved herself into the bow, managing to wrangle herself onto her knees in the narrow front space.

"Give me a paddle!"

Nadia swung the paddle up to her with enough force to nearly capsize them all, but Kermit held them upright by sheer force of will.

"Your turn," Serena told Kermit, jamming the paddle into the sand to hold the boat steady.

"There's not room," Jesse objected.

"Make room or get out," Serena spat back, the full force of her fury and her fear for Kermit snapping her head around to freeze Jesse in his place. "I don't care which."

"I'm pushing you out," Kermit said, his illustrative shove knocking her paddle free of the sand, though it caught enough to spin the kayak stern first. "I'll climb over the side when we hit the current."

"Kermit, that's not—"

A sputting noise turned her attention toward the kayak. A dime-sized hole started hissing air, inches from her knees.

"Stay down!" Kermit shouted, somewhat redundantly, as they all cringed downward at the hiss of bullets striking the water around them.

Serena felt the current snag the stern of the boat, abruptly spinning her upriver, jerking the kayak from Kermit's grasp.

"Come on," she shouted. "We're moving. Get in."

He lunged forward through the thigh-deep water, then stumbled, plunging headlong underwater. Serena knew the rocky bottom was treacherous, but this really wasn't a good time for Kermit's clumsiness to start up again—

He broke the surface, gasping, his face twisted in a grimace of pain. He pushed to his feet, but through the distortion of the swirling water, she could see his left hand grabbing at his lower thigh.

"You're hit!" Her paddle hit the water before she could even think, her arms straining as she dug into the water, but she couldn't prevail over the current.

She couldn't see blood in that dark water. That could only be her imagination. But Kermit's stumbling, slipping scramble forward was not.

She dug into the water again, with the strength of desperation, but the kayak only slipped farther downstream, farther from Kermit's reach.

Chapter 18

Serena redoubled her paddling, slowing the kayak's drift downstream, but not enough for Kermit to reach them.

"Use your paddle, Jesse. Help me." But when she shot a glance over her shoulder, all she could see of Jesse and Nadia were their shoulders, hunched down with their heads between their knees.

"Go on." Kermit stumbled to a halt, waving her on. "I'll catch up with you."

Trying to swim with a bullet hole in his leg, wearing water-soaked jeans and running shoes?

"Bullshit." She leaned forward against the bow of the kayak, shooting the paddle out in front. It almost reached his chest. "Grab on."

She saw the flicker of indecision in his eyes, gauging whether or not he might capsize them or pull her out of the boat if he took it. "Damn it, Riggs. No white knights. You're my backup, remember? Grab on, or I'm jumping out."

He met her gaze, and whatever he saw there turned his expression dark with exasperation, but he plunged forward, swinging out two long arms. His hands closed around the paddle.

The impact nearly unseated her, despite the assistance of his forward momentum, but her knees were lodged tightly enough into the front of the boat to keep her from flying over the bow.

She leaned back, hauling him forward until he could drop the paddle with one hand and grab on to the side of the boat. It sagged downward, nearly dipping the edge below water level.

"I'm too heavy," Kermit said, but Serena grabbed his wrist before he could let go.

"There's a bullet hole in that panel," she shouted, against his determination to sacrifice himself as much as against the gathering roar of the river. "Pull yourself down to the middle. It's sturdier there."

She hauled on him, helping him work past her and heave one arm over the side. He shook his head, gesturing forward with that hand. "We've got to turn the kayak around."

Serena glanced downstream, and her stomach lurched. It wasn't so much the spray flying off the boulders stacked against the cliff ahead to their left or the building noise of the river, like a train bearing down on them. It wasn't even the rocks poking up out of the water like the stubby teeth of a very old monster. Or maybe it was.

But what sent a sickening shot of fear through her gut were the rocks she couldn't see, the ones twisting the water into ropes of suction. If they capsized and got sucked into one of those pockets of tumbling death, if Kermit's legs slipped down and got trapped under one of those submerged rocks . . .

"Climb across the boat," she ordered, trying to stay low as she struggled to turn around.

"We have to turn it—"

"There's no time!"

The current had them now, beyond hope of escaping, and they were already shooting into the channel in the center of the river as it began its curve around the narrow bend. They had only a matter of moments before the river threw them against the opposite bank.

"Turn around!" she shouted, as Kermit nudged Nadia and Jesse. "Use your paddle, Jesse. We've got to stay off the rocks."

She dug into the current with her own paddle. Trying to transfer her Girl Scout camp knowledge of lake canoeing into steering an overloaded, bullet-riddled kayak through what was starting to look like Niagara Falls was sort of like trying to fly the space shuttle after taking high school driver's ed, but Jesse flung himself into paddling, too. He still faced Serena, with his back to their forward progress, but together they managed to pull the recalcitrant craft away from the rocks and back toward the center of the river.

Meanwhile, Nadia helped Kermit drag himself into the kayak. His feet still trailed over into the water, but at least his rear end was inside. The added weight brought the kayak's inflated sides almost down to the waterline, and several inches of water sloshed inside the craft.

"Turn around," she shouted to Jesse again. Then changed her mind. "Just paddle right, paddle right!"

For once, he simply did as he was told. Serena felt a thud as the kayak bumped against a low, black rock hulking in the fastest part of the current, but they'd reacted quickly enough that it was only a glancing blow. The kayak's rubberized hull growled as it scraped past, and the treacherous current tilted them precariously, but the fabric held and they managed to stay upright.

Jesse twisted himself around so he was finally facing forward. He used his paddle to push them away from another rock, and Serena had enough time to steer them past the next one.

"We're getting the hang of this!" Jesse shouted, as they

plunged into a narrow chute of fast water.

Don't jinx it!

Serena heard screams, her own included, as the kayak bucked and jumped forward, but Nadia cheered as they came through still afloat.

"Just like a roller coaster ride," Kermit said, grimacing as his feet knocked against a passing rock.

"A roller coaster ride in hell," Serena shot back.

He actually grinned at her, his blue eyes flashing. "Where's your sense of adventure?"

"Somebody shot it."

But the shooting had stopped, she had to admit. Glancing back, she saw they had come well around the bend from the beach, and they continued to rush downstream at a good pace.

Downstream to *where* became the obvious question. The previous summer, Roger, his two grown sons, Sarah, and Gemma had ridden inner-tubes from Roger's cabin all the way to Willow Creek, but it had taken them most of the day. Admittedly, it had been August when the river was low, and the kayak moved faster than an inner-tube, but despite Kermit's Ernest Shackleton–attitude and the pressure he was applying to his leg, she could see blood around his fingers.

They didn't have four or five hours to reach the hospital in Willow Creek, even if they could count on Bart Alexander's thugs being too stupid to find some convenient spot downstream from which to take potshots at them as they drifted by.

"We need to find a place to pull out," she shouted.

"Yeah, well not here." Jesse waved his paddle up at the cliffs pressing in on both sides. He had a point.

"There's a good place down at Hawkins Bar," Kermit

said. "We used to pull out there all the time when I was a kid. Or sometimes we'd put in there and go on down to the South Fork or Willow Creek. We can call the sheriff's department from the store up on the highway."

"What about Bart's gunmen?" Nadia asked, reaching the same problem Serena had. "Won't they wait for us there?"

Kermit shook his head. "I can't think of a public place for them to reach the river before Hawkins Bar. And they don't know the area. Hawkins Bar isn't exactly obvious."

"They found Roger's cabin," Serena reminded him. And how had they done that, anyway? She and Kermit had both kept watch when they left Hope Point that morning to be sure they weren't being followed, and they hadn't told anyone where they were going . . .

"How far is it to Hawkins Bar?" Nadia asked, cupping her hands to splash water out of the bottom of the boat. "I think we're sinking."

It had just been that kind of day.

"Can we quit the gab fest?" Jesse called back. "There's more whitewater ahead."

"What a surprise." Serena dipped her paddle back into the water.

Kermit leaned forward to peer around Jesse's back. "I'd forgotten about this section, but as I remember, it's not too bad. Not like the rapids we just went through. You just need to keep to the left."

"The left," Serena repeated, shifting her paddle.

"No!" Jesse shook his head. "Not left. There's a clear route to the right."

"Are you sure?" Kermit tried to hitch himself up, but they were riding too low for him to get a good view. "I remember lots of rocks on that side."

"No, it's clear enough. And it will keep us close to the

right bank in case the gunmen find a road that will take them to the cliff edge. They won't be able to see us."

Serena hoped Jesse had a better view than she did. It all looked much the same to her—impassable. And then they were shooting past a huge rock on their left and committed to the right-hand route. An impact jarred the kayak from the front, and another from the side. Serena saw Kermit bounce and felt a rock scrape by beneath her. Her paddle struck another boulder to her right.

"I thought I remembered rocks!" Kermit called back, bouncing again. "But the water's running high enough to get us through."

Almost.

Serena felt the jarring as the kayak struck yet another rock ahead of them. Jesse shoved at it with his paddle, but the craft's momentum had grounded its front end. The rear end wasn't similarly encumbered. Serena paddled furiously as the kayak began swinging sideways, but the current was much too strong.

They would spin off the rock, she saw. They'd be facing backwards once more, but there was smoother water ahead. They could turn themselves again . . .

Except the boat didn't spin completely. The front end pulled off the rock just as the kayak became perpendicular to the current. And then the craft's center, right beneath Kermit, struck another submerged rock.

The weight of the river behind them suddenly transformed into a lever. The kayak flipped, heaving them all forward into the churning water.

For a moment Serena couldn't think, couldn't hear, couldn't understand what had happened. Then her hip slammed into a rock and the air burst from her lungs.

Breathe. But as the water tumbled her forward, she couldn't tell which direction led up. Her shoulder banged another rock. Her feet struck one. Another. Another.

That was down. She pushed up, and her head broke water. She gulped air, but the rocks still battered her. There was the kayak up ahead, empty and upside down. Jesse was swimming toward it . . . swimming?

They'd finally struck smooth water. She could kick her legs without breaking them on the rocks.

"There's a beach! Swim toward the beach!"

Serena spun around at the sound of Nadia's voice. The woman was splashing toward the right bank where a rockslide had left a steep, dry patch of land.

Jesse, Nadia . . . where was Kermit? Serena spun in the water, her sneakers and jeans dragging her down, her hair, come loose from its ponytail, plastering across her face. From the river's surface, the rapids looked impassable, a huge, churning cauldron of violent water. She felt like she'd been tumbled through a washing machine.

But she'd been lucky. She could have been trapped under one of those standing waves of water, crushed to the bottom of the river, unable to fight her way to the top . . .

She flung herself back toward the rapids. But she was no match for the current. It thrust her back with ease. She would have to strike for shore. Climb along the rocks, try to work her way back toward that maelstrom. Precious time lost. She'd never get back in time, but she had to try—

The water broke in front of her. Kermit threw his head up out of the water, gasping for air.

"Kermit!"

He spat out a mouthful of water. "So much for the roller coaster ride."

"Can you make it to shore?" She was still frog-kicking in

that direction, but the current was so fast, she wasn't sure they could reach it before they were swept past Nadia's beach.

Kermit's head rose farther, then his shoulders. He reached out and grabbed her arm.

"I think I can make it," he said, half laughing, half choking. "I can stand up here."

Serena's feet banged against the uneven rocks as she tried to get her footing. If she slipped, it would be another ten yards before she would find bottom again, but she could stand, too.

With Kermit holding tight to her arm, they slogged toward the shore. Jesse reached it at the same time they did, and they all three dragged themselves over the rocks to the triangle of willow-shaded dirt and weeds where Nadia waited for them.

"I caught one of the paddles as it floated by," she said, holding it up in illustration.

Jesse shook his head. "I couldn't drag the kayak back. The current was too strong."

Serena glanced at the river, but the broad, green expanse showed no sign of their silver savior. Though the noise of the rapids upstream still thundered in her ears, the water looked almost tranquil here. The cliffs had eased apart and even gentled, sloping enough to allow shrubs and small trees to grow up their sides.

"A lovely spot for a picnic," Kermit observed.

"If we had a picnic," Nadia said glumly. "And a blanket and some sunscreen."

"I could use a roast beef sandwich right about now," Jesse agreed.

"An Italian sub from the Spicy Sicilian," Kermit corrected. "And a thirty-two-ounce root beer."

"Make that a real beer," Jesse suggested, "and you've got a deal."

"What we need is a first aid kit and a blood supply," Serena snapped. Her own stomach felt liquid with adrenaline, as unreliable as her shaky legs, but she managed a stern look at Kermit. "Take those jeans off, Riggs."

He grinned at her. "Anything you say, Davis."

"It would serve you right if I let you bleed to death."

"Probably." But his grimace as he leaned toward his feet stifled her reply.

Serena helped him wrestle off his waterlogged Sauconys and pulled the soaked denim down over his feet as he stripped off his jeans.

Navy blue Jockeys. A good choice for his athletic build. But it was the hole in his leg that got her full attention. As she feared, the water had kept it from clotting, though the water's frigid temperature had slowed the bleeding to a sluggish ooze.

"It went clean through," Kermit said, though he'd turned eerily pale at the sight. "I guess it didn't hit a major artery."

"You're the first aid guru," Serena said. "But I think the first order of business is to stop the bleeding."

"Elevate it. Apply pressure with a sterile, dry cloth."

"Right."

"Well, I've got cloth, anyway, even if it isn't dry." Kermit shrugged out of his denim jacket and t-shirt.

As she wrung out the t-shirt, Serena noted, in a purely clinical way, that though Kermit didn't have Jesse's tan, he obviously spent more time at the gym. And she couldn't help noticing that Nadia noticed, too.

By the time she got Kermit lying on his back with his leg propped on a rock, the t-shirt wrapped tightly around his wound, the bleeding seemed to have nearly stopped. But he still looked pale.

She glanced up the cliff sloping above them. It was steep, but just twenty feet above them was a strong copse of manzanita, and the entire top portion of the slope sported scrub brush. She thought it might just be possible to climb to the top. If one didn't have a bullet hole in one's leg.

Kermit dug through his sopping jeans and pulled out his cell phone. Serena figured the water pouring from it wasn't a good sign even before he shook his head.

"Dead."

"We're going to have to climb up and go for help, then," she said.

Nadia glanced up with a start. "Bart's men could be up there!"

"We'll have to take that risk. We can't stay here forever."

"The other side is a better bet for a climb," Jesse said, pointing across the river. "It looks like there might even be a trail."

"Maybe a deer trail," Serena said doubtfully. But Jesse was right. There was definitely a zigzag pattern through the scrub and up into the trees.

"Two-ninety-nine is just at the top of that cliff," Jesse said. "All we need to do is climb up there and flag down help."

As if to underscore his point, Serena saw a flash of silver through the trees, just above the cliff and below the hump of mountain beyond. A car passing on the highway.

"Do you think we can swim across in that current?" Kermit asked, hitching up on his elbows to take a look.

"No!" Serena was glad to hear Nadia and Jesse immediately echoing her objection. "You're not swimming anywhere, Riggs."

"I'll go," Jesse said.

"Not without me," Nadia said, glancing up behind them again. "I'm not waiting here for Bart to hunt me down like an animal."

"You go, too," Kermit said to Serena. "I'll be all right until you can bring back the cavalry."

Serena refused to dignify that with a response. "Just hurry," she said to Jesse. "This is your big chance to be a hero."

"What about Bart's men?" Nadia repeated. "This police officer is the one with the gun."

"Good point." Jesse gestured at Kermit's jacket where it was pillowing Kermit's head. "Let us take your gun. We're the ones who will be putting ourselves in danger."

Kermit snorted. "Won't do you much good. It's been swimming."

Jesse sighed. "We'll just have to be careful who we flag down, then. Ready for another swim, Nadia?"

It raised Serena's opinion of the woman that she was, indeed, ready. Looking at that expanse of green water, knowing the brutal power that lurked below, Serena wasn't sure she would have been so eager, even with a pair of gunmen on her trail.

The current caught Jesse and Nadia with chilling force as they struck out from shore. But angling downstream, they didn't have to fight the river's strength as they crossed. They dragged themselves from the water twenty feet downstream from the little deer track, but there was just enough of a bank for them to make their way back to it.

Nadia turned and waved as they began their climb, but once they hiked up into the trees, they were lost from view.

"I thought I'd be glad to get rid of them," Serena said, sitting down beside Kermit and drawing her knees up to her chest.

271

"Shared danger creates bonding?"

Her laughter surprised her. "Not hardly."

She reached out to touch the bandage around his leg. A pink stain marked the area near the bullet hole, but at least no blood ran down his thigh.

"It's just that I can't get you out of this by myself." She looked up at the sky, where the sun blazed overhead. "I'm so sorry for getting you into it."

"I recall volunteering."

She forced herself to look down to meet his gaze. "Just hang in there, all right?"

"I'm hanging."

"I can get you some water."

He grimaced. "Maybe if we get desperate. I'm not too excited about contracting giardia."

She made a face at him. "I'll be happy if we live long enough to have to worry about that."

He shifted up on one elbow to pull her hand from her knee. "Stop worrying, period. At the rate things are going, I'm more likely to die from sunburn than blood loss. The bad guys have no idea where we are. And Jesse and Nadia will be back with help in no time."

"Unless they get shot," Serena corrected.

"Or hit by a car."

"Or struck on the head by falling rock, causing them to suffer from amnesia." She shared a wry grin with him. "All right. I'll quit worrying. But I'd feel better if I could be doing something to make you more comfortable. How do you feel?"

"The truth?"

She nodded.

"My leg feels like somebody stuck a hot poker through it. And that water was pretty damn cold."

His hand was pretty cool in hers, come to think of it. She reached out to touch his forehead.

"Okay." She sucked in a calming breath. "I said I wasn't going to worry, so I'm not going to think about the fact that you could be going into shock from blood loss. I'm just going to try to keep you warm."

She shifted his arm out of the way and stretched out alongside him, laying her head on his shoulder, draping her arm across his chest.

"That ought to do it," he teased, but there was nothing teasing in the way he wrapped his arm around her, holding her close as she and the sun tried to pour heat back into his body.

Maybe she couldn't help noticing the way his sandy blond hair curled on his chest or the power in the muscles beneath her hand. Or the reassuring strength in his heartbeat as her own thudded through her.

But what she noticed most was how right it felt to be holding him so close. Not awkward at all. And although she had intended this to help him, she was the one who felt reassured and protected, held tight in his arms.

"I'm afraid," she admitted. "That bastard's frightened me. If anything ever happened to Sarah . . ."

"Shh." He shook her shoulder. "Pleasance can hold her own. And Garth will be checking in on them."

"But if we don't get back in time for Bart's call—"

"I don't think he needs your help in locating Jesse anymore," Kermit pointed out. "There's no reason for him to hurt Sarah."

"I don't think a monster like that needs a reason."

"He's going to have other things on his mind after this morning," Kermit said, speaking into her hair. "But even so, we'll be back if he decides to call. It will take a while for

Jesse and Nadia to hitchhike to Willow Creek. And it might take some time for the sheriff's department to figure out how to reach us. But they'll be here. Probably an hour. Two at the most. We'll be back in Hope Point before dark."

Of course they would. Serena glanced up at the sky. Just past noon. Logic said they would be back in Hope Point in time to share Pleasance's afternoon tea. She only wished logic were any more reliable than psychic predictions.

Chapter 19

Elongated cedar shadows streaked across the lawn in front of Mrs. Geary's house. The sky still stretched a clear blue toward the hills to the east, while thin white clouds streaked above the ocean in the west. A beautiful afternoon, shading toward a beautiful evening.

Sarah bit her lip against the fear that threatened every time she glanced toward the sun, slinking toward the sea behind the trees.

"C'mon, Sarah." Gemma came up beside her at the front windows. "Grandma made strawberry pie for dessert."

"They should be home by now."

"They'll be here. Waiting by the window won't make them come any faster."

"I'll *see* them faster," Sarah grumbled, but she backed away from the window. As she turned, movement on the drive caught her eye. For a second, she thought her wishing and her tattered prayers had brought her mom and Kermit home, after all. But the car turning up to the old farmhouse through the cedars resolved into a black Mustang with a bent right fender.

Not Kermit's car at all.

"Serena, it's too dangerous. Those men could still be around."

Serena shook her head, studying the steep cliff ahead of her. "I have to go now, to make sure I have time to get

275

back before it gets dark."

"Wait until morning. We'll be all right."

Serena glanced at where Kermit sat with his back propped against a rock. If she didn't look too closely, she could almost believe him. Getting back into his jeans had started his wound bleeding again, but only briefly. The jeans hid the bloodied t-shirt bandage, and his jacket hid most of the goosebumps from the breeze that had been sweeping down the river all afternoon.

The angle of the riverbank had cloaked them with shade for hours, which had protected them from serious sunburn but had sucked most of the ambient warmth from the rocks. The air temperature remained mild, but Serena knew it would drop uncomfortably overnight. Kermit's blood loss had to make him more susceptible to hypothermia. Not to mention that they were both suffering from hunger and dehydration.

To make it through the night, they needed rescue. Or at least blankets, water, food, and clean bandages.

And she was beginning to doubt that Nadia and Jesse would be returning with any of those items.

"Bart's men are almost certainly still searching for us. He's not the type to leave loose ends," Kermit warned. "If they caught up with Jesse and Nadia—"

"Then Jesse and Nadia obviously didn't tell them where we were, or they'd have found us by now. Maybe they told them we drowned." Serena tried to believe that. It meant Jesse and Nadia might still be alive. As opposed to the more likely scenario that the gunmen had simply killed them before they were able to talk.

"Don't worry," she said. "If there's anybody anywhere near the cabin, I won't wander over for a chat."

Kermit's lips thinned, but he didn't repeat the objections

he'd been making for the past half hour. Instead, he reached into his jacket pocket.

"If someone decides to initiate a conversation anyway, you might as well have something to answer back with." He checked the magazine of the gun in his hand and held it out toward her, butt first.

"But your gun . . ." Maybe his condition had deteriorated further than she thought. Maybe shock was affecting his cognitive processes. Or the wound might have started a fever. "Kermit, that won't do me any good. It got soaked."

Kermit shook his head, lifting the gun toward her until she took it. "It's a Glock. You can fire the police models underwater if you have to."

Serena frowned down at the gun, deadly looking and heavy in her hand. "But you told Jesse—"

"It was easier than fighting with him about it. I'm a police officer. I can't give a civilian my gun." His voice sounded as grim as his expression. "And I was sure he wouldn't need it. So damn sure."

Serena dropped to a crouch beside him. "It wouldn't have done him any good if he had taken it. You saw him with his gun on the beach."

The twist to Kermit's mouth held no humor. "That's not going to make me feel any better if he's dead." He shook his head to ward off her protest. "Forget I said that. They're probably just having a hard time hitching a ride."

Serena remembered Nadia's soaking wet, skintight dress. She knew Kermit didn't believe Nadia would have trouble hitching a ride any more than she did.

"Here." Kermit gestured toward the gun. "Let me show you how to use that thing. Hold it with your finger on the trigger. Yeah, like that. Steady it with your other hand.

Then all you have to do is pull the trigger."

"No safety?"

"It's just an extra tug on the trigger."

Serena jerked her finger away from the trigger, nearly dropping the gun. "Okay. Simple. Simple is good. Except when you might accidentally kill someone."

"You won't fire it by accident," Kermit promised. His brief grin held warmth this time. "I'm counting on you not having to fire it at all. It's still a police officer's gun."

"If anyone asks, I wrestled it from you while you were delirious from blood loss," Serena promised. She stuck the gun through her belt, where it jabbed awkwardly into her waist. "If this thing goes off and shoots me in the butt, I'm not going to be happy."

"Serena." Kermit's eyes held hers. "Be careful."

"Count on it." She didn't have any choice. If she didn't make it back, no one would know where Kermit was. He would die. She had no intention of letting that happen.

He'd saved her life, along with Jesse's and Nadia's that afternoon. It was time for her to return the favor.

"Grandma!" Gemma shouted, her voice high and reedy with tension. "Somebody's here."

"It's okay," Sarah called in reply, before Mrs. Geary could come running with her shotgun. "I recognize the car. It's Officer Vance."

But she waited until she saw Officer Vance actually get out of the Mustang, his reflective sunglasses glinting gold in the sunlight, before she opened the front door and ran out onto the porch.

"Have you heard from Mom and Kermit?" she demanded as he climbed the porch steps.

"Not yet." He paused on the porch to take a long look

around the property. "Everything okay here? You haven't seen any suspicious characters?"

"No," Sarah said, biting back her first answer: *Besides you?* Off duty, in his leather jacket and tight black jeans, Officer Vance looked more like a redneck biker than a cop.

"I haven't heard from them, either," Sarah told him. "I haven't been able to reach Kermit on his cell phone all day. They should have been back by now—"

"Maybe you should let Officer Vance catch his breath a minute before you dump the weight of the world on his shoulders." Mrs. Geary's voice came from the front door. The soft porch shadows turned the warm light of the hallway into a welcoming halo around her. "Why don't you come on inside, Garth? I've got some strawberry pie on the table and some decaf brewing."

"But—" Sarah hardly knew where to start as she followed Officer Vance into the house. "But Mom and Kermit! They should have been back hours ago. They must be in trouble."

Officer Vance glanced over his shoulder at her. "Kermit said the plan was to find Jesse and convince him to come back to Hope Point. They'd have come right back home if they hadn't found him, so they must just be having trouble convincing him."

Sarah glanced at her watch, as though she might have been reading it wrong for the past three hours. "It's past six o'clock. They've been gone since before nine!"

"It sounds like Jesse found himself some pretty big trouble." Officer Vance took the seat Mrs. Geary offered him at the big kitchen table. "That's beautiful pie."

Gemma slipped into one of the seats across from Officer Vance and Sarah plunked down next to her, though she knew she wouldn't be able to touch the piece of pie Mrs.

Geary placed in front of her. Fleur flopped down beside her with a sigh. At least the Lab looked properly worried.

"Bart Alexander said Mom only had until tonight to find out where Jesse was," Sarah said. She didn't remind Officer Vance of the part where Sarah was supposed to be the one who got hurt. She didn't want him to think she was only worried because she was scared. She *was* scared, but it was just for her mom and Kermit. Well, mostly. "Mom would make sure they were back before he had a chance to call her."

"I doubt they're too worried about this Alexander guy, Sarah. They know he doesn't have a clue where you are." Officer Vance's voice held that condescending adult sympathy that was designed to shut kids up. "Plus, Kermit arranged for me to be here this evening, if they didn't get back in time for him to keep an eye on you himself."

"That was for an emergency," Sarah said, exasperated. "So, if you're here, that means there *was* an emergency. They must be in trouble. We need to go look for them."

Officer Vance frowned around his mouthful of pie. "Look where?"

"Up at Roger's cabin." Sarah bounced up, unable to remain still with the worry vibrating through her nerves. "We could at least drive up and see if they're there. We should leave right away. The road's pretty bad. We need to get there while the light's still good."

"Sarah Davis." Mrs. Geary's voice could be as steely as her hair, even when she didn't raise it. "You told Agent Johnson this morning that you'd never been up to that cabin. You lied?"

"Um." There really wasn't a good answer to that. But surely Mrs. Geary had to see that grounding Sarah for life could wait until after they found her mom and Kermit. "Yes, ma'am."

Then again, based on her expression, maybe Mrs. Geary was beginning to think that allowing Bart Alexander to kill Sarah would solve all their problems.

"They've still got some time to get back before sunset," Officer Vance said, dismissing her concern.

"But once the sun sets, it will be too late to go look for them."

From the corner of her eye, Sarah saw Mrs. Geary lift a sturdy knife from the table and gesture at Officer Vance. Sarah winced when he nodded, but Mrs. Geary only dug back into the pie to cut him another slice.

"If we left right now, we'd probably pass them on the highway," Officer Vance said. "Your mom would go ballistic when she got here and found you gone. And when we got back, she'd slice me into little pieces for letting you talk me into going out looking for her in the first place."

Sarah could picture the scene perfectly. But it still looked better than sitting in Mrs. Geary's kitchen doing nothing while the light outside slanted ever more steeply toward the west.

"Sarah." Officer Vance finally removed his sunglasses, and his hazel eyes held hers with a steady confidence. "Kermit Riggs is more than a match for that Banos character. He might be a klutz off duty, but I've seen him in action. I'd want him watching my back any day."

Sarah couldn't argue with that. She'd seen Kermit in action, too. Even without loyalty factored in, she figured he could take Jesse in an even fight.

"Don't worry," Officer Vance said again. "They'll be fine."

"They will," Gemma added in agreement, pushing Sarah's pie closer to her.

Sarah sat back down in her chair with a huff of air. Sure

281

they would. Of course they would. *If* it was an even fight.

Mrs. Geary's heavy black telephone rang, catapulting Sarah up out of her chair. *Mom.* "I'll get it!"

So, she'd feel stupid for getting so worried. So, Officer Vance would give her that obnoxious told-you-so look that was already forming on his face. So, Mrs. Geary was going to give her a lecture for lying. She didn't care.

She grabbed the telephone receiver. "Hello. Geary residence. May I help you?"

"Sarah, sweetheart, one of the first rules of being in hiding is that you don't answer the telephone yourself." The amused male voice sounded vaguely familiar, but it definitely wasn't Kermit.

"Who is this?"

"I don't think we need to worry about names. Just think of me as an old e-mail buddy."

A chill began at the base of Sarah's back and worked its way up her spine. It couldn't be. He couldn't know where she was.

"Your mother hasn't been home all afternoon. I thought we had a little deal about that information she was supposed to share with me."

"She never made a deal," Sarah said, her voice hard with fear. "We don't give in to threats."

The voice laughed, a sound more terrifying than curses. "I do hope you're wrong, sweetheart. I truly do. I've developed quite a fondness for your mother, and I like that you've inherited her moxie. I bet you'll even grow into a beauty like her in a few years.

"But if she doesn't answer her telephone before sunset, we'll never have a chance to find out."

Chapter 20

Going up the cliff turned out not to be so bad. She could walk most of the way up, using shrubs and small trees for balance. Her thighs ached by the time she reached the top, but she didn't feel as though she'd defied death. Of course, after being shot at and taking the kayak trip from hell, she figured Death had already gotten his chance at her that day.

Then again, she still had to get back *down* the cliff, and the third time could be the charm. But she didn't plan on worrying about that until after she got back from the cabin without being murdered by brutal thugs.

There was something to be said for living a boring life.

She found the road to Roger's cabin without any trouble. It was closer to the cliff's edge here than it was by his place. Though the kayak ride had seemed both recklessly swift and endless, she didn't think they could have traveled more than a mile or two from the cabin. If she kept to a good pace, she should be able to reach it with plenty of time to return before dark.

Given the poor condition of the road, she felt confident she could hear an approaching vehicle and dive into the woods before anyone saw her, so she struck out along it, ignoring her parched throat and the exhaustion in her legs.

Her primary fantasy was that she could drive Kermit's car back to Willow Creek for help, but when she reached the drive to Roger's cabin, she saw immediately that wasn't going to happen.

Bart's men hadn't settled for slashing Kermit's tires. They'd also smashed in the Jensen Healey's windshield and dented the doors. Serena brushed tears of fury from her eyes as she leaned into the mutilated car to retrieve the plastic bag from Willow Creek's grocery store in the passenger's seat well.

Her mineral water, Kermit's soda, a pair of melted candy bars. Kermit had made a crack just that morning about the supplies saving their lives until rescue arrived.

"It's a start."

Her secondary fantasy had been that Roger's neighbor would be home to give her a ride to Willow Creek, but when she backtracked from Kermit's car to follow the other drive to the neighbor's cabin, she found it dark and locked up tight. Serena had to admit that it was probably better that way. If he had heard gunshots that afternoon and come over to Roger's cabin to investigate . . .

Serena shook the thought from her head. With the lack of recent rain, he would have to come over from the coast to water his garden over the weekend. If all else failed, she would climb the cliff again in the morning and return to wait for him.

She considered leaving a note on his door, but the possibility that Bart's men might return and see it was too great.

She returned to Roger's drive and slipped into the woods, following the same path she and Kermit had taken that morning. It seemed like weeks ago.

Peering out into the parking area beside the cabin, she saw that Jesse's car had received the same treatment as Kermit's.

"So much for testing out my hotwiring skills," she muttered to herself. On the upside, there were no other cars in evidence, which meant there were no more bad guys around. Or that the bad guys had left someone behind to lurk in the shadows and wait for their unwary quarry to return for their bathing suits.

It was a risk she was willing to take. She pulled Kermit's Glock from her waistband, and approached the cabin.

Bart's men had kicked in the back door and left it hanging awkwardly from a loose hinge. Serena feared the cabin's interior might have suffered the same fate as the cars, but when she entered, holding her breath to listen for other intruders, she found the destruction limited to Jesse and Nadia's luggage. Clothes lay strewn across the braided rug in the center of the room. Two piles of tiny plastic pieces were scattered around the bricks surrounding the wood stove.

Nadia's and Jesse's cell phones, undoubtedly. There went her third fantasy.

After making sure nothing big and well-armed skulked in the bathroom, Serena entered the kitchen and poured herself a huge glass of water. Two huge glasses of water.

The refrigerator yielded two more bottles of mineral water she could carry back to Kermit, and a block of cheddar cheese. Canned spaghetti and packages of macaroni and cheese weren't much good for a campout on the river, but the pantry also held a treasure trove of ready-to-eat snacks.

Salt, fat, and preservatives had never looked so good. Serena grabbed a bag of corn chips, a container of cheese dip, a package of Oreos, and a box of granola bars. She dug through kitchen drawers until she found a flashlight and some batteries.

She dumped her loot in Jesse's cloth carryall, conveniently emptied by the gunmen. She added Jesse's sweatshirt, dry socks for both her and Kermit, and a fleece blanket she found draped over the sofa bed.

Roger kept the bathroom as well-stocked as the rest of the cabin. The first aid kit held antiseptic cream, sterile gauze pads and tape, and alcohol wipes. In the medicine cabinet, she found a fresh bar of soap and a small bottle of ibuprofen.

She managed to lift the carryall to her shoulder without tilting sideways, but she wasn't going to last the hike back if she took any more.

As she headed back up the drive, she walked in the shadows of the mountains. The sky above was melting toward pewter. The distant rumble of the river and the first chirpings of insects drew a gentle peace over the world.

Serena struggled to unclench her jaw, to stop the panic in her head that wanted to scream against the peace. She couldn't fight the sunset. She couldn't haul Kermit up a cliff. She couldn't walk all the way to Willow Creek by midnight, much less in time to return to Sarah before Bart Alexander's promised call.

And with all that she'd found in the cabin, she still couldn't restore Kermit's lost blood, prevent an infection from setting into his wound, or guarantee that he would even be alive for a rescue by morning.

She could only take one step at a time. And pray. Pray that she hadn't waited too long to fetch water and medicine. Pray that Kermit was as resilient as he was pretending to be.

And pray that finding Jesse, even if his men had lost him again, had taken Bart Alexander's mind off of Sarah.

A sound jerked Kermit awake. A splash. A fish jumping or a rock falling. He'd thought he'd merely closed his eyes, but the shadows had deepened around him, and in the

ribbon of dusky sky far above, he could make out the diamond chip of a star.

The wind had finally died down, and the air was soft and
gentle against his skin, full of the scent of the river and
pierced by the good-night cries of a bird.

It was a beautiful evening.

His leg throbbed. He was thirsty enough that contracting
the *Giardia lambia* parasite was starting to sound like merely
a good way to clean out his intestinal tract. And the slight
dampness remaining in his jacket and jeans settled against
him with a steely chill.

Somehow, he couldn't make himself care. From a clinical point of view, that probably wasn't a good thing. But
every time he tried to get worked up about getting shot and
almost drowned and being trapped on a tiny strip of land
between a rock and a watery place, all he could think about
was spending the afternoon dozing with Serena's head on
his shoulder.

"Riggs, there is something seriously wrong with your pri-
orities." But the mere memory brought a grin to his face.

Another splash pulled him out of his reverie and up into
a sitting position. The river's roar didn't quite cover a scuf-
fling sound from up above. Someone was climbing down
the cliff.

Kermit grabbed a fist-sized chunk of granite from the
rocks scattered around him and pushed himself up so he
was half-sitting, half-leaning against the boulder behind
him. He imagined the picture he must make and dropped
the rock.

If the intruder wasn't Serena, he was pretty much toast.

She came down through a small thicket of trees twenty
feet above the little beach, a big black bag slung over her
shoulder. The light wasn't good for climbing, but she

scrambled down before he had a chance to worry.

"You shouldn't be up," she scolded as she picked her way across to him, but he didn't think he imagined the relief in her eyes. She dumped the bag on the ground near his feet. "They slashed the cars' tires and smashed Jesse and Nadia's cell phones, so I couldn't get help. But I brought a few things that ought to get us through the night."

"My white knight," he teased.

She looked up from where she had begun to dig through the bag. "I can turn around and climb right back up there, you know. There's a sofa bed in Roger's cabin."

"Is that an invitation?" Lack of concern about his physical well-being was one thing, but he was crossing the line into recklessness. "I could probably crawl that far, come to think of it, with the right incentive."

That earned him a snort of laughter. "You're delirious. Here, put this on."

She tossed him a navy sweatshirt with UC Berkeley printed across the front. A good reminder that her ex-fiancé had a master's degree. That she had graduated with honors in chemistry. And that his own education consisted of a four-year stint in the Army, graduation from the police academy, and an associate's degree from Pacific Coast Community College.

He shrugged out of his denim jacket and into the sweatshirt.

Reminders were good. While he was at it, he should remind himself that she earned more than he did. That she had a house and a car that started every morning. That she deserved the moon, and all he had to offer was a garage apartment with peeling linoleum and a thirty-year-old car. A car that was apparently going to need new tires.

He should remind himself that letting her see the

strength of his feelings for her would only make him look like a pathetic idiot. That admitting, even to himself, how much he loved her would lead to nothing but a broken heart.

Reminders were good.

Except that standing on a deserted beach with a bullet hole in his leg and the reality of nearly losing her lodged in his heart, he couldn't remember why any of those other things mattered.

He needed to distract himself. Ask her about what she had found at the cabin. Come up with a plan to find Bart Alexander when they returned to Hope Point. But at the moment he didn't think anything had the power to distract him from the soft fall of her hair over her shoulders, the beauty in the determined set of her jaw, the spark of humor in her hazel eyes, the—

"Here. Drink this." She handed him the bottle of lemon-lime soda he'd bought in Willow Creek that morning.

That worked.

The soda was even warmer than the air, making the flavor sickly sweet. The carbonation burned his dry throat. It was heavenly.

"More?" he asked.

"Just water." She stood up to offer him a bottle. "But there's chips and Oreos and some granola bars. And ibuprofen. You can have whatever you want."

Maybe his brain was clouded with pain and blood loss and dehydration. But what he wanted suddenly seemed very clear.

He took the bottle of water from her hand and set it down on the boulder beside him. Gently, he caught her waist with his hand. And he pulled her close.

Chapter 21

Mrs. Geary's extended-cab Dodge truck plowed through the crowding manzanita bushes like a bull mammoth. The front tires hit a deep rut, throwing Fleur across Sarah's lap where she sat in the back seat with Gemma.

"Are you sure this is the right road, Sarah?" Mrs. Geary asked as they dropped down another incline.

"Are you sure this is even a road?" Officer Vance grumbled from the passenger seat beside her. He turned to look behind them, though Sarah doubted he could get a good enough view to tell whether or not Deputy Chase, his friend from the Trinity County Sheriff's Department, still followed behind them.

"This is the right road," Sarah insisted, but a tickle of doubt had her clenching her fists in her lap. The road seemed longer than she remembered, and in the gloom of twilight beneath the trees, the landscape didn't look as familiar as it should. It had been almost a year since she'd been up here. She might have had Mrs. Geary turn off the paved road one dirt road too soon—

"There's Kermit's car!" Gemma yelped, pointing to the left as they reached a split in the road.

Sarah leaned around Fleur. Her heart jumped. There was no mistaking Kermit's beat-up Jensen Healey. He and her mom were here, after all.

Officer Vance wouldn't be able to make any more smart remarks about her detective instincts. After Bart Alexander's phone call, Officer Vance had wanted to stay at Mrs. Geary's farmhouse and trust the Hope Point PD to back them up if Alexander tried to besiege them there. But Mrs. Geary had agreed with Sarah that they'd be safer else-where—and as long as they were all getting into the truck, why not head out to Roger Avalos's cabin?

Kermit said that being shot by his own partner the year before had changed Officer Vance's cowboy attitude for the better. But Sarah had thought Officer Vance's calling Deputy Chase on the drive up to Willow Creek was closer to paranoia than caution.

Until Mrs. Geary pulled up behind Kermit's car.

"The windshield's smashed," Mrs. Geary said. "Looks like they hit a deer."

"Looks like they hit a baseball bat," Officer Vance said.

The tension in his voice frightened Sarah more than the sight of the battered car. She climbed out of the truck cab after him.

"Stay, Fleur," she ordered, pushing the Lab's nose back into the truck before shutting the door.

Officer Vance turned to order her back in the truck, but Mrs. Geary and Gemma had already climbed out the other side.

"You all stay back," he commanded instead.

Deputy Chase had parked his old Ford truck behind them. With his blond buzz cut and reflective shades, Deputy Chase looked like Officer Vance's twin brother as they examined the damage to Kermit's car.

"Slashed the tires."

"Dents in the door. Boots, y'think?"

"What a mess."

"No structural damage, though. Put some good tires on it, it'll still run."

No blood. That was the only thing Sarah cared about. The fading light softened colors with blue shadows, but she could see well enough to tell that much. No one had been in the car when the destruction had happened.

"We should check the cabin, see if Mom and Kermit went there," she said.

"In a minute," Officer Vance agreed.

He dropped down on his hands and knees to get a look under the car's chassis, while Deputy Chase walked around the other side, staring at the ground.

Maybe he was looking for footprints or something, but it seemed like a waste of time to Sarah. Somebody had attacked Kermit's car. Kermit or her mom or both could be injured somewhere. Or they could be right up the drive at Roger's cabin, waiting for somebody to come looking for them.

"The cabin is right up the drive—"

"Get back in the car, and wait, all of you," Officer Vance ordered, his voice clipped.

He thinks they might be dead. The knowledge knocked the breath from her.

"Come on, Gemma, Sarah." Mrs. Geary nodded back to the truck. "Let the officers work."

Sarah walked back to the passenger's side of the truck, anger fighting down the curl of fear in her stomach. How dare he think that? Kermit wouldn't let anything happen to her mom. Sarah had been with Kermit when a psychopath had attacked them and Aunt Destiny and Uncle Daniel with a crossbow. Kermit and Uncle Daniel had gotten them all to safety. Whatever had happened at Roger's cabin, he would have done the same for her mom.

Kermit's car made it obvious why they hadn't been able to drive back to Hope Point. And neither Roger's cabin nor the neighbor's had a telephone line. So, they were probably perfectly all right, but they just couldn't go for help.

Or they might be hurt, battered and bruised like the car. They might need immediate medical attention. And all Officer Vance and Deputy Chase seemed able to think about was whether or not Kermit's carburetor was still in one piece.

Sarah jerked open the truck door, and Fleur lunged out, legs scrambling as she took the long drop to the ground.

"Fleur!"

Tail waving madly, the Lab dodged just out of Sarah's reach and trotted around the front of the truck, snuffling excitedly at the weeds alongside the drive. Her ears pricked, and she turned her head down the drive.

The river. She heard the river, and smelled it, too, undoubtedly. Fleur could smell a rotting salamander a hundred feet off a park trail. She could pick the one stick Sarah had touched out of a pile of brush. But water was her passion. Fleur could smell a mud puddle from a mile away, and once she smelled water, the only thought in her brain was getting to it for a swim. Or a good roll, in the case of the puddle.

"No, Fleur," Sarah hissed at her. "Back to the truck. Hop in."

Officer Vance would kill her if Fleur took off for the river. Down the drive. Past the cabin.

She moved toward Fleur. Fleur skittered sideways, then bounced forward a few feet. Sarah stepped forward again. Fleur danced ahead of her, glancing back at Sarah with her tongue stuck out in a grin, eager for Sarah to be enjoying this game.

Sarah grinned back at her. Officer Vance might have had a good point about taking backup. If anyone but her mom and Kermit waited for them at the cabin, Fleur was at least as good protection as Deputy Chase.

"Sarah!"

She grimaced, turning to see Officer Vance striding toward her.

"I told you to get back in the truck."

"Fleur jumped out," she said, pointing at the dog, whose forehead was wrinkling anxiously at Officer Vance's angry tone. "I was just trying to catch her."

"Leave the dog, and get in the truck," Officer Vance snapped, pointing back the way she had come. He sighed, and his voice lost some of its harshness. "Deputy Chase and I are going to check out the cabin. I need you to wait for us here."

Sarah nodded. They were doing something. That was all she'd wanted. But she couldn't say anything, because something like tears suddenly clogged her throat.

She patted her thigh, and stepped back toward the truck. Patted her thigh, took a step. Fleur's ears drooped with disappointment, but as Officer Vance and Deputy Chase marched down the road, she ducked past them and returned toward Sarah.

Sarah slogged back to the truck, where Gemma waited with her head stuck out the passenger window. "They'll find your mom and Kermit. Don't worry."

"I know." Sarah didn't care if her voice sounded sharp. She didn't want any sympathy. She didn't need any sympathy. Only people who were going to get bad news needed sympathy.

Gemma pushed open the truck door for her.

"Okay, Fleur. Hop in. Fleur?"

"She's over by Kermit's car," Mrs. Geary called from her vantage point in the driver's seat.

Sarah dodged back around the front of the truck. Fleur stood by the side door of Kermit's car, her legs stiff, the hair on her back prickling with tension. Sarah's spine prickled, too.

"Fleur, come. Get away from there."

Fleur ignored her, stepping forward, her nose stuck out as rigidly as her tail, sniffing the air.

"Fleur, you're going to cut your feet on the glass." Sarah crossed the grass toward her.

A low growl rumbled from Fleur's throat as she sniffed at the car's dented doors. Then the dog's head tilted, and she whined, turning her nose into the soft evening breeze.

Slowly, her tail began to move again, waving back and forth as she trotted alongside the car back in the direction of the truck. Sarah followed, hurrying after her to grab her collar, but instead of slowing down at the truck, the dog hurried past, dropping her nose to the ground briefly before bounding across the road and burying her head in the weeds on the other side.

"Fleur!"

Sarah ran across the drive after her, but the dog only picked up her pace. She didn't glance back at Sarah, didn't even seem to realize Sarah was behind her, but she trotted just fast enough to stay out of Sarah's reach as she ran back up the rutted drive in the direction they had come.

Sarah heard the Dodge rumble to life behind her. If Mrs. Geary could turn the truck around, she would be able to keep pace with Fleur. Meanwhile, Sarah would keep the dog in her sights, in case Fleur decided to take off after a rabbit into the woods or she found a good place to head down the cliff to the river.

Officer Vance was going to kill her. But only after she killed Fleur. Her eyes burned again. Couldn't Fleur understand that something serious was going on, that this wasn't the time for games?

What if Officer Vance did find her mom and Kermit? What if he needed Sarah for something? What if he and Deputy Chase were in trouble? What if the men who had damaged Kermit's car were waiting in ambush at Roger's cabin?

Or what if they were hiding in the other direction? What if Fleur was leading her right to them?

Danger.

Serena's mind screamed it at her as she moved forward under the direction of Kermit's hand until her knees bumped against his legs. With Kermit half-sitting on his boulder, his gaze met hers straight on, yet she somehow felt as though she were falling into those blue eyes, as sure of drowning as she'd been after capsizing in the kayak that morning.

Self-preservation kicked her back to the surface.

"I'm worried about Sarah." As a diversionary tactic, it had the advantage of being true.

He nodded, solemn, but his hand remained settled on her waist. "I know. I am, too. But Garth won't let anything happen to her."

"I'd feel better if Grace was the one keeping an eye on her."

"Grace was on duty this afternoon." His fingers rubbed the small of her back, doing nothing to settle her suddenly unreliable pulse. "Garth's the best shot in the department. And he doesn't like bullies."

"Garth *is* a bully!"

Kermit laughed, but his eyes didn't shift from hers. "He is not, and you know it. He's just loud."

Obnoxious might be a better choice of words. But the rhythm of Kermit's fingertips against the muscles along her spine made words difficult to reach.

"I need to change the dressing on your leg," she said. She rested her fingertips on the bulge of the ripped t-shirt wrapped beneath his jeans.

"I know." His leg moved aside beneath her touch, and he pulled her between his knees.

"I can only guess how much blood you lost. I'm afraid—"

"I'm not dead yet. That's a pretty good sign."

She could feel the warmth of his hand on her back. The heat of his thighs seared hers, even through their jeans. Apparently she could stop worrying about shock. His blood pressure and temperature seemed high enough. Fever was a possibility, though.

She definitely felt feverish.

The evening breeze brushed softly against her skin, as soft as the brush of Kermit's fingers as he lifted his free hand to touch her cheek. Her senses expanded beneath his touch. The scent of the river filled her lungs, along with the sharp sagey smell of the brush she had climbed through coming down the cliff. Frog song trebled against the bass roar of the water.

But all she could see was the deep, evening blue of Kermit's eyes.

Her voice whispered from her, almost too low for her to hear it herself. "I'm afraid . . ."

Kermit's thumb brushed across her lips, silencing her. "Me, too."

She trembled, and it had nothing to do with the cool waft of the breeze against her bare arms. When his lips followed his thumb, closing gently on her mouth, she thought her knees would give way completely. Until his arms slid around her and pulled her against him, holding her steady.

Holding her as though he had been doing it all his life, as though their bodies had learned a space for each other as they lay together that afternoon, learned to fit together. It felt so right. As right as lying against his side, listening to his heartbeat. As right as breathing.

His mouth tasted of lemon-lime and salt and Kermit. She nibbled for more, parted her lips to taste him with her tongue. His arms tightened around her, crushing her chest to his. His tongue met hers.

And suddenly there was nothing safe about being in his arms. Nothing safe about the fire pouring through her. Nothing safe about the need that had her brushing her hands through his painfully short hair, trying to pull him even closer. Nothing safe about the heat in his hands as he ran them along her back.

And yet it still felt right.

But it was not nearly enough. She dropped her hands down, reaching under the sweatshirt he wore, needing the feel of his warm skin, his hard muscles under her palms. When his hands returned the favor, brushing up under her t-shirt, her gasp was muffled by his own.

She had to stop this now. Before she lost control. As if that hadn't happened already. But she had to try to think, had to try to remember why this was such a very bad idea, when it felt so very good.

She turned her head, pressing her cheek against his, confounded by the feel of his stubble, rough against her skin.

"Kermit." Her voice still worked, even if her brain didn't seem to. "We shouldn't. This isn't . . . I'm thirty-thr—"

"I know how old you are, Serena." One hand left her back to work its way into her hair as he pressed his lips close beside her ear. "If my age bothers you, I understand. But I really couldn't care less."

He should care. Or she should care. And she should tell him why. "Kermit, I—"

"I know you have a daughter. I happen to like her a lot. She's a good kid."

She blinked against his cheek. "That's not what I—"

"And I know you have a house and a decent car, and I don't. I know you have strange friends who think they're psychic and that you think some of my friends are a little red around the neck. I know you're a vegetarian and that I could be dooming myself to tofu turkey for Thanksgiving for all eternity."

Her arms slipped farther around his back as she leaned against him. The trembling had returned. "You're not going to let me get away with 'this is just a natural reaction to almost dying today,' are you?"

"Not a chance."

"That would be so much easier."

"Would it?" He pulled his head back, brushing the hair away from her face.

She shook her head, forcing herself to meet his gaze. "You don't want to get too close. My relationships tend to be disastrous."

Humor pulled at the corner of his mouth. "I'm certainly a disaster. I can't walk through a door without tripping over it. Can't even spend an afternoon at the river without getting shot. And if Lieutenant Marcy finds out I've fallen in love with Daniel Parks's sister-in-law, I'll never get promoted to sergeant."

She stopped breathing. He hadn't just said that.

His hands stilled against her back. "Did I just say that?"

She shook her head.

"Damn moon."

"Moon?"

His scowl was much too cute for her own good. "The full moon tonight. Callista said it was the . . . Well, the full moon always makes people crazy."

The lover's moon. Callista had mentioned it to her, as well.

Serena glanced upward at the wide strip of sky above them. "The moon's not up yet."

His lips found the sensitive skin of her neck, brushed up to her jaw. "I have no excuse then. I'm just crazy."

Her fingers dug into his shoulders as she held on against the heat that swamped her. She must be crazy, too.

"I've got a bad leg," Kermit murmured, his mouth moving at the corner of hers. "You can run if you want."

"No."

He pulled back an inch, so his eyes could meet hers once more. A furrow pulled his brows together. "No, you don't want to? Or no, you can't run? I wouldn't *make* you run, you know. All you have to do is say you want me to let you—"

"Kermit." She frowned back at him. "Shut up and kiss me."

She already knew the shape of his mouth, knew how he tasted, knew the tug of his lips on hers and the flick of his tongue, had it branded on her memory, but she found she still had much to learn about the effect of his kiss on her body, how it melted her muscles away and heated her bones until they felt light and translucent within her.

His hand found her hair again and she pulled on his shoulders, as their mouths moved hungrily together, but it wasn't close enough.

He caressed the small of her back, pulling her closer, until the hardness of his desire pressed against the heat pooling in her gut. She pushed forward, leaning into him—

And suddenly his weight shifted against the boulder behind them, slipping his rear end off the top of the rock. His hand left her hair, flailing for balance, for purchase on the rock. Serena braced herself as she felt his feet slipping out from under them.

For a moment they teetered on the edge of disaster. And then they were balanced again, leaning against the rock, panting as they clung to each other.

"Ow," Kermit said, gingerly lifting his hand from the rock to reach for his thigh.

"Did you jar it?" Serena demanded. She heard the river again, rushing by mere yards away. Saw the deepening shadows. Remembered where they were and why. "Are you all right? Are you bleeding again? Let me see."

But he held her tight against him. "It's fine. Just banged it a little. It will feel better if you kiss me again."

She put her hands against his chest, holding herself back against his gentle pull. "I don't think so, Riggs. That wound isn't a joke. I need to put a real dressing on it."

"Are you going to make me take off my pants again?" He slipped a hand under her shirt and slid it around to press against her belly.

She shivered at the touch, but held firm. "No jokes, remember? You could die." She glared at his grin. "Don't you dare say it."

He shook his head, still grinning irrepressibly. "I'm not ready to die. Life is too interesting with you around."

She would never be able to resist that grin. "What? Don't tell me I'm the first girl who's ever gotten you shot, half-drowned, and stranded in the wilderness?"

"Well . . ." He shrugged. "The only one who's done it all in one day."

"I'm not going to lose you to that bullet, Kermit."

Maybe too much of what she was feeling filled her voice, because even in the dying light, she could see the color brush his cheeks. His mouth twitched. "All right. I'll behave."

But he leaned in for another kiss. And she couldn't resist that, either. Gentler, this time, but no less powerful. Her hands slid up his chest and around his neck, leaning into his strength. She had to let him go. But just one more moment . . .

Like a couple of teenagers in the back seat of a car. Except the emotions tearing through her felt nothing like that. There was no wondering if this was right. If this was the right guy.

No guy had ever felt so right.

Yet what *should* be wrong battered her like the tumbling of the river. She wasn't ready for a new relationship. She'd just broken up with her fiancé. What would Sarah think? There was the age difference. Her disastrous track record with men. She'd sworn off them for good.

And if Lieutenant Marcy finds out I've fallen in love with Daniel Parks's sister-in-law . . .

She was lost. And terrified. And she'd been in love with Kermit for much longer than she had ever allowed herself to know.

She kissed him harder, tears stinging her eyes, before she pulled her mouth away, leaning her forehead against his.

"Kermit, I have to tell you—"

"Shh." He pressed a finger to her lips.

"This is important." And if she thought about it, she wouldn't be able to say it. "I don't know how—"

"Shh." He pressed his finger more insistently against her mouth, his own voice low. "I heard something. Moving in the woods up there."

Serena froze, her heart still pounding so loudly in her ears that she could hear nothing but the river. Just like teenagers, indeed. Panicked at the thought of being caught. But her parents would never have actually killed her.

"Bart's men?" she whispered.

"Maybe." He ran his hand down her back again, but this time it was to ease his Glock from her waistband. "More likely a deer."

"Or a bear." She nodded her head toward his arm. "You don't need a 9mm to fight off a deer."

His chest moved with an amused grunt. "Not the best defense against a bear, either."

Then she heard it, too. A rustling high above on the cliff. Not a rustling. A crashing noise. Something big, making no effort to move quietly.

"They've seen us!" she hissed.

"No. We're nearly in the dark down here. Don't move." He paused. "Animal. I heard it snuffle."

"No," Serena whispered back. "Isn't that a voice?"

Both their heads turned toward the sound, now echoing down the rocks above them and back from the other side of the river. Much too high-pitched for Bart's thugs. A familiar voice. Shouting familiar words.

"No! Stay! Come back here. There's no trail! Come! Fleur! Come!"

Based on the sound of scrambling dog feet skittering down the steep slope through the brush, Serena guessed Fleur wasn't listening.

Chapter 22

The chairs in the Green River Hospital emergency room waiting area had apparently been designed for some species other than *homo sapiens,* because no human form could possibly find them comfortable. But Serena couldn't muster the energy to lift herself out of hers.

The emergency room was quiet for a Friday night. A teenaged boy had come through with a broken finger from slamming his hand in a car door, and a worried couple had brought in a toddler with a fever from an ear infection. But now that Detective Ben Dillon from the Hope Point Police Department—and the small mob of concerned officers who had accompanied him—had left, only Serena, Sarah, Garth Vance, and Grace Martinez remained in the waiting area. The two officers paced like guard dogs on either side of the front door.

"Kermit's going to be fine, Mom."

Sarah had repeated those words at least a dozen times since the ER doctor had told them the same thing. Serena guessed she wasn't doing a great job of hiding her concern. As long as she'd had something to do, she'd been okay. But now she couldn't decide if she was going to sleep for a week or never sleep again. That probably depended on how fast Ben Dillon managed to hunt down Bart Alexander and his thugs.

"We're both going to be fine," she said, mustering enough energy to reach over and pull her daughter's ponytail. "Thanks to you."

"And Fleur."

She wasn't too tired to smile, after all. "And Fleur."

"I can't believe she followed your trail like that," Sarah said, another theme she'd repeated many times in the hours since the Trinity County Sheriff's Department had rescued Serena and Kermit from their little beach. "I thought she was after a squirrel or a deer or something."

"Knowing Fleur, I wouldn't be sur—"

"Mom! She rescued you."

Serena laughed at her daughter's outrage. "Yes, she did. You both did. And Pleasance and Gemma and Garth."

"Fleur's a hero," Sarah muttered, unappeased. "She shouldn't have to wait out in Officer Martinez's car just because she isn't human."

Serena didn't need to be psychic to see that there was going to have to be a dog, other than her sister's dog, in their near future. More than likely a big, hairy, drooly dog. Serena had said for years that Sarah couldn't get a dog until she was old enough to look after it herself.

Glancing at her lanky, pre-teen daughter, she guessed she didn't have that excuse anymore. Besides, Kermit was just as dog-crazy as Sarah, and she didn't have a chance against the two of them togeth—

"Are you okay, Mom?" Sarah's hand touched her arm. "Do you need to see the doctor again?"

She shook her head, though it made the room swoop dizzily. She and Kermit and Sarah all together? She'd seen it so clearly. Like a family.

Crazy.

She could still feel Kermit's lips on hers.

"I know you're worried," Sarah said, squeezing her arm. "But Kermit's going to be fine. And Deputy Chase has the sheriff's search and rescue team out looking for Jesse and Nadia—"

"Jesse." Serena jerked upright in her chair, not a good move for the health of her back. Guilt stabbed through her. She'd had other things on her mind, worrying about keeping Kermit alive, but now she had no excuse for forgetting about Jesse Banos so completely.

She might not know what was going to happen between her and Kermit. But at least they were alive to find out. Jesse and Nadia might not have that luxury.

"They'll find him," Sarah promised, obviously enjoying her role as comforter. "He's too much trouble to die. He'll probably call Mark from a pay phone in Willow Creek about four a.m.—"

"Mark," Serena repeated, the guilt escalating. "No one's even told him that Jesse is missing." She shook her head, trying to drive away the exhaustion. "I mean, he knows Jesse's missing, but that we found him and that he's missing again."

And might be dead or being held as Bart Alexander's hostage.

She pushed herself to her feet. "I'd better go talk to him."

"Mom!" Sarah stood with her. "It's after midnight."

"Still early for Mark." She dug into her jeans pocket for her keys, remembered that she didn't have her car. "His apartment is just a few blocks from here."

"Like a mile," Sarah objected. "You can't walk there at this time of night. And there are lots of weird people living in his building."

"Weirder than Mark?"

"What's wrong?" Garth Vance asked as he and Grace converged on them. "Did you think of something that might help us catch this guy?"

Serena shook her head. "I need to go see Mark Banos, tell him what's happening with his brother. Before . . . whatever."

"You're still in possible danger," Garth objected, but Grace cut him off.

"That's a good idea," she said. Her civilian clothing, a red tank top and blank pants, made her bobbed black hair look chic rather than military, but her words were crisp and efficient. "If anyone's heard from Jesse, it would be his brother."

Garth frowned. "I don't want Serena going out by herself. This perp—"

"Good plan, Garth," Grace agreed. "You drive her over. Sarah and I can wait for the doctors to spring Kermit. If they let him go before you get back, we'll meet you over at Serena's house."

"Serena's house?" Garth asked.

Serena caught the surreptitious, nudging look Grace gave Garth.

"We can't just send him home," Grace prodded. "Somebody's going to have to change his dressing, and it's not going to be me. You volunteering?"

Garth backed up a step, hands in the air. "Oh, no. No way." Then his eyes tracked to Serena, understanding clicked in, and his hands dropped. "Of course, I'd be more than happy to go out and get shot, if I could get a beautiful woman to invite me to stay at her house."

Grace grimaced in disgust. "Get out of here, Vance."

Serena was already heading for the door, too worried about Mark to be embarrassed by their teasing—even if her face did feel suspiciously hot.

Mark idolized Jesse. He wasn't going to take this well.

"Whoa. He just, like, left you there on the riverbank?"

Serena had made Mark sit before she started her story, but now he pushed himself up from the battered futon that served as his couch, energy rolling out the balls of his feet as he moved aimlessly around the cluttered room.

Mark's cramped one-bedroom apartment had a musty odor, probably explained by the damp stains on the ceiling from the bad roof, but Serena had chosen a plain wooden chair to sit on, rather than the lumpy, upholstered chair beside the futon. She would not have been able to move about the room without knocking against an end table or stepping on some kind of stereo equipment—or maybe that was a video game setup. Garth had taken one look at the mess and decided to wait outside.

But Mark's jumpy wanderings didn't so much as crunch the stray potato chips from the bag he'd been demolishing when she and Garth arrived.

"He just *left* you?" Mark asked again.

"He went for help," Serena said. She eyed Mark more closely. He'd been chatting on the phone when he answered the door, and she'd been glad they hadn't woken him. But now she wondered about the phone call, the chips, the nervous energy.

He'd practically jumped out of his skin when he'd seen them on his doorstep, nervously tidying up a pile of papers and envelopes on the coffee table before asking them in—a strange choice given the rest of the mess. She'd put that down to Garth's glowering presence. Mark's previous encounters with the county drug task force Garth worked with hadn't been warm and fuzzy.

But he hadn't reacted to her tale at all as she'd expected. He'd seemed confused from the beginning, and now he blinked frowningly at her as if she weren't quite speaking English.

She could remind herself all she wanted that she wasn't Jesse's fiancée anymore, that Mark was no longer her problem. But it would break her heart if he were back on drugs.

Then again, his strange reaction could simply be shock and denial.

"Jesse and Nadia were going to hitchhike into Willow Creek for help," she repeated. "They risked their lives to help us." That might be exaggerating, but not much. And Mark deserved to think the best of his brother, especially if . . .

She wouldn't finish that thought.

"But he never brought back help."

She shook her head. "If they'd reached the Sheriff's Department, Deputy Chase would have known. They must not have made it to Willow Creek. It's possible they just couldn't get a ride or something . . ."

The Sheriff's Posse, the groups of volunteers that worked the department's search and rescue missions, was scouring the stretch of Highway 299 between Roger's cabin and Willow Creek. She assumed they were checking in the other direction, too, in case Jesse and Nadia had gotten turned around.

"Maybe they got tired and fell asleep." She knew it was slim comfort, but until they knew otherwise, there was always hope. "I'm sorry, Mark. I wish I knew where they were. We just have to pray the searchers find them safe and sound."

Mark stilled for a second. "Oh. Yeah." Then his head nodded, and his feet bounced with it. "Well, hey, thanks for coming over to tell me and all. You, like, haven't been home yet, right? Are you going there now?"

"No." Serena stood, understanding the dismissal. She wished she could give Mark a hug, but he looked so tense she was afraid he'd fall apart if she touched him. "I'm heading back to the hospital, to wait for Kermit."

"He's going to be all right, right?"

"Yes." Relief flooded her again at the knowledge. "They're just giving him some fluids and some antibiotics, and I guess they'll stitch him up. They're not even going to keep him overnight."

"Tell him I said I'm, like, sorry about what happened. Man, that's so harsh."

"I'm sorry, too, Mark." Serena bit her lip against the emotion that threatened to overwhelm her. "Deputy Chase promised to call as soon as he has any news. I'll tell him to call you, too, but you're welcome to come over to my house and wait with us, if you don't want to be alone. I doubt we'll get a whole lot of sleep tonight."

"Your house?" Mark stared at her for a second, then his eyes darted away. "Yeah, sure . . . Like, I've got a couple of phone calls to make, right? But maybe I'll see you over at the hospital or something. Okay?"

"Sure. Come on by."

She stepped toward the door, but Mark darted forward, startling her with a brief, fierce hug. Then he dodged around the stereo equipment to open the door.

"It'll be all right," he promised, holding the door for her. "You'll see."

"We'll keep praying," she promised back.

He shut the door behind her with a solid bang, and she stood for a moment on the building's second-floor landing, fighting down the tears that threatened. Just that morning she had felt half ready to kill Jesse herself, but the pain his murder would cause his family would haunt her forever.

She took a deep breath and shook free of her paralysis. Callista would advise her to focus on positive thoughts, to send good energy out into the universe for Jesse and Nadia. But mental and physical exhaustion made that difficult.

She needed to soak her bruises in an Epsom salt bath while she drank a cup of lemon-ginger tea. And a shot of bourbon. Though her mental processes felt plenty impaired already. It was a good thing Garth was driving.

She started down the stairwell. The bare bulb on the second-floor landing gave just enough light for her to make her way down the concrete steps. The light on the first floor must have burned out.

As she reached the bottom and turned toward the back parking lot where Garth had parked his Mustang, she saw a flicker of movement to her right, in the shadows from the stairway.

She started, feeling silly for jumping, even as her heart pounded in her ears. "Garth? Are you ready to go?"

But the light chuckle that came from the shadows didn't sound like Garth, and she doubted the sinister glint of metal that caught the dim light came from the barrel of Garth's gun.

Sarah was the first to hear the faint whoosh of the emergency room doors opening into the waiting area. She unpretzeled herself out of her molded plastic chair and hurried across the room to give Kermit a hug as he hobbled through the doors.

"Crutches," she noted approvingly. "Cool."

"Deadly," Kermit corrected, taking an experimental swing farther into the waiting area. "I could kill somebody with these things. Like myself."

"You're doing great," Sarah assured him, trying to be unobtrusive about edging out of his way.

"Riggs!" Officer Martinez strode across the waiting room to stand grinning in front of Kermit. "They've let you out to return to fighting against truth, justice, and the American way."

"Ha, ha." Kermit adjusted his crutches. "Can we get out of here before they figure out I've escaped?" He glanced around, then down at Sarah. "Where's your mom?"

"She went to tell Mark what was going on."

"She went . . . By *herself?*" Kermit's crutches teetered ominously. "What was she thinking? We don't know where Bart Alexander is. His thugs are out there somewhere—"

"Garth's with her," Officer Martinez cut him off. She winked at Sarah. "I think he's going to ask the lieutenant for hazard pay after what happened to you."

Kermit's scowl didn't lift, and for some reason that made Officer Martinez's grin even wider. Sarah didn't have Gemma's intuition for boy–girl interactions, but if Officer Martinez was picking up on the same vibes from Kermit that Sarah had gotten from her mother, then something more had happened between them that afternoon than just getting shot and stranded. *Interesting.*

"How long have they been gone?" Kermit asked.

"Not long," Officer Martinez told him, though Sarah thought it had been at least half an hour. She would never understand grown-ups' concept of time. "I told her if you got out before she got back, we'd all meet at her place."

Kermit glanced at Sarah again. "Bart Alexander called Sarah at Pleasance Geary's house, long after he must have heard from his thugs. If he hasn't caught Nadia and Jesse yet, he might still believe Serena is his best bet at finding them."

"And I'd like to see him try to get past you, me, and Garth," Officer Martinez said. "Don't worry. Detective Dillon has backup ready for us if we need it. And we'll put a tracer on Serena's phone in case Alexander calls again."

"I can keep him talking while you send a patrol car to go arrest him," Sarah volunteered. When Officer Martinez raised one eyebrow, Sarah raised hers back. "He likes scaring kids. Might as well let him have a little fun on his last day of freedom."

Officer Martinez glanced at Kermit. "I tell you, this kid is the one who's scary."

Kermit frowned down at Sarah. "I'm just glad she's on our side." He shifted his crutches, and Sarah and Officer Martinez both scooted out of his way. "Let's go."

Sarah hurried to get the front door for him, but it opened before she could reach it. The slender man in the dark suit who stepped through the entrance barely spared a glance at Sarah, but his razor-sharp eyebrows speared together when he saw Kermit.

"Officer Riggs." His voice stretched with jaded annoyance, but Sarah saw the fingers of his near hand twitch with tension. "I heard I might find you here."

"Agent Johnson." Kermit suddenly looked blank, too, but Sarah noticed him shift his weight off of his crutches. "What do you want?"

"Wait." Sarah hadn't meant to snap out the word like that, hadn't meant to bring the shark-eyed man's attention to her. She tried an apologetic smile. "What did you say your name was? Sir?"

His eyebrows sliced together as he frowned at her. One positive thing about the past couple of days. The bullies at school were going to seem a lot less intimidating in the future. Jennifer Bright's snotty sneer had nothing on this guy.

"Agent Dominick Johnson." He cut the words out with cool precision. "Federal Bureau of Investigation."

Sarah feared she failed to show equal cool when she darted away from him to stand by Kermit.

"No, you're not!" And her voice squeaked, too. *Humiliating.* "Agent Johnson came out to Mrs. Geary's this morning, and that guy's not him."

The shark-man's frown changed, his nose wrinkling in surprise, but he didn't make any sudden moves toward a gun.

313

Possibly because Officer Martinez now had hers in her hand. Sarah didn't know where she'd hidden it in that Spandex outfit she was wearing, but she made a note to ask her later.

"I haven't been to see any Mrs. Geary," the shark-man said.

"That's what I said," Sarah reminded him. She glanced up at Kermit. "The real Agent Johnson is taller and has more muscles. He's got longer hair. And green eyes."

The shark-man's dark brown eyes snapped with anger. Maybe it was the "more muscles" comment. "I don't know what the hell your game is, missy, but *I* am the real Agent Johnson, and if you don't want to end up in a federal—"

He stepped toward her, but Kermit and Officer Martinez both stepped forward, as well, halting him in mid-threat.

He paused and took a calming breath before addressing Kermit. "Officer Riggs, we don't have time for a child's fantasies. I need to know—"

"Actually," Kermit interrupted, "I'm having fantasies of my own. How about you, Grace?"

Officer Martinez cocked her head, though her gun didn't move. "You mean about those telephone calls we made yesterday? To our buddies in the Federal Bureau of Investigation? Oh, yeah, I'm having those fantasies, too."

"It seems Agent Dominick Johnson isn't on a case investigating Jesse Banos," Kermit said, his face suddenly more steely than Sarah had ever seen it. "Agent Johnson is on vacation."

The shark-man blew out a frustrated curse, though he was smart enough not to move his hands out of Officer Martinez's sight. "Who the hell told you that?"

"I wish somebody had told me!" Sarah burst out, sudden shivers running through her at the memory of her interview with Agent Johnson. The other Agent Johnson. "You should have told me before you left to go find Jesse. What if I'd told him how to get to Roger's cabin?"

"Sarah, I—"

But she was too upset about being left out to stop. "You could at least have told me when I told you and Mom about him coming to Mrs. Geary's when we were driving back from Willow Creek. Mrs. Geary was ready to kill me when she found out I lied about—"

"My leg hurt," Kermit said, his unruffled voice cutting her off. "And I was still thinking of him as a real FBI agent, even if he was on vacation. But if there are two of him . . ." He shook his head. "I think at least one of him needs to go down to the station and have a little chat with Detective Dillon."

"There's no time for that!" the shark-man snapped. "I'm too close. I have to—"

"Find Jesse Banos," Kermit finished for him. "Well, we'd all like to do that, but—"

"I couldn't care less about Jesse Banos," the shark-man snarled. "I'm after the man who had you shot."

"Bart Alexander?"

The shark-man jerked in surprise. "You know who he is?"

Kermit shrugged. "Nadia Alexander's husband. Bart's been hunting for her."

The shark-man's face twisted in disgust. "You have no idea what you're dealing with. Bart Alexander isn't a scorned husband with a bad temper. You have no idea what he's capable of."

"Shooting a police officer?" Kermit suggested dryly. "Threatening children? Murder?"

Something in the shark-man's face shifted, as if he were suddenly hearing Kermit for the first time. "Yes. I've been trying to get proof. But it's too late for that, thanks to your interference. If he catches up with his wife and her lover, he'll kill them. We have to stop him."

"We?" Officer Martinez asked pointedly.

"I *am* Agent Dominick Johnson." Sarah heard his teeth grind. "Idiots."

"Then who came out to Mrs. Geary's?" she asked.

The shark-man glanced at Officer Martinez's gun. "Can I get out my billfold?"

She nodded. "Nice and slow. Two fingers."

He gingerly pulled a leather wallet from his back pocket. He flipped it open and pulled out a photograph. He extended it toward Sarah. "Take a look."

Kermit dropped a hand on Sarah's shoulder to hold her back. As if she were stupid enough to walk into the shark-man's reach!

Kermit leaned forward to take the photograph and handed it to Sarah.

The man in the picture had tousled blond hair and wore chinos and a striped button-down shirt opened to his chest hair, nothing like the dark hair and dark suit of the man who had questioned her on Mrs. Geary's porch. But she recognized the amused glint in those unblinking green eyes.

She almost dropped the photo. "That's him. He must have worn a wig."

"Bartholomew Alexander himself," Shark-man said as Kermit took the picture from her to examine it. "I'll just bet the bastard enjoyed impersonating me."

Kermit handed him back the photograph. "That explains how Alexander knew where Serena and I were going. Pleasance told him."

"Only because she thought he was an FBI agent." Sarah glared at Shark-man. Agent Johnson. Maybe it wasn't his fault, but he seemed glare-deserving, anyway.

"But it doesn't explain why you lied," Kermit said, turning his own hard gaze on Agent Johnson. "There is no FBI investigation of Jesse Banos."

Agent Johnson's sharp features twitched, but he gave a curt nod. "He called my office in Sacramento a few weeks ago. He wanted information on what evidence would be necessary to have someone arrested for conspiracy to commit murder and how to protect a material witness. He wouldn't give any details, but I checked into his phone records, found out he was in contact with Nadia Alexander, and put two and two together."

"You're saying Jesse then became part of an ongoing investigation?"

The muscle under Agent Johnson's right eye jerked. Sarah watched him swallow his automatic answer. He paused and shook his head. "When I took the information to my superiors, they said my personal vendetta against Bart Alexander was clouding my judgment, and I needed to take a nice, long vacation."

His mouth turned in a humorless smile. "I thought Jasper County sounded like a good vacation spot. But by the time I got here, Jesse Banos had disappeared with Nadia Alexander. I was afraid Bart Alexander would find them and kill them both before I could discover what evidence they had against him. So, I may have neglected to tell you and Ms. Davis that I wasn't, in fact, acting in an official FBI capacity."

Kermit's expression didn't soften. "It sounds like your superiors were right," he said. "It sounds like you've let this case become personal."

"That's because it *is* personal." Agent Johnson's eyes burned with intensity. "Very personal. Bart Alexander murdered my brother."

Chapter 23

The shadows shifted behind the stairway. Serena thought the gun was a Glock—at least, it looked like Kermit's, cold and deadly. But not as cold and deadly as the man holding it.

"Bart Alexander."

His unblinking green eyes glinted with amusement. "Here I thought Jesse and my wife might show up on his brother's doorstep, but instead he's sent you. What a pleasant surprise."

She could feel her brain slowing down, as it had that morning at the river. *Useless in a crisis situation.*

"Don't bother to run. My men aren't far away."

Run? She hadn't yet gotten past scream. *Get a grip, Serena.*

She could call for Garth. But Bart might shoot her. Or, more likely, his men would shoot Garth when Garth came running. And where *was* Garth, anyway? If he was waiting in his car, would he notice if Bart murdered her here in the stairwell?

"You're wondering about your redneck jock friend," Bart guessed. "What is it with you and law enforcement types, Serena? Or maybe you just like big guns?"

"I don't know what you're talking about."

"Really?" Bart's face contorted into a mockery of sorrow. "I'm sure he'd be disappointed to hear that, considering what he's suffered for you."

318

He turned his head, glancing down. Serena followed his gaze. Her eyes must have adjusted to the lack of light, because now she saw another shape below the stairs, two booted feet sprawling out from the shadows.

"Garth!"

"No, no." The barrel of Bart's gun jerked up to point at her head, halting her rush toward Garth's prone form. "No touching."

Fury and fear clogged Serena's throat, but she managed to spit her words through them. "He's a police officer. If you've killed him, you won't just go to prison. You'll get the death penalty."

"My, my. Aren't you a bloodthirsty little thing." Bart remained calmly amused. "No need to fret, though. He's got a hard head. He'll come around eventually."

She clenched her fists. "He'd better."

"Or what?" The amusement died in Bart's eyes, deadening them to hard, flat granite. "You've run right through your supply of viable threats, Serena."

He moved the gun barrel a fraction of an inch, centering it between her eyes. "I, on the other hand, am just getting started. Tell me where Jesse Banos has taken my wife."

"Your men shot them," Serena said, though his words raised her first real hope that maybe they hadn't. "Kermit and I barely got away with our lives."

"Mr. X and Mr. Y may not be quite such competent killers as I had hoped," Bart said, "but they're not liars. All four of you got away alive. Try again."

Serena shrugged. "I don't know where they are. I honestly thought you'd killed them."

"If that were true, it would make me very sad." Bart's mouth managed a parody of regret. "Because then I would have no reason at all to keep you alive."

His gun hand jerked, and Serena flinched, making him laugh. "Why don't you try one more time? And remember, if my foolish wife escapes from me, my life as an upstanding, law-abiding citizen is over. So I won't have any sense of peer pressure to keep me from taking my anger out on Jesse Banos's friends and family. Including his brother and your little girl."

Whoever said the truth hurts had it right. Her brain had revved back up to normal speed, but didn't have anywhere to go. She hadn't a clue where Jesse and Nadia might be. "Lost in the Trinity Mountains," wasn't going to satisfy Bart Alexander. But she had to say something before he got bored and pulled the trigger.

And reminding herself of that would get her nowhere. She forced her mind to relax, slipping into the quiet, open state Callista was trying to teach her.

She couldn't fool him into taking her to the hospital. He might wait to shoot her until after he checked it out, but then again, he might not. And the police station wasn't even a consideration.

She needed somewhere he wouldn't doubt Jesse and Nadia might be, somewhere she would have the advantage of knowing the terrain. Somewhere she might even expect a couple of police officer types to show up eventually. A vision slipped into that quiet space in her mind.

"All right." She dropped her shoulders in feigned defeat. "I'll show you where they are."

"He killed your brother?" Kermit felt the puzzle piece that was Agent Johnson finally fall into place. "Eddie Johnson. The labor organizer."

He remembered what he had thought was a snide comment of Agent Johnson's, the man saying he wouldn't mind having to drag Kermit's and Serena's mutilated bodies out of a drainage ditch, but he wouldn't want to have to do the paperwork. Eddie Johnson's body had been found mutilated in a drainage ditch.

"You're Eduardo Johnson's brother?" Grace's gun hand dropped to her side. "I'm so sorry. My cousin worked with him. She said he was a hero."

"He wanted to save the world." But Dominick Johnson's shark-like smile held more pain than derision. "Hell, look at me. An FBI agent. Maybe I did, too. Until I saw what the world did to my baby brother."

"The investigation showed he was killed by a drug gang," Kermit said, though Nadia's story had convinced him otherwise.

Agent Johnson's eye twitched. "That was the easiest solution. There wasn't enough evidence to prove anything else. But one look in that smug bastard Bart Alexander's eyes, and I knew the truth."

Kermit could picture how well that argument had gone over with Johnson's superiors.

"Look, I need . . ." Johnson paused, and Kermit could almost see his throat move as he swallowed his pride. "I need your help."

"To bring your brother's killer to justice," Grace supplied.

Kermit thought she suddenly seemed much too ready to grab her white hat and ride out into the sunset with their vigilante FBI agent.

"To make him pay?" Sarah demanded, her arms crossed over her chest. At least she hadn't forgotten Johnson's obnoxious personality.

"To keep him from killing anyone else," Johnson said. "That would be what Eddie would want first of all." He met Kermit's gaze. "You have to take me to Bart Alexander's wife. We have to protect her."

Kermit shifted his crutches, trying to stop them from digging into his arms. His leg ached. It was past his bedtime. The painkillers the doctor had given him were making the room too bright. Part of him would have been happy to loose Agent Johnson on an unsuspecting Jesse Banos and forget about the whole thing.

Unfortunately . . . "I'm not going to be able to help you do that," Kermit said. "We did find Jesse and Nadia this morning, but we split up. I have no idea where they—"

The waiting room door swung open behind Agent Johnson, causing him to jump sideways.

"Hey, man! Kermit!" Mark Banos stood in the doorway, blinking in the bright light.

"Hi, Mark." Kermit wondered if the meds were causing hallucinations. Which could mean that Agent Johnson was a hallucination, too. Maybe he was actually still back in the ER, unconscious on a gurney. The idea had appeal. "What are you doing here?"

"I'm, like, coming to be a total traitor. But what else can I do? He deserves it, man. The way he treated Serena." Mark squared his shoulders. "I'm here to take you to my brother. I know where Jesse is."

Her house looked peaceful, sitting quietly back from the street in a dark sea of grass. The living room lamp she'd forgotten to turn off that morning gleamed through the imperfectly drawn front curtains like a beacon calling her home.

If not for that single light, the utterly still, dark house might have brought other words to Serena's mind, besides peaceful. Words like empty. Lonely. Isolated.

"You're sure they're here?" Bart Alexander turned toward her in the back seat of his black Mercedes.

His two goons rode in the front. Serena hadn't gotten a good look at the men who had shot Kermit on the beach, but the one with the blond ponytail in the sedan's driver's seat was at least six foot two, and his shoulders seemed nearly as broad as his height, so she guessed he was the one Nadia had described as "hulking." The man on the passenger's side was big, too, but appeared almost inconsequential in comparison.

"I'm not playing games," Bart continued, uncharacteristically edgy with tension. "I have no intention of driving all over this miserable little backwater on your say-so. If Nadia isn't here, I will kill you."

Serena's fantasies of grabbing a kitchen knife and fighting off Bart, Hulk, and Mr. Bland had faded on the drive over from Mark's apartment. And Grace obviously hadn't brought Kermit to her house from the hospital yet, either.

But that was just as well. Now that her mind was working more clearly, she could see that two unsuspecting off-duty cops, one of them injured and on pain medication, wouldn't have a chance against Bart and his thugs. She didn't want to get them killed along with her.

And at least Sarah was safe with them.

"The only car I see is yours," Bart said, his mood growing rapidly darker.

"No kidding," Serena snapped back. She might be out of options, but she wasn't going down without a fight. "Your friends up front there slashed our tires. We had to hitchhike back from Willow Creek."

She couldn't see Bart's face well in the back seat darkness, but she felt his energy change as his expectations rose once more.

"Get out," he ordered, nodding to Hulk to release the door locks. "But keep quiet. Don't try anything. I don't need you quite so badly anymore, so you'll want to keep me happy."

He slid out the door after her. She'd hoped he'd leave one of his goons behind as a lookout, but both Hulk and Bland followed them up the walk.

"Why here?" Bart whispered, unable to keep his own stricture of silence in the excitement of the chase. "When you escaped my men, you must have known I'd still be looking for you."

"You didn't look here, did you, Einstein?" Serena hissed back. No reason to placate him. He'd know she'd lied to him soon enough, anyway. "We figured it would be the last place you'd expect us to return to."

But Bart only laughed, a silent chuckle, his good humor fully restored. "Touché. My resources are more limited up here in the hinterland. I had to allocate them carefully. Mr. X and Mr. Y drove by your house several times, but I didn't have them stake it out as I did with Jesse's house, dear Mrs. Geary's farm, and, obviously, Mark Banos's apartment."

He shook his head in regret. "I would have liked to question Mrs. Geary again when she returned this evening with her granddaughter—she was so forthcoming this morning. A counterfeit FBI badge is almost as useful as a gun in getting people to talk. Although it's not nearly so much fun.

"But then Mr. X alerted me to your arrival at Mr. Banos's place, and I had to make a difficult choice."

His smile held all the insouciant charm of a flirting frat boy. "I just couldn't pass up the opportunity to see you again, Serena."

They had reached the front door. Serena was surprised to find that her hand did not shake as she pulled her key ring from her jeans pocket. She had moved beyond fear. Or maybe she simply couldn't believe that someone as irritating as Bart Alexander was going to kill her. It didn't seem karmically fitting.

The door opened smoothly, the scents of orange cleaner and lilac candles welcoming her home. Safety. That's what home smelled like. Comfort and family. And maybe a little whiff of dog.

She'd have given a lot to have Fleur for backup right that moment. If she survived tonight, she'd let Sarah pick out the biggest puppy at the shelter if that's what Sarah wanted. The biggest puppy that didn't shed great clumps of long hair. Or drool too much.

"Where are they?" Bart demanded, reminding her of more pressing concerns than dog drool.

"How should I know?" Serena whispered back. "I just got here, too. They're probably asleep. Why don't you have X and Y check the guest bedroom while we check the kitchen?"

If she only got one attempt to skewer any of them with a kitchen knife, she wanted it to be Bart. Another thing she was going to do if she survived the night was to buy a bear-sized can of pepper spray to keep in a kitchen drawer. Or maybe a Taser.

"Move." Bart jabbed her in the ribs with his gun.

Or maybe an M-16.

She stepped forward into the entrance hall. The soft light from the living room lamp offered a much gentler welcome than Bart deserved. As she moved into the house, she saw that she'd left a light on in the kitchen, as well.

She couldn't work up much concern over her environmental sins, though. If she survived the night . . .

Quit kidding yourself, Serena.

If survival was unlikely, she could at least make sure Bart Alexander paid for his crimes. His blood on her floor. DNA under her fingernails. Something. Anything.

"Wait here," she whispered, "while I check the kitchen."

"Fat chance." Bart grabbed her arm. He turned to Goon X and Goon Y. "Check down the hall."

His unblinking eyes glittered in the dim light as he surveyed the empty living room. "I'm beginning to think Ms. Davis has played us, gentlemen, but be thorough. Feel free to shoot anything that moves." He grinned. "Just do it quietly."

"They're here," Serena insisted, her voice rising with her adrenaline as Bart's men disappeared down the dim hall. "At least, they were when I left. Maybe they left a note on the kitchen table."

She jerked her arm from Bart's grasp, and lurched toward the kitchen doorway. The anticipation of Bart's gun going off filled her so completely that the sudden appearance of yet another gun, lunging out from behind the counter as the kitchen suddenly went dark, almost failed to register.

"Freeze!"

The voice, though squeezed tight with anger and fear, still sounded familiar. She certainly recognized the face looming from the shadows, its high cheekbones framed with thick black hair. But her brain couldn't quite get around the idea that yet another gun was pointed directly at her forehead. And how willing this particular gun-toter had been to empty the last one.

"Jesse!" Bart's cheerful greeting caused the gun to jerk sideways, but not far enough to give her any relief.

The position of Jesse's aim told Serena that Bart Alexander had slid right up behind her. The feel of cold steel against the back of her head confirmed it.

"You must be Jesse Banos," Bart continued. "I can't tell you how pleased I am to meet you under these circumstances. And that pitiful puppy huddled behind you must be my soon-to-be-late wife."

As Serena's eyes became accustomed to the light, she could see a second form in the shadows of her kitchen, Nadia's blond hair gleaming above her perfect tan.

"Call your thugs out here and tell them to drop their guns," Jesse ordered. "Do it, Alexander, or you're a dead man."

Serena didn't have to turn her head to know that Bart smiled behind her.

"If you pull that trigger, Ms. Davis dies," he said, shifting the gun sideways against her head to bring it clearly into Jesse's line of sight. "Even if you don't accidentally kill her yourself."

"I don't care if I have to shoot through her to hit you. Just as long as you die." Jesse's desperate gaze flicked to Serena. "How could you do it?" he demanded, his voice twisted with emotion. "How could you lead him to us? Traitor."

Serena stared at him. "How could I lead him to you? That's a good question, considering I had *no idea where you were*. When you didn't bring help back for me and Kermit, we thought you were dead!"

If a flash of guilt crossed Jesse's face, it was much too fleeting for her taste.

Behind her, Bart laughed. "No. Tell me it isn't true, Serena. You were lying to me, after all? You really didn't know where Jesse and Nadia were?"

Serena suppressed an answering, wild laugh. "Of course I knew. I'm psychic."

She fixed Jesse with a sharp look. "It makes perfect sense, though. Jesse knew Kermit and I weren't going to be coming back here any time soon. Thanks to him. What better place to hide out?"

"You're so self-righteous," Jesse snapped back. "Nadia's life was in danger. You and Officer Riggs would have forced her to go to the police. I did what I had to do. We were going to call the sheriff's department in the morning to tell them where you were."

Bart's laughter was digging his gun deeper into Serena's skull. She didn't care. She could put up with anything that gave her one more moment before either Bart or Jesse pulled a trigger.

"Not that this isn't the best entertainment I've had all week," Bart said, "but I've already spent much too long hunting down my wayward wife. It's time for me to complete my business."

Jesse's eyes widened. "Call your men, and tell them to drop their guns," he ordered again.

"They're hiding in the shadows of that hall with their guns trained on you," Bart said. "And I think they're better shots than you are."

"No one's going to shoot anyone," Serena said, trying not to sound terrified out of her mind. "Bart, if you leave now, you have a chance to escape, to flee the country. But you have to run. Jesse and Nadia must have called 911 when they heard us enter the house. The police will be here any second."

Even an idiot could have interpreted Jesse's blank look as he glanced toward the telephone sitting quietly in its cradle on the kitchen counter. And, unfortunately, Bart Alexander was no idiot.

"Oh, God." Nadia's whimper echoed in the kitchen. "We're all going to die."

Chapter 24

Serena hated to admit it, but she had to agree with Nadia. They were all going to die. And she was going to be first, unless she did something soon.

"Did you hear something?" she asked, turning her head slightly against the gun. "I thought I heard something outside. Maybe X and Y should check it out."

"Serena, Serena." Bart sighed.

"Nadia, climb out the window," Jesse said, jerking his head toward the window over the kitchen sink.

"What?" Nadia frowned doubtfully. "It's too small."

"You can get through," Jesse assured her. "I'll hold Bart off until you get out."

"But he'll kill you!"

Jesse shrugged with heroic stoicism. "At least you'll escape."

"If she makes a move toward that window, I'll shoot you right now," Bart barked, his gun turning to lie flat against the side of Serena's head.

"Just give me your gun," Serena suggested. She'd wasted two years on this man? "I'll shoot him myself."

"Go, Nadia." Jesse adjusted his stance, steadying his gun.

Nadia glanced sideways, still unsure.

"Don't even think about it!" Bart's gun hand shot out past Serena's head to point his weapon straight at Jesse.

She'd never have another chance. She'd seen it on TV a

hundred times. With the speed and force of desperation, Serena reached up and grabbed Bart's forearm. She ducked her head, bent her knees, and jerked forward and down.

Instead of flying over her shoulder and landing with a satisfying thud on his back on the floor, Bart twisted away like a snake, wrenching her sideways, off balance.

Serena fell. But she still held Bart's arm, and he fell with her. She landed on his side, against his arm. His gun went off, so close she thought she could feel the brush of the bullet against her body. His arm jerked back with the recoil, but she held on.

She heard screams, something crashing in the kitchen. A dog barking hysterically. A door slamming. Bart cursing in her ears.

But the only thing that mattered was hanging on to the tightly knotted forearm twisting in her grip. He kicked at her calves, knocked his forehead against her temple. He worked out. She remembered his physique. He was taller, and he outweighed her.

Jesse had better move fast, or Bart would escape her grasp. Unless Jesse had already run, saving his distressed damsel. Those pounding feet had to be Goon X and Goon Y, coming to their boss's rescue.

Bart's head cracked against hers again, but when he jerked this time, she felt his arm muscles slacken, heard a clatter as the gun fell to the hardwood floor.

"Grace, get his weapon."

The hoarse order sounded familiar. The hand brushing her face, grabbing her shoulder, looked familiar.

"Let go, honey, let go. It's all right. Can you move? Are you hurt?"

With a sob, she dropped Bart's arm and pushed off the

floor, letting Kermit haul her to her feet and crush her against his chest.

"Don't move." Grace's order, sharp and professional, was directed down at Bart's groaning form. "Not that you're going to want to move very fast after a crack in the head like that. Nice work, Kermit, whacking him with those crutches."

"I told you I was going to hurt somebody with them," Kermit said.

But Serena heard the tense catch in his voice, and looking into his eyes, she could see the fear for her that caused him to clutch her so tight she could barely breathe, his crutches pressed against her back.

"Good timing," she gasped, squeezing him back for all she was worth. "We finally got some good luck today."

"It wasn't luck," Kermit said. "We had a little un-divine intervention."

"You shouldn't have hit him so hard," a male voice said. "He needs to move a little more before I'll have a legitimate excuse to shoot him."

"You don't have a gun."

"I could borrow yours."

Serena turned in Kermit's arms.

Grace Martinez stood with her gun drawn over Bart Alexander's prone form. Beside her stood Dominick Johnson, nudging Bart with one shiny black shoe, as if hoping to prod him into fatal action. Bart only pressed his hand to his head and groaned.

"Agent Johnson?" Serena glanced up at Kermit.

"I'll explain later."

Bart groaned again. "X! Y!" he shouted. "Shoot them! Take them all out!"

"X and Y?" Kermit asked.

"His thugs!" Serena jerked back from him. "I forgot all about them. They went back to the bedrooms." She'd already almost lost Kermit to one of their bullets. She wasn't going to do it again. "We have to take cover."

"That shouldn't be necessary."

She and Kermit turned to look across the living room. Mr. X and Mr. Y stood framed in the dim hallway. Or rather, they tilted in the doorway. Two shorter, stockier men in Harley-Davidson jackets stood beside them, propping them up.

"Tank!" Serena said, never expecting she'd be so glad to see the scarred biker. "Jimbo! What are you doing here?"

"They came with me." Mark stepped forward out of the shadows between the two men and their charges. He grinned.

Serena might have run forward to hug him, but another body slammed into her from the side.

"Mom!"

Serena loosed one arm from Kermit's waist to grab her daughter. "Sarah. Oh, baby."

Fleur's head pushed in between them, the dog's eyes bright with the joy in her people's voices.

"Sarah." Kermit grinned, then frowned. "Garth was supposed to keep you out in the car."

"You try keeping that kid under control when you've got a head injury," Garth growled from the open doorway.

Serena had to admit it; she was even glad to see Garth.

"Great," Jesse's voice held the faintest note of sarcasm. "This is just great."

Serena turned back toward the kitchen. She'd forgotten Bart Alexander wasn't the only man who'd threatened her with a gun in her own home that night.

Jesse still held his weapon pointed out at the rest of

them, Nadia pressed close behind him.

"Drop the gun, Banos," Grace ordered, changing her aim.

"I will," Jesse agreed. "As soon as you all give me and Nadia a clear pathway to the door. You've got Bart Alexander. That's what you wanted. Now let us go."

"You know it doesn't work that way," Kermit said, his voice perfectly calm, though he shifted out of Serena's arms to free his own. "Nadia is safe now. You'll both need to come in for questioning."

"I'm not safe," Nadia objected, looking nearly as afraid of Bart prone on the floor as she had of him standing with his gun pointed at Serena's head. "I'll never be safe. If I help you put Bart in jail, his father will kill me."

"The FBI can protect you, Mrs. Alexander," Agent Johnson said, his voice more gentle than Serena had ever heard it. Was it the blond hair? Or the helplessness?

"Like they protected your brother?" Nadia asked.

"My brother refused to ask for help."

"Brother?" Serena asked.

"I'll explain," Kermit assured her again. "Jesse, put down the gun. You won't be able to hide again, especially after threatening a roomful of law enforcement officers."

"Hiding isn't the plan," Jesse said. He looked past Serena and Kermit. "Mark, I told you not to tell anyone where we were. You see what happened? Did you at least bring the documents with you?"

"The passports and plane tickets and stuff? Yeah, man, I brought them."

Mark left Tank and Jimbo with their charges, and walked across the living room toward the kitchen. As he passed Serena, he gave her an apologetic grimace.

That had been his guilty secret. He'd been using his less-than-legal contacts to dig up false identification for Jesse and Nadia to use to flee the country. She couldn't be angry with Mark. Jesse was his brother. And Mark's bringing Kermit here tonight had saved her life. But she realized she hadn't yet reached the limits of her anger at Jesse.

"I can't believe this." Only Sarah's arm around her waist kept her from charging Jesse and his gun. "I mean, I can believe you'd endanger us all to hole up with another man's wife. I can believe you'd risk Kermit's life by abandoning him in order to protect your own hide. I can even believe you'd pull a gun on me in my own kitchen, when we were engaged to each other just a few weeks ago."

She shook her head. "But I can't believe you would leave Nigel and Lani and Roger in the lurch by running off to Brazil or somewhere and abandoning all your clients at the clinic."

"I'm not abandoning them!" Jesse's chin jutted out in indignation. "I'm only going to be gone long enough to get Nadia settled. Then I'll return to face the consequences."

His eyes gleaming with righteousness, he held out his free hand to his brother as Mark approached. "Give me the documents, and then get out. I don't want to get you mixed up in this."

"Like, isn't it a little late for that, man? You already did."

Mark's punch landed squarely on the point of Jesse's jaw. The gun flew across the kitchen floor as Jesse toppled backwards, only Nadia's deft grab at his shoulders keeping his head from crashing to the tile floor.

"That wasn't fair, Mark," Kermit objected from Serena's side. "I wanted to do that."

Chapter 25

"I don't know what's wrong with her." Sarah's voice came from high above Serena's closed eyelids. "She never just lies around like this. She's always freaking out about skin cancer."

Serena blinked her eyes open to squint up at her daughter and Kermit, both standing over her in dripping wet bathing suits. She edged herself up onto her elbows.

"I'm wearing SPF two thousand or something sunscreen," she informed Sarah haughtily, gesturing at the lotion bottle several feet away next to the red cooler.

"Auntie Dess is covered up," Sarah pointed out.

Serena turned her head to glance at her sister, stretched out on a towel beside her. Destiny still had on a long-sleeved chambray shirt over the t-shirt and shorts she'd worn since Serena, Kermit, and Sarah had picked her and Daniel up from the airport a few hours earlier. Daniel lay beside her, contentedly absorbed in his Robert Parker mystery, despite his show of grumbling about not needing another afternoon of sun and sand after two weeks in Hawaii.

"If Auntie Dess is trying to avoid skin cancer, it's a little late," Serena said, eyeing her sister's deep Hawaiian tan.

"You're just jealous," Destiny said, as relaxed and contented as her husband. She looked up at Sarah. "The shirt isn't to keep me from getting skin cancer, it's to keep me from freezing to death."

"It's hot!" Sarah objected, waving her hand in front of her face as a fan.

"For Jasper County." Destiny pulled her shirt closed and shivered dramatically.

"Score one for those of us who haven't spent two weeks in paradise," Serena said, unmoved. "We can enjoy a seventy-three-degree heat wave. The sun feels wonderful on my bruises. Natural healing."

She still ached all over from the disastrous kayak ride on Friday, even after sleeping most of Saturday away. The parts of Saturday that she hadn't spent answering questions in the police station.

"The water will feel good, too," Sarah said, plopping down on the sand between her and Destiny. "You should alternate hot and cold. That's what my softball coach says."

She shot a smile at her aunt, who coached Sarah's summer league team.

"Speaking of healing, Kermit shouldn't be getting his bullet wound wet." Serena glared pointedly at the bandage wrapped around Kermit's leg just below his flaming red swim trunks.

Kermit merely grinned as he settled awkwardly on the towel next to her, dripping cold droplets on her stomach. He'd given up the crutches after two near-disasters the day before.

"You said you were only going to wade," she accused.

His blue eyes widened with innocence. "I slipped."

"They're all like that," Destiny said, obviously not resigned to it.

"Men?" Serena asked.

"Cops," Kermit assured her. "You should have seen Grace after she pulled her hamstring chasing down a perp. She went out and played racquetball with Garth that afternoon. Couldn't walk for two days, but she beat Garth. Big time."

"Just don't expect any sympathy when you get gangrene," Serena grumbled, trying to tamp down her concern. The doctor had promised Kermit was healing quickly—and if he didn't, she'd sic Callista and her herbs on him. "And keep those drips to yourself."

"You, too, Sarah," Destiny said, edging away from her niece. "That water is *cold*."

"Then you better get up fast!" Sarah warned, as the ominous sound of ragged panting roared near. Sarah leaped to her feet, the only one to escape the sudden deluge as seventy pounds of yellow Labrador shed twenty pounds of water all over her too-staid humans.

"Fleur!" Destiny's shriek made Serena laugh, despite the icy drops spattering her own skin.

"No!" Daniel shouted, as Fleur moved toward him. "Down, Fleur! Down!"

Fleur complied with abandon, throwing her sopping body down beside him on his towel and rolling over onto her back, waving long, cream-colored legs in the air.

Daniel struggled to his feet, trying to protect his paperback from the wet dog. "Gee, thanks, Fleur. I'm happy to see you, too."

"Sarah!" Gemma's voice called from the boulders marking the swimming hole farther down the long, narrow beach. "Thirst, remember?"

Rolling her eyes, Sarah jumped across Serena to get to the cooler and dug out a couple of sodas. "Gemma's got some good gossip, and she won't share until I bring her a Coke. Come on, Fleur, let's leave these stick-in-the-muds to their sunbath."

She grabbed Fleur's collar to get the dog headed the

right direction, then picked her way after the Lab across the crowded beach toward the swimming hole.

"My own dog just sent me into hypothermia." Destiny climbed to her feet, rubbing her hands over the goosebumps rising on her arms.

"She was slow today," her husband said, brushing wet sand from his shorts. "It usually takes her less than five minutes from the time she hits the water."

"I'm so glad you're home." Serena smiled up at her sister. She had to admit she would miss Fleur's company, but she wasn't going to miss the mess. "As long as you're up, why don't you and Daniel go back to the car and get the picnic basket? The exercise will warm you."

"My sister. A regular Florence Nightingale." But Destiny reached down to rest a hand on Serena's shoulder as she passed. Serena caught her eye and squeezed her hand. She knew exactly how her sister was feeling. Serena had felt it herself after Destiny's narrow escape from a sociopathic would-be killer.

She watched Destiny and Daniel trudge across the sand and rocks toward the trees that shielded the river from the parking lot, picking their way among the other families that picnicked along the riverbank. Downstream, older teenagers swung on a rope from the opposite bank out over a deep pool. Small children shrieked as they splashed in the river's pebbly shallows under the watchful eyes of parents.

"Not quite as private and peaceful as Roger's beach," Kermit commented.

"And nobody's been shot at or nearly drowned in the whole hour we've been here," Serena reminded him. The Green River didn't have the exciting tubing or the deep water of the Trinity, especially not so close to Hope Point, but the peaceful flow seemed just right to her that afternoon.

"It's a perfect day for a picnic." Kermit gazed out over the water as she gazed at him, watching the laughter of the children and the soft brush of the breeze settle into the contentment in his face.

Her gaze shifted to where Sarah sat on a boulder with Gemma, sharing sodas and junior high gossip. Maybe some of Jesse's repeated comments about her failures as a wife and mother had hit home. She felt a stab of regret that she hadn't been able to offer Sarah the same stable, nuclear family life she and Destiny had shared as children.

But Sarah and Gemma were as close as two sisters could be, and today could hardly be any more normal and stable.

"It was good of Sarah's father to agree to wait a week to come pick her up," Kermit said.

"I don't think I could have let her out of my sight this soon," Serena admitted.

The night before, she had started awake at every creak the house made, terrified Bart Alexander had returned to make good his threats against her daughter. Reminding herself that Bart was in jail and that Kermit slept in the guest bedroom just down the hall had eased the fear, but not helped her sleep.

In fact, the thought of Kermit in the guest bedroom just down the hall had been a real sleep-killer. She felt her face flush at the mere memory.

"I don't think Sarah was ready to let you out of her sight, either," Kermit said, fortunately not reading her mind. "I saw how scared she was for you Friday night when we went back to Mark's apartment to pick up Tank and Jimbo and found Garth with that bump on his head."

"So much for her life being normal and stable," Serena muttered.

Kermit's blue eyes sharpened as he gazed down at her.

"Sarah is a smart, level-headed girl who knows both her parents love her and want what's best for her. She's not missing anything living with you." Humor sparked again. "Of course, if she was hoping for normal, she should have picked a different mother."

Serena made a face at him, but her words were serious. "We've done all right together. But it's never been just me and Sarah, even after the divorce. She's got a big family. Destiny and Daniel, Callista, Pleasance, and Gemma. And you."

"We'll always be her family," Kermit promised, and she knew he meant that, regardless of what happened between him and her. He grinned, sudden light sparking in his eyes. "The only thing missing in her life is a dog."

Serena snorted and pointed at the big yellow Lab chasing the pebbles Sarah tossed into the water. "Pardon?"

"A dog of her *own*." Kermit slanted a thoughtful look down at Serena. "I guess the question is whether or not she and I should each get a dog or we should get one family dog after you and I get married."

Serena sat up abruptly, nearly knocking her forehead against his, sputtering wildly, but unable to come up with a coherent sentence.

"I know." He nodded sagely, ignoring her gasping attempts at speech. "You're not ready for another engagement yet. It's too soon after Jesse." His jaw hardened despite his smile. "I wish you'd let me book him for breaking and entering and assault with a deadly weapon."

"It's not breaking and entering if you have a key," Serena reminded him, able to speak on that subject at least. "Besides, you couldn't very well charge him with anything relating to Friday night without bringing Mark and those forged documents into it."

And with Mark's drug record, he could have faced serious prison time.

"So, we'll take it slow," Kermit said. His eyes held hers with an intensity that made her shiver despite the sun on her back and the heat swelling in her heart. "I'm willing to wait as long as it takes for you, Serena."

Then he grinned that heart-cracking grin. "But I won't wait that long for my dog. And I don't think Sarah will, either."

"That's blackmail!"

He shrugged.

She struggled to tamp down her answering grin, struggled to hold onto control of her reason and her heart. "I'm still older than you are, Kermit. And I don't live an exciting life—"

She ignored his snort of disbelief. "I'm a hazardous materials technician. I think it's a pretty great job, but it's not glamorous. I'm not glamorous. I'm a mom. I'm never going to look like Nadia Alexander. You deserve—"

"Nadia Alexander is a bimbo," Kermit said, his eyes dangerous chips of blue flint. "You don't think I deserve any better than a bimbo?"

He crossed his arms, drawing her attention to his muscular bare chest, which had to be cheating. If she took off her bikini top, they might be even, but he'd probably have to arrest her for indecent exposure. Life was not fair.

"What about you?" he demanded. "You deserve more than a clumsy, junior cop without a college diploma."

"I don't care about that." Jesse had graduated *magna cum laude*. And look where that had got her.

Kermit raised one eyebrow. "You don't love me for my mind?"

"Stop that!" She growled. "I'm trying to be serious. You

341

want to know what I love about you?" Besides his bare chest and the way his grin turned her insides upside down. "It's this."

She waved at the beach. "It's the fact that you're here. That you don't mind spending your day off swimming with me and my daughter and sister and Daniel. That you'll take me out for a beer on a Friday night and aren't afraid to dance if I want to. That you never make me feel like there's somewhere you'd rather be than just hanging out with me."

He reached out to touch her cheek, the slight roughness of sand dust under his fingers. "There isn't."

"There isn't for me, either," Serena said, the admission both easier and more shattering than she expected. She lifted her hand to touch his.

"I want to see where this—" Tension? Passion? Love? She waved her free hand. "—feeling between us will lead. But I don't want to lose your friendship."

"You won't."

Her mouth turned wryly. "You sound so certain. But you don't know the future. And, Friday night not withstanding, I'm no psychic, either."

"It's not a psychic prediction." He brushed his thumb closer to her lips. "It's a promise."

He leaned toward her, and she tilted her face to his, letting the electric jolt of his kiss burn away her fears. She might not need a white knight, but she needed a man who would keep his promises. And she didn't need to be psychic to know Kermit would keep his. It was written in the heat in his eyes, the gentleness of his kiss, the tracings of honor and strength and compassion in his face.

A sudden high-pitched squealing caused Kermit to jerk backward. Together they turned toward the boulders down the beach, where Gemma sat staring with her jaw open and

Sarah frowned at them with her arms crossed over her chest in an uncanny parody of Serena as concerned parent.

"Maybe we should go back to the car," Destiny's voice sounded from behind them, not nearly as shocked as Serena thought she ought to be. "Give them some privacy."

"Maybe I should ask what his intentions are," Daniel replied.

"I would think that's fairly obvious."

Kermit grimaced as he turned back toward Serena, his face redder than his fire-bright swim trunks. "Of course, if you were psychic, you would have known they were all watching just then."

"Not all surprises are bad," Serena said. She could never in a thousand years have predicted the love for this unlikely man that filled her heart. "It occurs to me that being psychic may be highly overrated."

About the Author

An avid reader since she devoured (literally) *One Fish, Two Fish, Red Fish, Blue Fish* as a toddler, **Tess Pendergrass** wrote her first book in third grade. However she didn't follow up her dream of becoming a writer until graduate school, when she began writing her first novel as an antidote to the literary theory she was studying. She hasn't been able to stop writing since.

Tess grew up in the fog on the Northern California coast, in a small town much like the fictional Hope Point in her Hope Point Mystery series. She received a BA in Psychology and in Literature from UC Santa Cruz and an MA in Comparative Literature and Theory from Northwestern University.

She currently lives in Georgia with her husband, Dan, their cat, Shale, and Maggie the Devil Dog. Living in the South, Tess has learned to appreciate exotic entities like sunshine and sweet tea. She's also careful not to let Maggie swim in ponds with signs reading, "Don't Feed the Alligators."

Tess has written three historical romances and three romantic mysteries for Five Star.